Sleeping Partners

A special limited edition featuring the novels:

O.P.P.
Naomi King

Single Black Female
Yvette Richards

Published by:
The X Press
PO Box 25694
London, N17 6FP
Tel: 020 8801 2100
Fax: 020 8885 1322
E-mail: vibes@xpress.co.uk

Printed by Omnia Books Ltd, Glasgow, UK

Distributed in UK by Turnaround Distribution
Unit 3, Olympia Trading Estate, Coburg Road, London N22 6TZ
Tel: 020 8829 3000
Fax: 020 8881 5088

ISBN 1-902934-09-1

THE BIRTH OF TWO BESTSELLERS

With the publication of Victor Headley's *Yardie* in 1992, the X Press started the publishing revolution that was to herald a new dawn in black British fiction. Surprisingly, for a 'bad bwoy' book, *Yardie* was bought and loved by women everywhere. Naomi King was one such fan, and when she called X Press HQ and launched into a "my man ain't no good" tirade, she planted the seeds that were to become the first black British female bestseller.

It was a runaway success in high street booksellers, and in hairdressers, pattie shops and record stores. Guys were also reading it. Brash, sexy, raw, with balls and clubs and the Afro Hair and Beauty Show to visit, the novel's four bashment gals from Brixton burst onto the literary scene.

A year later, a mansucript entitled 'Woo Man' arrived at X Press HQ. Retitled 'Single Black Female', the novel became a must-read for young, black, gifted and single women in Britain and America, and in Yvette Richards they found a voice that was in tune with theirs.

Dotun Adebayo
The X Press, 2001

O.P.P.

"You down with O.P.P.?"

That was the last thing the bridegroom should have been asking one of the female guests at his wedding, but he couldn't help himself. From the moment she entered the church, his tongue was hanging down to the ground. Even as he exchanged vows with his blushing bride, he was mentally calculating the risk to his marriage of checking this exceptionally criss gal.

It was worth it, he decided.

"You down with O.P.P?" he asked her again. "You know, 'other people's property'..."

Maxine, Merlene, Andrea and Beverly were Brixton's 'It' girls in their heyday. They ruled the area from Stockwell to Camberwell and from Kennington to Streatham. They had the looks, the style and the intention. No women could test, and any how a man wanted to 'try a t'ing', he had to pay homage, pay for drinks and bow down low enough to eat off a 'two-foot table'.

Collectively, they were known as the Four Musketeers - all for one and one for all. But now ten years on from their glory days, these four best friends are brought together following the death of Winston, Andrea's other half.

Winston's death is causing more distress for Merlene

than the grieving widow however. Little does Andrea know that her 'best friend' had been having an affair with Winston, an affair that now threatens to land her in jail.

Maxine, meanwhile, has done well for herself, like everyone knew she would. She had always been the prettiest, the sexiest, the one that most men would leave their wives for. Now she's found her knight in shining armour. He's handsome, he's charming and he's very rich. The only thing is, he isn't black... Can he give her everything she really wants, or will she only find happiness with her 'soul brother'?

SINGLE BLACK FEMALE

For women who know that love 'still lives here'.....

High-flying executive Dee has been waiting to exhale for much too long. Getting a man isn't the problem. No man has yet turned down the offer of spending the night with her. But high calibre men are in short supply in the United States. They've all either been snapped up already, or they aren't into women. So when she is headhunted for a top job in London, she dreams of finding love there too. But the accent isn't the only thing that she finds hard to understand in England. The men she meets seem to be speaking a totally different language also.

Dee shares a house in Wimbledon, south London, with fellow thirtysomething Carol and twentysomething Donna. Carol had turned her back on her childhood sweetheart to marry the perfect man. But now she is a woman scorned by that perfect husband who informs her on Christmas Eve that he is leaving her for his secretary. The years she has spent as the dutiful and loving housewife have become worthless overnight. Well, almost worthless. She's determined to make her ex pay for every one of those years, starting with the home they shared and into which she welcomes her new friends. This new single life makes her realize how false her perfect marriage had been. Trying to turn back the hands of the clock, she embarks on a rigorous fitness regime and a search for that childhood sweetheart who wasn't quite perfect back in the day.

Barely out of her teens, Donna knows more about men than men know about themselves She's under no illusion: there are no good men out there. She should know, she's learned about men the hard way, through the 'school of hard knocks'. On the run from a murderous boyfriend, the last thing she needs is another man in her life.

O.P.P

Other People's Property

Naomi King

ONE

It was an unusually warm autumn day, but this was no picnic in the park. The large crowd gathered around the freshly dug grave were all dressed in black. Half a dozen limousines waited, bumper to bumper in a line.

Those who knew him couldn't believe he was dead. He had been so full of life and only twenty-seven. Winston's early death reminded them of their own mortality. Time was slowly ticking away for each one of them.

"It's not Winston inna de box, y'know," Fitzroy whispered to Rosie, his baby mother. "Me know him. Him can't dead." He took his turn to shovel earth into the grave.

Fitzroy had known Winston longer than most. They had attended school together and had even spent a spell together at a youth detention centre back in the day.

No way was Winston in that coffin.

Fitzroy knew his friend as the great escapologist. More tricks up his sleeve than Harry Houdini. Winston liked to 'tek chance', but always managed to get out of the stickiest situation, whether with the law or otherwise. Out on the street they called him the 'Don Dadda'. He was invincible.

Fitzroy smiled to himself, reminded of the time when a seventeen year old Winston had convinced a magistrate's court that the half a pound of prime sensimilla the police found on him was for his own personal use. It was a month's supply, Winston had claimed. When you divided it by thirty days, it didn't seem that much. A quarter of an ounce a day, that's all. He got off with a fifty pound fine.

He could get away with anything. Like the time an old girlfriend caught him on the job. Actually *on the job!* Winston carried on denying that she had seen what she had seen, until the girl was blue in the face. Winston's three cardinal rules in a relationship were: deny, deny and deny.

Fitzroy chuckled to himself. A wicked chuckle. His time was ticking away more rapidly than the others. He knew this. He had only a matter of time to find that big, elusive skank that would set him up for life. A true hustler, he made a quick mental note to get to the bottom of the mystery. If Winston was undercover with a stash of contraband, Fitzroy wanted to know. His cardinal rule was: never let friendship get in the way of a good skank.

"Mind yuhself." Rosie's elbow nudged him into the here and now. "Remember where we are."

Fitzroy straightened up and mimicked the placid demeanour of the other mourners. He wasn't in the habit of taking orders from any woman, but Rosie was his main squeeze. His number one baby mother. Circumstances forced her to have his best interests at heart. Besides, she was right. This wasn't the time and the place for reminiscing on his bredrin's comical escapades.

No, he concluded, it couldn't possibly be Winston in the coffin. He didn't know how it had happened, but somebody else must have been driving that car. For whatever reason, Winston was keeping a low profile. Maybe because of the police. Or maybe because of all that money he had mentioned.

A short distance from the grave, a solitary feminine figure had peeled away from the family and friends paying their last respects. Her carefully stooped gait gave the impression of a woman burdened by grief in moderation. Only Merlene's eyes revealed her true anguish. Fortunately, nobody had bothered to look deeply into them. Why should they? As far as everyone was concerned Andrea, not Merlene, was the chief widow here.

Merlene walked slowly to a bench and sat down. Her feet were killing her.

"Damn new shoes," she muttered to herself. "Is who

2

tell me fe buy dem?"

She sat wearily, easing her feet out of the shoes and leaning back, eyes closed, as the breeze soothed her aching toes. She sighed the sigh of a thousand hardships. If only the pain deep within her could be so easily relieved. Eye-water, which earlier had threatened to expose her, now trickled freely down her cheeks. She choked, covering her mouth hastily to stifle the moans which slowly erupted in the belly of her soul. As much as she wanted to bawl out with grief, the outward signs of her pain had to be tempered. Everybody would want to know why she was grieving so much for a man who was her best friend's boyfriend.

"Merlene," the voice spoke softly. "Girl, y'all right?"

Merlene looked up, surprised to see Beverly peering down at her, a look of concern on her face. She struggled to speak, but the words were not forthcoming. She could normally tell Beverly anything. But not this. How would Beverly react when she discovered that Miss Prim and Proper had engaged in an illicit relationship? Merlene held out her hand to her sister-in-spirit, who gave it a gentle squeeze.

"I know how you feel," Beverly chirped. "Funerals aren't exactly my idea of a good time either."

Who feels it, knows it. Merlene wasn't in the mood for good cheer.

"Just give me a moment on my own," she said, placing her hand on her stomach. "I've got really bad period pains. That and this whole thing with Winston, it's all a bit too much, y'know."

"Yes, I understand. Take your time, Merle. But the cars are driving off in a few minutes." Beverly hurried away to offer Andrea more solace.

Fists clenched, Merlene braced herself against the fever burning in her soul. What was she to do? After all the plans, the dreams… To be cheated in this way.

3

"I don't bloody deserve this." The words were no more than a sob. "Bring him back, I need him, I ache for him. Bring him back." The tears began to flow again.

"Winston, is how you do this to me, man? You always said that you would take me with you, wherever you were going. Now all I have is memories and problems."

Merlene's sorrow was for Winston, but the despair which gripped her was the result of more than just the permanent loss of a lover. By now, she had accepted the fact that Winston was gone and there wasn't a damn thing she could do about it. That her dreams and aspirations had been dashed so suddenly was more difficult to accept, however. Ashes to ashes and dust to dust was all that remained of her plans for the future.

She cast a critical eye at her best friends standing by the grave. Andrea, with the determined expression of a widow who couldn't wait for the last shovelful of earth to be tipped on her dearly departed's grave. Beverly, regarding the occasion as a 'potential husband situation', discreetly swapping numbers with a tall, handsome mourner.

At thirty, Merlene was feeling the anguish of a woman who now realised she would never drive through Paris in a sports car with the cool breeze blowing in her hair. She was too old to fantasise like younger women do. Winston was her last chance to fly away on a magic carpet and experience the freedom of life outside south London. It was a game of high stakes which she had played and lost.

"What am I going to do?" she sobbed softly. "What am I going to do?"

The seemingly endless procession of private cars followed the limousines back to Andrea's council flat. From the cemetery in Nunhead, the motorcade crawled to its destination in Brixton's 'Poet's Corner', grinding the midday traffic into a go-slow. Passing through Dulwich

Village, it attracted the focal attentions of a Japanese tourist with a camera. An elderly black couple stopped at the kerb. The wife couldn't resist observing that this was, "the only time a crowd of yout' nah play no reggae."

"But wait," her aged husband remarked, "half ah dem don't even wear 'at! What a disgrace, Betty. Young people really do not have any manners."

Winston was a popular man. A bit too popular if you ask me, Andrea thought, from the back of the lead limousine. There were too many 'widows' at the funeral. Too many grieving women she had never seen before. Everywhere she turned there was a woman avoiding her eyes from behind a veil. She had begun to feel pissed off.

"Some girls don't have no shame," she remarked aloud.

"What do you mean?" Merlene asked nervously.

"Didn't you see them at the graveside? Whispering loud enough for everyone to hear, about how close dem was to Winston and so on?" Andrea kissed her teeth. "Renk! No respect. Talking as if I'm deaf or sump'n."

"I know what you mean," Beverly added. "I heard a few of them talking like they were married to him."

"They think they can just rope into my yard and eat my food and drink my drink." Andrea kissed her teeth again.

"Do you want us to make sure they don't come inside?" Merlene offered.

"Nah," Andrea declined. "Let them come. I want everyone to see them for what they are."

The loss of a husband can make the most devoted wife cynical, when all sorts of slackness comes out of the woodwork for a burial. Like they can't live with themselves unless they attend. They can live with themselves when they steal another woman's man, but they can't live with themselves if they don't pay their last respects. Even if it means introducing suspicion in the mind of the grieving spouse.

Andrea had only herself to blame. She had suspected

Winston of playing away from home many times, but had done little about it, believing it would cease once her seven years of bad luck were completed. Today, the very day she buried Winston, was the end of her seven years. Can fate really be so cruel, she wondered.

It's impossible to keep a man on a leash. Throughout their seven-year relationship, Winston sowed his wild oats regardless, Andrea was sure. He had stayed out on countless nights and had come home smelling of cheap perfume too many times. But Winston had denied everything outright. He claimed he didn't know anything about the mysterious midnight telephone calls when the line would go dead if Andrea answered. Whenever Winston answered, however, he would close the bedroom door gently behind him, to make it difficult for her to overhear his whispered words in the hallway.

Being sure of her man's infidelity was insufficient. Andrea needed to catch him red-handed otherwise he would make her eat her circumstantial evidence.

Andrea gritted her teeth. Judging by the number of tearful women at the cemetery, Winston must have been having it away with half of south London. Pure slackness. There was no other word for it. She, at least, was tactful enough to make sure that the men she met didn't even have her phone number, much less her address.

Sinking into the limousine's deep leather seats, she comforted herself with the thought that at least she had her closest friends supporting her. At a time like this, she knew she could rely on her sisterhood.

He had been watching her silently from the other side of the room for some time. There was no mistaking the message in the disarming, dimpled smile and the warm inviting eyes. As she felt her bosom harden, Andrea readjusted her blouse and then blushed, realising that

6

Donovan was still observing her closely.

"Everyt'ing will be all right, Andrea. Trust me." Fitzroy's voice was like the Messenger of Doom, waking her from her private daydreams.

"Let me tell you somet'ing," he whispered. "I know for a fact dat Winston nevah dead."

Andrea was tempted to fling her glass of red wine in his face. She was tired of the gathering, tired of everything.

About thirty of the guests had crammed into her tiny living room for the funeral reception. Beverly and Merlene were helping out making sure that the guests all had enough to eat and drink. It was an ordeal that the next of kin were expected to go through. Why was it, Andrea wondered, that your friends and family always throw a great party for you when you're dead, when you're the one person who can't attend? Winston would have loved the plate of rice and soft boiled banana.

Andrea wished everybody would simply disappear, particularly Fitzroy. She needed time to pick up the pieces of a life without Winston.

She knew the youth from time. He was Winston's closest male friend. She didn't much like him nor the way he was always talking about 'the old days' — the criminal days — with Winston. They would sit and talk until the early hours, smoking weed and playing cards, while Fitzroy animated the conversation with memories of daring, illegal escapades from their youth. But whereas Winston had changed his ways, Fitzroy was still a baby gangster and a hustler. Not to be trusted one bit. He had even tried it on with her once, when Winston was away on business. After that she had tried to ban Fitzroy from the flat, without success. Winston wouldn't hear of it. Fitzroy was his best friend and that was that. Well, Fitzroy was somebody else's problem now. With his spar dead, he would have no reason to drop by Andrea's modest council flat uninvited.

"Winston told me he was going to pull a skank," Fitzroy continued at low volume, looking over his shoulders suspiciously for prying ears. "He said that he might have to stay undercover, low profile, for a while. Y'know. Dis t'ing is a set-up. Winston nah go ah no funeral. Ah no lie."

Andrea cast Fitzroy a dismissive look, sizing him up scornfully. Fitzroy liked to play big-shot, but unlike the big 'supes' who paraded up and down Atlantic Road in their shiny new motors, Fitzroy had not seen the fruits of his life in crime. He had no future, no prospects and he never had any money. He was condemned to a life of signing on, in between spells at Her Majesty's pleasure up on Brixton Hill. Jail was an occupational hazard for this small-time crackhead.

"What are you talking about, Fitzroy?"

More than anything, Andrea pitied him, because he hadn't grown up. He still hadn't understood why his contemporaries had all left the fantasy 'wild west' life of youth behind them. Everybody else was getting on with life, buying homes and starting families, while Fitzroy believed he was still part of a bad bwoy posse of Brixton outlaws. The brightest hope in Fitzroy's life was another spell on Brixton Hill. At least there he could learn a trade. He had been virtually illiterate when he first got sent down for a jail term. But he had learned to read and write inside. Fitzroy was living proof that detention works.

"He's not dead. Winston's not dead. He's alive." Fitzroy protested. "He had to bury the loot, seen? A whole heap ah money."

Frustrated by Andrea's casual manner, Fitzroy had blurted out the words a little too loudly. A deafening silence fell over the packed living room at the mention of money, with all the guests craning their necks to be within earshot.

"Yes, all right." Andrea smiled apologetically to the

guests. The situation now under control, they resumed their natter. "Find me proof of the money and I'll believe you," she assured Fitzroy, while taking the opportunity to start up a conversation with someone she hardly knew. She looked around the room casually, hoping to catch Donovan's attention, but he was nowhere to be seen. Andrea frowned. Once again, Fitzroy had come between her and a man.

Fitzroy's outburst had struck a chord in Merlene's soul. How did Fitzroy know about the money? Winston must have told him. The bastard. How could he tell anyone when he knew where it came from? She was the one who was going to go to prison if anyone found out. If he told Fitzroy about the money, who's to know what he told Andrea. How could she be sure of how much or how little Andrea knew? And where was the missing money? She had to find it. Quick time.

The skank was simple but original, the product of a fertile imagination and too many crime novels. Merlene had hit upon it during the course of a lazy afternoon at her job in the accounts office of the council. For her, the idea was sufficiently exciting. Winston's reaction, however, was far more serious. He had raved about it.

"Love the beauty of it," he had said. "Me jus' love the beauty and the simplicity. It's the perfect skank."

Winston eventually persuaded Merlene to put the idea into practice. A few weeks earlier, the first instalments of grant money had come through for the twenty fictitious students that Merlene had inserted onto the council's student grant list. Thirty-four grand in all. Winston had called her the night before his death and assured her that he had deposited the cheques through various phony bank accounts and that he would transfer the cash into her name in the next few days. But he died before he could make good his promise and now there was thirty-four grand in cash out there somewhere, just waiting to be picked up.

The ulcer in Merlene's stomach burned like crazy every time she thought about it.

Merlene didn't get a wink of sleep that night. By morning, she looked haggard. Good job she had taken the day off work.

She planned to pay Fitzroy a little visit, hoping that he might know something which could shed some light on her predicament. Perhaps there was something in what Fitzroy had said about Winston burying the money. But what if the secret of the money was buried with Winston? Time was running out.

Before she stole the money, Merlene had never seen thirty-four grand in one lump sum. She believed that in life everybody gets one chance to taste that crock of gold at the end of the rainbow — legally or otherwise. This was her chance.

She didn't have the guts to do it straight away, though. She needed someone to reassure her. That someone was Winston, her 'part-time sump'n'. He was so eager for the skank, he even promised he would leave Andrea and run off to the Caribbean with Merlene if they pulled it off. He had never promised anything like that before.

"Now listen, tek the money and leave the job," he had assured her. "By the time it's found missing, we'll be relaxing on our island in the sun. Where's your job going to take you? Back-ah-yard we could set up nice together. Buy a lickle piece of land by the sea. But we don't have no money. In life, you haffe tek chance. What better chance are we going to get? If yuh nuh ready, step aside. I can deal with the cheques myself, with no comeback to you."

That Merlene wanted to spend the rest of her life with Winston was beyond question. He was the best thing that had ever happened to her. He was right, she was in a dead-end job. She wasn't going to get promotion unless she took some more exams. As a thirty year old single parent, where was she going to find the time to go to evening classes?

10

Anyway, she could take all the exams in the world and still not get anywhere.

Like most people whose families left the islands for economic reasons in the fifties and sixties, Merlene dreamed of returning. But to do that successfully, you had to have cash money. Now, with no Winston and no money, her dream of running off to the Caribbean was shattered. With the money she still stood a chance of setting herself up in Jamaica. Back home her son, Marlon, would get a chance to grow up healthy and strong and conscious of his roots. Thirty-four grand would smooth the way.

It didn't even enter her head to return the money to the council. That kind of thing is out of date.

The weather had turned chilly, but Merlene refused to allow the biting wind to interfere with her resolve. It was the first time she had been on the estate since her school days. Back then, it was a nice, clean, newly-built estate. Now, the walkways and lawns had fallen into dilapidation and the residential blocks stretching from Brixton to Stockwell were considered the roughest in the area. The estate had seen better days.

She was looking for number one hundred and twenty-nine. One hundred and twenty-five... ninety-six... The numbers didn't follow any order.

"You know where Fitzroy lives?" she asked two youngsters who were leaning casually over the balcony.

The boys turned around. They were dressed in the familiar 'gangsta' style that was popular with south London youngsters — baggy jeans with bullet holes, baseball caps and hooded jackets — the type of clothes Marlon was always begging for. Merlene noticed the spliff that was being passed casually between them. The two boys weren't much older than Marlon and were already smoking spliff.

The boys grinned at each other. The taller, skinnier of the two spoke first.

"If me ah go do sump'n fe you, wha' you ah go do fe me?" he asked in a Jamaican accent learned in a secondary school in Camberwell.

"Look, I haven't got time to play games," Merlene snapped. "Do you know where Fitzroy lives or not?"

"Well, that depends."

"Oh, shut up," Merlene interrupted, turning around to continue her search.

"Okay, okay, hang on," the tall boy called, reverting to his natural south London 'cockney'. "Fitzroy's is the last flat along. The one with the big security gate in front of it. You can't miss it."

Merlene continued walking until she came to the door with the wrought-iron gate. The life Fitzroy lived, he needed at all times to keep a barrier between his runnings and the local police. They had tried to break down the gate several times, but without success.

"Fitzroy... Fitzroy! It's me, Merlene," she shouted through the gate.

As the door opened slowly, the sharp, acrid smell from a red-hot pipe gushed out.

"Come in, Merle," a smiling Fitzroy beckoned.

The flat was a pig-sty. Fitzroy used the floor as a sink, a wardrobe, a waste bin — whatever.

"I can't stay long," Merlene said hurriedly, "but as I said on the phone, I need to find out some things."

"Why you need to know about Winston so badly?" Fitzroy asked suspiciously.

"Because we had some runnings."

"It's like I said," Fitzroy interrupted her, "he's not really dead. He told me everyt'ing. He was involved in some lickle jugglings, seen? He was checking some part-time gal, some high class sump'n at the council. They skanked fifty grand. He was gonna disappear back-ah-yard an' lie low."

Merlene blushed modestly. There was no point in correcting the inaccuracies in Fitzroy's story. Right now it was more important to get the information she needed. She had to come clean.

"Look, Fitz, Winston is dead. Definitely. I saw him myself. There's nothing that anyone can do about it. Fitzroy, I have to find that money. You see, I'm that woman. I helped Winston pull the skank."

Merlene studied Fitzroy's reaction to the news. Almost immediately, she regretted confiding in him. She didn't trust him. But he was her best hope. She decided to lie. "Now that he's gone, I have to put the money back. I need to know where that money is. Did he say anything about where he hid the money?"

"Bumboclaat!" Fitzroy was clearly bemused. "So, is you dat?"

"Yes, yes. The important thing now is that I get hold of the money as fast as I can and return it. The whole thing could be found out at any time. I'm desperate."

"Put back the money? Cho! You're crazy, man. Put back fifty grand? Nah, man. We ah go find the money an' split it. Fifty-fifty. Seen?"

Merlene looked at him blankly. She realised she had made a mistake confiding in this hustler.

"Fitzroy, the money has to be returned," she insisted, nervously following his cocaine-propelled eyes as they spun around in their sockets.

"Easy," he reassured her. "We could be a team, t'raasclaat! Like Bonnie an' Clyde. You an' me."

Merlene stared at the youth incredulously.

"You must be joking, Fitzroy. You think I would waste my time with someone like you?" Merlene taunted.

"Tek a look at yuhself," Fitzroy replied. "You ah huff an' ah puff an' gwan like yuh chest big. But remember — how it go...? 'Thou shalt not steal, thou shalt not kill neither commit adultery. Ah nuh me seh so. Ah de bible seh so."

Merlene winced. "I can see I've wasted my time here. I'll wish you good luck and goodbye."

She brushed past him and headed out of the flat. Fitzroy called after her.

"An' how you ah go find the money widout me? You NEED me."

Merlene continued without turning back. Fitzroy was right, she didn't have a clue where to look. But she hoped she would never have to stoop so low as to ask for his help again.

Dancehall gals, with their barely-decent outfits and exaggerated make-up, have an incredible effect on men. They can make particularly stingy men lose their hearts, their minds and their wallets in an evening. Concrete Jungle in Vauxhall was a venue which always allowed women free entrance before midnight. On this mild evening in early October the ravers were out in force. The place was rammed. At the entrance, the promoter and his 'idren' danced a little jig, rubbing their hands gleefully and whistling 'tra-la-la-la-la-la-lee'. Everything in the dance was sweet. Security maximum.

The deejays were deejaying their gun lyrics when Fitzroy entered. The music relaxed him, as he took a swig from his can of Kestrel Export in the darkened, sweaty, smoky venue.

Fitzroy usually went raving to look for a woman. But tonight he went with backative. He had got word on the 'frontline' wire that Errol Holt suspected him of ripping him off. Nothing moved in Brixton without the say-so of the Holt brothers, Barrington and Errol. Barrington was cool, a real professional, but Errol, the youngest and wildest, was a feared bad bwoy. Fitzroy had to find him first and sort out the misunderstanding. But he needed his backative, just in case.

"Remember me?" A female voice caressed his ear.

Fitzroy turned to face a sexy, red-skinned girl with a blonde wig, a micro-mini skirt and one of those suggestive smiles men say they can't resist. He recognised her as a girl he had tried unsuccessfully to chirps a while back — same place, same time. A girl who was well aware of the effect her body had on men. Fitzroy licked his lips. Mmmm, maybe some other time. He wouldn't feel comfortable tonight until he had sorted out his business with Errol.

"Girl chile, nah bother run me down right now," Fitzroy spoke slowly and in a low, sincere voice.

The girl looked at him, practically saying 'I wanna ride you'. She wasn't used to being turned down. She eased herself close behind him, slipped her arm around his waist, reaching out to lightly pat his groin.

"Baby, I can stroke you where it feels good," she purred, caressing his earlobe with her warm breath. "You have the stamina?"

Fitzroy stiffened. It was tempting. The girl was lovable. But not tonight.

"Nah worry yuhself," he said with a smirk.

He felt her release the groping hand suddenly and heard her scream. Fitzroy spun around, his hand on his backative.

The girl lay sprawled out on the floor, the table she had been thrown across, on top of her. The glasses on the table had emptied their alcoholic contents over her blouse and micro-mini skirt, titillating the leering male idlers. A huge, angry man was standing over her.

"You bitch! I turn my back for one minute and you're rubbing up against a nex' man."

Fitzroy observed the man pitifully. He hoped he would never embarrass himself like this over a woman.

"Jus' cool, nuh man. Ease off," he said.

He didn't want to get mixed up in it, but at the same

time he didn't want to see the girl get battered further.

The angry boyfriend looked up. "Who the fuck are you?" he spat venomously.

Fitzroy shivered. The man was built like a big stone wall. But then again, he didn't know about Fitzroy's backative.

"Look, boss, true me an' you nuh have no argument. Seen? An' true, if your woman steps outta line you mus' manners her. But leave it inna yuh yard, man."

The boyfriend rolled up his sleeves. He knew that he could take on the skinnier man and flatten him with ease.

"So who's gonna bodyguard YOU, Mister Bodyguard?"

He lunged at Fitzroy. The smaller man was quicker and niftily stepped to one side, sending the boyfriend crashing into the bar behind him. By the time the man had taken a moment to compose himself, he was staring into the barrel of a 'matic, which Fitzroy had drawn with the speed of a bullet.

"Don't tes' me," Fitzroy hissed slowly. "You haffe mind how you ah talk," he continued in a drawl that Clint Eastwood would have been proud of.

All too accustomed to this rude bwoy business, the ravers had scattered. It was every woman for herself, their men nowhere to be seen.

If Fitzroy hadn't been acting out a scene from *Dirty Harry*, he might have seen one of the burly bouncers from Pitbull Security, the baddest security firm in south London, creeping up on the left flank, with a baseball bat in his hand. The bat came crashing down on the gunman's wrist. Fitzroy yelled with pain as his grip released the pistol, sending it clattering to the ground. The gun was picked up by another of Pitbull's bouncers and it vanished from sight. In a flash, the first bouncer had his victim pinned to a wall, the baseball bat at his throat. Fitzroy struggled in vain, realising now that he was in serious trouble. Pinned to the wall, the baseball bat at his throat, is how he remained until the police came to collect him and the gun.

The sound system had been switched off, the venue lights switched on. The restless crowd had no choice but to hang around, while the twenty or so officers had finished questioning each and everyone of them in turn. Everyone had their own version of events.

"Me warn the deejay, 'Stop boosting gun lyrics'. But dem nevah stop until the place get hot," said one man.

"It's time fe tell the politicians to stop giving the youth dem guns," said another.

TWO

Brixton talk. Rude bwoy chat. Contemporary Afro-Saxons favour a lingua that is a language of their own — a cross between Jamaican patois and yankee, blended with their local vernacular. Brixton talk is coming like a yankee yardman's cockney.

"So where d'you want to go raving tonight? We could check out Rampage."

"Nah, man. I'm reaching Night Moves if it kills me. It was the lick last week. Remember when the whole dance mash-up?"

"How y'mean? Course I do. All five, six hours an' nobody nah siddung. Pure niceness ah gwaning."

"Yeah, man. It was ruff."

"See't deh."

The two women laughed as they recalled a good night out.

"An' you 'member that nasty bwoy who was tryin' to chirps you?"

"Oh don't... Don't. I'm not having it."

"Yes, what was his name again, Dawn? Lancelot? Yes, him dance a lot, but me nevah see him lance a lot."

"No, that's just out of order, Angie. You know I don't like to be reminded of that. That's outta order. But that is not my biggest problem, because me can love any man."

"See't deh."

Andrea smiled at the two younger women warily. She didn't much like them. They were sneaky like a snake outta grass, but they were regular customers. They had to be. Looking sexy was their full-time occupation. They spent their mornings in the gym to stay trim and on

18

Saturdays they could be seen on Fonthill Road, Finsbury Park, shopping for the latest fashions at factory prices. They would literally starve themselves all week to squeeze into a size eight. But no matter how good they looked in their outfits, they didn't look their best until they returned to Brixton to get their hair done.

Ebony Hair salon was a tiny premises in the half of the Brixton Arcade on the north side of Atlantic Road. Wedged between a Nigerian grocery store selling red-hot chillies and gari on the one side, and Neville's Record Shack, constantly blasting the latest dancehall releases on the other, it was inconspicuous enough not to attract passing trade. But Andrea's reputation for doing wonders with a pair of scissors and a clump of weave-on hair was legendary. With a decent lick of paint, the salon would be packed constantly. But Sister Anthea was happy with the little money her business brought in. She was set in her ways, too old to be motivated by wealth.

Andrea loved and respected Sister Anthea, but she had outgrown the salon and was thinking of setting up her own place. There was no future for her at Ebony, not on her basic salary. Winston had only been buried two days but already the bills had started coming through her letterbox — including one for the next repayment on her car, which Winston, uninsured, had written off in his fatal crash.

"Girl chile, I beg you, nuh budda burn up me head with that stuff," Angie warned as Andrea applied the relaxer on her hair. Andrea simply smiled. They were her last two clients of the day and always thought they knew best. Angie wanted the type of short, relaxed cut that an American R&B songstress had made famous. Andrea couldn't work miracles. If Angie wanted that style, she had to be prepared for a bit of heat.

"Anyways," Angie continued, turning to Dawn, "tonight I'm going to take it easy. Unless Barrington reaches."

"Barrington?" Dawn queried. "Barrington? What about Linvall? I thought you were checking Linvall now?"

"Well me mash it up already, so it's no problem," Angie replied sarcastically. "Him is not advanced."

"I know what you mean. He doesn't know the first thing about making a woman feel nice. Y'know. I remember when I was checking him, he would always say, 'You are my number one. You are my number one'. Ah dat him call foreplay. Can you imagine? And he's got a padlock on his wallet too."

"He had the nerve to call me up to talk about how we could be a team. About how he needed a woman to wash his clothes proper an' cook his dinner proper."

"He nevah! Did he?"

"What d'you mean he nevah, when I'm telling you that's the kind of foolishness the man ah deal wid? No, man. I'm saving myself for Barrington. Yuh nah see how the boy sweet so? Dresses stush and drives a wicked Mercedes."

"So you're moving with Barrington now?" Andrea asked in passing as she treated her customer's hair.

"What's it got to do with you?" Angie snapped.

"I'm just asking, that's all. You know how he earns his money, don't you? An' don't you think he's rather old for you? Old enough to be your father."

Angie flashed Andrea a cold, dismissive look.

"I said, what's it got to do with you?"

Andrea got the message and continued with the hair.

"You see what I mean, Dawn," Angie continued. "Bush don't have ears, but someone always deh inna it, hearing you. Too much hypocrites deh 'bout, spreading rumours."

Andrea simply frowned. Angie's derision didn't faze her.

Angie and Dawn were only nineteen, but they had taken over the scene. Everywhere they went, men's dripping tongues were bound to follow. They practically threw themselves over any man willing to flash a fifty pound note in front of them.

For every new generation that passes another is waiting in the wings waiting to take over. Every day, some youth somewhere says goodbye to his or her crew and the things they used to do and settles down. Before you know it, a next youth is standing at the old spot hustling same way. When Andrea and her posse gave up their claim to Brixton, Angie and Dawn inherited the mantle and now spent their time fighting to maintain their position as the most eligible girls in south London.

The tangy smell of hair relaxer greeted Merlene as she entered the salon for a welcome break from the hustle and bustle of a Saturday afternoon at the market.

"Hi, Merle," Andrea greeted her friend. "What's occurring?"

"Nothing much," came Merlene's sedate reply. "How are you?"

"Well, you know, ain't got no shoes on my feet but still I'm dancing. You haven't come to get your hair done, have you? I want to get away early tonight."

"Don't worry yourself. I only dropped in to see how you were doing. I was shopping in the market anyway and passing by."

"Safe. Take a seat, I'll be done in a few minutes."

"Don't rush my hair, you know," Angie said quickly. "I've got to look my best tonight. I don't want no rush job."

"Relax," Andrea assured her. "I've finished the styling. You're nearly done."

Angie turned to Dawn and continued her conversation.

"Anyways, as I was saying, Barrington love me bad. Bad-bad. I didn't believe it at first, but actions speak louder than words."

The hair done, Andrea left Angie admiring herself in the mirror and went across to Merlene.

"Sorry about that," Merlene said, nodding towards

Angie and Dawn as they inspected Andrea's handiwork. "Those two are renk."

"Don't worry about them, they're harmless," Andrea assured.

"Slack more like. They want to mind who they disrespect."

"Without them I'd be out of a job. Anyway, we used to be just like them a few years ago. Remember?"

"I don't remember letting my tits hang out of my blouse when I went out," said Merlene with exaggerated modesty.

"Yeah, we stopped just short of that," Andrea reminisced with an exaggerated sigh.

"We at least kept our clothes on until we got under the sheets. Those girls may as well be streaking."

Pleased with the job well done, Angie settled the bill.

"He says he loves me, but the only thing that I'm worried about," whispered Angie as she and Dawn walked out the door, "is that he's a bit funny. He wants me to come with him to an orgy. No, it's not what you think. All I have to do is watch."

Exhausted, Andrea turned to Merlene with a sigh of relief.

"I'm burned out."

"You're getting old," Merlene teased, jabbing her younger friend's pert behind.

"It's all right for you, I'm working twenty-four seven, what with one thing and another. Look how your hair so twist up, Merle. Honestly, I'm rushed off my feet, but I still manage to keep my hair nice." Andrea pulled out a comb and began straightening Merlene's hair out. "If you don't take care of it, it will start breaking up."

"Yeah I know, I know," Merlene answered with a smile on her face. Andrea was always poking in her friends' hair whenever she got a chance.

Merlene turned serious.

"Are you sure everything's okay about Winston and the

funeral and all that?"

"Oh yes, yes." Andrea waved the question away with a hand. "Winston's dead, but life goes on. It's difficult grieving for someone you didn't even know."

"What do you mean?"

"I'm finding out something new about Winston every day. Things I should have known by rights."

Merlene had begun to sweat as she shifted uneasily in her seat. "Like what?" she asked, waiting to exhale.

"I got a call from a woman who claims she was his baby mother."

"You nevah!" Merlene cried out with relief.

"Yeah, man. Oh that was years ago, before Winston and me, y'know. The kid's eight years old now. It was his birthday yesterday. When she didn't get the yearly cheque for the kid's birthday, she called up Winston's mobile to cuss him. Can you believe that? She was living just around the corner until recently."

"I'm really sorry that you had to hear about it that way, Andrea."

"I'm not. It doesn't bother me at all."

Despite her friend's resolute words, Merlene could see that Andrea was vexed. She feared how Andrea would react if she discovered... No, no. That was unthinkable.

"The woman said that she thinks that Winston had another baby mother as well. But she's not sure where the woman lives."

The news upset Merlene. She couldn't believe that Winston had two kids. It was as if he had deceived *her*. Why had he not mentioned it?

Andrea felt precisely the same way and asked herself the exact same question. But neither of them knew what the other was thinking and, for a moment, neither cared.

"Then I told her Winston was dead. Can you believe it, she asked if he left any money."

Merlene's eyes lit up. The real reason for dropping by to

see Andrea, was to find out if she knew anything about a certain sum of missing money.

"A man dies and suddenly everybody starts asking for money."

"It's truly a shame," Merlene agreed. "So did he leave any money?"

"Money? Joke you ah joke, Merlene. When las' you hear about a black man leaving money? *Eeenh?* When las' you hear that?"

"I just thought, maybe. You know, Winston was always doing so many things, he seemed to have his finger in so many pies."

"Pies? You can say that again. Pies, with bodies shaped like a coca-cola bottle."

"I just thought he might have a bit of money lying around. So he didn't leave anything at all?"

"Do you know something I don't know?" Andrea asked suspiciously. "Winston never left a will nor no insurance. All he left was bills to pay, but no money to pay them with."

Merlene sighed. "I'm sorry to hear that," she said.

"Oh, forget it. Forget it. Look, honestly Merle, the sooner I get that man out of my system the better. I can't believe he deceived me like that. When we first started seeing each other I asked him straight whether he had any kids or not. He lied to me. Why?"

Merlene put her arm reassuringly around her friend. She didn't have the answer to the question, as much as she desired to know herself.

Wrapped in her girlfriend's warm embrace, Andrea broke down in tears. Winston had let her down badly. Call it delayed reaction, but she was finally feeling it.

"All I wanted was a good man?" Andrea blurted out tearfully. "Just an ordinary guy who was honest. How come there aren't any men out there like that, Merle?"

"There are, Andrea. Really there are."

Merlene's words did little to comfort the distressed woman.

"Let me take you home," Merlene offered eventually. Put on your clothes, girl, we'll go to a party."

"Thanks Merle, but I've really got to be on my own tonight."

"Are you sure?"

"Yes. Really. I'll be all right."

Merlene was reluctant to go. She hung around until Andrea had locked up and then insisted on accompanying her friend halfway up Railton Road.

"I'll be all right. You go on off home," Andrea insisted. It's a good thing the good Lord is around to pick us up whenever we go down, she thought to herself.

Merlene took her leave, ignoring the catcalls from the group of men hanging on the corner, each with a brew in his hand.

Andrea continued her way down Railton Road, pushing her way past the kerbside hustlers. No matter what anyone said, she adored Brixton. She romanticised it out of all proportion. It was the vibes. No matter the season, this was still a community that existed in black and white and pulsated to the beat of reggae. Brixton meant beautiful women and guys who knew all the angles. Even though Andrea enjoyed her trips 'home' to the land of wood and water, she knew that she could never leave Brixton permanently. It was her manor and it always would be.

Andrea was awakened early Monday morning by the insistent ring of the telephone. Shaking herself into full consciousness, she picked up the receiver to hear a firm, authoritative voice on the other end of the line.

"Miss Dunbar?"

"Er...yeah. Who's this?" Who had the cheek to be

calling this early?

"Notting Hill police station. You are registered as the owner of the black Volkswagen Golf which was involved in an accident on the Westway recently?"

"Yeah, yeah. That's right. What's wrong?"

"Nothing wrong. We've finished examining the vehicle. We'd like you to come down and sign for the contents of the car and arrange for it to be removed. As you know, it's a total write-off."

Andrea winced. What did he expect her to do with a total write-off?

"Can't this wait?" she asked irritably.

"Not really."

"All right, all right. I'll be down later today."

Andrea slammed the phone down and, despite herself, cursed Winston.

Even though she had been Winston's main squeeze for the past seven years, he had always refused to get married. He just wasn't interested in the 'm' word, yet they practically lived together as man and wife.

Nowadays, few black men walk down the aisle willingly. Andrea knew that. She had guested at more than one shotgun wedding.

"I don't need a piece of paper telling me that you're my queen," Winston had explained repeatedly. "I know that already. We don't need that. We're Africans, y'know. All we have to do is jump over the broom and it done." "It done" and "it finish," were Winston's ways of terminating any discussion.

They had even got engaged the year before. He didn't mind that. As far as Winston was concerned the engagement could last twenty years, just as long as they didn't have to walk down the aisle at the end of it.

Many women would immediately conclude that if a man shies away from marriage too strongly, get rid of him. But not Andrea. She held on to the hope that it would all work out in the end.

Winston was a smooth operator. He could sweet-up a girl nice.

"No matter who you see me with, you are still my number one," he had assured Andrea many times. "My main squeeze. No matter what the situation, we'll talk about it indoors. So I beg you, don't wash our dirty linen in public."

If only Winston hadn't got so under my skin, Andrea sighed.

She was still thinking about Winston's reluctance to get married when the taxi dropped her outside Notting Hill police station. A sense of guilt riddled her every thought. She ought to be playing the part of the grieving partner, rather than the suspicious girlfriend. It would do no good thinking about what could have been, or should have been, or may have been, when the truth is that nothing would come of that thinking. Winston was dead. That was the main thing. She'd rebuild her life, starting with the removal of her Golf.

"Can I help you?"

The voice from that morning's telephone call greeted her from behind the desk.

"You called me this morning. Andrea Dunbar. I've come to collect my Golf."

"Oh that's you, is it?" The policeman grinned. "Right mess the deceased made of your motor. Knew him well did you?"

"Yeah. What's it to you?" Andrea answered sharply. Ever since the unfortunate incident when she had boxed a feisty customer at the salon she worked at as a trainee, police stations had made her feel uneasy.

The officer looked at her and smiled.

"Well, Miss…" the officer trailed his finger down the record book. "Andrea Winsome Dunbar. Of Shakespeare Road, SE24."

"Yes, that's right," Andrea replied hurriedly. "Where do I sign?"

"Hold on, just one moment." There was a hint of triumph in the policeman's voice.

A scowl appeared on Andrea's face. She kissed her teeth and sighed in disbelief, as the officer motioned to a colleague in plain clothes behind him.

"If you don't mind… We'd like to ask you a few more questions about the vehicle. This way please."

Andrea stared directly at the officer. She was still angry, but her scowl was now tempered with a touch of humility. The cops seemed bent on wasting her time. There was no point in arguing.

She followed the officer to a tiny office in the building's inner sanctum, where she took a seat opposite the plain clothes detective.

"So, Miss Dunbar…" He jumped up suddenly, producing a briefcase from under his desk. He slammed the briefcase onto the table and popped the lock.

Andrea couldn't believe her eyes. It was Winston's case. There was no doubt about it. She recognised the jet black snake-skinned briefcase she had bought him for his birthday the previous year, with the initials W.P. inscribed in gold leaf on the side. But the inside of the case was lined with more money than she had ever seen. Fivers, tenners, twenty pound notes.

"Can you explain this money we found in your boyfriend's car?"

"What…? Er… I suppose it's money that Winston had with him for a business deal. He was a music promoter. He promoted concerts. He often carried large sums of money, to pay artists and that sort of thing."

"That's a lot of money to be carrying about." The officer's tone suggested that he didn't believe a word of it. "Five thousand pounds. Supposing he got mugged?"

"Well, that's the way he did business. What can I say?"

Andrea could think of no better explanation, but she had to buy time with some story or other. Otherwise she would never see that money.

"Have you got any proof?" the detective asked sarcastically.

"How do you expect me to have? He did business his way and didn't take too kindly to people knowing what he was up to."

The detective knew she was lying, but there wasn't much he could do, except use some delaying tactics.

"Well, Miss Dunbar. All we can do for the moment is hold on to this money, until my officers have made their enquiries and I am satisfied the cash doesn't correspond to any money reported missing recently. Meanwhile, if you come up with any more information please call the station immediately. You can ask for me, I'm Detective Constable MacInnes."

He wrote his name and number hurriedly on a sheet of paper, handing it to Andrea while he held the door open for her exit.

Outside, a heavy downpour had been sent down from the heavens to dampen the day. With the exception of the briefcase, the police had signed Winston's possessions over to Andrea. Looking at the downpour, she pulled her dead boyfriend's Burberry raincoat over her shoulders and raced down the road to Holland Park underground station, passing the remains of her once gleaming new Golf, now dangling unceremoniously behind a towtruck, waiting to be taken to its final resting place. She took a last fretful look at it before crossing the road to the tube station.

The image of the suitcase full of money flashed repeatedly through Andrea's mind on the journey home. What was Winston doing with all that money? Like most men, he kept his wallet close to his chest but she had suspected that he had his eye on a secondhand Mercedes convertible that a financially-strapped friend was selling.

She pushed her hands deep into the side pockets of the Burberry as she considered the possibility. Almost indifferently, she pulled out a postcard from one of the pockets and read it casually.

Darling Winston,

Looking forward to spending the rest of my life with you on our beach in the Caribbean.

Your future wife.

Andrea didn't recognise the handwriting or the words. She turned the card over and over, looking for clues. It had been sent to an address she didn't recognise. It had a West End postmark dated shortly before Winston's death. None of it made any sense. Who had sent it? What did it mean? What about the money? How did it all fit together?

Suspicion and an air of mystery consumed her thoughts as she waited on the southbound platform of the Victoria Line at Oxford Circus. The suspense was killing her. Taking a moment to think, she took off the raincoat and went through its pockets systematically. She recognised Winston's house keys. More interestingly, she found his cheque book in an inside pocket tucked discreetly into the lining of the coat. There it was, the entry on the last stub. The money in the suitcase. Drawn in cash! The police were so hopeless that they had missed the evidence. Andrea paused to read the postcard again.

Looking forward to spending the rest of my life with you, on our beach in the Caribbean. Your future wife.

It didn't make any sense. She rustled quickly through the plastic bag filled with Winston's effects, almost shrieking with alarm as she pulled out the dead man's passport. There could only be one reason for Winston to have his passport on him.

Old-time people used to say, 'when you pass away, even nanny goat know your secret'. Andrea sat on the thick-piled carpet of her living room rummaging through boxes filled with Winston's belongings. Fire burned in her eyes as she went through everything meticulously. Everything. She inspected his suits for unfamiliar strands of hair. She went through his record collection, reading the inscriptions for tell-tale signs. It no longer mattered that she didn't replace the albums in order. Winston couldn't lose his temper now. Seven years of their relationship lay strewn across the thick-pile carpet, but she didn't give a damn. There was badness on her breath. She had to find out who this 'future wife' was.

She thumbed her way hungrily, through the stack of unopened letters addressed to her late lover. A phone bill reminder. A car tax reminder. An indecipherable letter from someone called Junior. Unopened letters from Winston's bank manager reminding him of his overdraft limit, a couple of recording contracts and some letters from the Social. Winston was hardly a man of letters. Andrea then turned her attentions to the two books Winston owned, turning them upside down in case any incriminating slip of paper should fall out from between the pages. Then she went through his entire wardrobe. She studied the photos in the crumpled manila envelope. Photos of Winston at school, of him looking cool, drinking with the boys and with Andrea. There were several photographs of ex-girlfriends, few of whom Andrea recognised. Maybe one of these women...? The words on the postcard echoed through her thoughts:

Looking forward to spending the rest of my life with you... Your future wife.

No clues. What was the next step? She rolled onto her back, lying face up. Whoever said it was right, she thought to herself, the only man you can trust is a dead man. She picked up the photograph taken at their engagement party at the Roof Gardens in Kensington. Winston smiling seductively, his arm around Andrea's waist. Those were happier times. The pair looked like a couple of star-crossed young lovers on their first date. How ironic. She stared lifelessly at Winston's leery grin. It was a stupid grin. It had always been a stupid grin. The stupid grin of a stupid man.

The bastard. She understood now why Winston never wanted to get married all these years. She had provided him with a place to stay and spending money. All the time, he had been planning to elope with some other woman. He didn't even have the bottle to tell her. The bastard. To think that she was so cut up about him dying. She had cried for a week. Like a good widow she had stayed celibate, even though Donovan had left several messages for her in the last few days, wanting to start a 't'ing'. She had been tempted too. Like every woman, Andrea had physical needs. But she had not encouraged his advances, in deference to her dearly departed. All these things she had done out of respect for his memory. In return, he had reached from the grave and slapped her in the face. The bastard.

Andrea ripped the photograph down the middle. On the half from which Winston's smiling face now peered on its own, she wrote: *The only true man, is a dead man.*

"Men can be devious, y'know," she muttered to herself softly. "You can never know wha' ah really gwan with them." And she was right. Promise is a comfort to a fool. Looks are deceiving. Open up to the cold facts staring you in the face. Get a deeper reasoning before you deduce your conclusion. Always check his every move. The most obscure little detail could give you a surprise big enough to wipe the smile off your face when you realise what your man is up to.

Never again would she trust a man. She would sleep with men, use them then cast them aside, but never again would she speak of love to any man. All the diamonds and the pearls, all the sweetness in the world, would never again buy her love.

Oh well, backwards never, forwards forever and ever,

Andrea reasoned, picking up the phone and dialling Notting Hill police station.

"Detective Constable MacInnes? Andrea Dunbar. That money came from my late partner's bank account. I've got the counterfoil. Okay, I'll come down and collect it tomorrow morning."

Her seven years of bad luck had truly come to an end. She would cash in on Winston's death, she told herself, "respect is overdue." The money would help realise her dream. She would make Sister Anthea an offer for the lease of the Ebony salon. A safety net for the future.

"Yes!" she rejoiced. "Yes! Yes! Yes!!"

THREE

Half of Brixton knew that Max was back. You could see the guys on the corner, with their tongues dropping down to the ground when they heard the news. The reaction of their women was more like, "Why she nevah bother stay in Jamaica?" Because Max's return had upped the stakes. They would have to work harder to keep their man. Every man wanted their woman to look like Max. She was the measure for half of the women on the sunny side of the Thames.

Beverly got the news at the same time as the others. She recognised immediately the voice on the answering machine. "Hi Sugar. This is the Max, back from JA. I'm calling the crew together. At Dunn's River. Tonight at eight. You must reach."

Merlene and Andrea had received similar messages.

Beverly was looking forward to meeting up with the crew, she had some big news of her own to announce. It had been six months since she had seen any of the girls. Six months in which a lot had happened. For once, what Beverly had to say was as exciting as any new developments in Max's life.

Maxine Livingstone was Merlene's younger sister. One of the most stunning girls south London had ever seen, she was five-nine and carried it well. A stunner. She was also one of the posse's most lethal assets.

Since school days, Max, Andrea and Beverly had been the tightest of friends. Later, Merlene joined them to make up the foursome, even though she was five years older than the others. The quartet were inseparable. They went out together, stayed in together and shared each other's innermost secrets. Their friendship had earned them the nickname the Four Musketeers in their early raving days, when their appearance at any club or blues would turn women's heads, while the guys stood with their tongues hanging down to the ground. In their prime, the Four Musketeers were legal, crucial and bad like Rambo.

"Max, baby." Beverly waved as she entered Dunn's River.

Max jumped up, arms outstretched.

"Whoooaah Be-ver-lee!" she sang out. They paid each other loud compliments.

"Girl, you look good," Beverly said, admiring Max's trim body. She was truly impressed. Max seemed to look better every time you saw her. "It look like Jamaica treat you good."

"How y'mean?" Max quipped. "In Jamaica the people dem love me, any which part me go. The men treated me real good. I was wining and dining every night. It's amazing that I never put on more than a couple of pounds."

Walking arm in arm towards the table at the back of the bar where Andrea and Merlene were waiting, the two women continued to gossip in the mix of patois and cockney that was colloquial to south London's Afro-Saxons.

Dunn's River was the classiest little bar in Brixton. A cross between a coffee bar and a wine bar, it had become the place to be seen at. It was a little expensive for the area, but this ensured that only the right clientele bothered to pass through its doors.

"Yes, girl," Beverly continued, "you look stush. Next time take me with you."

"Things have changed over there y'know. Jamaica — land of wood an' water an' man slaughter, is how dem call it now. But the night life is firin'," she added quickly. "You won't believe what the girls over there are wearing.

Dressed to kill. You wouldn't believe it. They've got it all hanging out over there."

Beverly smiled. "Max is back," she said admiringly. "The return of the don*ette*. Original." Max had the ability to brighten up the gloomiest day. She was really good value.

If any of the other members of the crew were jealous of Max's good looks, they never showed it. Max naturally attracted most of the men, but that didn't matter. Since schooldays the others had used her to get whatever they wanted from men. They had encouraged her to tease any man who came bearing gifts. At the same time, they had been right at her side when some jealous girlfriend had tried to come test her.

"Ah you dat, Andrea?" A male voice came booming.

Andrea spun around. She didn't need to, she knew exactly who the voice belonged to. Donovan was one of her sweet boys. He approached the table, with his woman, Fay, dangling tightly on his arm.

"Andrea, I called you 'nuff times already, man. I was going to come check you."

"Well, now you've seen me, what can I do for you?"

Donovan stared at her sheepishly.

"Oh, you nevah met my woman yet, did you?"

"No, I don't believe I have," said Andrea politely, if somewhat indifferently. She stretched her hand out to the woman.

"The pleasure's all yours, I'm sure," Fay hissed and kissed her teeth. "So you know my man?"

Max was quick to sense the heat of the situation. She had seen too much of the world and had witnessed the subtle battles for supremacy between two women over one man so many times. She jumped to her friend's assistance by hugging the startled Donovan as tightly as she could. This gave Andrea the opportunity to game, set and match her rival, while Max gave the pleasantly surprised man a quick feel-up.

"Don't bother hug her too tight," Andrea addressed Donovan, "because you know you're a man dat don't know your own strength." The tease was aimed at Donovan, though Andrea couldn't resist casting Fay a triumphant smile as she spoke.

"I know some women who wouldn't know what to do with that strength," she concluded as she twisted the knife in some more.

Max released herself from Donovan's pawing grip and added purringly on behalf of her friend, "Andrea's certainly right, you are a man dat don't know your own strength. Hope to see you around sometime."

Fay shot Max a glance that spelt murder. Donovan's woman knew, however, that there wasn't much she could do. She wasn't the sort of woman that would baulk at a public scrap, but Max was surrounded by her crew. Together they could make mincemeat of Fay. Besides, Donovan had warned her about embarrassing him in public after the last time when she was seen rolling on the floor in a fight for her man in the foyer of Elroy's, the popular night spot at Clapton Pond. No, a deadly look would suffice — for now.

The four girlfriends could barely refrain from bursting out with laughter as Fay and Donovan turned to leave, tails between their legs. This was the kind of biting verbal assault they were so famous for inflicting in the old days. They had dispatched 'nuff potential threats in the same manner. Together, these sisters were tuff.

"So how long have you been dealing with Donovan?" Merlene asked mockingly.

"About three months." Andrea's answer was swift and defensive.

"So the two of oonuh is an item?" Max asked.

"We were an item," was Andrea's cool reply. "He told me seh, him an' her done."

"Is it serious?"

"Well, it was half-serious for me, but as you can see the man is on a leash. So me nah want him. He used to tell me how much he loved me and cared and then all of a sudden a nex' woman appears an' him expect me to stand aside. If you run out, you mus' know you can not come back in. From you is gone, a nex' man fe get the wedding ring. Man an' man haffe know dat ah we run this area."

"They never know the use of a good thing, until they lose it," Merlene agreed solemnly. "When they've lost it. They feel it."

Andrea had become a hard woman. Starting up a hairdresser's salon in the middle of a recession wasn't easy, but with Winston's money she had managed and was beginning to get a reputation in south London. She created new styles every week, outdoing her competitors with her cut-throat business acumen. She included several top celebrities amongst her clients. Soul crooner Kwame and supermodel sex kitten Pearl Jones were just two of the supes that had their locks washed and cut for free in return for their endorsement of Andrea's salon. It was a shrewd move. Once The Voice discovered where all the celebs went to get their roots seen to, the resulting feature brought in more customers than Andrea could handle. Every woman wanted their hair done "just like Pearl's."

But success had brought with it a change of character. She wanted to make up for the seven lost years. All the things that she went without, all the hardships she suffered. She wanted to make amends and quickly. She was harder — not only in business, but also socially. In the six months since Andrea discovered Winston's double life she had cultivated a voracious sexual appetite, dating men who were only too willing to satisfy her needs. She would treat her men ruthlessly. She discovered what all women realise eventually — that their strongest power over men is punanny power. She could make men stand with their tongues dribbling, just by promising them some. If they belonged to some other woman or not, it wasn't her look out. She didn't tell any of them to betray their women. That was their decision. She wasn't really out to take anybody's man, but men came on to her and if they said they were single then, as far as she was concerned, they were single. She accepted their word. She didn't have the time to cross reference or check. Andrea had become the kind of woman that men fear most, a woman prepared to take the money, break your heart and leave you alone.

Andrea even succeeded in turning some of her men into sex slaves. Those men she kept on longer than the usual one night stand. Donovan was such a one. He was so hooked on her, he'd jump up and down on his head if she asked him to. Andrea cast him a pitiful look as he left the bar. She knew that Donovan would now suffer the same fate as all the other ex-boyfriends who had lied to her about their 'marital' status. She needn't waste time in confronting him. She didn't have time for no dibbi dibbi man or a repetition of the Winston scenario.

It was barely six months since Andrea's man had died. Family and friends remarked on Andrea's speedy adjustment to 'widowhood' with more than a hint of snide. People expected a decent period of mourning. Andrea's behaviour since the accident was nothing short of scandalous. One man after the next.

"Andrea, when are you going to find somebody, you know, decent?" Beverly sounded concerned, but the observation came with a sting in its tail.

Andrea turned to Beverly, breathing irony with every word. "Decent? So this new man you have, him decent?"

"Yes, he is."

"Well if he's so decent, how come we haven't met him?"

"You will meet him very soon," Beverly replied confidently, mysteriously and somewhat snobbishly. "In actual fact, I'm going to invite you all to the celebration of my wedding."

The three other women were momentarily stunned by Beverly's news. Maxine boxed over her drink, Merlene choked on hers, while Andrea simply sat with her mouth wide open.

"Married? You mean as in 'piece of paper'? Married? As in 'church an' pastor'? Married?"

Beverly feigned surprise at her friends' reactions.

"What are you talking about? Why are you so shocked? I've met somebody, me an' him are a union. Therefore, we've decided to go in front of the pastor at the end of next month and get his blessing. Not everybody wants to live in sin."

The other women weren't going to let her off the hook that easily. Andrea was first on the attack.

"Oh, you're getting married? Now that you have two children by two different man, you're going to find respectability and get married?"

"How you can put it like that?" Beverly retorted. "Anybody can have two children by two different man."

"Exactly," Andrea was quick to reply. "Exactly."

Maxine decided to step in quickly before things got out of hand.

"Putting aside all of that, the important question is, do you love the man?"

"Of course I do."

"What do you mean 'the important question'?" Andrea butted in. "The important question is does *he* love her? Never mind whether she loves him. Is not who you love, is who love you."

Merlene had remained relatively quiet during the debate, thinking deeply as the others wrestled with the subject. She couldn't help feeling jealous about Beverly's marriage news. Merlene and Winston had planned to get married once they got to the Caribbean. He had promised that they would. She had no reason to doubt his word. He had explained that he and Andrea had never married, because he knew deep down in his heart of hearts that she was not the right woman. Not for him anyway. Merlene, however, was that woman. They would marry and spend the rest of their lives together on a small boat anchored in a tiny bay called Paradise, where they would start a new life, a new family. That was now never to be. Winston's car accident had put paid to that. Her possibilities had been shattered. All she was left with now was a heart that pined for a departed loved one and a thirty-four grand headache.

"How does he treat the kids?" Merlene asked finally.

"He's good with them," Beverly replied confidently, glad for the respite from the hostile questions. "He adores them, they adore him."

"Well, if you love him and he loves you, then we back you. That's all there is to it," the older woman concluded. "We're your friends. We're happy if you're happy and, if you're happy, we'll back you to the hilt. There's no 'whys' or 'buts', we're there for you."

An impartial observer hearing Merlene's words would consider her a hypocrite. But what else could she say? What can you do when you fall in love with your best friend's man? It's easy to say you would never do it, but what do you do if it happens anyway? She had tried to deny her feelings for Winston when Andrea introduced them, early on in the couple's relationship. She had tried, but without success. Since then, every word she spoke to her friends had sounded deceitful. It didn't matter if they were talking about the most trivial matter, like the latest reggae dance craze, Merlene always felt she was being dishonest. How could she tell them what she had done? She was the eldest in the crew. The one that the others came to for advice and support. She was the moral conscience of the group. She just couldn't face the shame of being truthful. Had she been honest at the beginning, when her affair with Winston was little more than a fling, she might have had to endure Andrea's wrath, but it would have been a weight off her shoulders by now. But she wasn't honest then and it was too late to come clean now. She didn't even have the bottle to tell Max, her own flesh and blood. Max regarded her elder sister with hallowed sentiments and a veneration which Merlene was not prepared to see diminished.

Raising her glass to a toast, Merlene continued, "We should celebrate the first marriage amongst our sisterhood. May I be the first to say, congratulations."

Maxine and Andrea were quick to join in the toast, laughing and embracing Beverly, then each other. This was how it had always been between them. They might joke and joust in mock battle, but the bottom line was they would always rally to support each other. At least in the old days. It was five years since the crew's glory days. Five years in which each girl had grown into an individual woman.

"Listen," Merlene raised her glass once more, "I've known you from time, the four of us, y'know we've been through some real trials and tribulations. So, I want to be the first to say I'm happy for you. I'm glad for you. I hope that this man gives you everything you want, everything you need, everything you deserve. Basically, we wish you all the luck. You deserve it, after all this time. Let's hope that this is an omen for the rest of us. That we'll each find our knight in shining armour."

Andrea raised her glass adding: "Seriously, I just want to say, I agree with what Merlene says. But you just mek sure seh, you keep your eye on your man. I don't mean to be funny, know who you're dealing with. Don't tek it the wrong way, Beverly. You're dealing with life here and this is a reality nowadays. Start as you mean to go on. Don't let the man t'ink seh you is any door mat."

Beverly understood well what her friend was saying. Andrea more than anyone knew how little the domestic contract of marriage would mean to a restless man. She had notched up more than her fair share of other women's men in a romantic history which read like a fearsome warning to women everywhere: Never trust your closest female confidante when your man is around. Beverly hadn't forgotten how Andrea had stolen the first boyfriend she ever had, all those years ago. But that wasn't important at the minute. Beverly was about to make the biggest decision in her life. The decision that would make her respectable.

She wanted a big wedding. "The social event of the year," she confided. "Everybody will be there. All three or four hundred at least."

"Personally I wouldn't have a large wedding," Andrea chirped. "When I get married, it's between me and my husband. I don't want to sleep with his family and he don't want to sleep with my people dem. Anyway, it's always other people saying, 'yeah have a big wedding', just so they can go there and work some science on you."

Some would say Beverly was acting wrecklessly, marrying her fiancé after having known him for only a matter of months. On the other hand, she already had two kids by two different men, both of whom, it was revealed after her pregnancies, had fathered several children between them, all over north London. A woman with that extra baggage is always on the look out for a potential father to her kids. If she can find a worthwhile man, best she grab him quick.

Beverly had a good feeling about Thomas. She was prepared to rush into the marriage because the man swore he would stay faithful and she needed to believe him. Her kids needed a father and, for that, she needed a husband. Thomas treated her and the children well. But at the end of the day, man is dog. They only need one sniff and they're away.

Beverly put an arm around Andrea, giving her a little

squeeze.

"I understand. I'm not taking it the wrong way. You're right, but I do know what I'm doing."

"Don't gamble with love," Andrea continued. "If it's loving that you want, you know you don't have to marry. When you're independent, you have your own key. Nobody can tell you not'n. Although me have my reservation about marriage, I support you same way. But remember two things. One, you mus' learn to satisfy, right from the start. You must always watch the woman that behind you… An' me nah tek back dem lyrics. 'Cause it's the original wickedness. Anywhere man go, gal pickney ah follow."

"There's nothing much left for me to say," Maxine quipped. "I'm looking forward to seeing this man, this Prince Charming who's going to make you Miss Respectable. Because we all know that's something you've wanted from time. You deserve this. My advice to you is to remember that diamonds are a girl's best friend. Talk don't mean a single thing. Put your glasses together again girls. Congratulations Beverly, we love you and you know seh we'll do anything for you. We will be there at the wedding, cheering you on and rooting for you."

Beverly turned to Max, grateful for the nice words and the renewal of this friendship with her oldest and dearest friends.

"It's really good to see you again, y'know. It's been a long time. Now I'm tied down with the kids, I don't get to go out so much."

Max more than any of the others had good reason to regret the demise of the Four Musketeers as a social force. She had missed the old days when they would go out together three or four times a week. That suited Max's lifestyle down to the bone. She was a good time party girl who liked nothing better than to go out raving with her best friends. But they hadn't really raved together since

44

back when. The crew as such was now little more than a faded memory from an adolescent dream. But that dream could easily be revived.

"Look, I know we've all moved our separate ways," Max said, "an' because of work and family pressures we don't have time to meet up as regularly as we used to. But why don't we at least try and meet up once a month? In fact I t'ink seh this is exactly what we need to do. Meet up every month, just to blow out the cobwebs and kick some dust off the heels. Y'know."

Andrea backed the suggestion immediately. She was now a free woman in several senses of the word and welcomed the revival of the old relationships with her soul sisters. Beverly and Merlene were reluctant to commit themselves to such an arrangement, citing various excuses. But it didn't take much coaxing from Max and Andrea to convince both women to acquiesce.

"It'll be just like the old days," Andrea chirped.

The four women spent another three hours at the bar, drinking cocktails and kicking up a storm as they steadily became tipsy.

"Big t'ings ah gwan fe everybody else right now, but not'n nah gwan fe me," Merlene sulked half-seriously. "Andrea, you have your new hairdressing business, Max has got her sugar daddy and Beverly's getting married. I've got nothing like that in my life."

"Your time soon come," Andrea assured her. "This is the black woman's time, y'all. An' me nah go tek back dem chat. Black women MEAN business. Yuh nuh see't?"

There was much gossip to be told and much fun to be had. For the first time in years, they played their own special brand of I-Spy, which they had devised as teenagers. Each in turn would spot a guy in the bar, giving him marks out of ten in three categories: looks, style and manners. The other three girls would try to guess which of the men in the bar the marks related to. They played the game for a while, interrupted only by a momentary loss of concentration every time new blood walked in, hungrily eyed up by the Four Musketeers.

It was past midnight when they departed and the April showers were pouring. Max was over the limit and decided to share a cab with the other women and return for her VW Beetle the next morning. The car, a jet-black, customised convertible, was typical of Max. While other women were slaving hard to buy a Golf, Max had to be different.

"That's a sweet car," Beverly complimented her.

"Yeah, Max answered. "You can buy it if you want. I'm getting ready to sell it. I want to get a Porsche next. You know, one of those really old ones from the fifties."

"Well, I do need some wheels," Beverly said, contemplating the offer. "How much are you asking for it?"

"We're sistren," Max replied. "Just let me know when you're ready and we'll reason."

Max looked fondly at the familiar sights of Brixton along the High Road, glad to be home amongst her friends. One by one the cab driver dropped them off at their respective homes, each woman promising, as they departed, to keep up the monthly nights out. They were all in high spirits, happy to have reaffirmed the close ties that had previously bound them together.

FOUR

The reception hall was filled to the brim with wedding guests. From her seat at the top table surrounded by family and friends, Beverly looked around the hall proudly, pleased that so many well-wishers had shown up. It was the happiest day of her life. The day she became 'respectable'. Thomas was now truly her man. Next morning her dream prince would be whisking her off to Gatwick Airport, where they would fly to a secret location. Thomas intended to surprise her. She wouldn't know where they were going until they collected their tickets at the airport. She was excited about the honeymoon and equally so about their wedding night, which they were to spend at an expensive hotel in the West End. Thomas promised that, even though they had been living together for three months, it would be a night to remember. It would be like the first time, he vowed. Outwardly a perfect, serene bride, Beverly felt a tingle of anticipation in her womb as she thought about the first time she and Thomas had made love.

The bride met her groom through a telephone dating line, four months previously. Before Levi, the father to her daughter Ashika, had gone AWOL, Beverly had spent her leisure time cooped up with her two kids, in her house down on the Camberwell end of Coldharbour Lane. Without realising it, she had let Levi turn her into an 'at home' person. He insisted that she stay in and look after the kids while he did his runnings. He very rarely took her out anywhere. Beverly literally went from being a raver one day, to being a working girl-housewife-mother the next. She didn't mind either. She was young and foolish and thought that was what love was all about.

Thomas, on the other hand, was a gift from Beverly's fairy godmother. Like Beverly, he was a browning. He was tall, handsome and suave, with a touch of sophistication. He was, however, prone to being a flirt. But then Beverly didn't know that yet. She wasn't looking to have her cake and eat it. She was looking for a man. Since Levi abandoned her, she had been through several relationships, which were all now dead stock. Thomas had arrived just as all looked lost. She would have given up on the male population entirely if she hadn't found a decent man, preferably someone who would be good to the kids and treat her like a queen, but most importantly, a decent man.

A woman who has got two children sees things differently from a woman with only one child. The more kids you have, the bigger a deal it is to get married quickly. It's all about prestige. Working nine-to-six at one of the top department stores on Oxford Street and then coming home to work as a mother, didn't leave much time for socialising but Beverly was still confident of her ability to go out raving and man-hunting with the girls. She had good looks and an ability to pull a good-looker on the dancefloor. Because of her busy schedule she had, of late, taken the scientific route to finding a man. A work colleague once slipped her a card advertising the services of the RSVP line and she was hooked soon after.

RSVP was the dating line most ambitious and career-minded black men and women used, not only to find romantic partners but also to meet social and business contacts. "Every contact you'll ever need," Beverly read on the card. Later that night, she dialled the dateline number and listened to the messages.

Telephone love, sounds so sweet on the line...

Thomas's message wasn't as slick as some of the others Beverly heard, but his voice sounded sincere. There was something intriguing about a man who described himself as 'Good looking without the ego', and 'looking for my soulful other half so that we can be joined together'.

Beverly took a deep breath as she cast her eye across the school hall. She wanted to laugh, cry or scream with joy. She didn't know which. This was the happiest day of her life. Thomas had come into her life at exactly the right time. He had given her that boost she so needed. She noticed her groom, now relaxed after the formal, almost sombre, church service, flirting with a couple of young women, dressed improperly in luminous green and pink dresses. Beverly didn't mind. Thomas was hers. They were now married. She felt that by marrying her, he had served notice to all other women that he was now another woman's property. That didn't guarantee that he would never play away from home, but rather that all other women knew that he belonged to her. So they would know damn well what they were getting themselves into. So they couldn't complain afterwards if they got burned.

Dawn and Angie, the two flirty-flirty women, were friends Thomas had invited to the reception. They were old friends, meaning he had slept with them intermittently over the years. They knew as much about his bachelor life as anyone. They weren't too concerned by his sudden conversion to marital vows for they felt sure he would still come by and spend the night whenever he felt like it. Had Beverly been sitting closer, she would have heard Angie urge Thomas to pay her a little visit tonight. "You know you're welcome, my door is always open to you, Thomas."

Beverly couldn't hear the words, but she saw the slimy smile of satisfaction spread across Thomas's face when Angie whispered in his ear.

Anyone who had seen Thomas and Beverly on their first date, would have rated them as the perfect couple. After setting up the date on the phone line, Thomas had taken Beverly to Roscoe's, a trendy restaurant in downtown Brixton. Even though she went past it almost every day, Beverly had never actually been inside. It had opened up while she was doing her child-rearing at home. The restaurant, one of a group around London owned by the king of the buppies, Russell Isaacs, followed the pattern of all buppie restaurants. They could rely on the odd black celebrity amongst their clientele and, therefore, attracted buppie wannabes looking to brush shoulders with the likes of ex-soap star Candi Clarke and former world light-heavyweight champ, Lloyd Daley. Daley's bankrupt now, but in his heyday, boy, he could whip up a storm at Roscoe's.

Beverly couldn't help feeling important surrounded by the intellect and ambition so clearly apparent in the restaurant.

"Oh, it's a nice place, isn't it?" she had remarked. "Do you come here often?"

"Yeah, it's just one of the places I pass through every now and again, y'know," Thomas lied. It was also his first time in Roscoe's. More at home in a pool hall than in an upmarket restaurant, Thomas had asked a classy friend where he should dine to impress a woman 'with high demands', as Beverly had described herself during their first telephone conversation. He was well impressed when he set eyes on his blind date for the evening. The gal criss, he thought to himself.

"Baby, you better go and sort the pastor out. He's standing over the other side of the hall waiting for his tip."

Beverly had decided to break up the mutual admiration club which had formed between her new husband and the ever-pouting, ever-flirting Angie and Dawn. The greedy look on Pastor Mason's face had been a perfect excuse. Thomas frowned as he turned and caught the pastor smiling in his direction.

"Yeah, you know seh Pastor Mason wants his pieces of silver," he answered sarcastically. He rustled in his pocket for some notes and swaggered over to the eager preacher. Beverly flashed Angie and Dawn that cold, knowing smile which spelled 'one-upmanship'. They returned the compliment and sauntered across the room to a group of Thomas's ragga-styled male friends, standing together in a cluster against the opposite wall. Beverly watched them closely. Some will eat with you and even drink with you, she thought, but behind your back they'll steal your man. The two girls spoke to the young men, pointing derisively at the bride as they shared a joke with the guys. Beverly was intimidated but kept her composure. Angie and Dawn were the competition. She knew that. Andrea had informed Beverly two weeks earlier, when she discovered from a reliable source that the two fresh girls had enjoyed relationships with her new husband. "An' me nevah hear yet dat him finish with either," the source had concluded.

Andrea dismissed Dawn as just a 'fancy gal', but warned Beverly to watch out for Angie, who reputedly could win the heart of any man and was not a stranger to fighting in public over a man.

Beverly took a sip from her champagne glass, deep in thought. She wasn't going to let some cheap whore be responsible for any misgivings she had about her husband. At the same time, she knew that no matter how much Thomas loved her, she didn't know if the man had yet been born who would turn up his nose if he's given a little sniff. She had lost her first real boyfriend to Andrea this way. Though she was only a teenager at the time, the memory still haunted her and deep inside she never forgave her friend for the hurt it caused. Since then, she had become possessive about her men, refusing to allow them the slightest possibility of a sniff. Like all men, Thomas's ego swelled any time a woman offered herself up to him. He couldn't turn it down. Come Angie and Dawn or any other women as they may, Beverly told herself, she was ready for them. She didn't intend to give up her husband without a fight.

"Mum!" Beverly heard Ashika call. "Mum, Ken keeps kicking me. Tell him mum, he just keeps kicking me for no reason."

Beverly turned towards her daughter who looked radiant but distressed in her bridesmaid's outfit.

"Kenyatta! Leave Ashika alone. All right? Behave yourself. If I hear her crying once more, you'll have to answer."

"What did I do?" Beverly's son cried sulkily from across the table. "I didn't touch her. I didn't do nothing. Why do I always get the blame for everything?"

"Oh, don't make out like you're innocent. This isn't the right time to be playing games. Just keep your feet to yourself, or you'll have me to deal with."

Still sulking, Kenyatta got up.

"I don't want to be at your stupid wedding anyway. I hate you. I hate you!"

He turned and walked away from the table.

"Kenyatta! Just turn back and sit down," Beverly commanded, but to no avail. The young boy was already halfway to the exit.

"I'll go and talk to him," Merlene offered, going after the kid.

As Beverly watched her son leave the hall, she wondered whether he would ever accept Thomas as his father. Ashika had readily embraced the idea of a replacement for her absent father. Her four year old mind no longer had any memories of Levi. As far as she was concerned Thomas was her father. But Kenyatta was two years older than his sister and had become increasingly troublesome since Thomas moved into their household. That wasn't through lack of trying on Thomas's part. He had bought the youngster gifts and had always made an effort to take him out. Apart from going to see Crystal Palace play on the odd Saturday afternoon, he seemed indifferent to everything Thomas did for him. Even that common ground vanished after Palace striker Egan Rowe was transferred to Arsenal. Thomas's allegiance lay with the striker, while Kenyatta was a diehard Palace fan. Since then, Kenyatta's hostility towards Thomas had come out in the open.

"Baby-boo, I love you sooooo much," Thomas had assured Beverly repeatedly. "I'm going to give my love to you and only you."

Before she was prepared to consider him 'legit', however, he had to convince her that he loved her even more than his car and his money and t'ing. For a sweet talker like Thomas, that was the easy part.

"You are my special lady. My very special, special girl." Beverly didn't fall for it immediately. He had gone on like this for weeks before she allowed him to sleep with her. How much sweet talk can one female ego take? Finally, she relented. She called him on the phone saying, "If you want me, then come and get me."

Once they had decided to marry, Beverly's only concern was that if Thomas was playing away from home, she didn't want to be the last to know.

"I don't want to hear them whispering everywhere I go," she warned him. "I've got my pride."

"How could I be unfaithful, when you mean so much to me?" Thomas had said.

Merlene returned, hugging Kenyatta. He was smart enough to avoid his mother's angry eyes which spelled 'fire'.

Beverly looked around the table at her closest friends Merlene, Andrea and Maxine. They were really in the same position as she was. None of them could be certain of their men. She hoped that marriage would make a difference, but deep down she knew that marriage or no marriage, she couldn't be a hundred percent sure her man wouldn't play away from home.

Thomas returned to the family table slightly ruffled from his 'business trip' to Pastor Mason.

"I gave him ten pounds and he said, 'the usual is twenty'." Thomas sounded annoyed. "He fleeced me. Cho!"

"Well he did do a good job at the church," Beverly replied, thinking Thomas was acting unnecessarily mean for a man on his wedding day.

"You look really beautiful," she whispered sweetly in his ear. I was so proud when I walked into the church and saw you waiting at the altar this afternoon. I hope you've had lots of rest, 'cause you'll need it tonight, I promise."

Out of the corner of her eye, Beverly could see the luminous electric-green of Angie's dress approaching their table again.

"Well, big boy," Angie spoke directly to Thomas, completely ignoring his bride. "Gotta go, dah-*ling*. Can't stay. You know I nevah eat food from strangers' kitchen. Here is your present." She handed him a lightly wrapped parcel. "It's a basket of your favourite toiletries — aftershave an' dem business. Don't forget, come up and see me any time." She planted a parting kiss squarely on Thomas's lips.

Angie intended Beverly to see and hear everything. Beverly was furious, but decided to keep her composure. She had hoped in vain that Thomas would have made some effort to cut the slackness down. That he would at least defend her honour. But he didn't. He simply stood there, taking it all in and smiling that stupid, self-important smile she had seen him smile so many times before. Angie had thrown down the gauntlet at her own wedding! She made a mental note to get even with that bitch one day.

Guests were still sauntering into the hall. The sound system boys were still humping their heavy speaker boxes on to the stage at one end of the hall. As sound boys always did at these functions, they felt that they were the highlight of the occasion, looking upon the wedding as a minor distraction.

"What a way Pastor Mason can deliver a wedding speech," said Mrs Henderson to nobody in particular. "It's the third wedding speech I've heard that man say. I've not known him to go wrong yet. You can tell he is a man of *h*uplifting qualities. A man of standing in the community. A man to look up to."

"Mmmn-unh," agreed Mrs Brown. "It's true. You nevah speak a truer word. An' you could see how the young people dem were... uhm... dumbfounded," she said finally, struggling for her words.

Mrs Henderson looked at Mrs Brown, as if to say, 'dumbfounded'?

"Yes. You nevah hear dat word before? You nevah know seh I could speak posh?" Mrs Brown added enthusiastically. "Yes, dumbfounded. You could see how the seriousness of the occasion rested on their shoulders."

Nobody at the reception cared for Mrs Brown's words. Even if they had heard them, they wouldn't have known what she meant. But it sounded good to Mrs Brown.

The two ladies were members of the pentecostal church which both Beverly's parents attended, her mother more diligently than her father. A group of a dozen or so older ladies from the church had got together to help organise the reception. Mrs Brown and Mrs Henderson would have continued their little banter all night long if not for the rude interruption from one of their colleagues walking past with a tray piled high with food.

"While you're both sitting there commenting on Pastor Mason's sermon, I could comment seh you're not doing nothing with your mouth other than fe work it. Just get your bottom off the chair and help me with these trays."

The reception was held at a local junior school a mile away from the church. Cars were parked tightly in what was normally the playground. Other cars were jammed together on the pavements around the school. There were at least three hundred people at the reception and none of them had walked there. The reception was held in the assembly hall, which was able to accommodate everybody comfortably. There were people everywhere. Some standing around observing, others gathering in groups. Groups of men, women, women with children, some of them scolding those children. Girls oozing sex all over to attract any stray men who might care to utter those three magical words, "I love you," and subsequently be led by the scruff of the neck to the church on time for another big wedding. The sound system men were up on stage, assembling the hi-fi, carrying boxes, posing, strutting and checking out the women.

Everybody had been barbered that morning. Andrea only just managed to cope with the twenty or so women who had booked appointments. Some Brixton women had to go as far afield as Streatham and South Norwood to find a black hairdresser who would give them an appointment.

Stronger than the faint aroma of Caribbean cooking was the heavy scent of expensive perfume. Everybody was dressed their best. Some people had spent hundreds of pounds just on clothes. You had to look your best or be the laughing stock.

Andrea and Merlene were respectably dressed in red and cream respectively, hoping to attract maximum attention without upstaging the bride, who looked divine behind the veil of a size ten white lace wedding dress with a long trail. Beverly looked the business. At the front of her dress was a daring split, going up to her knees. She wore dropped pearl earrings, which matched her necklace. She had taken Andrea's advice and piled her hair on top, giving her a much needed height increase as Thomas was a full twelve inches taller. Beverly's mother had made up a small bouquet which the bride wore pinned to her dress for the finishing touch.

Everybody agreed that she was a beautiful bride. Some of the older ladies could be heard muttering praises that she had finally married.

"Ah two kids she have now by two different man," said Mrs Brown.

"How the frock did look pretty," Sister Wright added.

Mrs Henderson cornered Beverly's mother and congratulated her on the occasion.

"Y'know Betty, your daughter look real nice today. I must say she look real nice. You must feel proud?"

Mrs Johnson turned to look at Beverly, realising that her daughter was now a respectable married lady. What she had always wanted.

"Yes, I am proud," she replied turning to Mrs Henderson, "but I have to say, it is all due to God's strength, why I'm here to see my one daughter in her greatest moment of happiness."

Before Beverly's mum could wallow in her pride, Mrs Brown interjected with a snide remark.

"It's a shame it couldn't work out even a lickle bit different, you know," she said with a tone of insincere sympathy.

The remark hurt Beverly's mum. The fact that her daughter had given birth to two children by two different men (neither of whom she had married), had caused her great embarrassment in her church circles. But she had accepted it nevertheless. Determined not to allow Mrs Brown's comment to upset her, she retorted, "Mmmn-hmm. I know exactly what you mean. But that is in the past and we are looking towards the future now. With God's blessing and my guidance, she will be all right."

Beverly certainly looked stush. She should have known that Max wouldn't dress appropriately for the occasion. No matter what the event, Max always dressed to suit her own moods. Once you've been in the spotlight, as Max had since she became a beauty in her teens, you still crave the attention even when you're way past your sell by date.

Wearing a short, short, short skirt with matching blouse and jacket and knee-length suede boots, Max seemed indifferent to the gasps and sniggers of the male guests. She wore a silver necklace, with a dazzling diamond teardrop centred on her cleavage. In her ears, were matching diamond teardrop studs.

At the head table were the immediate family and friends of the bride and bridegroom. Beverly's crew were naturally there, as were her two kids. The bride's closest friends, Maxine, Merlene and Andrea were as good as family.

Beverly's father, sitting in the middle next to his daughter, was rapidly becoming drunk on his own lethal mixture of Jamaican rum laced with gin. On the other side of the bride, Thomas the bridegroom had been watching the father casually.

"Go an' watch Beverly father. Go an' make sure seh him nah drink no more of that rum," he said nudging his best man. "Because once him taste the rum punch now, we're finished."

Thomas was the living black Adonis. A tall red-skinned man with an athletic physique, the gods had blessed him with more than his fair share of good looks which, complemented by a pinstripe moustache, made him irresistible. His near-perfect features were only marred by an unfortunate scar under his left eye. But that didn't put the ladies off. He was too good-looking to be true. Moreover, he was a charmer. He dressed to kill and had a deep sexy voice, with which he could use one or two slick words to turn a girl's head. Even now as he leaned back relaxed in his chair with his loosened tie and the top button of his shirt undone, his pose was studied and worked out. No sheer accident.

Though he was born in England, Thomas preferred to chat in the yard style he had learned while schooling in Jamaica during his early teens. Like all the other Anglo-Jamaicans at the wedding, he could switch at the drop of a hat to a cockney-yardman mix.

Red-skinned men are currently in vogue and Thomas had never been short of women, which is why his friends were surprised that this urban Casanova was willing to give it all up to marry this girl, Beverly. Why would a man who had women falling over him get married? Right now, though, he was happy. Marriage gave him some kind of pride. For a long time, he had felt that there was something missing in his life. That something was a woman to call his wife. He felt like a man now. Marriage proved his manhood.

Beverly's father stood up to make the first speech, microphone in hand. Slightly light-headed from the booze, he was filled with deep, tender emotion for his daughter.

"I'm so glad to see so many of my friends and my wife's friends here today, with my daughter and her friends and her husband's friends."

It was the typical long-winded speech, going all around the houses to make a point. You could already see people rolling their eyes thinking 'here comes another daddy about to make a fool of himself'.

"I feel it's only fair to seh," Mr Johnson continued, "dat I am very proud, very honoured, very… TOUCHED… yes, that's the word I'm looking for… TOUCHED."

Thomas's best man whispered loudly enough for the people around him to hear.

"Yes, you look touched," he grumbled with reference to Mr Johnson's unsober condition. A ripple of laughter followed the outburst.

"Yes, I am touched by the overwhelming emotions of the day. I feel, as these two young people embark on married life, they must realise the seriousness of the occasion. Dat when..."

Amongst the guests were some downright rude people. Mr Johnson must have heard quite clearly the comment coming from one of the men and directed at him: "Tell the man to shut up." But Johnson continued undaunted, his wife punctuating his every word with a rejoicing, "Oh yes, oh yes. Amen!" in acknowledgement.

"The seriousness of what you are about to go into," Johnson continued. "Marriage is a very serious situation to get into..." •

"You telling me, boss," came the impatient cry from one of the hungry guests.

At this point Beverly's mother urged her husband to hurry up. Unruffled, Mr Johnson continued. This was his party and he was going to enjoy it and speak 'til he was done.

"Beverly is my child, me lickle baby. An' I feel happy to know dat I can hand over the reign of responsibility to uhm... uhm... uhm... Terry... Terry, dat's it. So I can hand over the reign of full responsibility to my new son-in-law, Terry."

There was a sudden hush, followed by a great roar of laughter from the guests. Johnson's wife screamed hoarsely into his ear, "Thomas. The bwoy name Thomas. Your new son-in-law name Thomas."

Realising his mistake Mr Johnson composed himself quickly, diffusing the situation, by laughing at his own mistake.

"Yes, yes. Oonuh thought I was drunk, innit? I was only fooling you. I meant to say Thomas... my new son-in-law Thomas. Now, I would like all of you to join me in raising your... uhm... rum glasses and give a cheer to Beverly an' uhm... Thomas. Yes, I wish you all the very, very best, of the very best," he said, toasting and sitting down. He quickly got up again and turned to Thomas. With more than a hint of a threat he added, "She's my lickle baby, I'm putting her in your trust. So please tek care of her, or you'll have me to deal with."

There was polite applause from the seated guests, some of whom couldn't resist adding their own little bit:

"The rum isn't even flowing strongly yet and the man drunk. It's a damn disgrace, enh? Why man mus' stay so?"

"Dem know seh that the man can't hold his drink, an' still dem let the rum talk fe him."

"Typical, innit? Typical."

Some people just had to make their comments to downgrade the occasion. There are times when people do not think a wedding is a wedding unless they can complain about something.

Mr Johnson passed the microphone to Thomas's best man. A long time spar of the bridegroom, Danny was Thomas's bosom buddy and by now he had gotten over the shock of losing his boyhood friend to a woman. Thomas had assured him that nothing much would change in their lifestyle, had explained that the woman had a nice house and respectability. Those words had a calming effect on Danny, who had at first been reluctant to play an active part in the wedding. Indeed, the pentecostal women had all remarked at the way he had organised his part efficiently.

Taking the microphone, Danny began to speak. Sheepishly at first, in a mix of cockney and patois.

"Well, I'd like to say to everybody that Thomas is my mate. I've known him, y'know, we've been running around the streets from time. I just want to say to everybody that I never thought that this day would come," he said with a knowing wink for the benefit of those who knew Thomas from time. "I'm just joking... When Thomas said, 'come and be my best man', I had to say 'to who'? So, you ladies out there who've wanted Thomas, you can't have him. He's spoken for. I, as his spar, will defend his honour. I will fight off any woman for you," he continued, turning to Beverly. "So, just to let you ladies know that Thomas is no longer available, but I am sure that I can fill all your requirements..." Danny sat down, passing the microphone to Thomas.

"Hello... I just want to say to everybody that I'm glad you came here today to celebrate the wedding of me and Beverly, who was my woman and is now my wife. I just want to let everybody know seh, I'm not doing this under no pressure, y'know. I'M DOING THIS UNDER MY OWN STEAM, BECAUSE I'M MY OWN MAN. I've come to realise that there are certain qualities I admire and want from a woman. I've come to realise that Beverly is the woman who possesses those things."

The female section amongst the guests began to fire up in agreement with Thomas's tender words, expressing their approval with shouts of "Tell the people dem seh you love her. Jus' tell everybody seh you love her."

"Well, yeah I do," said Thomas, in response. "I'll say this to all the men out there, I am not standing here under any pressure, I'm standing here by myself to honour my woman, right? 'Cause me an' her is one. We're a unit, we're a unified force. If anybody wants to come and tear that force down, they'll have me to deal with. Beverly is the only woman that I want. No other woman out there can match her."

A stream of sunlight flooded in through the windows at the side of the auditorium. A dazzling flash of light resulted, as the sun exploded on an object in the auditorium. Thomas caught the dazzle in the corner of his eye. It made him squint momentarily. He lost concentration. Turning his head towards the light, his eyes locked on the sparkling diamond teardrop, dangling seductively on Max's chest and which now, with the aid of the afternoon sun, illuminated his thoughts. Every colour in the rainbow was filtered through that diamond, resulting in a sparkle of magnificent proportions. Thomas began to salivate, as his eyes followed Max's cleavage line. She observed him intently, a mischievous twinkle in her eye. Their eyes met and locked. Only for a moment, but a moment was enough. Thomas thought he detected a half-smile in her eyes. His eyes half-smiled back. He knew she was a friend of Beverly's, but they hadn't yet been introduced. She was the sexiest girl he had ever laid eyes on.

Remembering himself, he began searching for words. Above all the group of beautiful women at the wedding reception, Maxine alone had the power to send a hunk of man like Thomas gasping for air as he spoke. He couldn't help noticing that aura she had about her. Aura, or ambience, whichever. His voice wobbled as he spoke and his words become slurred. He had a reputation for being flash with words, so he wanted his speech to represent. He didn't want his guests going home and mocking the bridegroom's speech. But the more he struggled to find the right words, the more his voice quivered as his thoughts were distracted by the luscious black Cleopatra with 'wicked in bed' written all over her face. The guests, hanging on his every word with baited breath, realised something was up. But they didn't know what.

"I... I... thank you... all... thank you... I... I..." he stuttered.

"Beverly is the woman I want... an' adore... an'... I... respect her..."

Realising that he was faltering, he adjusted his tie and excused himself.

"I must apologise... the rum's gone to my head... I am overwhelmed with emotion by the occasion. Sorry I sound a bit off, but that's how emotions get you, when you're feeling and talking about someone, straight from the bottom of your heart. This is the happiest day of my life..." his voice trailed off.

Beverly realised that something had disturbed him and

knew that it wasn't what he had claimed it to be.

Max, feeling the intensity of the situation, lowered her eyes.

Still standing, Thomas had begun to look foolish. Beverly saved him by standing up and taking hold of the microphone.

"I'm glad that all my friends and Thomas's friends are here today just to celebrate our union," Beverly interjected. "I can only echo what Thomas has said. For me personally, he's the man I've been looking for. He's my Prince Charming, my knight in shining armour." She looked in his dark eyes and smiled. This was indeed her Prince Charming.

A sympathetic ripple could be heard amongst the women guests as they simultaneously whispered, "Aaahhh, ain't that sweet." Also audible were the cynical voices of some of the male guests who murmured, "Nah, nah rubbish, eenh!" Some bitchy females added their own comments by exchanging glances and skinning teeth as if to say, "What kind of foolishness is that? Which prince? You see any man ride armour? He ride the woman, he nah ride shining *h*armour." The sound men, still setting up their system on stage, stopped and sniggered as Beverly spoke of her devotion for Thomas. With his back bent almost double as he heaved one half of a gigantic sound box, Slim, the sound's main deejay, couldn't resist laying a wager with his partner.

"I bet you fifty pounds this wedding nah see out six months. I bet you fifty pounds it nah last. Mek me tell you nuh, you can mark it down, the wedding nah last." The pair were interrupted by one of the trusted ladies from the pentecostal church.

"Shhh!" she snapped. "If you don't want to say anything civil, you must leave the area."

Still standing and undeterred by the interruptions, Beverly continued.

"Yes, Thomas is my knight in shining armour and I know that he will treat me like he treats his mother..."

"I hope not," came a loud voice in the middle of the auditorium, "she don't want no baby."

The guests roared with laughter. Even Beverly's father joined in the merriment. Beverly got the joke, smiled and continued.

"I am happy that we can now go forward, that we're now respectable and that we're no longer just living together. Thomas has made a full commitment to me. He's telling all the world that he loves me. I love him too."

Again there are romantic gasps of "aaahhh" from the sympathetic female guests. Beverly's mother took over the microphone as her daughter sat herself down.

"I would like to take this opportunity to thank everybody who has assisted my good self and my husband in preparation of this wedding of my daughter Beverly and her new husband, Thomas. Please go ahead and enjoy yourself. Dinner is served."

Barely had she uttered those last words than there was a mad rush towards the long line of buffet tables along one side of the auditorium. The bigger the wedding, the more painful it is to see people rush to nyam-nyam. It was first come first served. The men, forgetting their manners, rushed to be at the front of the queue. The usual mutterings of, "Look how long you have to stand up and wait for food," and "Bwoy, me t'ink seh Beverly could have organised t'ings a lickle bettah, y'know," could be heard from the guests at the back of the queue whose stomachs were grumbling.

The calypso smell of curried goat and fried fish wafted through the air as one by one the guests sat down, with plates piled high. Every aspect of the wedding feast was chosen to put people in mind of the bride's Jamaican heritage. The hard dough bread known as 'duck bread' (because at weddings it's shaped as a duck), is staple diet at any Jamaican wedding. Beverly's mother had also added jerk chicken, white rice, tossed salad and watermelon. As the guests ate, the ladies from the church wandered between the tables, offering pieces of wedding cake.

The sound system boys were ready to take over the reception. They had reluctantly left their ragga clothes at home and dressed sheepishly in slacks, starched white shirts rolled up at the sleeves and fancy waistcoats, to blend in with the wedding atmosphere. Every few minutes one of them would disappear backstage and out the back entrance to charge up with a spliff. Like most parents, Beverly's parents wouldn't appreciate the sweet aroma of sensimilla at their daughter's wedding. So the bad bwoys congregated at the back of the building rolling blunts.

Beverly and Thomas took to the dancefloor alone for the first number, a popular lovers tune, which soon had the guests singing along as the newly weds held each other tightly across the dancefloor.

Whistles and cheers followed the bass intro to the next tune. Omar's 'There's Nothing Like This', had every man, woman and child who could walk joining Beverly and Thomas on the dancefloor. Then the newlyweds were cajoled into dancing with each other's best friends.

"I can't let you dance with this gorgeous man all evening," Maxine interrupted the newlyweds. "Ease up nuh?" She playfully shoved Beverly out of the way and whined slowly with the bridegroom. Thomas's old school mate, LaVern, grabbed Beverly by the waist and shuffled smoochily away with her in the opposite direction.

A lazy, soulful tune followed. An otherwise tacky new classic soul cover of an American R&B hit, it was the perfect excuse to hold your dancing partner tight, without offending moral decency.

"Are you down with O.P.P.?" Thomas asked cautiously. "What's O.P.P.?" Maxine enquired.

"Yuh nevah hear dat tune... how it go? You down with O.P.P.? Yeah, you know me."

"Oh that one... yeah, I heard it. What does it mean?"

"Other People's Property. Get it?"

"Other People's Property? Behave yourself, Thomas. You're forgetting that this is your wedding." Maxine laughed.

"O.P.P. don't have respect for wedding an' t'ing. You down with O.P.P.? Yeah, you know me." Thomas hummed the tune in Max's ear.

Maxine stared at him directly with a smile. She admired his tall athletic physique and his hunky good looks. Beverly had married a gorgeous guy. I could even fancy him myself, she thought. Then she thought better of it, remembering that this was Beverly's husband after all.

She slapped his chest playfully. "I said, behave yourself."

The dancing was still going on six hours later when the newlyweds sneaked off to their honeymoon suite at an expensive hotel in the West End.

Beverly looked at Thomas and smiled. "Darling, close the door. Turn down the lights. Come over here and hold me close. Let's do it like we did it that first night."

Thomas staggered out of the bathroom, feeling the effects of all the rum he had consumed. From the vacant look in his eyes, Beverly realised that her wedding night was not going to be the most romantic night ever. He stumbled onto the bed and passed out.

Thomas slept, snoring loudly. Beverly lay still but awake, praying that now they were married, Thomas would continue showing the warm, loving side he had previously always shown. Tears welled up in her eyes. Thomas continued snoring.

FIVE

The two naked bodies lay sprawled out on the bed side by side, sweaty and exhausted after a seventy-minute sex session. Maxine's eyes were open, staring almost lifelessly at the mirrored ceiling which reflected their contorted bodies, still tense after the climatic end to their physical passion. Her long and slender body, in colour the dark velvet of the midnight sky, contrasted against his light suntanned torso, like ebony and ivory. His eyes were closed, as men's often are after an orgasm.

Andrew was Max's boops, her sugar daddy. He was a handsome, slim but muscular man in his early forties. Good looks and good manners. His courteous disposition, correct posture and received pronunciation had been learned at one of the country's top public schools, a million miles away from the Streatham comprehensive where Maxine graduated with an 'O' level in art.

Everybody teased her about having a lover nearly twice her age, but it didn't bother Max. Naked or clothed, as a result of a daily workout Andrew looked good for his age. Max loved sex too much to pick up with any lazy body.

Max loved sex, but uncomplicated sex. She liked to be in total control of her own pleasure. It was pointless relying on a man for it. She was sure of that. However, Andrew was unlike most of the men she had met before. He put himself out to satisfy his woman. That was unusual. Even though you ultimately have to work at deriving your erotic pleasure yourself, it's a nice gesture when a man puts himself out.

For a moment, she let her mind wander to thoughts about the future. Would Andrew be part of that future? If so, what role would he play? What role would she play? Though they had been together for three years they were only a couple in the sense that they had good times together. Theirs was no ordinary relationship. There were no bad times. They were together only for the good times. It was either sex, parties, going out to dinner, going off on holiday and having laughs together. They never really fought. Their relationship certainly never got violent. There was never any need to break up. It was not so much a permanent relationship, more a permanently transitory relationship. For, when she thought about it, she hardly knew him and though she was as open with him as was possible, she knew deep down that he really didn't understand where she was coming from.

They had met a few years previously when Max had auditioned for a role in a television commercial Andrew was directing for a well-known French perfume company. His jaw had dropped as she entered his studio dressed in little more than nothing, with an attitude that men will always interpret as horny.

He was besotted with her. But as hard as he tried, the perfume company refused to use her for their television campaign and chose another model. Andrew wasn't to be put off. He called her regularly and took her out for drinks. She was a bit hesitant at first, but she found him too charming and witty to resist. He certainly knew how to make a girl feel good. After a long courtship, they finally consummated their relationship in a bout of frenzied intercourse in a bedroom at a party Andrew had invited her to. It was nerve-racking. The party was at the plush house of one of Andrew's film business contacts, but neither he nor Max could resist the urge any longer. They excused themselves each after the other, as if they needed to use the bathroom, but quickly ran into the bedroom and jumped onto the bed.

"Quick, quick," he had whispered anxiously. "Pull

down your skirt... someone's coming... anyone could burst in."

It wasn't the greatest sexual experience, but the element of danger turned Max on.

What she didn't anticipate, was the possibility of being addicted to the luxurious lifestyle Andrew could offer. She had never known so much wealth and financial decadence. But it didn't take her long to get a taste for it. Now Max was so accustomed to the champagne lifestyle they enjoyed together that she often wondered whether she could live without it.

When they first started dating, she planned to enjoy the ride and get out without anybody knowing about it. Because he was white, she had initially held back her emotions. Had he been black she wouldn't have hesitated. But six months down the road she realised things could work out quite sweet. She liked him. She was attracted to him. At the same time he was willing to splash out on her.

For his part, Andrew took his time when courting her before trying to get his leg over, which was all the more intriguing for Max. Sometimes, though, she felt like Eliza Doolittle being moulded into a lady. He introduced her to a life she was unfamiliar with, took her to restaurants with four course meals, seven spoons this side and two spoons that side and expected her to leave some of her coarser street culture at home when they went out. Though her modelling career hadn't really taken off, she no longer needed to work as a legal secretary if she didn't want to. The secretarial work was how she had made her living before she met her boops. Now, she would temp for two or three days every month just to keep from being bored and to give herself some semblance of economic independence. In reality though, Andrew took care of her.

After three years, Andrew still felt a slight lack of confidence around Max. She wasn't to know, because he kept it all to himself, while outwardly displaying the confidence of an ex-public school boy. When they first met he didn't believe that he stood a chance with her. That kind of attractive girl would never go for me, he thought. Since their relationship began his confidence in himself had grown tremendously. He had a guilt complex because if Max was a white girl, he would have probably set up home proper with her by now or even asked her to marry him. So he did the next best thing, by becoming her boopsie and setting her up in a luxury flat on Brixton Water Lane (where the prettiest houses in Brixton are to be found), with jewellery and more than enough pocket money to satisfy her every whim.

This man did love his black woman. For whatever reason. Initially it was more to do with the curiosity that white men have about black women, but that wasn't the main thing for him now. From the moment Max walked into his life he liked what he saw and started fantasising. He was willing to wait, no matter how long it took. Max had never had a man sit down and wait for her. No man had sat down and said, "mek me wait my several months", while driving himself crazy trying to get this woman into position. Moreover, Andrew was experienced — forty-three years old, yet physically fit

Max knew exactly why she was allowing herself to be a kept woman. She loved that four-poster bed she slept in. She liked not having to struggle or worry about money when she went to market. The allowance she obtained from this guy enabled her to send regular money home to her mother in Jamaica. If she pulled out now, how would her mother survive? That and the thought of going back to her nine-to-five life, making ends meet on an average salary, was enough to remind Max that bread was tastier on the buttered side. Unless she could find somebody who could, physically and emotionally, tear everything out of her, she would stay with Andrew. Max wasn't bothered. She would enjoy the ride while it lasted. In her own eyes, she was properly Andrew's woman. More than a bit of fluff.

Suddenly, without warning, she found herself thinking of Thomas.

Andrew enjoyed having Max as his woman. His friends were visibly taken aback when they first met his dark-skinned girlfriend. She was undeniably attractive and her smile made them wish they could get her into bed. Andrew enjoyed the fact, thinking to himself, 'yeah, you'd like to touch her, but you can't'.

On the matter of black guys trying to check his woman, Andrew was philosophical. "You can't offer her what I can offer. I've got the money, you haven't. I can open her eyes to a world you can't even imagine."

He wasn't street wise. He didn't have street cred but, nevertheless, he managed to hold a girl who any of those guys on the street would want.

Things would have been a lot easier for the couple had he been a black man and she a white woman. Some of the guys in the community weren't yet ready to deal with a black woman and a white man. What people thought didn't bother Max too tough. But Andrew, on the other hand, was always nervous and decided to keep a discreetly low profile whenever he drove to Max's plush apartment. It was all right going uptown together, but they rarely held hands in the community, at least not since a twelve inch machete was thrust in front of Andrew's face on the corner of Atlantic Road and Coldharbour Lane when the couple were out shopping together one Saturday afternoon.

Andrea and Beverly were surprised at Max's choice of a sugar daddy. Merlene, who knew Andrew quite well, understood why her sister was living as a kept woman. Merlene wanted more for her sister than she was able to attain for herself. She had always encouraged her baby sister to continue in education. The fact that Max wasn't a baby mother was down to her elder sister's influence. She took every opportunity to give Max a run-down of the things in life she could forget about once she had kids. "You've still got a lot of time to have kids," she assured her sister. "I should have waited as long as you and longer. Tek your time, sis." But more importantly, Merlene had tried to instil in Max the need to jump at any opportunities she was granted in life. "Women don't get too many chances," she had often said. "Take what you can get and set yourself up with pride."

She could see how happy her sister was. Andrew wasn't roughing her up, he wasn't milking her dry and she seemed to be enjoying herself. Max had always had difficulties finding the right guy, because she wasn't meeting anybody who could match her.

Max had been doing a lot of thinking. In three years with Andrew, she had amassed over twenty grand in her personal savings account. That didn't include any of the jewellery that she had received from him, jewellery which, it was understood, she would not have to return in any event. Twenty grand. Twenty grand just sitting there. Twenty grand she didn't need to touch. Max was truly safe, by anybody's standards.

She was discovering however, that the boundaries of the relationship had begun to be blurred. It wasn't just a cold, unemotional business deal anymore. She had begun to like Andrew. She had begun to catch feelings for him. That was something she wasn't too happy about. She liked Andrew a lot, though love was not quite the right word. She simply didn't want to complicate things by falling in love with him.

There was the question of her future with Andrew. She didn't want to have kids with someone who was not prepared to marry her. Merlene had taught her well. She had no intention of bearing a man's child on the same terms as her sister and was always more than a bit careful when she made love. There was no risk of any accidents happening.

Max could have been a younger version of Merlene, but different experiences gave the two sisters a different perspective. Merlene was serious, she had to be. She had been forced, because of their family's economic circumstances, to grow up fast, leave school in a hurry and work to make a contribution at home. Max's life on the other hand had been a laugh a minute. In her world, fairy tales seemed to come true.

Thinking about it, as she did this morning, Max didn't know much about Andrew. He seemed to have unlimited funds to provide for her. He had explained that as well as his television producer's income, he had an allowance from a fund his grandparents had set up for him as a child. His parents were farmers out in the country. But Max had never met them. He had already cleared the air by saying that he didn't intend for her to meet them. Meeting his mother was a no-no. "She's a bit funny," he had explained, preferring not to expand on the matter, "it would be better if we didn't go there."

Andrew awoke from his slumber to see Max smiling down at him. He kissed her softly and casually looked at his watch.

"Listen," he said, "I'm away on business for a few days, so I've topped up your account. It's balanced now."

She nodded appreciatively. He looked at her seriously.

"There seems to have been a very large purchase on the account…" He paused, looking at her intensely.

Max avoided his gaze.

"But that's cool," he continued, "as long as you don't keep going over the limit."

"Oh, I had some really major problems with the car," she lied, "and I had to take it to the garage. They fixed everything on it and it's running really well now."

She didn't have to lie to him, but sometimes preferred to not let him know her business too tough.

Max made him breakfast. Freshly squeezed orange juice. "After all that exercise, you don't want to put it all back on again," she teased. Andrew's doleful expression persuaded the cook to relent. She tossed some eggs into a bowl and fried the most basic of pancakes, with a twist of lemon and some almonds on top.

Andrew got up to shower. From the kitchen, Max could hear the rush of water and couldn't resist the welcoming sound. With one swift movement she removed the flimsy nightie from her body and dumping it on the ground, she joined Andrew in the shower, a mischievous twinkle in her eye. He smiled, caressing her ample but firm breasts with their bullet-size nipples standing to attention, revived by the morning shower.

With so much moaning in the shower they couldn't have hoped to hear the phone as it rang on the bedside table. Half an hour later when they both emerged, still steaming from the shower, the flashing red light on the answering machine caught their attention.

"Max, Andrea here," came the tape recorded message. "Do you still want that appointment later on this afternoon? 'Cause if you do, I'll stay in to do your hair personally. But if you don't, I'll go home early. Call me at the salon."

Max observed Andrew closely as he got up to wash the dishes. She admired his tennis-trained physique, thinking, "Mmm, his bottom is still tight, his legs are still firm." But again, without warning, she found her thoughts drifting to Thomas.

"You seem a bit distant," Andrew offered. "What's up? Do you need a bit more playing money?"

Max shook her head. "No, no. I've got enough." Then she changed her mind. "Well, I actually need about a hundred extra a week. I was thinking of finding more temping work," she lied, knowing that it hurt him to think of her slaving in an office for pin money.

Andrew looked at her hard, wondering what else was troubling her. He suggested that she could do with a break.

"Take some time out at the health farm, you might feel a bit better." He added that she could do with it as she seemed to be putting on a bit of weight.

The comment irritated Max.

"Some individuals on the set," Andrew continued, "keep mucking me about. Too much time-wasting. Acting so unprofessional. With no respect for my time."

Andrew came into regular contact with black people on a professional level, as his company had earned a fortune producing programmes with and for the black community. Having Max's insight into the community was a great asset for him.

Max looked at him frustrated.

"Set the time. If they don't like it, they can get out."

She sat down beside him, filling Andrew's glass once again with orange juice. She snuggled up close against him, nestling her head on his chest.

"So apart from the problems on the set, is everything else all right?"

"Yes. I think I also need to take a break though. Get away from everything."

"Well, I'm ready when you are," Max offered.

Andrew paused. It would be a good idea. But it was one thing wanting to take a break and it was another thing actually finding time to do it. His social life was currently at a premium. He barely had time to spend with Max.

Looking at his watch, Andrew realised he would be late for work. It was already ten-fifteen. He dressed quickly and after a brief kiss and cuddle with Max, rushed out the door.

Alone, Max's thoughts flashed back to Beverly's wedding. It was a grand affair. That's the way to get married, she thought. If you're going to do it, do it in style. She imagined Beverly and Thomas on honeymoon together, locked in a hotel room with a 'do not disturb' sign on the door. Max envied Beverly for having found a soul mate, even if he was a little naughty. One thing Max was sure of, Andrew could never do for her what Thomas was doing for Beverly.

Back from her daydreaming, Max phoned Andrea at the salon.

The voice of a bored teenager came down the phone line. "Andrea's popped out for a minute. Can I do something for you?"

"I'm Andrea's friend, Maxine. I want you to book an appointment for later on this afternoon."

The feisty girl at the end of the line didn't know Max and simply replied, "No chance, we're fully booked."

"Then you've got half an hour to unbook." Max spat the words out and slammed the phone down. She slipped a tight fitting lurex jumpsuit over her naked body before calling a cab.

SIX

Merlene awoke in a cold sweat. It was day, but her dreams were like a nightmare. It was always the same dream, detailed and concise. She would find love on a one way street, but lose it on a highway, alone and abandoned on the hard shoulder with fast, powerful cars zipping past her.

She found his charm irresistible. He was a maaga man, with sweet words and even sweeter moves. She was flattered that he had picked her over all the other girls. There were some good times. Times that felt better than anything she had ever felt before. Michael had made her feel like a queen. She was his queen, he was her king.

In the beginning of the relationship they romanced like a honeymoon. He was the attentive lover who couldn't do enough for her. They would cook and eat dinner together lovingly then share a night of passion. He'd sweet her so much she didn't want anybody else. Then one day the sweetness stopped and after that they were like strangers.

Merlene soon witnessed all the flaws in his character and began to form a picture of a man who was an incessant liar and a cheat. A man who was vain, conceited and irresponsible. A man who would lash out violently rather than take responsibility for his failings. Her battered and bruised body was testament to that. She became a regular visitor to the casualty department at the local hospital, once spending three days in intensive care.

Yet, she always took him back. When the police came to make their report she would lie and say she fell down the stairs. She never understood why. It didn't make any sense. Meanwhile her inner voice would echo from the land of reality, shouting, "The moment a man raises his hand against you, walk out."

Merlene was ashamed of what she had become but now understood the meaning of survival. She reclined on the leather settee, sweat dripping from her forehead. She had lain down hoping against hope that she could dream away her troubles. There had to be a way.

She had thrown her morals out the window in the last six months, in an attempt to stave off the alternative nightmare of a prison cell. She always imagined the same cold, dirty cell. She dreaded the lack of privacy.

She felt so weary, she didn't bother to move when she heard Marlon's key turning in the front door. Neither did she respond to his call of "Mum!" After a moment's silence, her son poked his head around the living room door and greeted her.

"I was calling you, mum. You didn't even answer me," he sulked.

Merlene frowned. This was not the time for a toe-to-toe with her young son. He was going through puberty. That's bad enough for a mother at the best of times.

Marlon entered the room, stepping aside to reveal a pretty young girl of roughly his age standing behind him. Merlene looked at the young girl indifferently. At Marlon's age it was good to be seen with an attractive young girl, or be seen to have a girlfriend. This was the third girl Marlon had brought home this school term.

"Mum, can I go upstairs with Melissa? We've got something to talk about."

Merlene would normally have said it was all right. But something stopped her. Something... something about the young girl that seemed vaguely familiar.

"Why do you have to go upstairs?" she barked irritated.

Marlon looked hurt. He couldn't understand why his mother was being so difficult and asked whether something was wrong.

"Why you ask me if something's wrong? I can ask anything about any young girl you bring through the door. I do not have to justify myself to you." Then she relented. "I'm going to see to the dinner," she concluded as she stood up, "so feel free to discuss whatever you have to discuss, in this living room."

Merlene gone, Melissa turned to Marlon and asked whether she should come a different day rather than upset his mother. She was a sweet girl.

They were classmates at the secondary school in Kennington. They had gone to the pictures with each other a couple of times, where they sat in the back rows learning to neck and French kiss so that they could return to school and lecture their respective friends on how to do it.

Marlon sighed. They really were only going to talk. If they had anything more 'interesting' to do, they had enough opportunities to do it elsewhere.

A stream of tears trickled down Merlene's face as she chopped the onions. She could hardly concentrate on the dinner. Everything she had worked for was falling apart. She needed desperately to hold it together, especially for Marlon.

She hadn't gone fifteen minutes in the last six months without thinking about the missing money. She now realised she should never have let Winston talk her into stealing the money. But Winston had a sweet way with words. The temptation had been too great. It had proved so easy.

"Mum!" Marlon's voice startled her. He stood right behind her. "I'm going to walk Melissa home. I'll have my dinner later."

"Okay, okay, whatever." Merlene just wanted to be left alone. "I've got to work tonight, so you'll find your dinner in the oven when you get back. Don't stay up too late."

She kissed her son hurriedly on the forehead.

"Thank you, Miss Livingstone," Melissa murmured

from the doorway.

Merlene turned to face the girl. Yes, Marlon had chosen well. There was no doubt about it, the girl was pretty, she could see the attraction for a young boy.

"Oh, I hope you come again. Come and have a chat when I'm not busy," Merlene offered. She couldn't put her finger on the button, but there was something about this girl...

Melissa cast Marlon a coy glance. You could see in her eyes that Merlene's young son was stirring her feelings.

"I hope so too," she smiled. The smile lingered long enough to torment Merlene. Why did that innocent smile make her feel so uneasy?

Merlene emerged from the subterranean twilight zone of Piccadilly Circus tube station and walked aggressively towards the neon haze of Soho. After a short walk up Shaftesbury Avenue, past the kerb artists turning out portraits of tourists by the truckload, she took a left turn into a seedy narrow street. She stopped at the gate to a basement club. The flashing neon lights above the entrance displayed the words, The Bowler Hat Club.

This was London. Sex City, UK. Soho, the sex capital of London. A billion pounds a year changed hands here, just for a little pussy. With a bit of luck, a girl who's prepared to spread her legs a little can get a raise and walk away after a couple of years with a nice little bundle. Some girls have all the luck and some girls have none.

"Hello Sugar, love," the cashier greeted Merlene as she wandered through the reception area.

"Y'all right, Venus?" Merlene smiled.

"Can't complain," Venus shouted after her.

Ozzie, the club's burly bouncer, nodded casually as Merlene swaggered past. She returned the gesture and made her way to the tiny office behind the bar, which doubled as a changing room for the girls.

The Bowler Hat Club was ostensibly a gentleman's club. In fact it provided a discreet atmosphere for gentlemen with more cash than sense to entertain ever-willing young ladies. In short, it provided everything that real gentlemen's clubs didn't.

It was a scam. The 'hostesses' would pester the wallet-packing punter to buy them drinks. The bubbly cost the club a fiver a bottle, but they re-sold it at a hundred and twenty pounds, of which the "hostess" would get twenty percent. A girl could make a hundred quid a night and more. The real money however, was made providing 'extras' for the generous male guests at a hotel nearby. The hotel concierge, who got tipped on a weekly basis, was always willing to turn a blind eye.

The Bowler Hat was popular, particularly amongst Arabs and Japanese businessmen, who were given 'free' membership to the club by taxi drivers retained by the club on a permanent basis.

It had happened a few weeks after Winston's funeral. Merlene had found a letter from Fitzroy waiting for her when she arrived home one evening. She was only mildly surprised to read that he was in prison on remand, following a gun incident at a night club. Fitzroy ordered her to make her way up Brixton Hill to pay him a little visit. The threatening tone of the letter sent Merlene into a panic. It was quite plain that he was blackmailing her with his knowledge of her misdeeds. She didn't waste any time in making arrangements for the visit. He was a desperate man and there was no telling what he was capable of doing with the information about the skank she had pulled.

It was the first time Merlene had been inside a prison. She had known people who had spent time within its walls, but she had never had the courage to go inside. Bad news carries fast in Brixton. As a precaution against bumping into any fellow visitors who might recognise her and carry word around, Merlene had disguised herself with wrap-around shades and a baseball cap pulled low over her eyes.

She sat inside the large visiting room alongside relatives and girlfriends. As the inmates filed in one by one to greet their visitors, she saw pain in their eyes. Their manhood now taken away from them, the mostly black inmates were only a shadow of the swaggering personas they had left behind on the street corners.

"Y'all right, Merle?" Fitzroy asked her when he appeared.

"Well, you should know," she barked. "You're the one who sent the letter. You're the one trying to blackmail me. You should know how I'm feeling."

Fitzroy simply smiled, glad that his carefully worded threats had done the trick. He didn't have much to lose.

"Yeah, well," he grunted.

He told her his story about the incident at Concrete Jungle.

"You know how long me sit an' wait for my court date? I can't tek it no longer. Me haffe spend Christmas with my woman and the pickney dem."

"Well, I don't see what that's got to do with me," Merlene interrupted.

The inmate looked at her hard, taking a long deliberate drag from a cigarette.

"Yuh evah find dat money?"

"No, Fitzroy. You can forget the money. It's disappeared. I've still got to replace it."

"Well, now you haffe find money to get me out ah here."

Merlene's face turned to stone.

"I don't have any money, Fitzroy." The words came out slowly and deliberately. "For the last time, I don't have any money. If I did, I would be getting myself out of my problem."

"Your problem is your problem," Fitzroy interjected. "And my problem is your problem. Ten grand for my bail money, or I talk to somebody. Yuh lucky it's not more. If I had bullets in the gun it woulda be more. Remember, before Christmas or else."

He got up to go, but Merlene raised a hand to stop him.

"Look, Fitzroy," she implored, "I would do anything to help you. But whát can I do, Fitzroy, what can I do? I haven't got any money."

Fitzroy stood for a moment, rubbing his chin and thinking to himself.

"Well, I have a friend… " he began. "He can help you. Him have a lickle runnings, y'know. Go an' check him."

"Fitzroy, I'm not interested in any illegal runnings, y'hear?"

Fitzroy smiled. He knew she was going to do it. He had been in similar positions himself. She didn't have much choice but to check Barrington. All she had to do was show up and Barrington would personally sort out his bail money.

"Don't worry," he assured her. "Barrington's safe, y'know. Him legally legal."

He told Merlene how to get hold of Barrington and got up to leave.

"If you see Rosie, me baby mudda, tell her I hope she's taking care of the children," Fitzroy concluded. "An' tell me 'idren' up ah street dat I soon step forward again. An' hail up Michael fe me."

Merlene was damned if she was going to extend his greetings to her ex.

The next two weeks were tense ones for Merlene. Bereaved, dispossessed and in peril of her freedom, she suffered extreme disorientation and teetered precariously on the very edge of mental collapse. When you endure misfortune, you reveal your true self. Every moment she spent at work was spent in terror of the auditors. They could arrive unexpectedly and the game would be up. Every moment she spent at home was spent working out how long it would take to repay the money. Now she also had to find the ten grand to cover Fitzroy's bail money. She had bumped into his woman, Rosie, in the part of the market down by Brixton Rec. Rosie had passed on a message from Fitzroy.

"Fitzroy tells me that you're going to put up his bail money for him," Rosie had said suspiciously.

"Oh well, I don't know… " Merlene began.

"Why would you do that for him, enh?" Rosie asked. "What have you and Fitzroy got to do with each other?"

"Nothing, really. Look Rosie, he's just an old friend. I never said that I would put up his bail money, but I'll help if I can."

"Well, he says I should tell you it's only four weeks to Christmas."

After that meeting, she had written an urgent letter to him stressing that she had tried everything but she couldn't get the money together. Fitzroy wrote back, 'Go and see Barrington. He will give you the money'.

Had Max been around, it would have been no problem. Merlene knew that her sister could have lent her the cash. But Max was still in Jamaica at that time. Andrea was the only other person Merlene knew of who had that kind of money. She couldn't ask her to lend the money without explaining how she knew about it. Her relationship with Winston had to be kept a secret at all costs. She had already lost her lover, she didn't need to lose her friend in the bargain.

On this particular evening, Merlene would rather not have been sitting with Mr Akiri, the Japanese businessman who was now ordering his fifth bottle of champagne.

"You show me good time after," he insisted, raising his glass for another toast.

Merlene smiled and promised that she would, but her mother's instinct kept sounding its alarm. She didn't know why she couldn't stop worrying about Marlon.

On entering the club earlier, Merlene had changed into the tight rubber dress, black fishnets, stilettoes, a long, straight wig, the trademark of her alter-ego, Sugar Brown. Merlene had invented the elegant, slinky character of Sugar Brown as a way of dealing with her moral objections to the type of night job she was doing. As Sugar Brown, she could swallow the shame of it all. Sugar Brown was a totally different person from Merlene Livingstone. The customers loved Sugar and, moreover, it was a good disguise. Just in case.

Merlene's work colleagues had noticed the change in her. She had started coming to work with dark shadows under her eyes and would often nod off during office hours. But nobody could explain how this previously diligent book-keeper had become so shoddy and slack. Her boss had called her in a couple of times and given her official warnings for coming in late and dozing on the job. Merlene gave an excuse about going through some heavy domestic scene. Six months later, the excuse was wearing thin.

By now, Mr Akiri was more than merry. He had thrown off his jacket, pocketed his spectacles and loosened his tie. With sweat pouring from his forehead, he was determined to have fun. He only needed half an opportunity to break into an off-key karaoke. Merlene did her best to smile and pretend to have fun. She hated working there, but she had no choice. She had to pay Barrington back the money and this was the best way to do it.

"I tell you something," Akiri began. "In Osaka, I have a very big house. You must come to Osaka and be my guest."

"What about your wife?" Merlene asked half-teasingly.

"Oh, you know, Japanese wife is very obedient. She do what I say. My wife is very good Japanese woman."

"Well, if you want me to come to Osaka, you'll have to buy me another bottle of champagne." Merlene purred.

"No, no more champagne." Akiri suddenly turned angry. "I drink too much champagne already. Now, you show me good time."

"Look, relax man. No need to get uptight. Of course I'll show you a good time. But sightseeing is extra. It'll cost you fifty."

"Ahhh money is no problem," Akiri hissed dismissively. "In Osaka, I own big factory."

Merlene asked Ozzie to call a mini cab and started getting her things together. She pushed her day clothes into her handbag and got Venus to sign eighty pounds to her credit. She was eighty pounds closer to getting Barrington off her back, she thought. Not bad for a couple of hours work. It was early yet. There was another fifty quid coming in before the night was through.

Outside, Akiri held the mini cab door open as Merlene jumped in. The night had turned chilly, few but the most ardent prowlers were walking along the narrow street. Merlene took a drag of her cigarette and looked around as tourists, kerbcrawlers and idlers passed around her.

"Just drive us around for an hour," Merlene directed the mini cab driver. "We want to do all the sights, London by night. Buckingham Palace, Trafalgar Square, Houses of Parliament. Everything."

The cab driver nodded, casually eyeing Merlene's nervous and heavily painted face, in his rear view mirror. He was used to shunting whores around town with their gullible punters.

The driver pushed the gears into drive and screeched away heading south. They passed prostitutes and the seedy signs of sex shops in Soho, in the direction of the the

Statue of Eros, with the bright lights of Piccadilly Circus'
Coca-Cola sign high up on their left. At Trafalgar Square,
Merlene pointed out Nelson's Column, for Akiri's benefit.
He craned his neck to see the figure at the top, all the time
remarking "ah so!" in wonder.

The Houses of Parliament, Westminster Abbey. West
towards Buckingham Palace, then back east again, over to
St Paul's Cathedral, the Tower of London and Tower
Bridge. Merlene glanced repeatedly at her watch, puffing
anxiously away at her cigarette. Finally the hour was up
and the cab driver was instructed to head towards Akiri's
Hotel on Piccadilly.

Akiri pulled out his wallet.

"Oh, I have only twenty pounds left," he cried out in
dismay.

Merlene gritted her teeth. She was tired and couldn't
wait to get home.

"It's all right," Akiri continued. I have more money in
the hotel. You come."

Merlene cursed under her breath. "Why you nevah
come out with enough money?"

"I use credit cards everywhere," Akiri protested.

Merlene cursed again. "All right," she said reluctantly.
"Pay the man. I'll get out with you."

The cab driver took the twenty and said they were
evens. As Merlene and her companion climbed out of the
car, the driver called out:

"Merlene. Ah you dat?"

The south London patois of the young Anglo-Jamaican
hit Merlene like a bullet through the heart. She stopped
dead in her tracks and turned slowly. She looked hard at
the driver, narrowing her eyes to focus. The face looked
vaguely familiar, but she didn't recognise him.

"It's me, Tony. You know, Pat's brother."

"Pat," Merlene exclaimed jumping back. She hadn't
twigged before, but now there seemed little doubt.

Melissa's smile, the dimples on her cheek, it reminded her of Pat. Pat was one of Michael's many baby mothers.

Merlene paced up and down impatiently, casting her gaze from the window to her watch and back to the window. Each glance was followed by a scowl as she kissed her teeth. Typical, she thought. You tell Michael to come at a certain time and you can guarantee that he's not going to show up until he's good and ready — if he shows up at all. The man's forty years old and still can't keep an appointment.

This wasn't the first time she had waited on Marlon's father, Michael. Their relationship had been one big long wait for something that never happened. She had given up on him since they split up and very rarely waited more than a few minutes. Sometimes, however, there were domestic issues to deal with, issues which he knew were too important for her not to wait. For all she knew, he was late on purpose, because he knew that she had no real choice but to pace up and down.

Pacing up and down in the tiny living room was tiresome. There wasn't really room to swing a cat, between the three piece suite, the stereo, the huge colour television and the drinks cabinet. Two paces this way and two paces that way. She eventually sat down. Standing increased her tension.

Her stomach was tight and getting tighter, she was angry. Here she was, eight years out of a relationship with the guy and he could still determine how she used the little free time she had available. She really didn't have time for this. Not this time. She had things on her mind. Waiting 'pon some man just didn't figure in the scheme of things.

Easing back into the armchair, she recalled the relationship with Michael. She thought back, wondering whether the position they were now in, the animosity, the anger and the contention that was there could actually have been avoided. She had loved him at one time. That fact was irrefutable.

When they first met, she was convinced that it was the big one. That Michael was the man she wanted to spend the rest of her life with. But then along came the bad times.

The things you said you loved, you're gonna lose. Michael showed very early on that he had a short temper and an almost cruel streak. Looking back on the relationship, she couldn't actually remember too many good times after the first couple of months.

After the first two months, Merlene and Michael never did anything together as a pair. He didn't take her out, he didn't even remember her birthday.

Yes, in the beginning he was good to her. But Michael was not unlike a certain type of man. Not all men, but a certain type, who use their physical side to subdue their women. This type of man shows his true colours very early. His cruel streak will manifest itself five months down the road. What usually happens is that his true nature reveals itself by way of isolated incidents which individually don't make sense. It often takes a woman several inexplicable, isolated incidents, before she'll accept that the guy she's hitched up with has got serious problems, sometimes dangerous problems. That his character isn't all there, or worse, that he is psychologically unbalanced.

When Merlene and Michael first met, she was still inexperienced. She was unable to read the warning signs. Or if she did, she misinterpreted them as insignificant, rather than seeing them for what they were — scenarios that would be repeated indefinitely.

He didn't take her out, yet she didn't see it as anything, because she didn't particularly want to go out. He would disappear for days on end, but she didn't mind, because it meant peace and quiet. She even allowed herself to accept his habit of spending all his earnings on clothes, raving and cars for himself, while any extra money she had was spent on Marlon. What she hadn't realised, however, was that deliberately or not, Michael was slowly taking away her self-confidence. She only had eyes for him. She never contemplated going to look anywhere else. But at the same time, by channelling all her emotions and thoughts to him, she neglected her own self.

Merlene was as gullible as the next woman. Despite all the sound advice to her sister, she used to let men walk all over her when it came to love.

With inexperience you've got nobody to learn from. You use your instincts. But this problem can be avoided. If you have a solid confidence thing from your parents, you'd soon realise that this kind of man is no good for you. Merlene hadn't got any of that stuff. Her father had run off with a younger woman just before Max was born, their heartbroken mother had returned to Jamaica ten years after, believing that to leave her daughters in England with their strict relatives was better than taking them with her to the Caribbean.

That's not to say the confidence thing works every time. So many women today will stay in a relationship even when they know it's no good. Behind every 'successful' relationship, there must be a woman.

Some women'll say they're staying in a rotten relationship because they can't resist the physical. That's fine, as long as they admit it to themselves. Usually, though, they're not even getting enough of the physical, in which case they'll say they're in it for love and meanwhile, the guy abuses them. If not physically, he'll abuse them emotionally.

Merlene lacked personal confidence, Michael was able to exploit that. He was able to convince her to have a child within their relationship, despite having already had several children prior to it, by getting up on his soap box and talking about how he was a righteous man and how he could do no wrong, how he knew about this and he knew about that.

A man has to be judged by his deeds, not his words. Michael's deeds stank. Yet he could always attract women. He was forced to admit that he already had five kids by three different women, yet Merlene decided it would be different for them. She shouldn't have ignored that kind of track record.

For a couple of years, she was willing to give everything of herself. But Michael would take little time with her. She tried to be the sweetest girl in the world, but she got nothing back in return. There's nothing worse than remembering your boyfriend's birthday every year, giving him a card and buying him presents until it dawns on you that this man has forgotten your birthday. Michael was that certain type of man who felt it's a woman's duty to remember things like birthdays. As far as he was concerned, birthdays were not his role in life.

Birthday cards are vitally important where certain women are concerned, because they show some sign of imagination. Even if you don't give a present, to actually take the time to go into a shop, pick a card and write something in it would smooth over a lot of creases. It doesn't matter if you haven't been getting on too well together, you'd be willing to give him a squeeze if he'd just remember your birthday. A lot of guys are quite clever at this. They'll spend a lot of time demoralising and abusing women physically, mentally and emotionally. But they diligently perform the small gestures which keep a woman under their thumb. Even if they forget the birthday, these men will always do some silly little things, like coming in with a box of chocolates. Now, when you balance that box of chocolates against all the times you've cooked dinner and had to chuck it in the bin, or when you've had girls ringing up who don't want to speak to you, or you pick up the phone and the line goes dead; balance that against a box of chocolates, it's pitiful. But it catches the women every time. If it's not a box of chocolates, you've begged him and begged him and begged him to go out with you and he doesn't want to go anywhere, y'know. He doesn't want to go anywhere with you. The one time out of the fifty occasions that he's come with you, you think that you've got through. But you had to beg him. What's the point of that?

Merlene remembered the nights she sat in by herself, watching paint dry. Waiting and waiting for Michael to come home. They were supposed to be living together, yet he was hardly ever home. When he would finally show up, she wouldn't question him. She would play the other game instead, which is, keep quiet and don't rock the boat and you'll eventually make things better.

When she looked back on it, Merlene realised she ought to have had it out with him. She ought to have torn shit out of him whenever he came home without a reasonable excuse. A man is only stronger than you if you let him believe he is. He might have physical superiority over you, but there are lots of ways women can put the fear of god into their men.

As far as their once hot sexual relationship was concerned, Merlene had learned to go through the motions without Michael being aware that she was passive. She knew exactly how to push the right buttons to make him think she was involved. She wasn't trying to avoid hurting his feelings. But she wasn't prepared to allow Michael the excuse of blaming her for their decaying relationship. He would probably have accused her of being frigid or some other stupidness. When they made love, he would roll over afterwards, while she lay passively. It was a long time since he had satisfied her. As far as she was concerned, there was nothing worse than a man on top of you once you realised you could have had more fun by yourself.

Slowly, she began to wean herself off him, until she finally gained the knowledge and the attitude to throw him out.

She had since had a couple of other relationships with reasonable guys, so she knew there were real men out there. You just had to search for them. There were men who showed warmth and generosity and gave her something. What she had with Michael did not compare.

Having somebody else to care about had made a difference. With the birth of their child, Michael changed in some ways. Merlene wondered how things would have been if she had given birth to a girl instead of a boy. Michael would have been less elated, unable to make the same proud comments after she gave birth, such as, "yeah, my seed's strong," and "this will keep my line going." The fact that Marlon was born a Leo, like his father, also seemed to have some mystical significance for Michael.

Merlene worried about having Michael as a role model for her child. She didn't want a rough, tough boy, with all that physical stuff. She wanted her son to grow up into a strong man, yes, but not to live just on his wits, but to realise that there were only a few occasions when you had to resort to using the physical. She wanted her son to grow up respecting women. She didn't want him to grow up, have children and not know why they were there, or to notch up another child that he couldn't feed. On the other hand, she felt that Marlon needed to have a relationship with Michael. She knew what Marlon wanted, but as for Michael, what he wanted was beyond her. He changed his stance so easily.

As soon as he heard the familiar rhythm from the door knock, Marlon ran down the stairs to greet his father. He was happy as children are when their fathers come to visit. It was Marlon's thirteenth birthday. His father had rung during the week to say he wanted to take the boy and to keep him for the weekend. He had told Merlene that, as he would be in the area, he would pass by and pick the boy up.

Merlene stood behind the front door, waiting for Michael to step in. Dressed smartly and sporting designer sunglasses, he approached the door cautiously. He knew he was late and, therefore, likely to get cussed. He had runnings to do and that's that. As far as he was concerned, he was big enough to take a cussin'. Anyway, he and Merlene were no longer an item. She could cuss the house down if she so wished.

Michael tried to enter, but Merlene stood stubbornly in front of him.

"You know somebody here?" she asked sarcastically. The edge on her voice put him on the defensive.

"Listen, right," he blurted, "Here I am and here I stand. When a man have something to do, him have to do it. I don't run my life by timetable. Right? Me said me gwan come, I come. Me reach. Me late, but me reach. You should be lucky seh me come here in one piece."

Merlene stared at him angrily.

"Time is getting rough, man," she said. "I don't have no time to sit down on a corner waiting for any man." She didn't want to engage in a full-length conversation with him.

Marlon stood innocently between his parents. He knew what was coming. He had seen it so many times before. He accepted it. What burned him, however, was that some other kids in his class who had been brought up by single parents, still had some sort of relationship with the absent parent. Marlon struggled with the fact that he had no relationship with his father, he didn't understand why it was that way. It wasn't like he was a demanding son or that he wanted his father to go out of his way to be with him. He simply wanted to pick up the phone and say 'Hi' every now and then and he wished his father would call him once in a while just to ask how he was.

Marlon was at the age when he needed his role model. He wanted to experience the stuff that the other kids were experiencing. He envied his classmates when they drove about in their dads' new cars. To them it was nice to say, "Cho, that's my daddy." That's what it's about for kids. Marlon had really looked forward to his daddy coming on his birthday. He stayed cool and collected all day though, because he knew his mum would get worked up if he showed too much enthusiasm.

Merlene couldn't hide her frustration even if she wanted to.

"This ain't good enough," she said finally. "What are you here for? We haven't seen you for ten months, even then, you only popped in for a couple of hours. Do you intend to take on the role of supporting your son? 'Cause if not, I can deal with that, that's no problem. I'll have my son to myself, I know how to keep him. Well, what d'you want?"

"Don't carry on like that, Merlene. Blouse an' skirt! Why you ah gwan so feisty? Me nuh trouble you, so ease off. You well an' know seh me come fe tek my yout out fe the day."

"What do you mean you 'come fe tek your yout' out fe the day'? Didn't you say you wanted him for the weekend? So what are you talking about? You come here driving in a brand new car on your son's birthday and you're prepared to disappoint the boy once again. What's wrong with you, Michael?"

"Now listen," Michael rejoined, "I didn't come here for no aggro. If me wan' tribulation, me go dung a bull shop, right? Stokey police station just love me."

"You should have been here from morning, you only just reach and immediately start chatting foolishness about taking him out for the day."

"Well me have runnings fe do. I don't want to hold up no argument with you. I just want to take Marlon out and spend the day with my son."

"You mean one of your sons, don't you?"

The door was still open, Michael kicked it furiously, slamming it shut.

Merlene realised that his temper was rising. When he took off his sunglasses, she saw in his eyes that he was ready to fight. Michael loved to cuss and pop too much style.

She hadn't meant to lose her temper, but she found herself getting angry. Just looking at this man, seeing him roll up in a brand new car, while she was worrying herself sick trying to pay Barrington back, as well as supporting a kid. She felt that Michael could at least, not so much for her but for his son, make the effort, regardless of any feelings he may have for her. Whether he liked or hated her, he should make the effort for his son. He didn't have to make a great show of it. He had never fed the child or clothed him. He was never around when the child was sick. He wouldn't even know if the child, his child, was taking penicillin.

Merlene decided that the best policy was to keep as calm as possible. She could feel Michael's temper rising. Marlon, totally ignored until now, looked up at his dad and said, "Hi, dad."

That burned Merlene. She kissed her teeth as if to say, 'Ungh, ah dat what you call dad'? She decided to let it go, however.

"Marlon, go back upstairs, I just want to say something to your father."

Merlene led the way into her front room, followed closely by Michael, who again slammed the living room door shut.

Merlene reminded him that he was in her house, her home.

"Personally, I don't give a shit about 'fe your house", Michael replied. "I don't give a shit if you're sleeping with man or the whole sound system posse. Right? You're still my baby mudda. Because right now, I'm telling you, I don't like the way you talk to me. I don't like the attitude you ah show me."

Merlene shook her head, her mouth open incredulously.

"I heard someone talking down the road, saying they saw you just the other day, an' you were talking about how you come into my house to run t'ings same way. There ain't no stopping you, is there Michael? Well let me tell you, you can forget all that nonsense. This is my house, as long as I'm around, there's no way you're coming back in."

Michael cursed. "You better show me some respect," he warned again.

"Show respect? You seem to forget Michael, that respect has to be earned. How can a man who has so many children who he doesn't maintain, by several women, know respect? How can a man who can drive on the same road that his child lives on and not even come in and pass the time of day with his pickney, know respect? How can a man who can not even remember or acknowledge the day his child was born, know respect? How can a man who drives around in a new car, when he knows that his ill child needs some things to aid with his learning or to widen his horizons, not even bring forward the money or the time to help that child, know respect? Michael, you have no right to stand up here in front of me and tell me about 'respect'. You can't spell the word. Go back to school."

Michael fumed.

"Look Merlene, any time I want I can just take my son and go about my business. Any time."

"Come. You come take your son, you come feed your son, you come take your child to school. You come speak to the teachers and make sure he's learning. You make sure that your child has the right clothing on his back. You make sure that your child has the emotional, the physical, the mental and the moral support that is needed day in and day out, to make that child grow. To bring that child through adolescence into manhood and to make his way through this world. Right? If at any time you think you are bigger, badder and broader than me, you come and you do that. But we both know seh you do not possess the skill, nor the knowledge to do that fe your own child. You only sit back in your easy chair and make like you care. 'Care', that's another word you ought to learn."

Unable to withstand Merlene's verbal onslaught, Michael picked up the ornamental marble ashtray on the coffee table and flung it across the room. It smashed against the wall, breaking into a thousand pieces.

Merlene, suddenly afraid, realised that she may have gone too far, however true the words. She would have to backpedal slightly to pacify him. She could see that he was riled up and that his muscles were flexing. Like any angry man he wasn't thinking straight.

She finally managed to calm him down. He moved nervously from one chair to another as he paced the room. Pulling out a cigarette, he lit up and threw himself on the sofa, with his feet sprawled across the arm. He searched inside himself for insults he could throw at Merlene, whether they were true or not. But he couldn't come up with anything.

"Just tell me something, Michael," Merlene began cautiously. "Just how many children do you intend to have and how do you intend to feed your pickney?"

He sucked hard on his cigarette. He wasn't in the mood to exchange pleasantries, or discuss his failings. 'Love is all I have, so love is all I bring', he told himself. As far as he was concerned, in the eyes of every other woman, he was fine, charming, physically and emotionally there for them. Merlene was just a ginal.

"Listen," she continued, "I don't really give a damn

how many children you intend to have, but the one thing you should do is tell your children of their other brothers and sisters. The earlier you do, the better it will be for those involved."

Michael simply kissed his teeth. He really didn't want to hear all this crap. Merlene could see his indifference. He felt she was ranting as usual and that this was just another one of her moments.

Merlene studied Michael hard, trying very hard to restrain herself.

"Marlon came home last week, with his girlfriend…"

Michael kissed his teeth. What did this have to do with him?

"Listen, Michael, you think I've got nothing better to do with my time, than run over old arguments and old issues with you? Your son, our son, brought in a girl to my house as his girlfriend. The girl's called Melissa."

Michael froze for a minute, unable or unwilling to figure out where Merlene was coming from.

"De gal named Melissa. So what?"

"Yes, Michael, as far as I can see she appears to be the same age as Marlon."

"Yes, Merlene, the girl is the same age as Marlon and she named Melissa. So what?"

"Bwoy, you're a big fool, y'know, Michael. Seriously to God, you are one of life's biggest fools. Out of all dem gal that you did run around town with, how much of them you breed? Or have you forgotten that you have a child called Melissa?"

Michael looked at Merlene, it registered now that she was talking about his daughter, but the implication still didn't connect. Merlene sighed heavily and walked away from him.

"Yes, Michael, as I was saying, one of the world's biggest fools. Your son, our son, brought in a girl… That Melissa is your daughter."

Michael said nothing. He simply wiped his brow and stood up. He took his hand to his jaw and rubbed his chin, pacing up and down the room.

"How you know it was my daughter, enh?" he countered finally.

"Listen, Michael, let me describe your daughter and you tell me if it's the same person. She's got relaxed hair. She's a little taller than Marlon and of a dark complexion like myself. She's got a strong resemblance to Pat. Same dimples when she smiles." Merlene saw the realisation dawn on Michael. "Yes," she continued, "The sowing of your wild oats has come to haunt you. But let me tell you something. Let me make myself loud and clear. I don't want your stinking shit on my doorstep. You shit anywhere you want, but just make sure it don't reach my door. I can't rely on you to take an active role in your son's upbringing, or his moral standing. But you make it clear to Melissa what the connection is. I've already told Marlon why nothing cyaan't go on."

Michael didn't say anything. What could he say? Merlene was right. He had ruled out the possibility of an incestuous relationship between his various offspring by different mothers. But here it was, it had happened. As a rule, Michael made sure that his baby mothers didn't know each other. But Merlene had found out about Pat by chance years ago.

Well, what was done was done, Michael figured. The important thing for now was not to allow Merlene to get one over on him. He had to somehow put a dent in her armour.

"Look Merlene, I don't know why you've come here with some bee in your bonnet. The boy come home with some girl, an' you assuming it's his girlfriend. It might be one of them boy girl things that don't lead nowhere. What's the point of telling Melissa seh Marlon's her brother? All you want to do is go bus' up in the hornet's nest, innit? Why gal, you love to get sting, innit? You just love to see my life mash up. Innit? You nah know seh there are times when certain t'ing nah fe move? An' all this just because I have pickney with different woman. All dat sump'n deh happened from time. We've talked about it, you've raised hell about it, you've cussed about it. I shout 'bout it meself, it done, it finish. I'm not telling Melissa not'n. It don't make no sense. What am I telling Melissa for? How do I know she's looking at Marlon as boyfriend? The boy's thirteen. If she wants something to go practice on she'll choose somebody older, innit?"

Merlene looked at him and shook her head in dismay. Which fool did this man think he was talking to? Melissa was his daughter, Marlon was his son. The man was so blind, he couldn't or wouldn't see the importance of telling Melissa that Marlon was her brother. She made her way to the door, turned around and looked at Michael.

"I hope you reap the very best of what you sow. The very best. You see all like you now, Michael, your dick should just drop off when you think of woman. It should just drop off, because you don't have no use for it. Forget about how you feel, or how your reputation is going to stay. Think about two young children living in close proximity to each other and how they feel, when they find out they were not told they were half brother and sister. You certainly didn't think about your shame when you was fucking Pat, so why fret about it now? That's your shame, you take it on your head and you live with it. A'right? But I don't want my son to live like that. I don't want my son to pick up the dirty standard of living that you've elected to live."

"Well before you talk woman, you mus' learn to behave yourself. I hear seh you was out all t'ree o'clock at night with some man in the West End. Tell me, where was our son then? Alone by himself in the house? So what kind of mother are you, enh? Answer me dat, Merle?"

It was a low blow and it hurt Merlene. She had nothing to say. She had dreaded that Tony would mention their late night sightseeing tour to Michael. The two men were friends. She hadn't prepared herself to have it thrown in her face moments after cussing Michael out for his behaviour. It was checkmate.

After a while, Michael collected Marlon, and father and son departed, leaving Merlene to ponder her situation.

She had a vision the night before that she was walking on a beach of golden sand. This beach that she saw was where she should have been with Winston. Instead, she had ended up owing thousands of pounds to Barrington.

Mr Akiri had persuaded her to follow him to his room in the expensive hotel on Piccadilly. She wanted the fifty he owed her so she didn't want to let him out of her sight. She felt safe and secure in the hotel.

Inside his room, Akiri had immediately reached for a pouch in the bottom of a suitcase, from which he pulled out a bundle of notes and dutifully counted out fifty pounds. As Merlene turned to leave, he called her back.

"I give you fifty pounds more if you show me your titties," he declared.

The offer threw Merlene off balance. Clients were always asking for the 'extras'. She had always refused to provide them. Most of the other girls at the club chose to sleep with the punters, because it was easy money. Merlene didn't mind the hostess bit, but she wasn't prepared to whore herself for any amount of money. So Akiri's offer peeved her.

"Look, I don't do extras, all right?"

"No, not extras," Akiri insisted. "Just show your titties. One hundred pounds?" He counted out another hundred and pushed the money towards her.

Merlene looked at the money and kissed her teeth. It

was easy money though.

She hurriedly lifted up her blouse, exposing her naked breasts. Akiri's eyes lit up as he ogled her, saliva dripping from his tongue. Just as hurriedly, Merlene pulled down her blouse and grabbed the hundred pounds from Akiri's outstretched hand.

Again she turned to leave and again Akiri called her back.

"Wait, please. I give you two hundred pounds if you let me touch your titties."

Merlene was furious. But Akiri calmed her down as he counted ten twenties and pushed the money towards her. Merlene decided that the request wouldn't do much harm. She had already gone this far and the money seemed so easy. It wasn't as if she was actually whoring herself. She snatched the money from Akiri's outstretched hand and lifted her blouse up, this time more cautiously.

Akiri didn't need any more encouragement. He pounced on Merlene, pinning her against the wall, and grabbed one of her breasts with an iron grip, pushing it up towards his face. He dived in immediately, biting the breast roughly, mercilessly. Merlene struggled, trying to push the man's head away. But it was impossible. Akiri clung to her breast like a vice. The pain was unbearable. She eventually managed to free herself sufficiently to direct a perfect hit with her knee. Akiri bent over double holding his crotch as he howled in pain. With her breast throbbing like it was on fire, Merlene turned quickly and rushed out, still clutching three hundred pounds in cash in her hand, to hail a black cab.

Once she was safely home, the full distress of what she had gone through hit her. She broke down crying, trying hard not to wake Marlon. She couldn't allow him to see her this way. She rushed into the bathroom and turned on the shower, stepping under the warm water, still dressed in her party clothes.

She felt dirty. She despised herself for what she had become. Oh, if only Winston had driven more carefully on that fateful night, she wouldn't be in this mess. She didn't know how she would manage to repay Barrington, but she resolved never to go back to the Club again.

SEVEN

The Four Musketeers met up the next evening. Beverly had just arrived back from her honeymoon in Jamaica and there was lots of gossip from back-ah-yard.

They sat at their usual table at the back of the bar in Dunn's River, each woman sipping from a different cocktail.

"Max, I hope you haven't sold that beautiful car while I've been away," Beverly enquired about her friend's customised Beetle.

"Nuh worry yourself," Max reassured, "Cause it's criss and clean and waiting for you, when you're ready."

"Well, I can't exactly say that you look like a married woman, Beverly," Andrea offered. "Look like you've put on a little bit of weight. I thought honeymoon was to make you shed weight?"

Dunn's River was packed to the brim with its curious mix of buppies and white trendies. The Four Musketeers stood out amongst everybody. They could steal any show dressed the way they were. However, they ignored the attentive glances from the lecherous men in suits doing their lizard thing at the bar.

"How can you ask the girl a personal question like that?" Merlene interrupted. "Beverly, did you enjoy your honeymoon?"

Beverly hesitated before answering. "Yes, it was really wonderful, a bit strange at first, but things worked out nice. We were a bit distant but things are cool."

"What do you mean 'distant'?" a surprised Merlene asked. "It was your honeymoon. Y'know. You don't have no children 'round your heels. What do you mean 'distant'?"

Beverly simply shrugged her shoulders.

Merlene studied Beverly's distant eyes long and hard, before asking, "Do you think you've made a mistake?"

"Of course I didn't make a mistake. I just told you, things were fine and he was just a bit nervous. I know it sounds silly, but..."

"Well, if I get married and my husband's acting a bit distant on our honeymoon, I'd have to ask the man why." Andrea warned casually. "So Beverly, you start turn fool now. Since when you can have man in your quarters behaving this way? What kind of rubbish is that?"

"You just want to read something into nothing. It's no big thing," Beverly countered, wanting desperately to get off the point. "I mean we've been together four and a half months... I'm just saying that the man was a bit distant, that's all. Maybe he was finding it all a bit strange or something. No big deal. Everybody's entitled to a little bit of nervousness about being married. But anyway, since we've been back, he's been cool. There's been no problem. He loves me madly and I feel the same."

Sudden silence fell over the girls. In their experience, men who were distant were usually playing away from home.

Beverly broke the silence by adding, "Well, we did manage to go out to Port Royal and Ocho Rios, we even climbed Dunn's River Falls."

"I don't believe you, Beverly," Andrea retorted. "How you can manage to climb Dunn's River when you're too afraid to go on the big wheel at the fair ground? You climbed Dunn's River?"

"Yes I did. But you have to remember that I did have my husband with me," Beverly added mockingly. "I wasn't frightened because I did have my husband with me."

"It's all right," Merlene interjected. "You don't have to

say 'husband' so many times, like you is the only person good enough to get married."

Beverly continued talking about the holiday—about the food they ate and what they didn't eat, who they saw and so on.

"Every time I think of Jamaica, it brings water to my eyes," she reminisced.

"So," Andrea asked, "how you get on with him people? How him people stay?"

"What a Waterloo! If I had stayed at their house any longer I might have lost my life," came Beverly's exaggerated reply. She was relieved that she had successfully changed the subject.

They all started laughing because the girls knew that here was a juicy bit of gossip.

Beverly began. "Let me tell you the truth, they never liked me. The moment I got through the door, his mum insisted that I call her 'Sister King', because, believe it or not, she belongs to the church. Thomas had never told me that his parents were church people, y'know. So when I came along and started forgetting myself and my p's and q's, it was a big shame and disgrace. You know what his mum had the cheek to ask me? She said 'Thomas tells me you already have two children'. She had the nerve to ask me if they were from the same man."

"She what?" Merlene asked incredulously.

"No, she nevah?" Andrea couldn't believe it. "What did you say to her?"

"I looked her straight in the eye and told her yes, they were from two different men and what about it? I simply told her that I love my children and they are well provided for materially. They will want for nothing. When she realised I had two children, as far as she was concerned I was bringing her son down and fire, brimstone and whatsit would hail down on him for fraternising with a low-life woman like me. That's the way the woman saw me, I'm telling you, I could see it in her eyes. There's no way I could mistake it. She even wanted to tek me to church to baptise me. You ever hear anything so stupid? You go on your honeymoon and your mother-in-law wants to baptise you."

"Well," said Andrea teasingly, "There's no redemption for you. Two pickney by two different man. Now you're getting married you're bound to have baby, that is three baby for t'ree different man," she giggled holding up three fingers to stress the point. "So, she could baptise you, but the water will have no use."

They all started laughing. Even Beverly saw the funny side of it.

"Even when I got up in the mornings, you could hear the woman saying her prayers," Beverly continued. "When we had breakfast we had to have one long prayer over the food. By that time the food cold."

Beverly paused for a moment, reflecting.

"I love him and I'm glad that I married him. But I have to admit, the way that his mum treated me — and she treated me a way — was out of order. To him, it's important that his mother likes me, so I tried hard. But it didn't matter what I did for this woman, she just did not like me. Her son chose me as his wife, so she will have to accept it."

"What about his dad?" Max asked. "How did the dad treat you?"

"Now I come to think about it he was hardly there. It could have been a woman. But I do not wish to get involved in people's dirty business. I keep myself to myself."

"For somebody who keep dem self to dem self," said Merlene, "You love wash you mouth 'pon people."

Beverly's eyes narrowed. Merlene's passing comment with the sting in its tail had burned her. She waved her left hand dismissively in front of Merlene, seemingly emphasising the wedding band on her finger. It was a simple gold ring with two interlocking hearts set in diamond. The other women marvelled at it, but resented Beverly's emphasis. Beverly was telling them that come rain or shine, joy or pain, at least she was married.

Beating teasingly about the bush with a glint in her eye, Andrea asked the newly-wed, "So, does Thomas eat off two-foot table?"

The other girls were horrified. Andrea had gone a bit too far.

"How could you?" Merlene stuttered. "That is too strong, that is too strong, Andrea. Because if you evah ask me such a question, I would lay you out same place. All twenty-four of your teeth would box out and lay down at the bottom of your stomach."

The four of them roared with laughter. But though they laughed heartily, Max, Merlene and Andrea still wanted to know.

Once the hilarities had subsided, Beverly replied loftily, "I am a married woman, you should respect the privacy of my marriage."

"You just full of fart, Bev," Andrea retorted mercilessly. "Either the man eats off a two-foot table, or he don't."

"Him eat off a two-foot table," Max interjected triumphantly. " 'Cause from when she says 'respect the privacy', that mean fe seh him can eat off a two-foot table."

"No, I want Beverly to answer me dat," Andrea demanded.

"I'm a married woman," Beverly repeated snobbishly, "So therefore, anything that happens within the confines of my marriage is private."

Andrea wasn't going to be put off easily.

"If you don't tell us whether Thomas eats off a two-foot table, I will put him to the test."

"That is out of order you know," Beverly replied coldly. "That's like incest."

Realising that she had overstepped her mark, Andrea decided to let it go.

Oral sex is still taboo in the community. Few men will admit to going down on their women orally. These four experienced women each knew the opposite to be true. The very same men who, upon commencing a relationship will remind you forcefully that they don't eat off two-foot table, are the same men who will practically think that they've been cheated if they're not given a blow job. They'll feel as if you've robbed them.

Yes, they enjoyed oral sex and their men enjoyed giving it as well as receiving it. Still, cow nevah know the use of him tail till the butcher cut it off.

The conversation continued in the general direction of men's sexual inadequacies.

"Men don't mind the woman doing all the work while they stand back and simply enjoy it," said Merlene.

"In the case of some men, foreplay is just like saying, 'let's go for tennis'. They're not aware of what the word foreplay is. Especially men who have this habit of doing the job mechanically and snoring afterwards. Literally, they gone completely fast asleep. Some guys will swear blind that the adrenaline that's flowing causes some chemical reaction which puts them to sleep, said Andrea."

"They just use that as a damn excuse, because as soon as they've got what they're concerned about, that's it. It releases them from any physical commitments afterwards. As far as they're concerned, 'I've got there, I've reached, I've conquered. I don't need to play around now, I can just go to sleep and everything's cool'," said Beverly.

They talked about the lack of sensitivity of some men.

"Some of them have to be taught to eat off a two-foot table," Andrea offered. "They're not aware of what they're doing, so you do have to teach. But that's only if they're prepared to be taught. Some men's egos are so fragile that it takes loads of sessions and it has to be done very

111

carefully, because if a man suspects that you're guiding him, or you're teaching him, or you're doing different moves, he'll think you're either sleeping with somebody else, or you're saying there's something wrong with the way he performs."

"It's true though," Merlene interrupted. "Some of them don't know how to perform. As far as they're concerned, any mistake, they never made it. They simply woke up one day at the age of sixteen and knew how to do it perfectly."

"You have to be very careful," Andrea continued. "You can't just turn around and tell a man that what he did was rubbish. Not unless you're very brave, or unless you really don't want that man."

The women's convivial banter was interrupted only by Beverly's abrasive enquiry directed at Max.

"What's it like, sleeping with a white man?"

"What is what like? A man is a man." Max was unwilling to be drawn into Beverly's line of questioning.

"No, you can not just come with that and expect us to take that," Beverly insisted. "You're screwing a white man. That is big 'tory for anybody. You're screwing a white man, so what's the difference?"

Andrea couldn't resist a little tease.

"Oh please, Max, the thought. Y'know — pink."

The four women burst out laughing.

"Come on, does it look the same?"

"It's a man. A man's thing is going to look the same, unless its smaller, bigger, taller whatever," Max assured them. Her three companions sat contemplative for a moment, until Beverly pursued the issue.

"Are you trying to tell us that this white man, just does the same thing as a black man? If so and he delivers the same goods as a black man, then why are you with a white man? You might as well have a black man. What's the difference?"

"Well, there is a difference," Max said trying to be frank.

"Not a lot, but there is ja little difference. I can't really speak for any other white man, because I don't know a lot. But this particular man, he's sensitive and caring, he's prepared to take time. It's more than just a screw. There's more than one way to skin a cat. There's a limit to how many times you can do the same thing in the same way at the same time, y'know, week in week out. That's not enjoyment, that's not learning, that's not discovering one another's bodies."

"Discovering one another's bodies?" Andrea couldn't believe the stupidness she was hearing. "Not'n nah go so. A fuck is a fuck. What is that?"

"You don't have to put it like that," Merlene rallied to her sister's defence. "When she says 'discovering one another's bodies', she means making love."

But Andrea wasn't giving up.

"Me fail to see what she means by 'discovering one another's bodies'. A fuck is a fuck is a fuck, right? There's no two ways about it."

Max turned to Merlene for more support. The elder sister simply rolled her eyes helplessly, finding the subject a bit too close to the knuckle. Anyway, if she got entangled in it, she might have to divulge her personal tastes, which she was not prepared to do.

With too many black men unwilling to treat their women with respect, where white men are concerned, some black women are no longer prepared to say nevah.

Beverly looked at Max, unable to let the subject drop. It wasn't her business who Max dated, she just felt that a good black woman could always find a good black man.

"Why have you got a white man in your bed? There's black men out there. I'm married to one."

"Only five minutes," Andrea added.

"Yes, I've been married five minutes, but I'm married to a black man. 'Cause that's how things are supposed to go."

Beverly fumbled for words. She had never been able to

express herself quite as eloquently as her three soul sisters.

"Yes, that's how things are supposed to go. You're supposed to marry your own black man. Just tell me what your white man is delivering that my Thomas couldn't do? The only thing that man's giving you more than the black man is money."

Max looked at Beverly hard, with pain in her eyes. That was the point that hurt her most. Andrea was anxious to hear Max's response.

"Well, is it money?"

Max hesitated before finally giving in.

"The money is a big factor, I'm not going to deny it. But what I'm saying is, at the beginning the money was a t'ing, it did entice me. Yeah. To get all the things I never had before. Yeah, of course it did entice me. Now, it's a bit more than that. Now, I feel a bit more for the man than just straight sex and money."

"Are you saying that you actually love him?" Andrea asked.

Max didn't answer.

"Well I'm sorry," Beverly continued. "I don't agree with you Max. There is no way I would pick up myself with some white man, knowing there's some serious looking black men out there. Some serious looking black men and you go and pick up some middle aged white man, who, just because he can eat off two-foot table, you go and give him credit. You're not telling me that when you turn over in the morning you wouldn't rather have a black man in your bed."

"Well," Andrea added, "I know seh, if I pick up with white man, him have fe go cook, clean, wash. Do everything fe me. He'd have to offer me more than a black man. He'd have to put himself so high up that no black man standing up on ten man could reach."

"I would agree with you, Beverly. There is good black man out there, but I can't find one. So what you going to do? You can't sit down and wait forever," Max interjected.

It was two against one. Merlene being the eldest felt she had to come down on the side of Max, not just because it was her sister, but to keep a balance.

"Max says she went with this man first of all for the money," Merlene chose her words carefully. "You can't judge her for that. Beverly, when the father of your first baby disappeared, you were cleaning floors to make extra money. That man didn't keep you. You've got two children, two different fathers. That's your black man for you, what have you got for it?"

"Yes, that's true," said Beverly defensively. "Things didn't work out. But I now have a black man who I'm married to and I'm happy to be married to him. What I'm saying about Max, is that I don't see how she can really in all honesty seh the white man is better. Bettah she turn to Bajan," she added in humour.

"Don't seh that," Andrea added mischievously. "Can you imagine, turning over in bed to hear some man tell you in that squeaky Bajan voice, 'me love you'. Well I don't know, y'know. If me have to wake up every morning to a Bajan man, I would go to white man. That's enough to turn you to white man." The girls all laughed.

Merlene thought long and hard, before concluding on a serious note:

"I would have said, before, that I would never go out with a white man, but I would never say never anymore. It just doesn't seem right to say never anymore. It's cosmopolitan out there. If I can't get no man at all and I'm on my own and a white man comes and offers me his time, then I can't categorically say that I wouldn't take him up on his offer. Let's face it, white or black man, they're all dogs. Once they sniff it, they're there. Nobody questions the black man going for white women. Everybody says 'Cho, dat common now, that's no problem. You just deal with it'. Well, what's the problem with a black woman going out with a white man, if that's what she really wants? Don't only talk about the problems in the world, you've got to help solve them."

Beverly bowed to Merlene's greater wisdom, but with one reservation.

"I agree with everything you say, but speaking for myself, I'm going to say I would never go with no white man. I would rather take the worst of the black man, than take myself and put myself in some white man's bed. There is no two ways about it. My parents never came to this country to work hard and suffer so much, so that I could just turn round and say, 'Here, mummy, look at my blond hair and blue eyes man'. It just doesn't wash. In Jamaica, some lickle white man come and said he's going to try and do a thing with me. When Thomas saw him he just cussed the man's b-c and his d-c and told him, if he wanted to live, to get out the area and never come back. In Jamaica people don't ramp with those things."

"That's not saying anything," Merlene said drily.

The other three women were irritated by Beverly's childish self-righteousness.

"If you were put to the test, supposing Thomas never came along, and you did physically check for that white man? What would you say?" asked Merlene.

"No way," Beverly insisted. "There's no way I would have gone with that man, or even begin anything with that man."

"No, no, no. What we're saying, is suppose this man's exactly the type of man you're attracted to, the only difference is the colour of his skin. What we're asking you is whether you would have been able to say categorically, with your hand on your heart, that you wouldn't check for this white man?"

"I wouldn't have checked him. I would rather check any other black man walking on that beach. You've got to stand up and fight for your black man, or you ain't gonna get no culture."

"The white man is no different from all those red men that you take a particular liking to," Merlene reminded her.

"That's rubbish. That's rubbish." Beverly's voice had taken on a hint of rage. "What's red man got to do with this? I am telling you that I don't go for white man, you come and tell me about red man."

"What's the difference between a red-skinned man and a fair-skinned man? With your preference for red man how can you say you wouldn't go for white man?"

"I don't have a problem with colour, so I don't know how you can say I only check for red men?"

"Beverly, since when you ever go out with any dark-skinned man? Because in all the years I've known you, you have never, never picked up any. If I am wrong, be not afraid to say so."

"Anyway," Merlene continued. "We are all sisters, so what are we fighting for? Nuh skin up. We can't skin up. We've got to work things out together. Forget what colour you may be, let's us talk about love."

A heartless observer aware of the problems on Merlene's mind, may have felt that she had an ulterior motive in commending unity amongst her sistren.

"We've got to stick together, it's a crazy world. It's rough out in the streets where our children go and play," she concluded.

This was the last happy evening they were to spend together. Dark secrets were tearing at their relationship.

EIGHT

As usual, the annual Afro Hair and Beauty Show afforded an opportunity for the ladies to parade their new style and fashion and to criticise those who do not quite have the right dress sense.

"But wait, look 'pon Sharon now," one girl dressed to impress in a micro-mini skirt and halter-back, whispered to her friend in matching attire. "Whoever told her that dress look good 'pon her?"

For many women, the show is the important calender date of the year. Forget Christmas, Easter and birthdays, giving the midsummer Afro Hair and Beauty a miss is like missing out on the most important opportunity to model and pose. You can't just go in anything either. You have to dress up in the latest style, with 'nuff jewellery and make-up on your face like an Apache Indian. A lickle dis, a lickle dat, a touch of beauty.

Few women can resist posing at 'celebrity' events. For some, these events are a way of netting the right calibre of man. Women will claim to their friends that they're not going to bother wearing anything special for the occasion. "I'm just going to pick some thing out of the wardrobe. Anything I put on will do." But that's a load of rubbish. Nobody's going to an event dressed in just anything because 'nuff men and women will be there, ready to criticise what you wear. If something ain't right about your clothes, the punters at the Afro Hair and Beauty will comment. You'll hear someone commenting about how 'your outfit's holey-holey', for example, or that 'it tear'. Or you'll hear someone else cuss you for wearing 'cheap clothes' to the event when you're supposed to look criss.

Worse still, there are photographers at these occasions and nobody wants to appear in the next edition of The Voice wearing clothes that make you look like you were only there to sweep up.

To turn out in the best outfit possible is so important, that a certain class and category of women will even ask to borrow their friend's best frock for the show. The point is, you want to look good, yet you want to look as if you have made no effort at all. For years, Jamaican girls have run that style twenty-four seven. Whether they live in Jamaica, London, or New York City, Jamaican girls love to lead fashion, they do not follow fashion.

Men pretend they're different, but the reality is that they love crissness as much as the women. If you don't look good, they'll be the first to say you nevah ready, yet still they'll talk 'bout you love vanity.

Max knew before she got there that she'd be head and shoulders above the competition — quite literally. The fact that she was tall and dark always stood in her favour at these events, where the emphasis was on a middle-class Afrocentrism. Though dressed simply, she looked stunning as usual. A dark-skinned ebony princess in white cotton jeans and bold African jewellery. She felt that this was her year and that nothing, nobody, no woman, could stop her, no matter how much they big up their chest. She certainly didn't feel like competing with the new kids on the block, those young ragamuffin girls who are prepared to wear practically anything and do anything to themselves in the hope of looking appealing to a man.

Things had changed a lot since the days when Max was the unofficial Miss Black Brixton. In the past few years there had been a massive increase in the number of girls going around in posses dressed identically. These girls were generally not even size ten let alone size twelve. They're often a size eight, with lanky limbs, all because they don't want their man to say, "Eh baby, you ah put on

119

a little bit of weight."

Max kept in trim. She didn't want to hear anybody calling after her, "Bwoy, you nah see how the fat suit you."

In the old days the Four Musketeers would have gone to the Afro Hair and Beauty as a posse. But Beverly had been unable to get a babysitter in time and Merlene had given some excuse at the last minute. Andrea, however, had to go. In her new role of salon proprietor, the Afro Hair and Beauty would be both business and pleasure. She would get a chance to see which new hair products were coming in from the United States and check out the creative hair designs. Max, of course, wouldn't dream of missing the event. Miss Ready and Waiting, Andrea, and Max, Miss Ready To Go, made quite a fearsome combination, something that didn't go unnoticed amongst the attendant men.

As they entered the venue, the two women checked everything a final time to make sure they looked their best. Their hair was in place, make-up in place, lipstick matted, stockings without a snare and heeled shoes still gleaming. Andrea, with her usual habit, took a comb from her handbag and made slight adjustments to Max's hair.

With an inviting wink of the eye and a seductive lick of the lips they pushed their way past the bouncers without paying, the hint of expensive perfume trailing behind them.

Max always wore the most expensive perfumes, but even Andrea had thought it wise to pull out a bottle of Chanel for this event. As she caught a glimpse of herself from the reflection on a glass door, Andrea was secretly pleased to see the effect of the ten-day diet she had embarked on, in order to look just that bit trimmer for the event. She hadn't mentioned the mini-diet to Max, who noticed the difference and commented that her friend did look 'particularly nice'.

Andrea's outfit was a little more daring than normal.

She revealed a lot more cleavage than she normally would, with her hemline a mere wisp above the knee. She was quite clearly out to get a man. But not just any man.

She could no longer cope with younger men. When she told Max this, the more extrovert woman was astonished.

"I don't know how you can say that," she had remarked.

But Andrea had a point. Older men are more experienced than the younger boys. If nothing else, they've used the same lines over and over again. The young men haven't had time to learn their lines properly yet. Also, Andrea was determined not to be the old bike for any young man to ride.

Winston was two years older and she was confident that, had he not died, he would have grown old quickly. If a man's older, he'll still find you attractive when flab has long since turned his belly into jelly. Young men on the other hand, are ignorant, immature and generally can't see beyond an equally young woman. If you pull up your blouse and show a young man your stretch marks, he won't even know what they are. He'll say something like, 'What, somebody take a knife and cut you?'

The vast and cavernous venue lilted slightly to the mixture of soul and reggae that floated freely in the background. There were women everywhere you looked and the atmosphere was tight with the aroma of various scents. In truth, it was the ideal ground for casual liaisons. Unattached men stood around, circling the available, fit women. In return, the women threw inviting glances at the fit, unattached men. Those who got there early were those who were desperate for action. As all latecomers know, the trick was to arrive late, composed, confident and ready for that unexpected stranger.

The girls came in all shapes and sizes. Tall, short, stout, fit and pencil-slim, each woman mingling amongst her particular crew. Naturally, the younger girls were there in force. Girls who hadn't yet kissed puberty goodbye. Girls still holding hands with each other, yet intent on doing battle with their older counterparts. Uninhibited by their small, rounded, pert breasts, their lack of hips, and their undeveloped calf muscles, they pouted for a man, craving for the excitement and maturity they thought the older girls enjoyed. Girls of fifteen and sixteen years of age. Little teenagers, who believed they were ready for womanhood. Despite their lack of hips, calves and chests, they made sure the little they had was out on parade, standing to attention. They were accompanied by their boyfriends who played 'big 'bout yah', sported tiny little yabba-you chins, and posed with their arms around their waif-like girlfriends, while staring nonchalantly over their sunglasses at the latest piece that walked past.

Groups of older guys stood around with their hands resting lightly across their mouths as they whispered things conspiratorially to their friends: "See dat piece over desso… pure niceness."

Every hairstyle imaginable was in effect. From the girls with short-cropped hairstyles with a pattern going around, to the full length weave-ons.

The pungent smell of people having their hair done filled the hall. There were some eighty stands selling a variety of hair products. At some stands women were having their hair done with protein conditioners, to enable the different exhibiting salons to do their 'before' and 'after' demonstration thing. A couple of stands were selling food — patties and cold drinks. At the far end of the hall, a fashion shoot was under way. Hair conditioner and hairspray freebies were handed out and a lucky woman screamed with joy as the winning raffle ticket was called out. Up on the stage, minor celebrity guests were paraded to a lukewarm response from the audience, and before long the PA and t'ing was brought back, to the approval of everyone present.

Everybody who was anybody was there. Some had turned up just for the sheer hell of seeing the thing collapse, because sometimes that's entertaining enough. Men go to something like the Afro Hair and Beauty, even though it's a female event, because they know there's a whole heap of women there and they're bound to pick up sump'n.

For the men, the Afro Hair and Beauty was a talent scout. It was high summer and every man wanted to be seen cruising around in a sweet convertible car, with something squeezable in the passenger seat.

Once the guys realised that they could get a much better view of the local talent from the gallery above, up they went, each one pretending that he was going up to consume alcohol in the gallery restaurant. Several of the women responded to the men's newly discovered bird's eye view by flirting from a distance, tossing their weaves back on their shoulders and their plaits from left to right.

Women, who are the consumers in the community, have slightly more reasons for attending such events. Some will go just for a good laugh, because there's bound to be people making fools of themselves. Others go to see who's gone with who, or more to the point, who hasn't taken who with them. Then there are the starfuckers who go to meet celebrities and chill out. Before he disappeared following the scandal over a steroid-laced urine sample, sprint champion Danny Henry was a regular at all these events. He knew he could always score amongst the women who were only too happy to oblige. Just like the men, a good portion of women attended because they knew 'nuff men flock to such events.

Thomas's eyes were the first thing Max saw when she and Andrea emerged from the ladies' room. He was standing way over on the other side of the hangar-sized hall, but even at that distance, his eyes melted any resistance she could have put up. They were locked in eye contact, all sorts of emotions and sensations running between them. She remained paralysed for some seconds, before quickly composing herself, remembering that she was not alone.

Loosely followed by his crew, Thomas walked over to the two girls. He was dressed in deep green balloon trousers with a matching waistcoat. The usual array of sovereigns hung from his neck, while his hands glistened from the gold rings on his fingers. Thomas, knowing that he looked good, swaggered that bit more. His crew were dressed equally sharply. There were even a couple of two-piece-suited super-dudes amongst them.

Thomas's crew were slick teasers. They puffed up their chests, confident about the way they looked, and admired the women present, talking loudly about 'what a girl have a sexy body', and about 'how her hips are broad and her batty nice and big'. They would call out to the talent and if the girls didn't stop, they would turn an cuss them, in front of their boyfriends if necessary. As far as they were concerned, no other crew could test them. Not today, anyway. They were sure they could pick up plenty of women, 'cause they looked better than the competition.

It was clear to Max and Andrea, having powdered their noses, that the two guys hanging lecherously outside the ladies didn't hold a fresh before they went out that morning. As one of them went up to Max and rested his arm on her shoulder, she became acutely aware of the repugnant smell that oozed from his armpit. Andrea remarked that "the boy stinks." Max turned around, addressing her admirer in a low but audible voice.

"Unless you have the dollars to entertain this merchandise, remove your hand from the equipment."

Andrea roared with laughter. It was quite clear from the 'cuff-up shoes he was wearing that the man couldn't afford her. Max's condescending expression was enough to brush off the unwanted admirer.

Thomas walked up and greeted each girl with a kiss on the cheek, asking them how they were doing. They exchanged pleasantries and both groups remarked on the event. The atmosphere between them was light hearted. Thomas was cool as ever on the outside. But, inside, he was not at ease. He knew that what he had made up his mind to do could backfire, with unforeseeable consequences. But he had always been a chancer, especially when it came to affairs of the heart or, more precisely, affairs of the sexual kind.

Max acted casual, while deep inside her a tingling sensation told her that she was anything but relaxed. She was fully aware that the slightest hint of any sexual chemistry between Thomas and herself would be picked up by her companion and give the game away. Max always preferred to be discreet, especially when playing with other people's property.

The two groups merged into one as together they walked around the exhibition hall. Gradually, Thomas managed to separate the two women. While Andrea's attention was drawn to an Afrocentric bookstand, Max sneaked off at a discreet distance behind Thomas, looking over her shoulder to check as she did so. The pair went to a great deal of trouble not to be seen together as they slipped out of the building.

Outside, the warm summer evening had drawn people out of their homes and into the many restaurants of north London. Magic was in the air — and what men call 'love' and the gods 'adultery' is much more common when the climate's sultry.

Thomas and Max made their way to a little wine bar halfway down Upper Street. They sat opposite each other in a booth near the back of the bar, where they were only partially hidden from the view of the people around them. Neither of them knew what to say, so they began by talking about anything but what was on their minds. Each was unsure about how far the other was prepared to go.

After a couple of hours of talking about nothing in particular and sharing some polite but false laughs, Thomas made the first move. He took Max's hand in his and caressed it. Slowly, nervously. Max felt the smoothness and warmth of Thomas's hand as he massaged her fingers and she wanted it to go on. At the same time, she refused to admit it to herself, so she hastily removed her hand.

Thomas couldn't make out the gesture. Was she game or wasn't she?

Max regretted withdrawing her hand and wished she could take that move back, but all the time, her conscience was telling her that this was her best friend's husband.

In the meantime, back at the Afro Hair and Beauty, Andrea had become aware that they had lost Max and Thomas, but she was not unduly worried. Besides, she had herself found something to engage her amorous inclinations. Something in the shape of a youthful but mature man called Spence. Andrea loved nothing better than a flirt.

The show was coming to a close and the event had turned into a dance with a deejay spinning the tunes.

"Give me some of your somet'ing and me give you some of my t'ing," Spence teased as he took her on to the dancefloor.

Andrea had been standing by herself watching the dancers all doing the latest dance to have taken the community by storm. Originated in Jamaica by the lame-legged man from whom the dance took its name, the new reggae dance had swept like a tempest through the community. The poor guy who had started it had all but missed out on cashing in on his creation, because while the dance took off with unprecedented momentum, he was sitting in the General Penitentiary back-ah-yard after an unfortunate altercation with the law.

The best way to do the dance (a variation on the old

'mating dance' theme) was to pretend that you yourself had a lame leg, as the infectious reggae dancehall rhythm which made the dance popular pumped out from the speakers. The dance had become so popular that if you couldn't do it, or a variation on the original, you had better not even try to step out on the dancefloor.

With some guys, if they see you standing by yourself at a dance and they don't see any other men dancing with you or going up to check you, they think there's something wrong with you. Because how come no other man is checking you, if there's nothing wrong with you? Women do the same too. If you see a man standing there by himself and no other women are interested in him, then you don't want to admit that you are into him.

So, Andrea stood around, waiting for a man to have the courage to come up and beg her for a dance. She occupied the time by marvelling at the sheer lack of clothing on some or most of the women there. It was a new fashion style, to go with the new dance style — the object apparently being to have as little clothing on as possible while only just remaining decent.

Spence finally picked up enough courage to ask Andrea if she'd like a drink.

"Yes," she answered, after allowing for a respectable pause, "I would like to have a drink or three with you, if you're paying." Spence turned to his friend standing close by, announcing, "Yuh nuh see how dis gal renk an' feisty. Offer to buy her a drink and she come tell me one or three."

"She will feed 'pon your pocket like termite feed 'pon carpet," the friend warned. But the advice came too late. Spence was already smitten, he just wanted to find a way of getting around paying for the drinks.

He turned to Andrea and said, "Haven't you heard, this is the modern day, love. Are we going Dutch?"

Andrea looked at him from his toe to his slightly receding hairline and kissed her teeth. She had forgotten how tight men could be when it came to buying a lady a drink.

Nowadays, Andrea expected men to pay for everything. She didn't have too much extra cash to go out raving and paying. No, that was the man's job. In no way did this influence her newly found independence. It was just that the hairdresser's salon took all her available money. Like any new business, there were cash flow problems and she wasn't actually earning much. But she had accepted the decision because she felt that she had to move quickly, before she hit thirty. So she decided not to go out and rave anymore, unless a man was prepared to pay for everything.

Unlike a lot of girls who go to clubs and are really into it, for Andrea it was no big deal. She would go to a dance without meeting any men and still feel good. She could go to a dance without dancing with any men and that was all right by her. She certainly didn't need the tight-fisted aggro that Spence was coming on with.

Women are tired of pushing men to do things they should be doing anyway. Buying drinks is man's responsibility, from time.

"Dutch? Dutch not in my vocabulary, y'know dahling. If you can not afford to buy me a drink, I suggest you keep your mouth quiet."

Spence found the loud-mouthed girl irresistible and decided reluctantly to get the drinks in.

Spence and his friend Roger escorted Andrea upstairs to the bar. Roger was a great deal more attractive than Spence and, for a moment, Andrea considered him as a possibility, but he had an unfortunate stammer, which convinced her that he had little chance getting off the starting block. Andrea was likely to devour him. She was never really into unsure men, least of all one who couldn't even get his words right. He tried unsuccessfully to broach several subjects with her but to no avail. Andrea, fully aware of what his ulterior motives were, turned her attention completely to Spence, as a way of giving Roger a polite brush-off. They observed the crowd down below and proceeded to pass their worldly knowledge on how people should or should not dress.

"Check that girl over there for instance," Andrea observed, "the one in ah the blonde wig, you're telling me that you don't think that looks good?"

Spence looked at Andrea to check if she was serious. How she could think a black woman dressed in a blonde wig, with those clumpy boots that she was wearing, could look alluring to a man like him? He had to do a double take. Was she joking or was she deadly serious?

"Is that for real, man? Are you trying to tell me that looks good?" Spence enquired.

"Well yeah, it nah look bad," Andrea insisted. "I've got one."

"You an' God one would be sleeping with that blonde wig," Spence said. " 'Cause I certainly wouldn't go near no women with no blonde wig."

Andrea didn't believe him.

"Are you telling me that, regardless of how sweet or how good the woman was, you still would ignore a woman if she had a blonde wig?"

Spence rubbed his chin softly and finally concluded, "Weeeeeell, you know how it go, Andrea. If somet'ing sweet y'know, it nah matter what disguise it come in, you still ah gwine check it same way."

"Well, there goes my black man," Andrea thought. "Ever ready, ever foolish."

They continued to slag off the crowd below, most of them now whining in rhythm to the music being played by Ladies' Choice Hi-Fi, the most popular sound system of the day.

Jamaican girls are the sweetest whiners. When some girls whine, they will only move a hand or a foot, or their chest, and it still looks good. They can switch from whining fast to whining slow without batting an eyelid. Regular clubgoers will swear blind that they have seen some women doing the whine on their knees, but you'd have to see that to believe it.

How come Jamaican girls whine so good? That's one of the great mysteries of the world and they're not prepared to reveal their secret. If you know you can't work up a storm on the dancefloor same way, then step aside. Leave the Jamdown girls to show you how.

"Won't you come dance wit' me again?" Spence begged, angling to turn his liaison with Andrea into more than just a chat show.

Andrea smiled, knowing what was going through his mind. On the dancefloor, he would want to come wheel and turn her, whispering sweet words of love. He didn't need to. Spence had bought the winning card in the O.P.P. game. She had already made up her mind that she would allow him to share her bed this night. But she had a particularly sadistic pleasure in seeing men sweat it out.

"You ah de best," Spence whispered in Andrea's ear as he escorted her on to the dancefloor. "You deh 'pon me mind, twenty-four seven. No girl can test you. But me's man who like to know where me stand in a line. Do you want to be my woman?"

"Do you want to be my man?" Andrea asked in response.

Spence laughed a little. He knew now that he had got a result, so he was cocksure of himself.

"Well, yeah, you tickle my fancy. If your love was currency, I would accept bribes."

Remarkable what a sweet woman and the right music can do to a man. Suddenly poetry starts emerging from a mouth more accustomed to cussing bad words. Andrea did look fit, but she probably couldn't have provoked such eloquence without the help of Ladies' Choice Hi-Fi, which was pumping its lovers music with a vengeance. The couples on the dancefloor had abandoned the popular reggae dance for some serious smooching. Anywhere else, their dancing might have been considered obscene.

"You say you full up of action," Andrea teased, she had begun to take a real fancy to this guy. "Well, food soon ripe for you to take your bite. Now's your chance to prove yourself."

Spence didn't need any more hints. He hurried Andrea off the dancefloor, out of the venue, and into his Ford Granada. He was lucky not to get pulled, the speed he was driving.

Nightfall had darkened the skies by the time they left the bar, but little had been resolved. Thomas offered to drive Max back to Brixton. She accepted and he directed her towards a BMW parked along a dark, narrow back alley a short distance from the venue.

Inside Thomas's newly-acquired dream vehicle, the two paused for a moment. They knew what they had come there to do and had no doubt that they were going to succeed. But each felt obliged to give the other a moment to opt out. It was exceptional circumstances. They were getting themselves into something big.

Thomas broke the impasse by kissing his conquest lightly on the back of the neck. Max enjoyed the oral caress a little too much. She dropped her hand down to touch his, very lightly, looking at him hard as she did so. At this precise moment, words were not necessary. As Thomas's hands softly caressed her body, the ache she had for him spoke much louder than words.

Now let's get this clear: Max loved Beverly like a sister. But Max also loved good sex. It was like a drug to her. You know how it is with some drugs, you'd sell your own sister to get a bit. She had enough experience with men to see that Thomas was good sex. He was handsome, he was fit. Blood would run if Beverly found out, she warned herself. If she slipped up, she'd slide and break her back. But it was too late now. Something like a stream was running through her heart, making her as happy as she could be. No amount of good sense can rule when a woman follows her heart. Love was in the air, she felt totally at ease with Thomas. She felt there was something quite fantastic about him. It was the perfect situation for a love affair. She would take the chance. In love, all is fair, she concluded, as she began a brand new episode in her life.

"Oh no, it just can't work," she moaned as Thomas's hands slipped down the front of her jeans.

Thomas continued undaunted. His heat was on and he was in a hurry to lay it on. To his pleasant surprise, he discovered that she didn't have knickers on. He was ready. When he felt her womanhood oozing wet on his wandering fingers, he knew she was ready too. He looked her in the eye and replied, "Hush darling. Even if it hurt, don't cry."

"But Thomas... Beverly... My friend..." she gasped.

"Me nah response fe dat, Max," Thomas insisted. "Ah jus' so it go." He wasn't interested in talking about Beverly. As far as he was concerned, none of his doings was ever wrong.

"I don't want the news carrying," she begged. "I don't want to lose Beverly. She's my friend."

He looked at her incredulously. "You t'ink seh I go telling everybody wha' me know?"

"Oh, just give it to me Thomas," Max sighed, a mischievous twinkle in her eye. "Just give it to and do it to me. I've got to have you right away."

With that she pulled him towards her, diving into his warm and willing mouth with her tongue. The course they were embarking on was one they would have to endure, whatever the eventual outcome.

Love is not for the swift, but for those who can endure it. Max and Thomas had endured the long wait since his pass at the wedding, but only just. There was no time for foreplay. She had genuinely only intended to have a ten minute feel-up, to release some of that pent-up energy. But once they had started, she knew it was going to be good and intensive. She intended to start from the beginning and take her time reaching the end.

One moment, he was reclining the seats and the next moment, he was easing his rock hard manhood into her inviting heaven, oblivious to the fact that they were parked in a public street.

They started moving in the groove. Slowly and deeply at first, then faster and faster and faster. Then slowly and deeply again. They were just starting to get to know each other.

He made her respond to his every movement and she, incredibly frustrated as she was, wanted his body more and more with every thrust. She finally found out whether Thomas ate off a two foot table. In fact, he loved oral sex. It was wild, animalistic. One position after another.

From the summit, they slowly, twitchingly, returned to the calm of complete satisfaction. They both lay perfectly still, she on top of him. Thomas had exploded into her like a Scud missile, though much more accurately. Her simultaneous orgasmic moaning had assured him that he was spot on. He never knew she could 'whine' so fine.

Hundred percent hot loving. Illegitimate loving, but hundred percent nonetheless. Neither of them was prepared to feel like a criminal.

"I will keep you warm," he whispered in her ear. "Whenever you want me."

Max put her forefinger to his lips, telling him to hush, but he continued with the pose up.

"I love you."

Max hadn't completely recovered. Thomas had touched

her soul and the tingling hadn't stopped. Her pussy throbbed with pain, but tingled with pleasure.

"You sure know how to do it to me," she smiled. "There's no other lover quite like you. You do it so good that I really want more."

She had feelings for him she couldn't understand. The girls nowadays don't want no minute man. She wanted his loving and wanted it non-stop.

He was only too willing to have another one for the road.

Andrew was asleep in the living room when Max returned home late that night. He woke as she slammed the door shut.

"Oh," Max exclaimed as she saw Andrew's silhouette rise up from the sofa. ""I didn't know you were coming by."

"Where've you been all this time," Andrew asked suspiciously. "It's after three."

"Oh, I was out with the girls. Remember I told you, I was going up to the Afro Hair and Beauty. Well, we went for some drinks afterwards. You know how it is. How comes you came around?" she asked changing the subject quickly.

"I wanted to see you, because I've got to leave town at the end of the week for a few days and go to my parents' place. My father is very ill and I have to help sort out his business affairs. I spoke to my mother yesterday. She seemed quite distressed. He's been ill for a long time, but he's always managed to carry on with the business. Apparently, he's just bed-ridden now."

"I am sorry." Max's tone turned to one of genuine sympathy. "You never told me that he was seriously ill. I hope he'll be all right."

"Parkinson's disease," Andrew answered. "He's not going to be all right, these things go on for years."

"I'll come up with you and help you."

Andrew looked at his concubine seriously. She had overstepped the boundaries of their relationship. She was genuinely concerned and didn't stop to think.

"You know that I don't ever take women to meet my parents," he replied slowly. "They're old-fashioned. They'll start poking their noses in."

Max looked at Andrew hard. What was his problem? The man's father is dying and he's got to rush off, but he's not prepared to take any help from her. What was the big deal? Plenty men would jump at the chance of having their woman at their side during their time of grief.

"Come off it, Andrew. How long have we been going out together? You're afraid to take me to meet your family. Look, I don't give a toss about them and their ways, I'm big enough to take it all. But I'm not big enough to have you being ashamed of me, or whatever else is on your mind. If that's the case, you can forget it. I'm coming with you. It's about time I met your family, unless you think that I'm your prostitute, or somebody who just provides bed service. If you think it's only bed service I'm providing and that is my only role in this relationship, then you can just get the fuck out of my life."

Andrew could see the anger boiling in Max's mind. What a drag. All he wanted out of life was a woman who would put up and shut up. Not this grief.

"I just don't think it's a good time, that's all," he said.

"When then, eh? When? Come on Andrew. Your father's seriously ill, it's not like I'll get another chance to meet the guy, is it? Look, all I'm offering is to help. Don't pretend that you couldn't use me at your side when things are getting a bit tough. What's the big problem?"

"All right, all right," Andrew exclaimed. She didn't know what the big problem was, she'd have to find out. "All right. We'll leave on Thursday. I need to drive all the way, because I've got some business in Manchester on the way up, otherwise I'd say we should fly."

"Fly? Where the hell do your parents live?"

"Scotland. Four hundred miles away. It will be a really nice drive. Have enough clothes packed for a week. Nothing fancy. Nobody up there would appreciate it."

Max looked at him long and hard, trying to figure out if he really wanted her to come, or whether he had simply given in under duress.

"I'm going with you to your family, because I want to see what your family's like, I want to know them and I want them to know me. 'Cause if I am as important to your life as you keep saying, I want a clear commitment. I'm not prepared to be hidden away. I want an acknowledgement of who I am and what I do for you, not just on a business level but on a personal level as well."

Thomas returned home at four in the morning. He was on a high after scoring with Max earlier that evening. But his high was laced with a feeling of guilt which he would rather have been without.

Making his way to the kitchen, he poured himself a glass of malt from the fridge, listening intently for any sound of Beverly moving about upstairs.

"She's asleep, so I won't have to face her," he concluded, relieved. He finished his drink and sneaked upstairs to the bedroom. Beverly appeared to be asleep. The thought crossed his mind that she may be faking it, but at that precise moment he didn't particular care whether she was or not. He began to remove his clothes and sat on the edge of the bed in his boxer shorts, contemplating the night's adventures for a moment. He knew that his feelings for Max were more than a passing whim. So strong in fact that he knew that he and Beverly could not continue living together. He had ceased making love to her the previous week, because he was tired of her. He didn't find her attractive any more, she was dead stock. Though Beverly was initially glad for the respite from the indifferent encounters Thomas had turned their magic moments into, after the third day she began to be worried. Sex, however dull, was all that remained of their relationship. She knew how much Thomas loved his sex. He could hardly go through a day without it. If he wasn't getting any from her, he had to be getting it elsewhere. If so, what was left of their marriage? She needed their marriage, to give her the respectability she craved so much.

She opened her eyes and sat up in the bed beside Thomas putting her arms around him.

"Listen, is something wrong?" she asked innocently.

Thomas simply kissed his teeth. She tired again.

"Is there something wrong at work, or is there something troubling you that we can talk about?"

Thomas simply climbed into the bed and turned his back on Beverly saying, "Right now I want to sleep. Seen?"

Beverly said nothing. In fact, she really just wanted to remain silent, but her heart was saying no. This was the third night this week that Thomas had come home in the early hours of the morning. No explanations as to why or where he had been. Considering they were newly-weds this was unusual to say the least.

The thought crossed her mind constantly that it could be another woman. Her previous experience with men suggested that Thomas's change in attitude, his changed manner, his continued indifference towards her, was to do with a woman. But she hadn't seen Thomas with any woman. Nobody came to mind. She hadn't been getting any mysterious phone calls from women asking to speak to him, or slamming the phone down as would be usual.

While Thomas fell asleep, Beverly stayed awake. As he slept, she listened to his deep, even breathing. She had previously found this very irritating because it kept her awake. Not tonight though, she welcomed the sound, using it to cradle her body as her heart cried silently.

There was something about his offhand manner after coming home late without so much as an apology or an excuse, that alerted her feminine instincts. Close to him in bed, she could just about smell the faint fragrance of expensive perfume as it mingled with his body odour. The perfume reminded her of Maxine, but she put the thought aside. No, not Maxine. Whoever it was, though, had a taste for the best perfumes and probably a lot of money to go with it. Beverly laid her head gently on the pillow. She felt dirty and betrayed. How could Thomas do something like this to her? They had only been married a couple of months and she was already sure that he had been intimate with another woman. She couldn't take it anymore, so she pinched Thomas awake.

Never wake a man in his sleep, not if you love your life. Waking a man in his sleep is asking for trouble. Ask any black man, or ask their women who have had to learn the consequences. Thomas had a look of death in his eyes which terrified Beverly, but she tried to sound as casual as possible. Even to her own ears, her question sounded limp.

"Where were you Thomas?" she asked. "You know, you could have been anywhere. You could have fallen under the wheels of a lorry, you could have been in hospital. I'm not turning into a moany cow, I just want to know where you were. I don't want to make a big deal out of it."

Thomas simply stared at her, with murder in his eyes. Beverly continued, tense but undaunted.

"Look Thomas, what's the big deal? This is the third night this week that you come in after four in the morning. You know, if you have a woman, then I want to know about her. If you've got some other problem, then let's talk it out. Let's sit down and try and see if the two of us can work it out."

Thomas could feel the anger in Beverly and he sensed that she really wasn't going to give in. In fact, she was just warming up.

"Thomas," Beverly barked indignantly, "I'm trying to talk to you, man. Wha' do you? Can't you show a bit of manners and answer me? I'm supposed to be your wife and you're treating me like I'm some stupid girl."

Thomas eased himself off his pillow and towered glaringly over Beverly. But she was not about to let this put her off.

"Thomas, just speak to me man. I just wanna know where you were. You have to go to work every day, yet you come in, this is the third night in a row, at four o'clock in the morning. What kind of lifestyle is that? What am I supposed to say to the children when you come home in the early hours of the morning? Then, when you come in, you just come bring in your stinking self and park it in my bed. But Thomas, that's not right. You're seriously out of order."

"Well, Beverly, it look like seh you set for me t'night, don't it?" Thomas said menacingly. "But right now, all I want to do is go to sleep. I suggest that you do the same."

Beverly, aware that her husband was on the threshold of losing his temper, wanted to let the discussion go, but she just wasn't able to. Something inside of her was telling her that something just wasn't right in Thomas's behaviour, she wouldn't or couldn't let the issue go.

"Thomas, this can't go on," she insisted. "It's ridiculous. I thought that being married or taking the steps to being married, you'd want to... you know... We're supposed to be making a commitment to each other. This isn't making a commitment. Coming in, early hours of the morning. Not saying where you were. Stinking of cigarettes and perfume. It don't make sense. Have I done you something?"

Thomas kissed his teeth again.

"Beverly, shut the fuck up. I don't want to listen to what you have to say, I am going to sleep."

Beverly sat there for a few moments. She pondered.

139

Should she pursue it, or should she fall asleep and let it go? But if she fell asleep and let it go, this would give Thomas the right to cuss her down whenever he felt like it. Whereas most women would have brushed off their husband's swearing as being a man just trying to talk his way out of an argument, Beverly saw it as a big insult. A major insult. A major spite on her as an individual. How could her husband tell her to 'shut the fuck up'? She got up angrily off the bed and put her hands on her hips.

"Thomas, when I talk to you, I don't swear. So what makes you think that I, even though I am your wife, should have to sit back and take that kind of rubbish?"

She waited for a few moments, edging for a response from him. But the response she got wasn't quite what she was waiting for. Thomas got up quickly from the bed, stood squarely in front of her. She looked up at him. Waiting.

Before she could think of anything else, the blow to her face with the back of Thomas's hand struck her squarely on the face. She didn't even have the chance to raise her hand to protect herself. The blow had come swiftly and sharply.

Her crying had little effect on Thomas. In fact, it seemed to make him more angry. He looked at Beverly whimpering on the floor. He felt nothing. Nothing at all. He turned and got back into bed and fell into a cold sleep.

Beverly felt so helpless, there was nothing she could do. Thomas had never showed any violence to her before and his assault left her stunned. What the hell was going on? She did not understand any of it.

Beverly put a hand to her mouth. The throbbings from her lower lip seemed to be intensifying. She got up and went to the bathroom. In the bathroom mirror, she examined the swelling that had already developed on her lip. She looked at herself and shook her head. Even to her own eyes this was unbelievable. She'd only been married months and already she was being knocked about by her husband. This was completely new to her. She had never been hit by any of her previous men.

She lowered her head into the sink and splashed some cold water on her face. She tried to rationalise what had happened and thought that, possibly, Thomas was under some kind of strain at work. Not knowing how to get rid of his pent up frustrations, he was taking it out on her. But even to Beverly it was a pitiful excuse.

Tears welled up in her eyes as she made her way timidly back to the bedroom and silently got into the bed.

Beverly stayed awake most of the night. What was she to do? As she considered her options, a deep sleep came over her and she slipped into dreamland.

Beverly got up as usual at seven o'clock that morning to get the children up. Thomas had got up and left for work an hour before. She was baffled by his Jekyll and Hyde transformation. Pride would not allow her to think that it was another woman. After all, in her book, Thomas was supposed to be her knight in shining armour, or the closest to it. Her heart wanted to hold on to the past, but her brain was saying get out fast, there's danger.

NINE

Thomas picked up another heavy box, his brow beaded with sweat. This was his daily toil at the warehouse where he worked. It was good for the muscles and kept him fit, but it was a job he despised. Carnival was still a couple weeks away, but a rare tropical heatwave had put Brixton on red alert since the beginning of the month. Thomas would rather have been driving along Acre Lane with his top down than working in a steaming warehouse where the temperature was eighty-six degrees in the shade.

After depositing the box full of alarm clocks on a shelf, he decided it was time for a tea break. Fari was already in the tiny alcove they called a tea room, immersed in his copy of The Voice with a cup of tepid coffee in his hand. Thomas sat down opposite the elderly rasta, hailing him up as he did so. They exchanged the usual pleasantries as one does at work. They discussed a dance that they were both at the previous week. Shaka, the indomitable lion of Deptford, was on the wire and as usual the session had been rammed to the max.

"Fari, did you get any overtime?" Thomas asked, changing the subject.

"Overtime? It's just like that fool boy, Smith. I could just set for that boy, y'know. Truly, I could just set for him."

Thomas tried to calm his dreadlocked workmate down, "Cho, just let the man carry on about his ways. There's no problem, you know. That's how he stays, he's the boss. There's nothing we can do about it."

The pair spent as long as they could get away with in the tea room, before going back reluctantly to work, the irate Fari even more reluctantly than his workmate who'd had little sleep the night before. As they went about their job of picking up boxes and lifting them onto their allocated shelves, Thomas watched his colleague out of the corner of his eye. He was rather worried about him. The glazed look in the rasta's eyes suggested that he was stoned. But that was nothing unusual. Fari was a man who loved his sensi. He was always stoned. But he could handle it. Today, though, there was something different about him. He was muttering loudly to nobody in particular about the boss, not caring whether anybody heard him or not. Fari was ranting ceaselessly, like some of the characters that walk around Brixton all day long screaming passages from the Bible.

Thomas and Fari had worked together for about eight months. In that time, they had become good friends and learned each other's idiosyncrasies. Though from different backgrounds, they were still able to meet on a level. They had a common enemy, the management at the warehouse, and a common bond, the management was giving both of them a bit of trouble. To both men, it seemed like Smith, the foreman, was constantly looking for a confrontation. Not directly, but indirectly. Smith's tactics were so subtle that an objective observer wouldn't have picked up on them, but as far as Smith was concerned, he was paying these blacks good money and he expected them to 'work like niggers'. As far as Fari and Thomas were concerned, he was getting on their backs for no reason. It seemed to them that he would prefer it if they didn't work there. For whatever reason, Smith saw Thomas in particular as some sort of threat to his manhood. All the secretaries at the company loved Thomas, because he looked fit. The way the young black man swanked into work every morning, dressed in some crisp clothing, made Smith look like shame. He disliked the younger man's confidence. He hated the strength of character he saw and resented Thomas for his potential in life. The fact that Thomas was filling in time at the warehouse, until something better came along, irritated Smith even more.

Fari continued to ramble on, forgetting himself totally and getting himself more and more worked up, as the shift ticked slowly away. He didn't notice Smith walking up to him. He stood for a moment, listening to the abuse Fari was hurling at him. Thomas tried to get Fari's attention, but the rasta was in his own world. Smith walked up to him, his face red with fury and told Fari that his allocated overtime was no longer available. Fari said nothing. But when Smith turned his back to return to his office, Fari hissed in a low, but audible voice, "You're full of shit."

Smith stopped dead in his tracks. He couldn't believe his ears. He turned around and faced Fari.

"I beg your pardon?"

"I said you're full of shit. You're just full of it. Listen, if you have a genuine argument to come to me with, let me hear it. But don't come and give me this kind of hassle. You're fuckries. You have a personal vendetta and you're ignorant. I don't know what kind of inferiority complex you're suffering from, but don't come and heap it on me, right? Anyhow you tell anybody that this conversation took place, only me and Thomas is here to witness it. I'll swear blind it never occurred. So you just take your two little short leg and fuck off! Seen?"

Thomas had stopped working and now stood beside Fari, to form a common line of defence. He could see that Smith's forehead had become moist and there was a trickle of perspiration rolling down the side of his face. Thomas enjoyed seeing Smith squirm. Thomas's first instinct was to box the man one time. But he decided against it. Though Thomas was unconcerned about losing his job, he wasn't sure that Fari was prepared, or could afford, to lose his. Smith tried to speak, but Fari wasn't finished yet.

"I've been slaving in this warehouse for so many years, y'hear? So me nah really appreciate a lickle bwoy like you.

Y'hear? For so long I've been living in this dump yah! Me ready fe die you understand? But jus' t'rough you nah know. Otherwise, you wouldn't come trouble me."

Smith looked at the two men staring at him, waiting for him to make his move. He knew he had no move to make but to back down. There was no telling what they would do to him if he put up any resistance. He didn't have the bottle to sack them either. The last time he had sacked a black man for no reason, the guy had waited for him outside the warehouse with five of his friends. The nervous foreman decided to drop the whole thing and walked back to his office, defeated. Fari didn't bother to savour his victory. He continued griping to himself.

"It's t'rough seh dat man don't know what I can do to him," he confided to Thomas, a menacing tone in his voice. "It's only because I'm trying to keep my spirit calm by standing firm. Anytime that I want to do that man, I can deal with him. There's more than one way to skin a cat. When me ready to rain in blows on that man, I don't have to use it a physical way."

Thomas listened. He had often wondered about Fari. The middle-aged rasta was old enough to be his father and had much wisdom and worldly knowledge. Thomas always listened to him and gave him the respect he would give his father. Although he was a quiet man and said little, what Fari did say, he meant. He wasn't a man to waste words. If he said something, he had a reason for saying it. But sometimes Fari spoke in mystical sentences that needed a mystic man to unravel. Thomas had an idea of what Fari meant, but he wasn't altogether sure.

"What do you mean?" asked Thomas.

"How you mean, what do I mean? You nevah hear what I said? I'm not going to repeat it. You heard what I said. So jus' hold your calm, because I don't want me an' you falling out."

Thomas calmed Fari down. He could see that the older

man wasn't in the mood for any games.

"I heard what you said. I don't disagree with what you're saying, either. If the man play with fire, he must get burned, an' if you know any way to burn him, then that's fine.," Thomas paused, allowing the old man the chance to say something, but nothing was forthcoming. He proceeded cautiously. "You know, I have a problem. Uhm, me have somebody give me a lickle trouble, you know. An' try as I might, I just can't warn them off. I just want them fe lef' me alone. You know wha' I'm saying?"

Fari looked up at Thomas. Yes, he knew exactly what his young friend was saying. Although he liked Thomas, he knew that the youngster was just a bit too hot-headed. Ruled too much by his emotions. He never really took time to feel his way around a problem properly. He knew that the smallest power in Thomas's hands could lead to disaster. But he liked the young man too much to turn him down, so he decided, 'well, all right'.

"Well, Thomas, what you asking me?"

"If you know somebody, that could maybe put me on to somebody to… you know? I just want my path clear so I can see through an', y'know, carry on with my day to day living. Because I'm finding that this person is blocking my view, y'know. I can't make headway. You know when you feel seh crosses deh 'pon you? An' you find seh bad luck ah tek you an' you don't know why?"

Thomas did his best to explain himself without giving anything away. However, Fari knew what he was dealing with and took a pen from his pocket. He wrote down a number on a piece of paper which he handed to his workmate. Thomas nodded gratefully.

"Just tek in dat piece of paper and when you done, jus dash it way. This is a serious t'ing, not to be messed with," the older man warned.

"That's cool by me, man," Thomas assured him. The two men resumed their hard labour, as if the conversation never took place. Both were relieved that they didn't need to continue such a dangerous conversation.

That night, Thomas rang the number and made an appointment for the following day.

He set off early, because he didn't know the area well and because he had only asked for the morning off work. The address he had been given was in deepest east London, over by Plaistow side. He made his way down there and pulled up in his car, taking the precaution of parking around the corner from the terraced 'two up, two down' house. Sometimes, it didn't pay to leave your calling card outside the place you were going. He smoked a large spliff.

He was at least half an hour early, but the front door opened as soon as he had touched the doorbell. The large middle-aged woman who stood before him looked fearsome. She had a knowing sneer on her face. Thomas tried to look inconspicuous but he felt uncomfortable. She ushered him through the door. The array of people inside all sat motionless. Nobody daring to look in the eyes of the other people, for fear of being recognised at a later gathering. He would rather not have been there, but at the moment it was his only option.

The house was not uncommon in the community. It was the type of place that many know exists, but nobody admits to ever going to. Many at some time or other go to seek a little guidance, or a little help from a specialist to give them some direction. The spiritual world is not something to scoff at. This is a serious world, no joke business. Even those who do not participate in it could not deny that there was a certain power to be had in the world of obeah, or juju as the Africans call it. Most people believed in it. Even the ones who treat it with scepticism are wary of it. The most committed Christians claim that their belief is the only spiritual belief they hold, yet they are too afraid to confront obeah. They would rather take the line, 'don't trouble trouble unless trouble trouble you'. Few would deny that there are certain forces in this world that have no logic to them. There are those forces which no one understands.

The large woman held open the door to the back room. Thomas peered into the dark room, not knowing what to do, as he had never been to such a place before. He half-expected someone to come through the door, but nobody came. The door remained open. He could see a silhouette beyond the entrance, but nobody presented themselves. The large woman explained that she didn't have all day and ordered Thomas to step inside or leave the premises. He thanked her nervously and reluctantly made his way into the dark room, taking fright as the door was slammed shut behind him.

Now he was in complete darkness. He tried hard to adjust his eyes, but he couldn't quite make everything out. The silhouette had disappeared and now he couldn't tell whether the person was standing in front of him or behind him. The sensimilla on his brain was playing havoc with his mind. He tried to shake his head into full consciousness, but it was good weed, and he was now truly under its spell. His brain had expanded too much and his eyes were too relaxed to focus properly. Using the other senses available to him, Thomas noticed first that the room was filled with the smell of incense. Although he used incense regularly himself, he had never smelt any with such a bitter-sweet scent. Suddenly a voice boomed out of the darkness, "Please take a seat, and state your business." A flashlight appeared out of nowhere and shone its beam onto a chair. Thomas, grateful for the light, hurriedly took his seat, trying to seem as relaxed as possible. But he wasn't fooling anyone, least of all the man who was now shining the flashlight directly into his face, and who could see the fear in the young man's eyes.

A cackle of laughter broke the silence. A wall switch

was thrown, and the light from the overhead electric bulb threw its stark glare, illuminating the room.

The old man cackled uncontrollably. Thomas could see him clearly now. He was dressed somewhat shabbily and eccentrically in a dark brown gaberdine two-piece suit covered almost completely with small mirrors. Thomas looked at him, and saw himself reflected a hundred times in the man's jacket.

"It works every time," the man giggled. "Every time. People expect mystery, so I give them mystery."

The old man smiled, observing Thomas from underneath a wide-brimmed hat. Thomas was new at the spiritual game and felt decidedly uneasy. He clenched his teeth together, sniffing nervously. He looked about the room. There were candles everywhere. Candles and bits of mirrors littered every available space. A plethora of other meaningless objects cluttered the small room. There was nothing in particular that Thomas could focus on. Apart from the junk, the room was simple and nondescript. He waited nervously for the man to speak. The old man also waited. He was looking for a sign of the hunger in Thomas's eyes.

"How can I help you?"

"I... I'm not sure what you can do," Thomas stuttered.

The old man looked at Thomas through steely eyes.

"Well, if you tell me what your problem is, I will try and see what I can do. I'm sure you realise that this doesn't come cheap. But you must speak the truth. Conversations with clients are treated in the strictest confidence, like any confession to a priest."

Thomas nodded.

"Well, I'm in a relationship," he began, "and I don't want to be in it no more."

The old man looked at him hard. Thomas felt that he was possibly being judged. But that was not the case. After all, there weren't many stories the old man had not heard.

Nothing surprised him anymore. He got all sorts of requests. It was the nature of the business. The old man was, however, troubled by the growing number of young men that had come to him recently, all saying that they wanted to get rid of their woman. He sometimes wondered why they simply didn't walk out and leave their girlfriends, instead of insisting that he should do things to make the women get vexed, and leave of their own accord. What never ceased to amaze the old man was the apparent contradiction in the manner of the men he saw. Despite their so-called strength, and their claims that they knew how to handle and deal with their women, men still flocked to him begging for help. If they really were as strong as they made out, they would simply walk away from a relationship that wasn't going too well.

"I just want to get rid of her, right?" said Thomas finally. "Because there's somebody else right now who I want, who I want to be with, and she's the only person I want."

The old man looked at Thomas, searching for some doubt in the young man's eyes. If there was the shadow of a doubt, he could change the youngster's mind. He searched and searched, but couldn't see anything. Thomas was resolved to go through with it.

"Do you have something that belongs to your woman, or should I say your wife?"

Thomas looked down at his wedding ring. It had given the game away.

"Yes, we are married, but with your help, it won't be for much longer."

"I need something that belongs to your wife," the old man repeated. "Something personal. Have you brought anything like that with you?"

"Well, no, I haven't."

"I need something personal from her. What exactly do you want to happen to her?" the old man enquired hesitantly.

"Well, I want the woman out of my life. I want her out. I just want her out."

In his dream world, Thomas wanted Beverly to disappear so that he could move in with Max, with whom he could make a new start. He was crazy about his new-found love, the long-legged unofficial beauty queen of Brixton. He realised that he had made a mistake with his marriage, and right now, he couldn't stand the sight of his wife.

The old man asked Thomas if he was sure he wanted that. "Because what is done can't be undone," he stressed.

Thomas nodded his head in a slow, deliberate manner.

"All right, maybe I can help you, but once you go on this road there's no turning back. Do you understand? I presume that you just want her confused enough to go elsewhere, yeah? But you have to bring me something that belongs to her, and when you come back, I'll tell you what you have to do. So if you don't mind, just leave the money on the table."

"That's cool, how much do I have to pay you?"

Thomas counted out the notes and left. After he had gone, the old man shook his head and smiled to himself thinking, "What a young fool. They just never learn." The old man was blessed with certain gifts, which he would rather have put to a positive use. But human nature being what it is, he made most of his living from the misery of others, by practising the old ancient crafts handed down by a thousand generations, in a bad way. Sometimes, people brought misery on themselves. These ancient arts had started out as a way for people to protect themselves and each other, but today were being used to do harm, in a world where people were prepared to do almost anything to someone they disliked. Most of the old man's customers were people wanting to teach their friends a lesson. It was a pity, the old man thought to himself, that more people didn't realise and learn that it's not your enemy that's the most dangerous to you, it's your friends. 'Cause only your friends know your secrets, so only they can reveal them. Only your friends have the inside knowledge of what you're doing and how you think. Only those closest to you can use that knowledge to do you real harm. Keep your friends close, and your enemies even closer.

The phone had rung several times before Max woke up.

"Max?"

"Andrew. How are you darling?"

"I'm all right. And you?"

"Look, I haven't got time to speak very much right now, because I'm just about to go into an important meeting. I was trying to get hold of you all last night, but there was no answer."

"Oh, I must have been fast asleep," Max replied.

"Look, I'll pass by at noon to pick you up for the trip up to Scotland."

"What? Oh, yes, of course." Max had forgotten about the trip to Andrew's parents place. She remembered the fuss she had made about accompanying him on it. Right now she wasn't in the mood for going up to Scotland. Thomas had been a regular thing for the past six days. They had such a good thing going, she had clean forgotten about Andrew's sick father. She preferred to stay in London, with Thomas in her bed the whole weekend. "Look, are you sure that you don't want to go up there on your own, if you feel it would be better?"

"No, not at all. You were quite right, Max. I ought to share my emotions and my family life with you a lot more. I just wish we weren't going up there in circumstances such as these. They say that my father's very ill."

"Perhaps it's not a good idea if I come this time?" Max offered. But Andrew insisted. She had brought it on herself by demanding to go earlier in the week, and now he expected her to follow him. There was no way out. Andrew couldn't figure out why Max suddenly sounded reluctant. Oh well, he had other things on his mind for the moment. They would perhaps have a chance to reason it out later.

The conversation over, Max replaced the receiver on its cradle, rolled over to the other side of the bed and pulled out a pack of Silk Cut from the bedside drawer. She hadn't had a puff in a month. But she could feel a nicotine urge. This was going to be a drag of a weekend. She just wasn't in the mood to play wife to Andrew's family. She resolved to take with her the whole quarter ounce of weed that she was saving for her sexual liaison with Thomas. She imagined that she would need all the help she could get to kill the boredom of a weekend in the countryside.

Max's travel bag was packed with the usual toiletries and waiting in the hall, when Andrew arrived to pick her up.

They drove off in his 3.5 litre Rover. It was one of the old ones, with thick leather seats and a walnut dashboard. In its earlier life, the car had been used by a former prime minister. The ideal car for a long journey. Andrew slipped the motor into drive and roared its hundred and fifty horsepower engine along the streets of Brixton. He headed north.

In all her twenty-five years, Max had rarely seen more of Britain than the inner cities. Locked in her own thoughts, she took in the country views. The air was fresher and clearer than she was accustomed to in south London. As they got deeper and deeper into the countryside, she could feel that she was leaving the city tensions behind her. She was getting more and more excited about the prospect of meeting Andrew's family. She felt that in the mood she was in she could take them on. Little did she knew that she was inadequately dressed for the occasion.

They stopped in Manchester for an hour, and then back on the road again. A few more hours, and the motorway gave way to a trunk road. Another hour or so, and they were on a tiny country road.

"We're really in Scotland now," he informed her. He had said very little during the journey. Almost nothing about what she should expect at his family home.

The roads got smaller and smaller. Eventually, the Rover was brought to a halt by a herd of sheep trying to cross the road. Max couldn't believe it.

"It's just one of those things you have to put up with in the countryside," Andrew explained.

The shepherd raised his flat cap to extend his thanks to the driver. As the Rover pulled alongside, the shepherd peered in and immediately recognised the driver.

"Master Andrew," the man said, totally ignoring Max. "Well, what a surprise. It's a long time since we've seen you up this way. I hope you'll be staying a while this time. Make sure you drop by and see myself and the old lady before you go back to London, won't you?"

Andrew assured the shepherd that he wouldn't dream of departing without popping in to see him. They bade each other farewell.

Max noticed that the shepherd had not acknowledged her presence. But she didn't know if it was down to her colour, or because he didn't actually know her and, like some men, just speak to the person they're addressing and not any other companion.

A road sign loomed ahead, indicating that the Fern Lodge Estate lay to the left up ahead. The south London girl noticed the sign, but it meant nothing to her. She simply eased herself comfortably into her seat as Andrew swung the car into the left bend. The Rover bumped along the gravel road. They passed a huge oak tree, beyond which Max caught her first glimpse of the huge mansion up ahead. She looked inquisitively at Andrew and back to the house. Andrew remained silent, saying nothing all the way up the drive. He stopped the Rover in front of the great oak door of the mansion.

"Is this it?" she asked in amazement.

"Yes," Andrew answered solemnly. "Big, isn't it? Too big, if you ask me."

Max sat motionless in the passenger seat, shaking her head slowly. She was expecting "to go ah country, to tek a lickle rest in her boopsie's parents' shack." Nothing could have prepared her for this. It began to dawn on her that Andrew was worth much more than his producer's salary. She felt like patting herself on the shoulder and saying, 'well done Max, you didn't just pick a sugar daddy, you picked the biggest daddy around'. She eased herself out of the car without taking her eyes off the house. With her hands on her hips, she took in the full view from an upright position. She could not believe how wide the mansion was. All she could think was, 'this man doesn't make money, he is money'. She had surpassed her good fortune by having a man like Andrew fall for her. He got out, stretching his hand to her. They walked up to the house hand in hand.

Before they had even reached the great oak door it was swung open by an elderly man in a butler's uniform.

"Master Andrew, welcome. We've been expecting you, and your guest." The butler threw a cold half-glance in Max's direction.

"I see, Wooton," Andrew remarked dismissively, "that despite your age, your irreverence is as sharp as ever."

Max stepped into the huge hallway. In front of her a magnificent curved staircase, divided into two sections, rose towards the left and the right of the house. She had to arch her neck all the way back to see the ceiling on which was painted a mural representing scenes from the Bible. Max allowed herself to take in the sheer opulence of the place. Oil paintings which had no meaning to her, but were quite clearly expensive, hung on the walls. The marble floor she stood on was in its own right like a work of art. The character of the house exuded money. There was nobody else to be seen, but Max could hear the hushed murmur of people talking in another room.

"My mother is here?" Andrew asked the butler.

"Yes she is, sir. She's in the drawing room at the moment, with your sisters."

Andrew gave Max a reassuring squeeze of his hand. Wooton sniffed at this open display of affection for the black woman.

"Dinner will be served presently," he announced, turning on his heels to collect the couple's baggage, and leaving them alone in the hallway.

"Servants?" Max whispered to Andrew. "You have servants?"

"Well, in a house this size, you didn't expect us to do everything on our own, did you?"

Andrew realised that this return home would be tense. It had been five months since he was last there, and he expected a certain amount of hostility from his family for not keeping in touch, although he had kept his eye on the family finances via their solicitor. If there was going to be heat, he'd have to take it, he decided, as he led Max into the drawing room.

Andrew's mother sat at the table, pretending to read a newspaper. She had already been informed by her daughters, Lucinda and Abigail, that Andrew had arrived with his black woman in tow.

Max stood in the gigantic room, feeling very uncomfortable. None of its occupants looked up to acknowledge the newly arrived couple. Lucinda sat motionless with her legs flopped over an armchair, pretending to read a book. Max noticed that the book was upside down. Abigail stood by a window peering out.

Andrew could feel the tension in the air. His mother, Hannah, observed Max silently. Max got the message. She was unwelcome and wasn't sure how to deal with it. What she was sure of was that the next couple of days would be hell if this treatment continued.

Andrew's mother continued looking Max up and down, her nose in the air. The angle of her nose spoke contempt for the girl's dress sense: the slim heeled shoes, the very tight striped trousers and matching jeans jacket, the fake gold jewellery or 'cargo'. Max felt the heat of the examining eyes, and looked to Andrew for some moral support. He took her by the hand, leading her across the room to his mother, for formal introductions. Hannah looked coldly at Max and said, "I'm not entirely happy about you being here, but there are certain matters that need Andrew's urgent attention, matters of legality which can not wait. So I would appreciate your making yourself at home in the guest room. The staff will attend to your needs."

"Oh, thank you," Max replied with overstated gratitude, a mischievous twinkle in her eye. Pulling Andrew towards her, she gave him a very long, intimate kiss. She turned to face Hannah triumphantly, executing a perfectly overstated curtsy followed by an exaggerated bow.

The shock on his mother's face made Andrew grimace. He knew that his woman would be unwelcome at the family home, but had hoped that Max would use her own sense of survival to deal with it. The heat was really centred on Max, but he was well aware that she could hold her own. Unless she was able to come out on top by herself, his sisters and mother would make liquorish allsorts of the unworldly Max. The Scottish wilderness was unchartered territory for most Brixtonites.

Abigail moved away from the window. She walked around Max in a wide circle, looking her up and down as she did so. Finally, she walked out the room haughtily with an exaggerated gesture of disgust.

The gesture completely floored Max. She had come across prejudice before, but to actually have someone eye her up and down, and treat her with such disdain was too much. The girl was lucky to be standing up, because in any other situation, Max would have just hauled her back into the room by her collar and given her what for.

Now it was the other sister's turn to deflate Max. Looking up from the book she was pretending to read, Lucinda addressed her.

"I presume you have a name?"

"I presume you have manners," Max retorted as she left the room. She had exchanged pleasantries enough. Now she needed to find a bathroom somewhere, and get to her room so she could enjoy a cool, relaxing spliff.

Back inside the drawing room, Andrew's mother was fuming.

"What the hell do you think you're playing at? Your father's on his death bed, there are important papers and documents that need to be signed, the estate has to be sorted out, and you have the audacity to bring your black whore back with you. It may suffice in London, but it won't do out here."

"There was really no need to treat her like that," Andrew protested half-heartedly.

"I'm really not the slightest bit interested in which whore you happen to have picked up this week," his mother replied.

"She's not a whore, she's my, er..."

"She's your what? She's your what? For god's sake Andrew, don't tell me that is your girlfriend. She couldn't possibly... Your bed partner, yes, but she certainly can't be your girlfriend."

Andrew didn't see the point of arguing with his mother on the issue. She really wouldn't have been able to comprehend his need for Maxine. Their relationship, for him, was no longer just a physical thing: he had an emotional investment in her. Affection for a black woman, was something his family could not understand.

"She *is* my girlfriend," he insisted.

"She may well be your girlfriend today, Andrew, and she may well be your girlfriend tomorrow. But if she's not your girlfriend in a month's time, she's a whore," Lucinda interjected. Not that she ever had anything of any consequence to say herself. Lucinda echoed her mother's every word like a parrot.

Andrew sat on his favourite stool and asked about the deteriorating health of his father. They had been expecting his death for some time now, but the old codger had hung on in there.

"My purpose here is to make my peace with father, sort out the estate's paperwork, and be here for the funeral," Andrew stated. "How much time has he got left?"

They went over the formalities. Andrew spent an hour looking over the legal papers, and felt quite drained when he left the room in search of Max.

On leaving the family to themselves earlier, Max had made her way up to her prepared room, escorted by Wooton. The butler had informed her that "M'lud of the house is an Earl."

Though Max had an idea that Andrew's parents might be wealthy, she could never in her wildest imagination have anticipated that they were a titled family. It was quite an awesome thing for her to walk leisurely up the beautiful staircase, with large paintings of deceased ancestors peering down on her from the walls. She found the house quite breathtaking. Built in the late eighteenth century, its interior design belonged to the more recent Edwardian age.

As it dragged on, the weekend proved more and more oppressive. It was far worse than Max had anticipated. She was unprepared for the hostility that Lucinda and Abigail always found time to hurl her way, despite their dying father. Max decided to lock herself in her bedroom, in self-imposed imprisonment. Andrew had attempted to make love to her on their first night at the mansion. The fact that his father was lying down the hall on his death bed did nothing to suppress his sexual appetite. But Max wasn't having any of it, and played dead. It seemed no amount of caressing, kissing or other manipulation had any effect. She felt bitter that Andrew was not supporting her, and told him so. This led to a heated argument.

"It's just not bloody good enough," Max said angrily. "You'll just have to tell your posh family — your high and mighty family — that I'm not your whore. I'm not some black wench that you picked up off the street, right? I'm a black woman who shares your bed, your life, and who you care for. Because the way I see it, Andrew, unless you tell your family so, and that you're in love with me, and that we have a loving one-to-one relationship, I can't see where the fuck we're going."

Andrew rolled over onto his back and let out a heavy sigh.

"I don't need this right now, Max. My father's on his death bed, I've got mountains of paperwork which has to be done, and the last thing on my mind is to involve my family in my relationship with you. I know how I feel about you, I'm secure in that knowledge. I do not have to explain myself to my family."

"I don't give a fucking shit what you think," Max spat venomously.

"I know from the way your family's treating me... It's like a way of telling me that we're going nowhere fast. Are we? Can you imagine the look on your mother's face if you were ever to entertain the thought that you might marry somebody like me. You may not have noticed that I am black, but she has."

"No, of course I didn't notice that you were black Max, and I'm a bloody Chinaman," he said sarcastically.

They went on for a while throwing small insults at one another. Max was deadly serious. Andrew tried unsuccessfully to defuse the situation by pacifying her in a low, seductive voice. In the end, he was overcome by tiredness and gave up his amorous intentions as he slipped into slumberland.

The next morning, Andrew thought he was dreaming. Could this be the same woman who last night played like the vestal virgin? He was laying on his stomach and woke up to the series of very gentle butterfly kisses Max planted on his back, his shoulders and his ears. Could this be the same beautiful young woman who rejected his most amorous advances just hours earlier? He wanted to play hard to get, but Max knew better. He began to wriggle under her as she kissed and caressed him. She knew that his body was reacting to her.

"I've changed my mind," she said with a mischievous twinkle in her eye. "I want you to prove just how much you care about me."

Andrew turned to her and smiled.

"Your wish is my command. I'd be very happy to oblige."

They showered and went down to breakfast. The morning of passion had put Max in a good mood, which evaporated the moment she clocked Abigail and Lucinda across the breakfast table. She could tell that they weren't going to let up. Lucinda enquired about the type of job she did for a living. Max's first reaction was to tell her that she worked in a supermarket, but she thought better about it because she felt it would only reinforce the stereotypes Andrew's sisters quite obviously had.

"I do work," she answered guardedly. "I am employed,

and it's none of your goddamn business what I do for a living."

Lucinda responded to Max's outburst with a triumphant look on her face, but kept silent. She had managed to game, set and match the black girl with her first serve of the day.

Max endured the scrutiny throughout the long breakfast. Even though the sisters and Andrew's mother ate their breakfast in silence, Max clearly understood that her presence there was not needed or wanted. The whole episode made her feel somewhat insecure about her relationship with Andrew.

By Sunday morning, Max had decided that nothing could be accomplished by remaining at the mansion a moment longer. The situation was quite intolerable. She tried on several occasions to strike up polite conversation with Andrew's mother, but Hannah was not forthcoming, reiterating, rather, that it would be best all round if Max returned to her "housing estate in London. Only the fact that Andrew's father was dying upstairs had stopped Max from throwing an insult at the mother. They weren't going to let her in, she decided.

Everything came to a head when Andrew told Max that he had to leave on business and that she'd have to spend the night at the mansion without him. Max told him plainly, there was no way she was staying there on her own.

"No way. This house? With your family, who have no wish to have a black woman at their table? It's just not on. It's just not going to happen. Andrew, you've been acting like a little boy all weekend. I'm supposed to be your girlfriend. You should be able to tell your mother where to get off."

"Grow up," replied Andrew coldly. "If my father doesn't die today he'll more than likely be dead by tomorrow, or the day after that. There's a great many things that must be dealt with in the meantime. If you don't like it, then go back to London."

Max looked at Andrew coldly.

"Drive me to a train station," she said. "I'll leave now."

Andrew was reluctant to oblige, but agreed. Nothing could be achieved by having Max stay any longer.

Max sat motionless throughout the bumpy ride down to the local railway station. Andrew could feel her anger. He had never seen her this upset. He hoped that he hadn't lost her for good. But he didn't exactly know what to say.

"People say I'm not the type of man to be your lover," he said slowly. "But Max, you and I are good for each other."

Max said nothing. Andrew decided that perhaps now was not the time for words. The two sat in silence until Andrew's Rover pulled up at the small railway station. Without a word, Max took her bag from the car and walked through the station entrance.

Back in London, she called Andrea's and booked an appointment at the salon. She was literally going to wash Andrew right out of her hair.

TEN

It was the day before Carnival. To Beverly, it seemed like the whole of Brixton was in festive spirits except her. She had become increasingly desperate about her marriage. She didn't know where to turn and found herself taking her anger out on the kids. She knew it wasn't really their fault, but as she had no one else to hit on, they were easy targets.

Beverly washed up and got the kids ready. She made a call before leaving.

"Hi, mum."

"Beverly? Is you? What's wrong?"

"Does anything have to be wrong? I'm just ringing to say that I'm bringing the children down for the weekend if that's still okay. You can still take them down to the Carnival tomorrow?"

"If you say so, Beverly. I'm not going anywhere, so you can come."

Beverly slammed down the phone, irritated at her mother's self-righteous tone. She had put up with it since she was a kid, but felt like she was a big enough woman now. Her mother didn't have to continue treating her as if she was ignorant about life.

She got dressed, slipping on a pair of leggings and an oversized t-shirt. She looked around for the new pair of high-heeled shoes, but couldn't find them in the wardrobe. After a few minutes searching, she found them under the bed. She was puzzled as to how they came to be there as she was certain she'd put them away in the wardrobe.

She slipped the left shoe on, but found it to be a tighter squeeze than she expected. It felt like there was something jammed in the toes. She removed the shoe and examined it, shaking out a clove of garlic as she did. She couldn't figure out how it got there, but thought nothing much of it. It was probably Kenyatta and Ashika fooling around, she reasoned.

"Why do we have to stay with grandma for the weekend?" Kenyatta asked angrily as they made their way over to Beverly's mother, his sister Ashika running behind them.

"She wants to see you, that's why. She is your grandmother. Just behave yourself."

"I don't like to go there," Kenyatta persisted. "She's always singing prayers. All the time. She tries to get me to sing too. I never get to do anything I want to do there."

"That's too bad," Beverly gave him short shrift. "You're going and that's the end of it."

Kenyatta looked at her with tears in his eyes. Beverly could see that he hated her as she had often hated her parents when she was his age.

Beverly looked at Kenyatta and remembered how difficult his father had been during her time with him. Wesley was a man who liked to get his own way and when he didn't, he would sulk for days like a child. Their eight month relationship was generally a happy one until another woman came along. Within weeks he had packed his bags and left with the woman. A month later Beverly discovered she was pregnant. The last she had heard was that Wesley was married and living in JA.

"Don't bother give me no screw face, either. I'm warning you, Ken."

Kenyatta burst into tears uncontrollably, unable any longer to take his mother's verbal onslaught. His sister, unsure of what was going on, took fright at the sight of her elder brother sobbing, and began to cry herself.

"You're just making us go there," Kenyatta sobbed. "I don't want to go and Ashika doesn't want to go. But you're making us and that's not fair."

Beverly finished her preparations and ordered the reluctant children out of the front door. Outside Kenyatta continued his protestation.

"It's not fair. It's not fair. It's not fair." He complained.

"Don't talk to me about fair," Beverly retorted, walking briskly and forcing the two tearful children to run in order to keep up. "And anyway, Ashika likes going, don't you darling."

Still crying, Ashika shook her head hoping that it was the right answer.

Beverly simply sighed. She realised that she was making the children suffer because of the emotional crisis she herself was going through. It wasn't their fault. But there was no way she could be responsible for them tonight.

"So, are you staying for dinner?" Mrs Johnson asked when her daughter arrived at the family home on the Stockwell Green end of Landor Road.

Beverly looked at her mother hesitantly. She didn't really want to stay to dinner, but on the other hand, there was nothing to go home for. Thomas didn't want her. He was quite obviously eating elsewhere.

With the kids occupied watching telly in the living room, Beverly sat down in the kitchen, making small talk as her mother prepared the evening meal. But her heart wasn't in it. Her mum realised this, but couldn't figure out what was troubling her daughter.

"Where is Thomas now, I suppose he's gone to work?"

"Yes," Beverly replied. In truth, she didn't know where Thomas was. He had gone out two nights previously and hadn't returned home.

"So, you're definitely not going to the Carnival?" Mrs Johnson asked.

Beverly studied her mum casually, wondering whether she was the right person to confide in.

"No, mum. I don't feel too good this weekend."

"You know Mrs Morris's daughter is expecting a child?" Mrs Johnson announced.

"Is she?" Beverly answered without enthusiasm.

Her daughter's indifference hadn't gone unnoticed by Mrs Johnson. She sighed aloud, guessing what lay at the core of Beverly's lack of humour.

"So you thought marriage was going to be easy?" the older woman began. "You made a choice, a decision, and therefore, you should stand by that decision. Well, Beverly, nothing in this life is easy."

Beverly realised her mother was going to start lecturing her. At this stage, there was nothing to do except sit back and take it.

"I love you to my heart, Beverly," Mrs Johnson continued, "but you must realise, it's two children you have by two different man. Now you've chosen this man, Thomas, to marry and the likelihood is that you will have more children. The likelihood is that the road will be rocky, but you will just have to grin and bear it. You have to deal with it as best you can. Like we all do.

"Just remember that marriage is a beautiful creation. If you choose the right man, hopefully you have, then things will work out right eventually. Nobody put a gun to your head, Beverly. You went into your marriage with your two eyes open. So now you've made your choice, you'll just have to stick with it." Mrs Johnson paused. "So, did you want my advice about anything in particular, Beverly?"

Beverly shook her head. What could she say? How could she tell her mother about how Thomas was treating her? She felt isolated, confused. She was going through a nightmare, yet there didn't seem to be a way out. She couldn't wake herself up. No one to turn to. No one to ask for help.

In her heart, she knew she loved Thomas, despite everything. Physically, she loved him. Mentally, she adored him. Emotionally, he overwhelmed her.

However, the strain of the contention between them was beginning to show on Beverly. She was even beginning to lose weight, a fact that had not escaped her mother's attention though she chose not to mention it.

Home alone that evening, Beverly got increasingly distressed pondering her marriage. She eventually picked up the phone and dialled Max's number. The answering machine was on, but Beverly decided against leaving a message. She called Merlene instead. Marlon answered.

"My mum's not in, Auntie Beverly," he informed her. "She's always out in the evenings."

"I didn't know that," Beverly said, looking at her watch. It was eight o'clock in the evening. "Just leave a message for her to call me when she gets back, or just to come 'round. I'll be in all evening."

"That's if she doesn't come back too late."

Merlene must be seeing a man, to be staying out all hours, Beverly assumed.

"Whenever. Just leave the message. You all right yourself, Marl?" Beverly enquired of the boy.

"A bit bored on my own, but I'm okay."

"Like I say, I'm here all evening, so if you get too bored, just call up. You going to Carnival tomorrow?"

"Yeah," Marlon answered nonchalantly. "My dad's taking me."

"Oh that's good, isn't it? All right, take care Marl."

For a moment, Beverly wondered what kind of a man was so important that Merlene would leave Marlon alone by himself all night? Then she dialled Andrea's number. She was probably not in, as usual. She had a good thing going on with Spence, who had turned out all right. He took care of her well and couldn't get enough of her. As far as Spence was concerned, every day was an Andrea day.

"Hello," Andrea's voice came down the line.

"Andrea? It's Beverly."

Andrea was the last person Beverly wished to discuss her private life with. Since they fell out all those years back, Beverly had excluded Andrea from her intimate thoughts.

"Hi, Beverly, how's things? Enjoying married life?"

Beverly said nothing.

"Are the kids all right?" Andrea asked, sensing that something was wrong.

Again Beverly said nothing.

"Are you in trouble, Beverly?"

Beverly waited a few moments before answering.

"Andrea, if you're not too busy, will you just call round and see me?"

"Yeah, no problem. I'll be there in about half an hour."

Beverly hung up the phone.

Andrea guessed that married life wasn't as sweet as Beverly expected it to be. She wallowed slightly in her friend's misery. Thomas had seemed to her like the type of man who would give trouble. He was just a little too slick. Nonetheless, that's who her friend chose as her partner. At the end of the day she had to back her.

A mini cab tooted its horn outside the flat and Andrea left for Beverly's house.

On arrival at Beverly's, Andrea was shocked to see the dishevelled state her friend was in. Beverly had obviously been crying for hours.

"Just look at the state of you," Andrea said, concerned. "Just look how tangled your hair is. The first thing we're going to do, is sort you out, Bev. We'll have you looking fine in no time."

Andrea always carried a comb in her handbag in case she was called on in an emergency to draw on her talents. Beverly, however, was in no mood for beauty tips.

"Please, just sit down, Andrea," she begged.

"I was going to ask Spence to drive 'round tomorrow afternoon and pick you up for Carnival," Andrea said, throwing the unwanted comb on the coffee table.

"I'm not going to Carnival," Beverly informed her dispassionately.

"A lie!" Andrea exclaimed incredulously. "Since when you nevah go to Carnival?"

"I'm not going!" Beverly repeated, a little more determined.

Andrea stopped joking and looked deep into Beverly's eyes. This was serious, she thought. Beverly must really be feeling it.

Beverly offered Andrea a cup of tea.

"Yes, just mek sure you mek it sweet, I need to keep my sugar level up," the guest said, trying to cheer her friend up.

"Because a young lady like me needs all the energy that she can get."

Beverly poured the tea and they sat down.

Andrea waited for Beverly to talk, but nothing.

"Why did you call?" Andrea asked eventually.

Fresh tears welled up in Beverly's eyes. Andrea wasn't sure what she was about to hear, but as Beverly wasn't the type of woman to cry easily, she knew it was important. She sat there and waited, until Beverly regained her composure.

"It's not working, Andrea," she whispered.

"What's not working?"

"I'm talking about the marriage," Beverly persisted.

Andrea wanted to choose her words carefully, but her conscience wouldn't allow it.

"What do you mean it's not working? What's not working? The whole thing? The children? He's not working? The sex life? What is it, Beverly?"

"Well everything. He's not coming in any more, or he's getting home in the early hours of the morning, with no explanation as to where he's been. He won't touch me. Anything that I say or try to talk to him about, if I talk to him about it too strong, the man's ready to raise hand."

Andrea's mouth fell open.

"What did you say?"

"You heard what I said, Andrea. Stop playing fool."

"You mean, in the short time you're... you..." She couldn't find the right words. "Are you trying to tell me that this man was hitting you prior to getting married and you still went ahead and married him? But Beverly, I thought you had more sense?"

"Look Andrea, he didn't hit me before we got married," Beverly protested.

Andrea was not convinced.

"He never hit you before you got married, and now all of a sudden, for no reason, he's decided to hit you? That don't make sense, Bev."

"You don't make sense." Beverly knew how far-fetched it sounded to Andrea, but it was the truth. Thomas hadn't been violent before the wedding. Yes, he had a temper, but if she thought at the time that he would ever lift up his hand and hit her, she would have gone. She'd never been out with a man that hit her. She knew other women it had happened to, but she had always maintained that she wouldn't stay in a relationship where she was being used as a punchbag. The fact that she had married Thomas made it slightly different, however. She couldn't just walk away because he had hit her, after all the expense the family had been through for the wedding. It would burn her parents. She would be made a laughing stock. Married six months and then divorce.

She had to try and work it out.

"Well, what do you want to do?" Andrea asked. "Because you're the one who's in this marriage. Decide what you want to do, and take it from there."

Beverly knew that Andrea was right.

"Well, has he got another woman?" Andrea asked.

Beverly said she wasn't sure. Maybe, but she couldn't say for definite.

Andrea felt uncomfortable about being alone with Beverly at a time like this. The two women's relationship had been strained during their days as students at Brixton College. That's when Andrea first got off with Winston.

He had no connection with the college, but he used to hang around outside with his spar, Fitzroy, taking in the breeze as the female students went home for the day. Andrea had seen him a couple of times and hadn't really taken too much notice. But one day he called her over. She was just eighteen and happy to be seen with this cool ragamuffin.

Winston sweet-talked her into bed within a few days. He was a charmer when he wanted to be and gave her roses and chocolates, and picked her up from college in his red BMW. By the end of the week they were making love two or three times a day.

The following Monday, Beverly came in to college after being off ill for a week. Stepping out on Brixton Hill after classes, she couldn't help but see Andrea and Winston snogging openly in his car parked right outside. She freaked out, screaming and tearing at her friend's hair. The situation soon developed into a full-blown fight, fanned by students pouring out of the college to urge the girls on.

Winston managed to come between the girls, separating them. Beverly, still screaming, spat in Andrea's face.

"You bitch," she hollered. "You dirty bitch."

Andrea was too dazed to take in everything around her. She didn't know why Beverly had attacked her, but friend or no friend, she was going to fight back.

"Oh just shut up yourself, bitch," Andrea retorted.

Later on that evening, Merlene called Beverly. Max had told her about the fight. After speaking at length with Beverly, Merlene then called Andrea and explained that Beverly claimed to be going out with Winston. Andrea couldn't believe it. That was the first she had heard of it.

When she confronted Winston later, he admitted he had slept with Beverly just before he met Andrea.

"But it was only a one-off," he insisted. "Me nevah seh not'n to her 'bout no relationship."

It took Merlene weeks of mediating to get Beverly to accept that it was all a misunderstanding, but she finally succeeded. The Four Musketeers went out raving together and Andrea and Beverly made up.

Though all that was in the past, Andrea still felt uncomfortable talking to Beverly about her marital problems.

"I'm not going to tell you what to do," Andrea declared finally, "but first of all, you should find out if there really is another woman, just in case something else is going down. Maybe it's something to do with drugs or whatever."

Beverly looked at Andrea shaking her head slowly. Thomas was a 'one spliff and a Heineken' man, he never touched drugs. They both knew this was to do with another woman.

"If it's a woman, can you think of anyone it might be?" Andrea suggested.

Beverly searched frantically through her mind to remember anything about anyone Thomas had taken a particular interest in, but she could think of no one. She hadn't seen him behave funny towards anyone, and she had not received any strange phone calls — nobody hanging up suddenly — so if there was a woman, where was she?

"So you definitely didn't have these doubts before you got married?"

Beverly answered honestly. "No."

"But Beverly, even to your mind, nobody can change that quickly. If he has changed that quickly, then get out. Tell the man to fuck off and get out. Right? You don't have to sit down in this kind of shit. I know that if man lif' up his hand and say he's coming for me, him haffe dead. Him can't live. My mother never give birth to me so that any man can come and just say lif' up his hand and box me down, like seh him a box pickney. I wouldn't take it."

Beverly knew this to be true. Nobody could get rid of men as quickly as Andrea could. It left her with a rather dubious reputation since Winston's death because she was far from discreet. There was no denying that in her relationship with Spence, Andrea was boss. Ah she run t'ings, t'ings nuh run she.

"Beverly, if you won't kick him out, I suggest that you and Thomas sit down and try and reason this thing through."

"Andrea, you don't understand, the man won't talk to me. I've tried everything. I cook, I clean, I wash... I do everything I'm supposed to do, it doesn't make sense. Y'know?"

"But tell me something, what happened on your honeymoon? Was everything all right then?"

Beverly looked at Andrea and began to squirm a bit with embarrassment.

"Well, if you don't want to tell me, cool. But you brought me here to talk this out. What I'm trying to find out here is where this thing went wrong. Because it couldn't be no sudden thing."

"I can't even put it into words. The honeymoon was okay, but he was kind of rough. Y'know? He didn't handle me like he was supposed to. He was rough, like one of those men who don't really care about you. On the honeymoon, I put it all down to the pressures of the wedding and getting organised and so on. I couldn't really put my finger on it. Since we came back from Jamaica though, it's been worse.

"We got married for better or for worse, and a few months down the road now, this man's decided that he wants to get violent.

"Look don't get me wrong, Thomas has hit me only on

one occasion but I'm worried that he might do it again.

"I just don't know why this is happening to me. I need to know. I even phoned up one of them tarot card business, just to cheer myself up."

Beverly reached across for her handbag and pulled out a flyer advertising a tarot card reader. 'Prince Elijah's Tarotscope'.

Tarot cards? It didn't surprise Andrea, who remembered that Beverly had always been superstitious but at the same time dismissive of the pop mystics who read the cards.

"You phone them tarot cards?" Andrea asked incredulously, taking the flyer and reading it. "You who said they were rubbish? You who said only misguided woman will turn to those things? You who said they couldn't help anybody and asked how could a sensible, right-thinking person phone up one of those places and expect another person on the other end of the line to put their life in order for them? Now look who's calling the kettle black!"

Beverly had to smile. Andrea was quite right. She had previously run them down. But she was desperately clutching at straws. She had tried everything else, to no avail. So she tried the unconventional. All she wanted was to be given some insight into what the future held for Thomas and herself. A little insight to ease the pain.

Andrea held the flyer up to her nose and sniffed it. "Boy, even their paper smells funny."

"How d'you mean?" Beverly asked.

"Well you smell that and tell me if you don't think it smells of garlic," Andrea said, handing the flyer over.

Beverly took the flyer and sniffed casually. She had to agree, it did smell funny.

Beverly had called and made an appointment for the Tuesday morning after Carnival. She was going to see somebody who would either tell her "yeah, 'tings are going to work out," or tell her if there was a woman involved, or say if there was something she was supposed to do to make things better. She would put her life in the hands of the cards and let them decide.

Andrea admitted reluctantly that she had also gone for tarot readings, but she didn't want Beverly to think that she frequented such places regularly.

"From time to time everybody needs a little help, a little guidance," Andrea said. She had gone for a reading when she first bought the salon and business wasn't going too good. "I just needed a little luck, y'know. I was talking about that with Max just yesterday, when she came in to have her hair done. She reckons there's nothing in it, but let me tell you, there's more to the tarot cards than meets the eye."

The women joked together for an hour, with Andrea succeeding in cheering Beverly up a little. However, Andrea felt she had to ram home her advice.

"Beverly, it can't go on," she began. "It's tough out there as it is. I'm not ramping over this. If you want to stay in this marriage and play stush, then cool, you stay there and play stush. But I know that if you come ring me in the middle of the night and come tell me seh Thomas box you, or I get urgent phone call from hospital to seh you in there and you're unconscious, you can stay there. I will come, pick up your kids and take them where I live or take them where your mother yard or somewhere else, but don't expect me to come visit you in hospital, right?

"I don't business what other girls want to do. If they want to stay in their house and mek the man beat the shit out of them, that's their problem, right? You is my friend, and as a friend, I'm telling you get out. If the man's hit you already, him done. Him finish. I don't care if it only happen one time, he will do it again. You know that and him still here.

"It can't work, Beverly. If you want to sit down and

work it out I'll allow you and say well, all right, do it. But nobody else can get you out of this kind of trouble."

"Look, you love Thomas and I'm sure seh before this, you thought Thomas loved you. But Thomas is a man and a man is a dog. Now I've had enough of man to know that what you've just told me shows signs that Thomas pick up with somebody. It's not important who it is. The fact is that he's done it. What you have to do is tell him that he can either drop her or get out."

Beverly knew that Andrea was right, but this was different.

This wasn't some man she picked up off of the street. This was someone she had married. This was someone she had vowed to spend the rest of her life with. Beverly wasn't prepared to give him up without a fight.

Beverly shifted uncomfortably in her chair and toyed with her wedding ring, twisting it nervously around her finger. Tears eventually welled up in her eyes. Within seconds she had broken down.

"Andrea I love him, that's all there is to it," she blurted. "I want him, I love him, I want him to be daddy for both of my children. I know things are uncomfortable at the moment, but I'm just hoping that with a little commitment, with some effort from myself, it's going to work out. I know what you're saying Andrea, and I agree with you. But I can't live my life the way you live your life. I don't really think it's fair to say I'm being stush. What does stush mean? If stush is wanting your lover to be your husband, your keeper, your soulmate then, yeah, I'm stush. If stush means to be part of one whole unit with Thomas, then I'll stand up to be counted. I can't explain it to you. I can't justify it, but Thomas is the man I love. For whatever reason. Maybe it's not another woman. Maybe it's just pressures getting to him. After all, he's only just got married, he's taken on two children that are not his... So for the time being I'm just going to cool, y'know. Just let things ride. There's nothing I can do. He won't talk to me. He's not a big talker anyway. So…" Beverly's voice trailed off.

Andrea observed her friend closely and shook her head. All Beverly said was bullshit. Had anybody else been in the predicament she found herself in, she would have seen the stupidity of it.

"Let me know how things go, and, if it gets rough, then we'll just have to see what goes down from there. But I'm telling you straight, Beverly, if the man lifts his hand up to you again, set the police on him."

It was a sunny Tuesday morning when Beverly left home to make her way to the tarot card reader. Brixton to Plaistow was one of those long and complicated tube routes that made you wish you owned a car. Beverly made a mental note to give Max a call about her Beetle. She had the money and she wouldn't mind having a car to cruise around in during the last few weeks of the summer. It would take her mind off her marital problems and, now Thomas was never around, it would help with the kids and shopping.

She emerged from the underground and with the help of an A to Z, found her way to a terraced 'two up, two down' house.

The front door was opened the moment she touched the door bell, by a large, fearsome-looking, middle-aged woman who ushered Beverly through the door and into the dimly-lit room. An old man sitting down behind a desk opposite the door welcomed her. There was a hint of mystery in his voice.

"Come in faith and seek the wisdom of the tarot cards and all will be revealed. Sit down," he commanded, pointing to a chair.

Beverly did as she was told. Seated, she folded her arms anxiously and crossed her legs.

The man looked at her long and hard. He could sense

that she was tense and he knew why. People were always tense on their first visit. They didn't know what to expect.

"Unfold your arms and uncross your legs," he ordered. "Folded arms and crossed legs put up a barrier. You have to be totally transparent. Nothing is to come between you and the cards."

Beverly unfolded her arms and spread her legs slightly apart, apologising as she did so. She was still tense and the old man knew it.

"Just relax, girl. That's the best way."

On a desk in front of him was a pack of cards. The old man picked them up and handed them to Beverly.

"Shuffle them," he instructed her.

Beverly nervously accepted the pack and began shuffling slowly. When she had shuffled sufficiently, she looked at the old man. He took the pack from her hands and placed them on the table, cutting the cards into two packs, putting the bottom half on top and vice versa. He handed Beverly the cards once again and told her to shuffle some more. Beverly obliged and once she had shuffled sufficiently, once again handed the cards back to the man. He once again cut the pack in two and counted out seven cards from the bottom pile. The seven cards were spread out on the table.

"Pick a card," the old man ordered.

Beverly did as she was told. The old man flicked the card over and studied it momentarily.

"There's a man in your life," he said. "And you're having problems."

Beverly nodded her head.

He invited her to select another card. She picked it and handed it to him. He glanced at the card.

"There is no bondage between you and your husband," he said. "Are you living in separate houses?"

Beverly shook her head.

"But you don't share the same bed?"

Beverly nodded.

"Resolve your differences," the old man advised her. "Resolve your differences quickly, or he will never be in your bed again."

Beverly chose another card.

"Your man has been mistreating you."

As sceptical as she was, hearing her marital problems being described so perfectly by this tarot card reader had twanged the chords of Beverly's heart. Tears welled up in her eyes. Unable to contain herself any longer, she broke down, crying uncontrollably.

The old man sat through her weeping dispassionately. He was used to this. For some women a tarot card reading is like the Catholic confession. People often got emotional.

"Never mind, dear," he tried to comfort her. "I told you that this tarot was a serious t'ing."

"I just want to hear some good news," Beverly blurted through the tears. "I need to hear something positive. What's going to happen tomorrow, next week, next month. Please..."

The old man got up and walked over to Beverly to comfort her.

"It's all right," he said with a sympathetic arm around her. He noticed the wedding ring on her finger. It reminded him of another ring he had seen recently. Then it slowly dawned on him...

"An' your husband," the old man continued, "he mus' be six feet tall and maybe more?"

Beverly nodded.

"He's a light-skinned breddah, an' he has a cut, jus' a lickle cut under his eye, soh?"

Again Beverly nodded.

The old man looked at her incredulously. Could this be possible? Not only was it possible, it had happened. On the one hand the world is a huge place, he thought to himself, but on the other, it's as small as your own back yard. Life

180

is full of unbelievable coincidences. Some just dismiss it as chance, while others call it fate. Only the gods know. They alone would know why fate had brought Thomas and Beverly to the same house in east London.

"I'm afraid I've got some bad news for you," the old man stuttered eventually, studying the cards with a worried look on his face.

"Those that hate and persecute you, are lying awake, plotting to steal your soul. They want to mess up your life. Watch your step, chile."

Beverly couldn't believe what she was hearing. She looked at the old man rambling on. He had gone too far. He had a manic look on his face, and he was sweating profusely. She shifted on her seat, wishing he would just stop talking. She was paying good money to hear something positive. The old man had succeeded in destroying any hopes of that. She opened her handbag and got up to leave hurriedly. She pulled out some notes from her handbag and counted them. A clove of garlic had stuck onto one of the notes. She shook it free, making a mental note to remind Kenyatta and Ashika to stay out of her handbag, and counted out the agreed fee.

"Tek care chile," he warned her desperately as she departed. "Tek care. Nah lend anybody your clothes to wear go pose, 'cause that can bring sudden destruction. Tell your friends to bring back the clothes weh dem borrow. Once you get them back, throw them away or burn them. If you can't get them back leave it and only accept a new replacement."

The old man rambled on and on, but Beverly had already switched off. She got out of the house as swiftly as she could, and breathed a sigh of relief.

She made her way quickly back to the tube station. She had planned to spend the afternoon at Andrea's gossiping, but it was too early. Andrea would still be dealing with her early customers.

She decided instead to give Max a call to see if she could go round and give the Beetle a spin. If it drove well, she would stop by the bank and draw out however much they agreed on. She found a payphone that worked and dialled the number.

"Hello."

Beverly recognised Thomas's voice immediately. She was speechless, her heart pumping so hard that she became nauseous.

"You bastard," she exclaimed defiantly.

It was Tuesday morning after the Carnival. Thomas lay relaxing on Max's silk sheets after spending the night with her. They had a great time together, bumping waists with each other for hours, to the sound of the mighty Observer sound system over by Westbourne Park way.

Max knew what she was doing was wrong, but she could not deny how alive she felt when she was with Thomas. The fact that he was married to Beverly didn't deter her. Beverly's two children did not matter, not when she felt like this. She had never been so elated. She not only wanted Thomas, she needed him, no matter what the cost. She ached from longing when she was without him, and she ached from pure pleasure when she was with him.

She was pretty sure that she loved him. He gave her the love she had craved for. The secret dream she had perceived was now a reality. Who said life was easy? Nobody walks a straight road. Maybe the price to pay for Thomas was the cost of her friendship. If so, it was a price she was prepared to pay.

She stood motionless in the shower, allowing the rush of hot water to gently caress her body. She and Thomas would make beautiful babies, she thought. She would gladly allow her flat stomach to swell for the love of her life.

She wrestled with her thoughts, conjuring up pictures of a future with Thomas. Try as hard as she could though, she couldn't imagine a picture of the future without Beverly's familiar figure beside him. The dutiful wife. Nevertheless, Thomas, in her mind, was still a free agent. Free to choose whoever he wanted to be with. He had chosen her.

Despite a tingling of guilt, Max's feeling for Thomas was stronger than any remorse she might otherwise have felt. For Max, everything about Thomas, his manner, his speech, his touch, his petting, reminded her of the things Andrew could not give her.

With Thomas there was a lot more spontaneity. A lot more rawness. Quite simply, Andrew lacked fun. Max allowed her mind to wander back to that morning's sexual encounter with Thomas. With Thomas she found it easier to let herself go, get passionate and start talking dirty. With Andrew, it was always, 'Do it again, please'. She had to be a bit more 'refined'. With Thomas she didn't have to beg for it. She could just be herself and allow her animal passions to show through.

One thing about Thomas, he wasn't your usual street yardman, because like everybody knows, yardman just don't like to eat off a two-foot table. There are guys out there who still believe that as long as you 'lick' the neck of the womb twenty times, that's the sex done. Roll over and draw a snooze. You've come, so that's the end of the job. As long as the woman feels a bit sore, you've made it. But Thomas? Well, he was a different kettle of fish. He was sweeter than sweet. He was strong, firm, tender, titillating, arousing, sexual. All of those things rolled into one.

He had woken her early that morning, whispering sweet nothings in her ear. His warm seductiveness succeeded in pushing all her buttons. That was something she was unused to.

When you first start seeing them, men like to think,

"Cho! Just get my leg over and it done." Whereas Thomas, with all his bravado, was sensitive.

He took time to engage in small talk, asking her how she was. She replied that everyt'ing was cool, y'know. He wrapped his hand playfully around her head. She could hear her heart beating fast. He talked casually about some hassle he was having with one of his spars.

"There are times when you shouldn't tell people all of your business," he remarked, contemplatively.

He tried to sound relaxed, but he had already decided that the relationship with Max was just too damned sweet to let it go in five minutes. 'Hold up,' he thought to himself. 'I want to taste this. I want to savour it, I want to enjoy it.' Thomas was one of those men who preferred to take his time when tasting something sweet.

One thing he had learned in all his years as a man, was that you take your time with a woman of pedigree. Pick up with a street girl and you can just raise your leg and go over. They're not going to mind. They're just happy that they've even got a man. Thomas had been taught by the very best. He knew that with a woman like Max, he had to take his time and make his move right. Make it slow and execute it with confidence. Despite his level of experience, Thomas trembled as he lay in the bed, Max in his arms. 'If I don't get hold of myself,' he was thinking, 'I am going to squeeze up, and I don't want to squeeze up. 'Cause I have waited so long for this girl. I even dream about her.'

Ever since that first time together after the Afro Hair and Beauty Show, Max had followed him in his thoughts. Last thing at night and first thing in the morning, a vision of Max was always with him. He couldn't look at photographs in magazines without seeing her sexy body. He couldn't even pee in peace, 'cause Max was right there with him. He would be just about to go, when the vision of Max with no clothes on would appear. Then he would stiffen, peeing all over the toilet seat as a result.

Thomas turned and admired the sleepy beauty beside him. 'The girl has some nice legs,' he thought. 'Those calves are well defined. She has a nice, rich complexion. The curve of her buttocks is tantalising. *Tantalising!'*

Thomas didn't waste much time to go down on her. One moment he was resting his chin on her shoulder, with his arm slipped around her waist, and gently, very gently, nuzzling her. All the while, he was thinking about how much he wanted to put his tongue in the water and test the temperature. The moment he got what he wanted, bell number one rang saying, 'Mmm hmmn! The temperature sweet in here.'

Max meanwhile, was trying her best to look as cool and as calm as she knew she should be. But Thomas could feel her convulsions and thought to himself, 'Yes!' He had hit the right button. He looked up at her and saw the stars dancing in her eyes.

"I will take you to heaven and bring you back and take you there again and bring you back again, then we will glide together," he promised in a whisper.

He ran a finger around her eyes and with the same finger, caressed her nose and her lips. Then he listened for her heartbeat, which was so loud it echoed. With his tongue, he slowly caressed her lips waiting, waiting, until finally he thrust his tongue into her warm, inviting, salivating mouth. He kissed her so lightly, she shuddered. In that gentle movement, he had awakened all her senses. She could have sworn that she had found a new sense, because the feeling she had in her soul could not be explained by the others.

'This man is good,' Max thought to herself. Thomas looked inviting. Max sat on top of him gently, then even more gently rocked her hips up and down and round and round.

"You're heavier than you look, y'know," he teased.

She slapped his wrists playfully. As she did so, Thomas

185

could feel her hand trembling, ever so slightly. It was hardly detectable, but for Thomas it was enough proof that, as for him, the feeling was so good for Max it chilled her bones. He thought, bwoy this is good.

He hadn't felt this good for so long. What he and Beverly had just didn't have that buzz. That buzz you get when you see somebody that you fancy. The buzz that gets the juices running. The buzz that makes you come alive. When your stomach hums "hmmmm!" When your heart says "mmmmn!" Thomas took her hand and very slowly sucked her fingers, one by one, then proceeded to kiss her on the arms and chest. 'She is lighting my fire,' he thought. 'Everything she wants she can have.'

It didn't take them long before they were having intercourse. For every thrust he made, Max would gasp in desperation. Thomas was taking her so high. It was like she hadn't been anywhere before.

Thomas had to use all his imagination to keep himself in the flow. 'Bwoy, if I take off now, I'll miss my timing,' he warned himself. 'Bwoy, that would be such a sin with a gorgeous girl like Max.' He unbuttoned the top of her blouse with his teeth. She was so eager, she reached behind her back to undo her bra, but he caught her and held her hand firmly in an arm lock. He nuzzled and nipped at her neck. Max wanted to take the initiative and she wasn't prepared to wait but he just held her down and took her steady, guiding her. She knew her business, but Thomas was now in the driver's seat. So she relaxed and allowed herself to be teased, thinking, 'Andrew could never have done this to me. He couldn't have made this vibe happen.'

Few words were exchanged between the two illicit lovers, the desperate sound of each other's breathing was enough conversation for their purpose. Thomas made Max feel so good inside. She would have given him anything he wanted. Absolutely anything. That's how good his sweet, personal touch was to her. All the time, he never took his eyes off her, as if he was only interested in her pleasure. 'Bwoy,' she thought, 'this man can do some wicked things with his tongue,' and yet he hadn't even reached the serious parts of her body. He was going to get her going first. He wasn't going to touch any of her erogenous zones until he was good and ready. She lay half-naked, his eyes still firmly fixed on her, touching her and kissing her all the time. Then he rolled her onto her stomach and began massaging her toes and running his fingers along the balls of her feet. She wriggled at his touch. He ran his tongue slowly along the back of her legs, just so that he could then blow them dry. He stopped suddenly at the buttocks. She quivered. He was teasing her mercilessly. She whispered his name and tried to turn over, but Thomas held her down. As he moistened the full length of her spine, he gently removed her panties. She wanted him to take her there and then, but Thomas feeling how wet she was, decided to hold it a moment longer. It turned him on. He eventually turned Max onto her back. He got up off the bed and undressed, without removing his eyes from her once. She lay there waiting, anticipating. This man wanted her to beg. His eyes seemed to penetrate right through her. His eyes surveyed her body. She wanted to pull him down towards her. This man was too much. She allowed her eyes to rest between his legs as she stretched out her arms. As the word "please" escaped from her lips, Thomas knew this woman was his.

They made love for hours. In so many different positions, trying out new things all the time. Before long, Max was screaming "Mercy!" This guy was the most. When she was ready, the two of them took off at the same time.

By the time they were finished, beads of sweat covered their bodies. He carried her to the bathroom so gently, so masterfully, that she was thinking, 'This man is addictive.' How could she give him up? His seat was solid and he was broad shouldered. A perfectly formed shape of a man.

Thomas, meanwhile, had spared a thought for Beverly and his marriage. If only a marriage licence was like a Jamaican driver's licence which expired every two years, he thought to himself wishfully.

Max knew what she wanted from a man. She could attract whoever she wanted, so she went for the best. She only wanted the *crème de la crème.* Some girls would look and say, 'Well, what's she doing with that attitude? How can you only pick the cream of the crop?' Max's argument was, 'If you think you're the queen, then surely your partner should be the king'. What could she possibly want with the peasant? That don't make no sense. If you aim low, you'll get low. If you aim high and you get somebody who falls short, you're still making it. You're still coining it in. Some would say Max was selfish, self-centred, conceited, full of her own opinions. On the other hand, you could just as easily say she was single-minded, strong, determined. That's what it's about, or else she'd be left at the starting post. The world is divided between those who think about doing something and those who do it. Max was one of those people who do it. Of course, like everybody else, she wanted love, children and marriage — eventually. If it could work that way.

As a rule, Max never allowed men to answer her phone. But she was on such a high after a great carnival, she couldn't be blamed for allowing herself to slip a little. She threw caution to the wind together with her oversized night shirt and stepped into the shower. The rush of hot water from the shower tap made her deaf to the world. Thomas, who had returned to a deep slumber in Max's comfortable bed shortly after carrying her to the bathroom, was awakened by the persistent ring of the telephone. He didn't know where he was at first. He was so sleepy, he thought he was at his own house and reached clumsily for the phone.

"Hello." There was a momentary pause on the other end of the line, Then he heard Beverly's unmistakable voice.

"You bastard," she yelled.

ELEVEN

Merlene had been expecting the knock on the door for a couple of weeks now and she was almost relieved when it finally came.

"So wha'ppen Merle, you nah come to work no more?" Barrington asked as she opened the door.

"Look, Barrington," she began. "I've been meaning to phone you and explain everything, I've just had a lot of problems."

Barrington invited himself in, taking a swig from his can of brew as he did so.

Dressed in a cream coloured off the peg Burton suit and a full length black leather overcoat, Barrington was a refugee from another era. He would have been better placed in a seventies blaxploitation film like *Shaft* or *Superfly* than in downtown Brixton. But you didn't take the piss out of Barrington. He was one of the local dons whose business wavered along the thin line between legality and illegality.

Barrington made his way through to the living room and looked around studying everything Merlene owned in between swigs of brew. There was silence between them for a moment. Barrington took his time, then began nodding his head slowly.

"So you nevah manners?" he asked. "Me come ah your yard an' you don't even offer me tea."

"Oh, I'm sorry," Merlene said anxiously. "I thought you were drinking." She pointed at the can. "I'll just go and make some tea."

She rushed to the kitchen to put the kettle on the boil. She had been expecting Barrington, but now that he was here in her house and making himself very comfortable, she was nervous. She didn't know what he was capable of doing, but she had heard the stories. It was one thing to owe the guy money but it was a totally different thing to cross him. She hoped he didn't see it that way. The kettle filled with water, she turned and walked smack into Barrington, who had crept up behind her.

"I want all the money now," he hissed threateningly.

In the early fifties, Jamaicans still believed the streets of England were paved with gold. People reasoned that, with their colonies and the slave trade and all, the English must have had so much money they didn't know what to do with it. So they paved their streets with gold. On arriving on these shores and finding nothing but squalor and concrete paving, the hordes of new immigrants walked around dazed, wondering where all the money was. Several Jamaicans and other Caribbean newcomers walked around for years asking any Englishmen they bumped into, "Where's all that money?"

For Barrington Holt, however, the streets really were paved with gold. He was forced to make a hurried departure from Kingston in 1956 aged sixteen. A whore by the name of Pussy Blue had skanked him. She had lifted a wallet from the breast pocket of an American client in a crowded bar, but the Yank soon realised his cash was gone. In the panic that ensued, she shouted out that the yout' Barrington was the sticks man. She had seen everything. Barrington, who was just leaving the bar, had to make a hasty retreat as the Yank and every hustler in town chased him to get their hands on the loot. Kingstonians love a good yarn. By the end of the day, the story was that Barrington had lifted fifty grand from the Yank's wallet. Remember, this was 1956.

Barrington first decided to lay low in the country for a few weeks until things died down. Unfortunately, the story had reached the ears of Sergeant Eric 'Eradicator' Rodney of the Jamaican police force. Eradicator heard that it was a hundred thousand dollars and had vowed to seek and recover the money for himself. Word got through to Barrington that he was on the Eradicator's hit list and the young hustler knew that his days in Kingston were numbered. That night he and a friend had stowed away on a banana boat to England or, more precisely, Tiger Bay. On arrival, Barrington swore that no woman would ever skank him the way Pussy had done.

After only a short time in London, Barrington had acquainted himself with the small but blossoming black underworld community. In 1957, Barrington became the first black man to bus' gun in a bank robbery in England. By the end of the fifties, he and a posse of other Jamaican rudies were working for slum landlord Roger Goldstein, doing the strong arm bit for him any time his tenants were late with the rent. It meant violently evicting whole families from their homes around the Notting Hill area. These families were mainly black, but Barrington had no remorse about his job and carried it out like a professional.

By the early sixties, Barrington was a pimp, controlling half of the women working on the All Saints Road. But he was set up by one of his girls and the Metropolitan Police who planted drugs on him and accused him of being a dealer. Six years of nothing but pigswill is enough to make any man feel bitter. Barrington blamed his incarceration on the whore who was "dumb enough to play policeman's nark." While doing his time he took a solemn oath that 'any bitch who crossed this man again was one dead bitch'. His half-brother, Errol, Barrington's junior by twenty years, came over from Kingston in 1975. Together they had built an empire that included girlie clubs in Soho and running raves in Brixton, as well as their shady dealings.

"Me nah leave your yard before I get every penny," Barrington said coldly.

"Easy, man. I've got the money, all right?" Merlene

found it distasteful discussing money with someone like Barrington, but she had made her bed and now she had to lie in it.

She walked back into the living room, Barrington following close behind. She walked to the back of the room and lifted up the carpet in the corner by the French windows. She pulled out an unmarked white envelope and handed it to him. He opened it and pulled out a bundle of fifty pound notes held together by an elastic band. He looked at Merlene quizzically as he gently tossed the bundle up and down in his hand.

"This feels like five grand," he said.

"It's five thousand five hundred," Merlene replied. "That's all I owe after deducting the money from my commission at the club."

Barrington chuckled to himself and pulled out the contract from his breast pocket. He slowly unfolded the soiled sheet of paper and handed it to her.

"Read the small print," Barrington commanded. "You broke the terms of the agreement, so two hundred percent interest me ah deal wid."

Merlene held the contract shakily. She suddenly felt ill. She wished she had never borrowed the money, but at the time Barrington was the only person she was able to turn to. He may have had a dodgy reputation, but, faced with Fitzroy's blackmail, Merlene conveniently forgot the stories she had heard about him being this and that, and about the clubs and bars in Brixton which paid a 'donation' to him for 'security services provided'.

So Barrington had put up the bail. In return, Merlene had signed a contract to work at his club until the money was paid off. In effect, he had bought her for the duration. After the incident with the Japanese businessman, however, Merlene had not returned to The Bowler Hat Club. She had been expecting Barrington to show up since then. Max had withdrawn a large sum of her savings from the bank after her sister told of her predicament. But could Merlene really have been so desperate that she never realised she would have to pay an extortionate amount of money back?

"You're crazy, man. You don't expect me to pay two hundred percent interest for money I borrowed not even a year ago." Merlene was foolish to dismiss the proposition out of hand. Barrington had been in this game longer than her.

"Okay," he said slowly. "I'm going to give you until twelve o'clock tomorrow to get the rest of the money. If you haven't, I'll be making one phone call to Brixton Town Hall about a certain number of students who don't exist." He smiled at Merlene, knowing that he had just played his trump card.

Merlene felt nauseous again. It seemed like everybody in Brixton knew the skank she had pulled. It was just a matter of time before the police would find out.

Still spinning from the recent revelation, Beverly walked around Brixton in a daze for what seemed like hours. Somehow, she had managed to make it back to Brixton from Plaistow, but she had no memory of the journey. Even amid the familiar surroundings of Brixton, she found it hard to distinguish dreams from reality. She had walked mechanically up Brixton Hill to the old windmill. Even though she had lived in Brixton all her life, she had never visited the windmill, just a stone's throw away from her home. She hadn't even known it existed until a couple of years ago when a friend had asked her if she knew that the last working windmill in London was situated just halfway up Brixton Hill.

Beverly hadn't come to sightsee, however.

When she first heard Thomas's voice on the phone, she thought she had mistakenly dialled her own number.

When she realised she had dialled correctly, everything suddenly fell into place. She had been blind, but she could see clearly now. Thomas hardly knew Max. There was only one reason for him to be at her flat that early in the morning. As far as she knew they had only met once, at her wedding. The wedding? Beverly wondered whether her husband and her best friend had been getting off with each other since then, but decided it was inconceivable. They couldn't have. It must have been a coincidence that Thomas began to brutalise her on that night, she convinced herself.

She couldn't remember how she got there but by early evening, Beverly was standing in front of Merlene's house, looking like a woman who needed answers to some questions.

Merlene was surprised to see her, but thought nothing more of it.

"Hi, Bev," she said cheerfully. "What a nice surprise. Come in. I've only just got back from work." Beverly entered Merlene's house, walking slowly and deliberately. "You already know, don't you?" she said.

Merlene paused for a moment, studying her friend closely. "Look, come through," she said eventually, "I'm in the kitchen."

Beverly followed her friend silently down the narrow hallway to the rear of the house. Once in the kitchen, Merlene resumed the preparation of the evening meal. The silence between them was deafening. Merlene could feel Beverly standing right behind her, though her friend said nothing and did nothing.

Merlene's heart pumped fast and furiously. The moment she had been dreading had finally arrived, but no amount of planning could have prepared her for this. Questions fired through her mind mercilessly. How was she going to play this? Could she say it was none of her concern? Should she admit that she knew about the situation, or deny it outright? She didn't know how much Beverly knew, but her friend's question was so vague it didn't mean anything.

"I've always looked at you as one good sister," Beverly broke the stalemate nervously, "and the rest of the crew, just like sisters. But I know Thomas is seeing Max. You see, Merlene, what nobody seems to understand is that I'm the one who can't sleep. I can't eat, I can't think straight. So, answer me. It's true isn't it?"

Beverly's eyes had become moist. Try as hard as she might, she couldn't hold back the tears and began to cry uncontrollably. Merlene wanted desperately to put an arm around her friend and comfort her, but her conscience wouldn't let her. There was nothing she could say. She had known for some time that Thomas was sleeping with Maxine. She didn't approve, but there wasn't a lot she could do about it.

"Beverly, I can't help you. I wish there was something I could do. All I can say is, do what you have to do. I wish there was some way I could wave everything away."

Beverly dried her eyes slowly.

"Merlene, I know you're Max's sister, but... there are so many... Max could have anybody. Why Thomas? I expected him to play away from home, but not with Max. Not with Max. I mean, that is just like... I can't even find the words to explain how I feel. One of my best friends? With my husband? It's sick. Merlene, it's sick, it stinks. How the fuck am I supposed to feel about it? Tell me. How am I supposed to feel about this?

"I tell you one thing, Merlene, she's not having him. I don't care what it takes. Y'know. She's not having him. I can't even begin to say what I feel about that girl. I just wanna... You don't do that to a friend. I don't deserve that. She can have the pick of any man. Why? Why did she have to do this?

"She already has her rich sugar daddy. What's the

matter with the girl, she ain't satisfied? I'll fight her for him. I want him by my side, I need him by my side. Merlene, you don't know how bad I feel, y'know. To wake up and look at this man who professes to be my husband..." She broke down sobbing again.

Guilt had got to Merlene and she comforted her friend with a gentle embrace. She realised that Beverly already knew, so there was no point in confirming or denying anything. At the same time, Max was her sister and blood is thicker than water. Beverly couldn't expect her to take sides against her own flesh and blood.

"All I can say is that you should speak with Max," Merlene advised. It was a problem for Max, Beverly and Thomas to resolve. She didn't want any part of it.

Beverly shrugged off Merlene's embracing arms and said coldly, "If you knew you should have said something earlier. This is somebody who I intend to spend the rest of my life with and you did not deem it important enough to come and tell me what was going down. I look a bloody fool."

She had tricked Merlene into confirming her suspicions, but the fact that Merlene hadn't said anything previously burned her.

Beverly departed. Max was the person in the forefront of Beverly's mind. She had to see her, speak to her and make her understand that Thomas was 'other people's property', that Beverly could not allow her to have him.

Alone in the kitchen, Merlene wondered if she could have done anything to prevent Max's affair with Thomas, but remembered her similar situation with Winston. Nobody could have stopped her at the time. She was crazy about the guy, as simple as that. If Max had determined to have a thing with Thomas and he was happy about it, there wasn't much anybody else could have done to stop it. They were two consenting adults who knew what they were doing. They were prepared to take the risk and, now that they were found out, they would had to pay the price, whatever it was.

Andrew reclined on Max's sofa. He looked troubled, not paying much attention to Max as she ironed a pair of jeans by her living room window.

Max felt uncomfortable. She knew that something was bothering him, and she had a good idea what it was. But she didn't want to bring the subject up. She threw a glance out the window onto the street. It was a clear, sunny day and people were out in force. From her first floor flat, you could get a good view of the traffic outside on Brixton Water Lane. She watched as the BMW posse cruised by slowly in brand new cars, their booming systems providing a roughneck ragga soundtrack that disturbed the neighbourhood. Max's windowpanes shook threateningly as Buju Banton's voice blasted out from below at three thousand watts. It was the Saturday after the Notting Hill Carnival. Max was preparing to travel up to the Birmingham Carnival with Thomas. He had assured her that the Birmingham Carnival in Handsworth Park was really something special.

"It's different from Notting Hill," he told her. "You don't see any cops around at all, they just let people get on with enjoying themselves. People are a lot more relaxed, Max, I'm tellin' you."

Max had to admit it sounded like fun and she was looking forward to going. He had promised to come by and pick her up that evening. Evening couldn't come soon enough for Max. But then Andrew showed up and insisted on parking himself on the sofa without saying much.

It was the first time he had come round in weeks. Since the disastrous visit to Scotland, their relationship had become strained, which suited her fine as she had found pleasure with Thomas.

Her relationship with Andrew was stale. You outgrow things, she reasoned. It happens.

She wanted to tell Andrew that she loved Thomas. She wanted the world to know. She was confused, and no longer felt she knew what that word 'love' meant any more. Nobody out there knows what's going on, she told herself.

"How ya feeling?" she asked Andrew eventually.

He snapped out of his silent meditation, rubbing his eyes.

"I'm just irie," he answered nonchalantly.

Merlene grunted. She hated it when Andrew tried to be hip and use words that were trendy. 'Irie', means you rule your internal, she thought to herself. From the worried look on his face, it looked like Andrew's internal did run t'ings.

"So you're going off to Birmingham with this guy... what's his name?"

"Thomas," Max replied with a sigh. "And yes. I didn't know you were coming. You haven't called, you didn't let me know. I've got my life to lead as well, y'know."

"You've been seeing this guy recently, have you?" Andrew asked.

"Every now and then," Max answered, seeing no reason to avoid the truth. "Why, are you spying on me?"

Andrew knew the rules. She was there for him, but she wasn't tied to him with a ball and chain. What was she going to do if he didn't show up? She had urges too. Anyway, she didn't ask the same questions of him.

As far as Max was concerned, her relationship with Andrew was over in everything but name. She had decided, however, to keep it going. The mortgage had to be paid on the flat. She couldn't do that without his help. What's more, he had the contacts she needed in the modelling world. But she wasn't going to hang around waiting on him to marry her anymore. Oh no, all that was over with. She didn't care, either, if he no longer shared her bed.

All this was not lost on Andrew. He had stayed away because he had been seeing Max long enough to pick up on her vibes. But he was dejected because he didn't want it to end this way. In his heart, he knew it was over. They had lost whatever they had. The flame had fizzled out. He was hoping that Max would say the words to make their relationship null and void.

"Look, we have to talk seriously," Andrew began, jumping off the sofa and walking over to where Max was busy ironing. She could feel his warm breath on her neck. "Just tell me what's going on. If something is wrong I want to know. If you've found somebody else, then fine. It will hurt, but I'm a man. I can take it. I'll survive." Andrew placed his hands gently on her hips and kissed her tenderly on the nape of the neck.

Max stopped her ironing. Andrew wanted to compromise her and make her feel guilty, but she wasn't having any of it. She had thought about ending things after the disastrous trip to his family, but felt sorry for him. However, this time she was determined. 'Why should I feel guilty about this?' she asked herself. 'It's ridiculous.' Life was too short to feel guilty. You've got enough time only to do what you've got to do.

"Look, this is crazy. I really can't do this anymore," she said. "Our relationship isn't going anywhere. I haven't seen you for weeks, but I'm supposed to be here waiting when you show up. I'm beautiful and I'm bright, Andrew. I don't deserve this."

He looked at her sympathetically.

"What do you want me to do?" he asked.

For a moment, she thought of telling him exactly what she wanted. She wanted him to open her up sexually when they made love, as Thomas did. She wanted him to stop in the middle of a sex session so they could take time to bathe each other in a hot bath, massaging each other with oil until they were both relaxed and ready to go again. She wanted him to flirt with her. She wanted to make love all night long, to find out how many times a night he could do it. She wanted them to share a spliff together before intercourse, because, since discovering its joys with Thomas, she couldn't bring herself to have sex without a spliff again. She thought of all the things she could ask Andrew to do, but decided against it. He was dead stock.

"Nothing," she answered finally. "Our relationship is going nowhere fast."

"So, you want us to stop seeing each other? I'm not angry. I knew it was going to end this way and now that it's happened, I'm upset, but I'm not angry. I'm just glad that one of us had the nerve to end it."

The entryphone buzzed.

"Who is it?" Max answered speaking into the receiver.

There was a pause.

"It's me," Beverly replied.

Beverly wasn't expected. The sound of her voice threw Max off balance. She didn't know for sure why Beverly had come round, but the tone of her friend's voice was ominous. The hairs on the back of her neck stood up. She was anxious, but decided that if she played her cards right she could get Beverly out of the flat without getting a black eye, or losing some vital part of her body.

Her legs unsteady, Beverly walked slowly and deliberately up the stairs to Max's flat. She hadn't decided how to play things. She trembled slightly, knowing she was capable of doing something lethal.

Max met Beverly at the door. They stood there for a moment, simply staring at each other, neither knowing how to play the next move. Out of the corner of her eye, Beverly saw Andrew standing in the background.

"I don't want to talk to you," she warned him over Max's shoulder. "Just get out."

The beef was between herself and Max. If she was going to let rip, she didn't want anybody there.

Andrew hesitated, looking at Max as if to ask 'Do you really want me to leave you in this room with this girl, when quite clearly she's upset?' With a nod of her head, Max signalled that it was all right. Andrew got his things together hurriedly. On his way out, he kissed Max lightly on her cheeks.

"If you need me, just call on the mobile," he said, obviously reluctant to abandon Max at a volatile moment. He didn't know for certain what the whole thing was about, but he guessed that it had something to do with the guy Max had been playing around with. He was old enough to see that Beverly's eyes spoke the murderous intentions of a wronged woman.

Beverly held the door open for him, waiting for him to leave. He frowned at her as he left. Luckily for him, her eyes were superglued to Max, because in the state she was in she couldn't really business with no frown from anybody.

Beverly entered the flat, slamming the door shut behind her. Max thought it best to keep her mouth shut. She led Beverly into the living room.

Beverly looked at her coldly. She had forgotten the words she'd prepared. She couldn't remember any of it. If she opened her mouth there and then, nothing but expletives would come out.

They must have stood facing each other silently for a full minute before Beverly managed to utter the one word, "Why?"

"I don't know Beverly, what are you asking me?" Max answered innocently, hoping that there was still room to manoeuvre. There was no point in admitting to anything if Beverly didn't have any concrete evidence.

"You've not answered my question. I want to know why." Beverly repeated forcefully.

"Look Beverly, I don't know what you're talking about. 'Why' about what? How can you come to somebody's house, be rude to their guests and just say, 'why'?"

Beverly looked at Max in disgust.

"You're fuckries. There's no other word for it, you are fuckries. Don't tell me no shit about 'why'. I've known you from time, you've known me. You've known how I stay. I knew you before you start spread your legs for white man. So don't come with me and tell me you don't understand what I'm talking about. We talk the same language."

She drew closer to Max.

"I want to know how long Thomas has been fucking you."

Max tried to speak, but no words came out.

Beverly continued.

"Yes Maxine, yes Miss High and Mighty, yes the kept woman. Obviously your boops with all his money isn't fucking you good enough, so you feel it necessary to take the husband of one of your best friends. Out of all the men you could have taken, why my husband? Why shit on your own doorstep?"

Max said nothing. What could she say? Beverly, who usually refrained from profanities, was in no joking mood.

"I want you to keep your fucking hands off my man. Right? As far as I'm concerned, you've taken our friendship and spat on it."

Max was a good five inches taller than Beverly. Beverly had to almost stand on tiptoe to look into Max's eyes. Despite her diminutive figure, however, there was no mistaking which of the two was the most threatening.

"Tell me something Maxine," Beverly continued. "When you lay down with Thomas, do you not see my face. Did he never accidently call my name instead of yours?"

Max sucked her teeth.

Undaunted, Beverly continued. She was beginning to

warm up.

"You feel it necessary to take my man from my bed. To entice my man from his home, his family? I've got news for you, Maxine, Thomas is staying in my bed tonight, tomorrow, next week, next month — for the next twenty years until I have finished with him. The man belongs to me. "

Max sighed heavily.

Beverly realised she wasn't making her point forcefully enough. She wanted to cut the lecture and just thump Max again and again, until there was no strength left in her body. But she had to work herself up to it.

Max remained silent, hoping that would take the heat out of the situation.

"Can't you get a man of your own, Maxine?" Beverly challenged, pacing around the room with her hands on her hips. "Can't your slim figure, pretty clothes and flash car get you the man you want?"

Max had had enough. She felt she had to say something. She spoke slowly and deliberately to let Beverly know she wasn't running scared.

"I'm a grown woman and I can do what I like."

Beverly didn't need to be prompted. Max had thrown down the gauntlet and she was going to pick it up and slap her about the face with it. She walked over to Max slowly and took position. A moment later, a trickle of saliva trickled down Maxine's face. Max lifted up her hand as if to hit Beverly. Undaunted, Beverly moved up close and repeated the gesture managing to secrete a lot more spit the second time. Before Max could respond, Beverly had slapped the taller woman down with the palm of her hand.

Max lay crumpled on the floor, with Beverly standing menacingly above her.

"People like you make me vomit, Maxine." A heartbeat later Beverly sounded remorseful. "Poor Maxine," she began with overstated sympathy. "Poor little Maxine. Why don't you let me help you Maxine?"

She offered Maxine her hand. Max looked up from the floor wondering what Beverly was scheming up now.

Beverly knelt down as if to lift Max up, but instead pushed her hand in Max's face, smearing the saliva all over.

Enough was enough. Max lashed out at Beverly, with a blow to the ear. The blow triggered Beverly's stored up emotions. She lost it completely and jumped on top of Max, kicking, punching and screaming relentlessly. She wanted to hurt her. All the anger and frustration she had stored up for Thomas was let loose on Max.

Max was the bigger and stronger woman, however, and in a matter of moments, was able to restrain Beverly. She pushed the hysterical woman aside and got up.

"Get the fuck out of my flat," Max commanded threateningly. "There's no way you can fight me in here and you live. Right? Just take your arse out of here and go home to your Thomas."

Beverly, subdued by Max's efforts, her rage temporarily abating, turned and left the flat, slamming the door behind her.

Thomas was incensed when Max told him what had happened with Beverly.

"How did she find out?" Max asked.

"Me nuh know," Thomas lied. He hadn't mentioned Beverly's phone call while Max was in the shower. There was no point in mentioning it now, either. Not when they were on their way to a sweet weekend together. The motorway sign indicated that Birmingham was one hundred miles away. Thomas smiled to himself, thinking he could make it in an hour. He depressed the throttle some more and the BMW responded eagerly, its speedometer twitching past the speed limit untethered.

Max reclined the passenger seat and lay back dreamily. She was excited about their first weekend together.

"I don't even want to think about Beverly for the next two days," she insisted.

"Don't worry about her," Thomas promised. "I've started sorting things out. She's going to be out of our lives permanently. Just give me a bit of time."

Max had no idea what Thomas was talking about. She didn't know anything about the obeah man and she didn't know about the cloves of garlic Thomas had been leaving around the house. Neither did she know that, after weeks of waiting around for the chance, Thomas had finally found a lock of Beverly's hair on a comb she had left on the coffee table at home. It was a stroke of luck. He had gone home to get a few clothes for the weekend and there it was, lying there. He grabbed his chance immediately and drove out to the old man in Plaistow. The obeah man had reluctantly carried out a ritual with the lock of hair and assured Thomas that the woman would leave his life forever. Max didn't know about any of this. She was only interested in a dirty weekend with Thomas.

It was already getting dark when the BMW cruised into the maze of motorways that criss-cross Birmingham town centre. Thomas suggested that they check into the hotel and wait until the next morning to drive out to Handsworth for the carnival. That was okay with Max. It had been an eventful day. She couldn't think of anything better to cheer her up than a whole night of passion with Thomas.

Max was pleasantly surprised to see the hotel they were staying in. It was one of the grandest in Birmingham, just a stone's throw away from the Bullring. Thomas knew how to impress a woman. He had to entertain Max in the fashion she was used to, and had borrowed five hundred pounds to impress his dream princess. The hotel suite alone was a hundred and fifty a night, but it was worth every penny. There was a king size bed which you could sleep on (or make love on) widthways as easily as lengthways. There was a sunken Jacuzzi in the sumptuous bathroom and they had their own private balcony outside. The room was made for lovers.

Max threw her arms around Thomas's neck and kissed him impulsively, but deeply and passionately.

"Bwoy, you really know how to turn a girl on," she giggled, winking at him as she pulled him down onto the bed.

"Nah worry yourself, Max," he assured her. "Everyt'ing's going to be cool between us."

They rolled around on the bed, kissing and caressing. Thomas turned her on, the way only he knew how. His hand wandered in her jeans and he very gently caressed those spots that drove her wild. He massaged her all over, thrilled to be stroking that body Max had developed through hard work — an hour's exercise a day and a fat-free diet. Starvation couldn't get you a body like Max's. Hours of aerobics couldn't do it either. Max's motto had always been 'an hour's sex a day, keeps the droopy breasts and droopy bum at bay'.

"Don't wait, Thomas," she whispered breathlessly. "Give it to me now. Please Thomas, give it to me now."

She was as hot as she would ever be, with sweat oozing out of every pore in her body.

Thomas turned to sit on her, pulling down his trousers with one swift hand movement. It was then she noticed his droop.

"What's the matter, Thomas," she asked, gulping for air "Aren't you ready yet?"

Thomas looked down at his briefs and realised that he evidently wasn't. Strange, he thought. He felt ready and willing but he was far from able.

"Just a minute, just a minute," he said. "It'll come in a minute."

He took her hand and placed it in his briefs. Max didn't need any more prompting. She went straight to work, holding and caressing and pumping away. Thomas rolled over on his back and urged Max to go down on him. She obeyed dutifully. Now, when it came to blow jobs, few women were as skilful as Max. But try as hard as she might, she just couldn't get it going on for Thomas.

For him, there was no better feeling than Max's tongue working its way around his manhood and scrotum. It was a sincere pleasure for him.

"Just keep going on," he whispered. "It's coming on, just a bit more. Just a bit more."

So it went on for the next two hours. Max could feel him stiffen momentarily and then lose it. What was happening?

Finally, they both collapsed on the bed from the effort.

Max lay on her back, exhausted, staring at the ceiling.

"What are you thinking?" Thomas asked nervously.

"I was just thinking about something I read recently, that everybody is bound to everybody else in this world by a trail of just six people. Six degrees of separation between me and everyone else on this planet. Isn't that crazy? A trail of just six people connects me with the President of the United States, the Queen, or the starving kids in Somalia. It's scary when you think about it."

Thomas didn't get her drift, but dreaded that it had something to do with his failure to perform.

"I don't know what's happening, Max," Thomas said apologetically.

"Don't worry about it," Max reassured him. "It happens like that sometimes for everybody. We'll try again in the morning."

She was too tired for anything now and promptly fell asleep.

Thomas, on the other hand, stayed awake all night long, terrified that his worst nightmare had come true.

The same thing happened the next day. Max tried for

hours to get him going, but finally gave up. Thomas couldn't believe it. His manhood had never let him down like this before. He could see on Max's face that she was disappointed. They were together in an expensive hotel for the weekend. It was like their dreams had come true. The one thing missing was sex. If he couldn't get it together, he knew he would lose this woman. For a moment, he thought about the obeah man. He had instructed the old man that he wanted Beverly out of his life. Nothing untoward had happened to Beverly. Instead, it looked like Max would be out of his life. For the whole of their long weekend together Thomas tried to make love to Max. Time and time again his manhood let him down. For Max it was the ultimate insult and she began to think that the love affair with Thomas had been a dreadful mistake. One moment she had been madly in love with Thomas, now she felt indifferent. She began to question whether she had ever really been in love with her best friend's husband.

By the time they began to journey back to London, Max had decided that she had to try and get Andrew back. Thomas was no good to her now. Her best hope was to secure her financial future.

TWELVE

Barrington ordered his driver to stop off at Tasty Patties on Acre Lane. There was nowhere to park outside, however, so the Mercedes stopped abruptly in the middle of the road, double parked. The burly driver jumped out, cursing the angry motorist behind as he held the back door open for his boss. Barrington stepped out with a big smile on his face. The sun was shining, business was good, and he had just received the news that a local Chamber of Commerce had nominated him as their Man of the Year for 'services to the community'. He was definitely in a good mood. As he filled his lungs with a sharp blast of south London air, he considered himself invincible. 'Brixton is mine', he assured himself, and made his way into the restaurant.

Tasty Patties was an important stop on Barrington's daily runnings, because he loved his chicken and his goat well curried, and nobody cooked a better portion than Tasty.

Merlene rushed around the house in a state of panic. She didn't have much time to play with. Barrington could arrive at any moment. The photos and ornaments were unceremoniously swept off the mantlepiece and into a plastic shopping bag. There was little room for sentimentality. She stopped in front of the fireplace where, until last night, her stereo system occupied pride of place. She pondered on the events of the last year and how quickly she had lost everything she had worked hard to build up. The stereo system, like the television and video, had been sold at a ridiculously low price. All her jewellery and other valuables had gone the same way. It was either that or ask Max for more money, something Merlene wanted to avoid.

It was the middle of the month. Though Merlene was reluctant to forego her next pay check, she couldn't afford to wait until the end of the month to get paid, so she had spent the last few days selling her belongings.

"Here's my rucksack like you told me, mum," Marlon said on entering the living room.

"Great," Merlene replied. "Look, go upstairs and pack just the important things you're going to need with you."

"Are you going to tell me what's going on?" Marlon asked solemnly.

"I told you already," Merlene insisted. "We're going on holiday, that's all. We're in a hurry, so go upstairs and bring anything you need for a short trip. Okay?"

Merlene kissed her son reassuringly on the forehead, but his fears were far from allayed.

"So how comes we're going so soon? You never told me anything about this. You've never mentioned it before."

Merlene sighed. "Marlon, I'll answer all your questions once we're out of here, I promise. But if we don't leave very quickly, we'll be in trouble. Do y'hear me? So pack as much as you need into your rucksack."

Marlon turned to go upstairs, still unconvinced, but aware that his mother meant business.

It was a risky move, but one Merlene had to make. If she stayed in Brixton, she would have both Barrington and Fitzroy blackmailing her.

"Let me know as soon as you're ready so I can call a cab," she called up the stairs to her son. Fumbling for matches in her pocket, she lit a cigarette and took a soothing drag as she peered anxiously out the living room window.

Max turned down Queensway, walking in a daze and looking for a taxi. The words of the doctor kept echoing in her thoughts: "Miss Livingstone, I'm pleased to inform you that you are about to become a mother."

To her surprise she had learned that she was pregnant, though she couldn't figure out how it could have happened. She took precautions with both Andrew and Thomas. Yet, here she was, pregnant. She had gone up West to the clinic, because her regular-like-clockwork period was two weeks overdue and she had begun to feel peculiar. Now the doctor had confirmed her worst fear, she didn't know what to do. She didn't know whether to call Andrew or call Thomas. For crissakes, she didn't even know whether the baby would come out black or coffee-coloured. What was she going to do?

Max climbed into the cab and mechanically gave instructions to be driven to Brixton. She sat back, unable to make sense of her pregnancy. Her mind wandered off and, for a moment, she began thinking about what she would call the baby. She knew that she would definitely go ahead and have the baby. There was no question about that. She wondered whether either Andrew or Thomas would offer to take care of the baby. She couldn't see Thomas offering to support the baby financially. In a way, she hoped it was Andrew's. At least that way she could rely on maintenance.

"I'm telling you, man, somebody put some obeah on me." Thomas was exasperated. He had tried for an hour to convince the doctor that the loss of his virility had nothing to do with the male menopause, but the man wasn't having any of it. 'Ah dat dem call 'specialist',' Thomas thought to himself. The guy just didn't have a clue.

"I can assure you that it's quite a common complaint," the doctor repeated. "It's not as bad as you think. Really, I wouldn't worry about it. It could have been worse. Why, just the other day a Jamaican gentleman came in here, with far more reason to be distressed than you. His penis had actually broken in two during intercourse. A painful experience, I can assure you."

If the doctor had meant to ease Thomas's mind, he was doing a bad job of it. Thomas could think of nothing but the loss of his manhood. Which woman would want him now?

Barrington walked the half block to the bookies to check what ah gwaning. Ailey, of course, was in there along with the other smalltime hustlers who virtually lived in the smoky betting shop. He spotted Barrington straight away.

"Yes, boss!" the youth called out.

Barrington nodded casually in response. He didn't have anything against the youth, but knew well that such an eager greeting from Ailey was usually followed by a request.

"Beggin' you a fifty pence, boss."

Barrington sighed. He had heard it all before.

"You too beggy-beggy, y'know, Ailey. Ev'rytime I see you it's the same thing, 'Beggin' you dis, boss, beggin' you dat.' Cho!"

"Respeck, boss," the youth said humbly, "but this time you bound to get the money back." Ailey waved the tipster's page of the daily paper in front of Barrington. "Dangerous Liaisons in the two-thirty at Kempton Park."

Barrington glanced at the paper dispassionately.

"Don't budda with that, Ailey," he started, "The las' time you guaranteed a winner, the horse run like it only have t'ree leg!"

"It run like it kick the bucket," Horsemouth chipped in. "If only I had t'ree leg I woulda win the race meself."

Barrington and Horsemouth enjoyed the joke, while

Ailey shifted uneasily from one foot to the other. He only had a couple of minutes wait before Barrington relented and tossed him a fifty pence coin. Barrington didn't really have time for chit chat. He had far more important things to do, like paying Merlene a visit and collecting the outstanding money.

"I bet you, twenty pounds dat the third person to walk through that door is a woman," Horsemouth challenged, facing Barrington with a mischievous glint in his eye.

Barrington smiled. The bet didn't surprise him. He had known Horsemouth long enough to know that the man would bet on anything.

"Okay," Barrington agreed, humouring Horsemouth. "A'right."

The two men shook hands on the deal.

Both men fixed their gaze in the direction of the door, as the punters sauntered in and out. A scruffy, elderly man came through first, followed closely by his shabbily dressed partner. Both men tensed up in anxious anticipation as they waited for the third person to cross the threshold, Horsemouth more anxious than Barrington. Twenty pounds was a lot to lose for a man who lived by his wits alone. For Barrington, however, the money was insignificant. He was a betting man that regarded losing as an occupational hazard. You win some, you lose some. The bet was the thing. You cast your die and you lived by it. It was the law of the jungle, but Barrington would lay his life on it.

"Yes!" exclaimed Horsemouth in victorious jubilation as a drunken woman crashed through the doors with a midday Tennants in her hand. "Yes. See my gal deh?"

Merlene paced back and forth, too restless to sit down while Marlon got his things ready. An echo of tension filled the whole house. Constantly her eyes swept out through the living room window, where she watched the garden path, dreading that any moment the doorbell would ring, waiting and panicking, like a woman expecting a time bomb to explode. There was a terrifying feeling in her mind that Barrington would arrive at any moment and her plan would be exposed. What would she do then? He wouldn't take her attempt to escape lying down. His reputation went before him, and if he realised that she was trying to abscond from her 'debt'... Merlene knew she had every reason to fear what his response would be.

"Mum, I'm ready!" Marlon called out as he made his way downstairs.

Relieved, Merlene rushed out to meet him in the hallway. She hugged her son and told him everything was going to be just fine.

"We're going to Jamaica to visit grandma," Merlene explained as she rushed over to the phone and called a minicab. "You'll love it."

No sooner had she put down the phone and relaxed, than the droning buzz of the front door exploded throughout the house.

"What you have?"

"Three aces, now," Jeremiah answered, confident that he held a winning hand.

Lucky Chester stared down at Jeremiah's hat trick of aces thoughtfully. They were both veterans of the informal poker sessions in the back room at the bookies. They both knew how to lengthen the reflective moment that every gambler is allowed before calling his shot.

Realising that he had stepped through the door at a crucial stage in the game, Barrington observed the unwritten rule of silence, allowing Lucky to savour every second of the delay.

"Come nuh, man." The suspense was too much for

Jeremiah and he lost his cool. He was already down eighty pounds. If he lost this hand, it would bring his losses to ninety-five. "Play your cards, man."

Unruffled, Lucky slapped his cards down slowly but purposefully on the table.

"I-man have four jacks, rasta. Jack of hearts. Jack of clubs. Jack of diamonds. Jack of spades!"

Jeremiah stared at the upturned cards in disbelief. No matter how much he wanted them to disappear, they remained as confirmation of the losing hand he had been dealt. Losing four games in a row was too much of a coincidence to contemplate. He knew he had been hustled, but he didn't know how. Lucky seemed to know every card in the pack

"But Lucky, where you find yourself with so much jacks man?" the losing man shouted as if his life depended on it. "You ah steal I. You ah teef, man. Me nah come back again, y'hear? Nah rasta. Me nah come back inna it again."

The back room was a private member's club for hardcore gamblers. Not satisfied by the tepid thrill of a legal flutter, some of the old-timers had convinced the manager to let them use the store cupboard at the rear of the shop as a 'coffee room'. The manager was cool about it as long as it was just 'members only'. It didn't do any harm to business and, apart from anything else, the regular money that this handful of old-timers spent on legal gambling was the bread and butter of his trade.

After placing his legal bets, Barrington had sauntered over to the back room to see if he could get in a game of seven card stud. But he could see that Lucky and Jeremiah were about to drag him into their argument, so he left. He didn't have time to discuss who was or was not cheating. It was time to go and collect the money from Merlene.

He hailed up the few members of the Brixton Punters' Association standing in the doorway as he left the shop and stepped out into the fresh air. His driver was waiting patiently in the car for him. The powerfully-built man with the funki dreds lifted his huge bulk out of the driver's seat to open the door for Barrington.

"You ready to go, boss?" he asked in a deep, booming voice.

"Yeah, drive over to that daughter's yard. We still have some business to finish."

The big man grinned slowly. This was Corbin, Barrington's driver and minder, an ex-con who now worked full-time for Barrington. He had proved himself a good man to have covering your back. Corbin was a solid heavyweight. Only a hustler with scant regard for his personal safety would attempt to take him on. That had been one of Barrington's considerations when he employed him.

Merlene's heart sank, as she dropped to her hands and knees in terror. She motioned to Marlon to hide behind a door and to keep quiet. The startled boy watched as his mother made her way to the living room on all fours to peer through the window. It was only Max. Relieved, Merlene jumped up and opened the door for her sister.

"Max, oh, I'm so glad it's only you," Merlene said as she embraced her sister.

"What's up, sis. You look like a wreck," Max replied, taken aback by the obvious distress on Merlene's face.

"Come in. Come in quickly. I can't stand on the door chatting," Merlene said, casting a furtive glance up and down the street to make sure there was no sign of Barrington's Mercedes.

Max followed Merlene into the house, stepping over a pile of clothes in the hallway.

"What's going on, Merlene?" she asked anxiously. "My goodness, look at this mess. What's going on?"

Merlene looked at her sister thoughtfully. She knew

that her sister would try and help her out if she explained everything. But she didn't want that. She had already borrowed enough money from Max. No, this was her problem and she had to sort it out by herself.

"Well, you know after you gave me that money," she began slowly and deliberately, "I paid Barrington, but he's claiming that I still owe him money."

Max remained silent, digesting everything her sister told her about Barrington's threats, how she had come to the conclusion that Barrington and Fitzroy would always be able to blackmail her if she remained in Brixton, and how she had decided to take Marlon and run off to Jamaica until things cooled down.

Merlene paused when she came to the end of her story, wondering whether she had the guts to fill Max in fully. Merlene finally decided that she couldn't keep her secret from her sister any longer.

"I was having an affair with Winston," she blurted.

"Never!" Max exclaimed. "Does Andrea know this?"

"No, I haven't said anything. I doubt if she suspects anything. But that's how come I got myself in this mess in the first place. Me and Winston tried to pull a skank..."

Before she could continue, there was a repeated honk from a car horn outside. The taxi had arrived.

"Look, sis, I've got to go before Barrington gets here. I'll call as soon as I get to mum's. I'll write you a letter and explain everything, I promise."

The two sisters embraced hurriedly.

"Take care of yourself, sis," Max advised. "And Marlon, promise your Auntie Max that you're going to be a good boy and look after your mum."

Marlon nodded his head sulkily. Max grabbed the boy and gave him a hug.

"Don't worry, Marl, I'll come over and see you both as soon as I can."

They said their goodbyes and Max helped them out

with their luggage.

"We're going to Gatwick Airport," Merlene shouted at the cab driver. "As fast as you can, we've got a plane to catch."

The cab pulled away and sped off. Max stood on the pavement for a moment, waving at its passengers until they were only a speck in the distance. She turned and walked back to her Beetle parked a few houses down the street. What a day it had been, she thought to herself. Max stroked her stomach with a hand to see if she could feel anything then remembered she had totally forgotten to mention her reason for stopping by to her sister.

Barrington's Mercedes pulled up outside Merlene's house. Corbin got out and dutifully opened the rear passenger door for his boss. Barrington stepped out and walked up to the house, motioning to Corbin to wait in the car.

Barrington knocked on the door but nobody answered. Straight away he smelled a rat. He had given her strict instructions to be in at noon and he didn't believe that she had the bottle to test him. He tried to peer in through the windows, but his vision was obscured by the net curtains. He bent down and looked through the letterbox. Again he saw nothing. He walked around the side of the house and niftily jumped a wall that a younger man would have found difficult, landing in Merlene's back garden.

In this type of situation, everything is done on the spur of the moment. It wasn't that Barrington was an expert housebreaker, simply that he wasn't prepared to allow anything to stand between him and money. He found a window and simply broke it, gaining entry to the house.

Once inside, Barrington walked slowly and purposefully around, the scene before him confirming his suspicion. It was evident that the bird had flown in a hurry.

There wasn't a soul in sight. Clothes and other

belongings lay strewn everywhere. Barrington rushed upstairs. On entering Merlene's bedroom, he cast a cursory glance at the clothes piled several feet deep on the floor. But there was no sign of Merlene or her son.

Barrington walked back downstairs into the kitchen. The refrigerator door stood open, its contents recently raided.

The anger boiled within him. In his rage, he grabbed the refrigerator by its open door and dragged it towards him, sending it crashing to the ground. He then turned his fury onto the plates, which lay stacked neatly in a cupboard, and sent the lot of them crashing to the ground with a deafening smash.

He looked quickly through the house for anything he could sell, but soon discovered that there was nothing but useless trinkets remaining.

"Did you take care of business?" asked Corbin innocently when his boss emerged through Merlene's front door.

"She tek me for a fool," he growled, trying to control his agitation. "Giving me the runaround. No, man. Me nah take dat from any woman. When I get her, I'll knock all her blasted teeth out."

"You just missed them," a shaky voice squeaked from a first floor window of the house next door.

Barrington spun around to see a little old lady peering down on him.

"What did you say?" he asked her.

"Merlene and that son of hers, they left about five minutes ago. In a cab," the old lady repeated.

"Do you happen to know where they were going?" Barrington asked anxiously. "I'm a friend of theirs."

"It don't matter to me who you are," the old lady said. "They've gone to the airport. S'pose they're off on holiday."

"Airport?" Barrington looked genuinely worried. "Do

you know which one?"

"I heard them tell the cab driver when he come," the old lady informed him. "Gatwick it was. Gatwick Airport."

Barrington jumped into the front passenger seat of the Merc. "Gatwick. Fast!" he instructed. Corbin responded immediately by shifting the car into gear and roaring away.

The Mercedes raced through the south London streets, the speedometer flicking past seventy as they screeched around corners, weaving between cars and ignoring traffic lights while scattering pedestrians with a blaring horn. They missed disaster several times by a matter of inches.

Corbin hunched over the wheel with ice cool concentration. Barrington remained silent while gently caressing a half empty can of Heineken. He rolled the events over in his mind. He could come to no other conclusion than that she was trying to skank him, in which case she would have to pay.

Barrington didn't like being skanked.

Merlene sat in the back of the minicab, relaxed and happy to have left all her troubles back in Brixton. She didn't know what she would do in Jamaica or how long she would be there, the main thing was that she would be away from Fitzroy, away from Barrington and all the other worries. She had never intended to take Barrington's exorbitant demands lying down. She knew, also, that he wouldn't take her flight lightly. Crossing Barrington was like skating on very thin ice, but she had no choice.

An unexpected storm had sent rain pouring down as Thomas drove slowly along Peckham High Street, contemplating his situation. He had tried to call Max over and over again, but she was avoiding him. After umpteen phone calls, he got the message. Max had dumped him, there was little he could do about that. But, he resolved, if she breathed a word about his condition and it got around, she wouldn't live to see the next year. He would make sure of that. His mobile phone suddenly sounded its shrill alarm. "Who dat?" he answered. "Thomas, this is Beverly. Your belongings are in black plastic bags outside the house." Beverly had replaced the receiver before Thomas could respond. "The bitch!" he cried aloud. This was serious. He managed a nifty u-turn on the narrow street and headed back to Brixton at breakneck speed.

By the time he arrived, his belongings were piled neatly around the dustbins in Beverly's front garden, the rain pouring down on them. He was furious, yet despite his anger, he counted himself lucky that it wasn't a Thursday when the dustmen came. He meant to go in and give Beverly what for but discovered he had been locked out. His key no longer matched the front door keyhole. This incensed Thomas some more, and he began to pound furiously on the door with both fists.

"Beverly, open up! Beverly!" he commanded through the letterbox, but to no avail.

Soaked to the skin, he finally gave up and decided to at least save his belongings from the rain. As he picked up the first bag, he noticed the wet 'Post It' still clinging on to it. The message was still legible despite the rain: 'I don't want you to set your foot back in my house.' He frowned as he read the note, then swung 'round as he heard the front door creek open. He couldn't believe it. Beverly was standing there as bold as anything, sneering down at him with her hand resting tauntingly on her hip.

"I'm going to kill you," he threatened as he started up the garden path.

Beverly responded immediately, producing her other arm from behind her back and pointing it viciously at her husband. Thomas stopped dead in his tracks, his eyes fixed on the bread knife in his wife's hand.

"Read the note," Beverly said coldly, "I don't want you to set your foot back in my house."

For a few moments, neither of them said anything, each occupied with their own thoughts. Thomas decided that the best approach was to play for time, he just couldn't be sure of what Beverly was capable of.

"Look, I'm sorry, I made a mistake," he began, taking a few cautious steps towards her. "I did you wrong."

Beverly looked at him pitifully. 'Sorry' was all he could say. After all the hell he had given her, after all the suffering words still didn't come easily.

"Don't test me," she warned, jabbing the knife in his direction. "Just don't test me."

Thomas's eyes darted from Beverly to the knife and back to Beverly again. It was obvious she meant business. Thomas backed off hesitantly; he couldn't afford to test her. He casually straightened his coat, keeping his eyes on the knife and slowly began to pick up his belongings.

"All right," he began with a sinister threat in his voice. "Put down the knife and we'll see how tough you are?"

Beverly didn't bother responding. Thomas continued.

"Me gone for now. But nah worry yourself, anywhere you go I'll be right there behind you, until one day, you're going to get what you asked for."

Rain water dripping in his eyes, Thomas dumped his belongings on the back seat of his car and sped off.

Driving conditions had been made hazardous by the downpour, but that didn't worry Corbin; they had driven down the motorway at a hundred miles an hour. He steered the Mercedes expertly around the roundabout on the approach road to the airport, without slowing down. Barrington sat beside him stony-faced.

He was thinking about Pussy Blue and how she skanked him back in Kingston all those years ago. He was thinking about the whore who had juggled things so that the police could frame him. It burned him to think that these women had played him in a man's game and won. And now Merlene. 'I won't be responsible for my actions when I catch up with her', Barrington convinced himself. He could feel the anger rising in his chest, reaching out to take a vicelike grip on his throat. His jaws locked so tightly that his teeth ached.

"There she is!" he screamed as he saw Merlene and Thomas jump out of a car up ahead.

Corbin's eyes darted around the airport terminal, but it was too late, Merlene and her son had already scurried into the building."Where?" he asked finally.

"Over there," Barrington yelled frantically, pointing to the spot from which Merlene had now departed.

Corbin raced in the direction his boss was pointing. Barrington leapt from the car before it had stopped rolling and sprinted determinedly after Merlene. For an old man, Barrington still had a healthy body, which manifested itself in the pursuit of money.

Inside the crowded departure lounge, Barrington had to stop a moment to get his bearings. Suddenly the calm voice of a woman came over the tannoy system. "This is the last call for passengers on British Airways flight BA 765 to Miami."

He rushed around looking for the British Airways desk. Most travellers to the Caribbean travel through Miami. It was just a long shot, but it was somewhere to start.

A letter from Andrew awaited Max when she got home later that afternoon dripping with rain. The neatly typed letter was just his style. She opened it casually. The letter came straight to the point, their relationship was no longer working. He offered to pay the mortgage for the next month, but explained that he wanted her out after that so that he could sell the flat.

Max sat down slowly, taking it all in. She wasn't expecting this. It was typical of Andrew to end their relationship in a letter. He always liked to avoid confrontation. It took a while for the full impact of her situation to sink in but, when it did, Max couldn't contain herself. She broke down sobbing. She had lost her friend, her lover and her financial security and she was strapped on her own with a baby. Everything she had planned for her future was now lost.

Thomas drove to the address he had been given by the estate agent. The house was a four storey Victorian building in the no-man's land between Stockwell and Clapham North. A sign in a downstairs window announcing "Rooms To Let" reassured him that he had come to the right place. Thomas had managed to get a front room on the third floor.

The landlord met him at the front door and led him up a flight of unevenly carpeted stairs to the dingy room with a faded rug on the bare floor, a rickety bed and a wicker armchair.

"Home is what you make it," the landlord insisted with a broad grin. He collected the two month's rent and departed.

Alone, Thomas peered through the greyish shroud that served as a lace curtain, to the cars that cranked noisily past on the main road outside. It was hard to believe that he had fallen so swiftly from grace. He winced as he looked around the dingy room, its stained wallpaper in a huge flowered design, unrelieved by anything but a pin-up calender tacked to one wall.

Thomas giggled to himself nervously. The thought crossed his mind that Max and Beverly had somehow got together with the obeah man to do this to him. He had lost his wife, his lover, his home, and something was wrong with his virility. How can anybody have so much bad luck? Maybe they were all in this together and were now laughing at him.

"Yes sir, Miss Livingstone has checked in. You've just missed her, she should be on her way to the departure lounge."

Barrington barely waited for the check-in attendant to finish what she was saying before he resumed his chase at breakneck speed along the terminal towards the departure lounge. The speed at which he was going he probably couldn't have stopped even if he had seen the trolley piled high with suitcases.

Barrington hit the vehicle full on and sent cases flying everywhere. He himself landed sprawled out on the floor, a painful exercise for an old man, even one as fit as Barrington.

"I'm a'right," he cried out, dismissing a helping hand and climbing to his feet unaided. He resumed his chase. He hadn't got very far however, when he felt a sharp tugging on his jacket. Barrington spun around to see the chubby, sweaty face of the traveller he had just collided with.

"What about my camera?" the man insisted in a yankee drawl while hanging onto Barrington's jacket as if his life depended on it.

"What the hell…" Barrington began, ready to thump the man, but deciding against it at the sight of a policeman coming towards him. "What you ah talk 'bout?" Barrington hissed angrily.

"My camera," the traveller repeated, waving a damaged camcorder in Barrington's face. "You crashed into me. You weren't looking where you were going and you sent me flying. So what are you going to do about it?"

By the time Barrington had managed to placate the

American with a fifty pound note, he had lost a few valuable minutes. He raced on undaunted towards the departure lounge. Then he saw her standing at the front of a queue at passport control. Barrington rushed forward past other passengers waiting obediently at the queue. He would get her now.

"Passport and boarding card, please," came the passport officer's voice as an authoritative hand halted Barrington's progress.

"Merlene!" Barrington called as she walked through the passage into the departure lounge. "Merlene, you fucker, you!"

Merlene turned momentarily but continued walking through, ushering Marlon ahead of her.

Beverly popped open a bottle of champagne and quickly poured the bubbling liquid into their glasses. Andrea didn't feel like celebrating too tough, but Beverly had insisted.

"Here's to you, and to the Ebony Hair Salon," Beverly announced merrily, clinking glasses with her friend. "May she sail through the recession and come out a gold mine at the other end."

Andrea wondered whether Beverly had forgotten the significance of the date. It was exactly a year since Winston died. It seemed inappropriate to be toasting each other's good health and good fortune today of all days.

Beverly had become a regular visitor to Andrea's salon during the last month. She would arrive religiously at two in the afternoon, every day, to have her hair done. Andrea was now Beverly's most intimate friend, and they enjoyed their afternoons together, more for the gossip than the beautification. Andrea was only too glad of the company.

"Guess what? I got a letter from Merlene." Andrea announced enthusiastically as they emptied their glasses.

"She's in Jamaica. Can you believe it? All this time, we're here wondering what's happened to her and the bitch has gone to Jamaica without telling anyone."

Beverly merely grunted. "So, what did she have to say for herself?" she asked. "Why did she disappear? She must have explained something."

"It's a strange letter, I'm telling you, Bev. I couldn't make head or tail out of it. She seemed... well, you read it."

Andrea pulled the neatly folded pages of the letter from her pocket and handed it to Beverly, who slipped on her reading glasses and read aloud:

Dear Andrea,

I hope that this letter finds you in good health, and that things are looking up for you generally. You have no idea how my life has been hell the past year. No one knows the pain I have felt and suffered. Until recently, I was smoking cigarettes by the pack and drinking spirits heavily. I couldn't face anybody. I was ashamed of certain things I had done, and I didn't know how even you, my own friend, would take it when everything was revealed. I couldn't take another day under those conditions so I've decided to be with my friends and family out here until things cool down for me back in London.

Here, life is hard but easier than London (I haven't got a penny in my pocket, but I feel like a millionaire). True, Kingston's hot, and that's no joke thing. But out here in the countryside, I live amongst people who greet you in the morning with "God bless you chile." I live amongst people like that. No fussing or cussing or fighting, just plain good and decent people.

It's taken me all this time to realise how low I had sunk. In London, I was lying and cheating and stealing, all kinds of rubbish. Not any more.

Out here, people know the true meaning of love, Andrea. Love is caring, sharing, crying, laughing, all those things and more. Real love will blow your mind, just you wait and see. True devotion, honesty, fidelity, gratitude... I never really understood that love was all those things, Andrea. Please be honest with

228

yourself, neither did you. None of us loved wisely, Andrea, we loved too much. I've had to lose those closest to my heart to realise. I once thought I had love but when I check it now, I was blind to the light of the world. I just couldn't or wouldn't understand the signs. Andrea, friends may tell you bad about me, but please, judge me as you knew me.

Max arrived here yesterday. She's pregnant and depressed. I just hope she'll be all right. None of us is perfect, but we should stop blaming each other for what we have done wrong. Max was wrong sleeping with Thomas, but I've done wrong things as well, which I have to take responsibility for. But no woman is an island, Andrea. No woman should have to stand alone.

Marlon found it strange out here at first and missed his friends. But he has made some new friends and is settling in well at his new school.

At last I have found peace in my life. I'll stay out here for a while. I made my mum a solemn promise to try my best to take care of Max.

Andrea, I've had to learn the hard way that a good friend is better than pocket money. Even though we're far apart, there's a place for you in my heart. Always.

Love

Merlene.

"Well, jeezus," Beverly exclaimed. It was the longest letter she had ever read. "So Merlene turned poet now. What is she saying? I don't understand any of it."

"Innit," Andrea agreed. "It's like she's trying to say something, but she doesn't get to the point. It's like we're supposed to unravel some kind of message from what she wrote. She mus' t'ink we deh 'pon Mastermind or sump'n."

"Songs of Praise more like. So Merlene turned poet and she turned Christian all in one go. Can you believe it?" Beverly knew well that Merlene's letter was a cry for help. But she didn't have much sympathy for her or her sister. Not since the way they had treated her when she was at her lowest ebb.

Max had betrayed her, and Merlene had turned her back on her when she most needed her. Beverly didn't know what trouble Merlene had got herself into and didn't care. As for Max, Beverly's conclusion was that the deceiving whore had been given a taste of divine retribution. 'Pregnant,' she thought, 'I bet the bitch don't even know who the father is'.

"She's out of order," Beverly exclaimed. "I'm telling you. Talking 'bout how Max is depressed. Bettah she sits down and thinks about how I feel after what her sister did to me. If your works are evil, God will cut you down. Don't take it from me. Ah de Bible seh so."

Andrea didn't want to get into any slanging match. She knew how Beverly felt about Max's infidelity with her husband. Nothing Andrea had to say would ever erase the pain her friend felt. The Four Musketeers could never be again. Beverly had vowed that she would never find it in her heart to forgive Max her indiscretions. Andrea suspected also that Beverly held Merlene guilty to some extent. "Merlene is her sister's keeper," Beverly had insisted several times. Andrea had to agree that Merlene had always held her younger sister by a tight leash, and that Max's behaviour followed Merlene's example. If Max was capable of sleeping with her best friend's husband, then wasn't Merlene capable of the same thing? Beverly certainly did have a point there.

"I just think that you should let bygones be bygones," Andrea offered. "We were all best friends before. You can't just throw all that away. Friends do things bad to each other sometimes. Oh, Beverly, at least try and forgive them. Anyway Max and Merlene have come out worst of all."

"That's easy for you to say, Andrea. You don't know what it feels like to discover that your husband is sleeping with your best friend. I don't give a toss about Thomas. I can accept that he was a bad choice of husband, but I'm the one who has got to live with the shame of having my friend, someone who I ought to know and trust well, sleeping with my husband. I hate Max, Andrea. That's not going to change, and Merlene happens to be her sister, so I'm not exactly over the moon about her either."

Andrea could see that Beverly wasn't going to shift her position. She couldn't argue with her. Whenever someone throws in the argument, 'How would you know unless you experienced it?' there's nothing much you can say. To be honest, Andrea didn't know how she would have reacted. She would have hoped she had enough generosity for her friend, that she would have forgiven her eventually. But then it's easier to say that when it hasn't really happened to you. As far as Andrea was concerned, it wasn't all Max's fault. Max didn't exactly rape Thomas, did she? She didn't drag him into her bed. He went there of his own free will, knowing full well what the consequences were. As far as Andrea was concerned, Thomas was Beverly's responsibility. She should have had him on a short leash. But, the mood Beverly was in, Andrea didn't have the bottle to say it to her face.

"Not'n nah happen, y'know Beverly. Whatever you see, it was there before. Thomas was bad from before, but you married him. Max was that way before, but she was your best friend. An' before you found out what was happening between them in bed, you were able to live sweet with the two ah them. You've got to dash way those bad vibes and try to live positive and be nice. 'Cause, you see me? No gal nah badder than me. I could box down anybody who mess wit' my man. You understand? If my friend and my husband ah go sleep with each other, me should know from time. Me should see dem intentions inna dem eye. Me know which friends you can look 'pon an' see if dem is a real friend, more than girls who just ah hustle it. Yeah, me know dem. Don't get me wrong Bev. I'm not saying we mus' remain friends. Personally, I can survive without Max and Merlene as friends. Me was all alone, by myself long before me meet any friend."

"We were four girls," Beverly answered after a long pause. "We were four girls who went through some real hardships in the old days. But we stuck together through joy and pain, through pregnancy, through births, marriage and even death. Now two girls leave. Well, that's all right. Whoever moves with us is the crew. If four of us formed the crew, and the four of us can't work together, then it's better not to waste time. Thinking about the things we've been through just gets me vexed. I don't care if Max don't come back. She made her own decision. Nobody wants to talk about what really happened — Max stole my husband. I'm her best friend. That's not supposed to happen. Up to now, I don't know the reason. Friendship is supposed to come first before all other considerations. Love doesn't come first, friendship comes first, I don't care what the situation. When I begged Merlene to speak to Max, she seriously dissed me. I can't forget that. 'Cause I'm a woman who suffers same way. No man protect me from my friends, now that I know all my enemies."

Andrea didn't know what to do. Beverly was her only true friend now. They had all lost out. She had lost Winston, Beverly had lost Thomas, and Max had lost Andrew. Andrea showed Beverly a photograph in one of the national papers. The picture showed a smiling, handsome man and his fiancée. The man was Andrew, who had become an Earl on the recent death of his father. He had announced his engagement to a wealthy heiress. It had been covered by most of the press. The papers described Andrew as one of the most eligible bachelors in the country. No mention of the black woman he had been seeing for the last three years.

"Well, if you ask me," the still bitter Beverly offered, "that's where all her troubles began. From when she was with that white man, she just lost her mind. She needs to know her culture, the way she just put up herself with the white man and started acting stush when she find out seh him have 'nuff money. You know how much she love bling-bling, Andrea. Max was always shine eye. Her eye was bigger than her belly. She deserved what she got.

"I found out what Max is the hard way and I've made up my mind that I can get along without her. I may have to work seven days a week just for my pickney to have some place to sleep an' eat. But still, I would rather live poor and clean. Look at Max now. She's lost her money and she's lost her friends. It's like her whole life is finished. But I'll never forget what she did."

Andrea's mind had wandered off. She had resigned herself to the situation. There was no point in thinking that the four of them would one day be friends again. Nobody could tell Beverly 'sorry', 'cause sorry couldn't satisfy her. She had come to her verdict. She was both judge and jury and had found Max guilty without a trial. She hated Max with a passion.

If only Beverly would accept that anybody could have done what Max did. Because, no matter what you say otherwise, morality goes out the window when it comes to love. Max wanted to have her cake and eat it. But that's how the youth of today were carrying on a way. An' it noh funny. You never stop to think, 'Who is getting hurt?' Andrea couldn't swear to God that she wouldn't deceive a friend. They had all played O.P.P. when they were younger. Nowadays those things seemed dumb. Some women will come hold you 'bout dem man. They should know puss, dog, and stray cat keep good company. If there was one thing Andrea's discovery of Winston's infidelity had taught her, it was that, when the rice nuh swell, man's belly nah go full. You give a man too much free time, he's going to look elsewhere. Andrea counted herself lucky that she and Spence had a good thing going. He had turned out real sweet and couldn't get enough of her. Andrea was experienced enough to know that this was the real thing and she had accepted his proposal. However much she trusted Spence, Andrea made sure that every move he made she was right beside him. Whether he was going up town or down town, whether going up country or going to foreign, she would tell him to bring her. She had learned from Beverly's mistake.

"What make your face so long?" Beverly asked after a while. The words shook Andrea out of her day dream.

"Oh, I was just thinking that everything you do in life you're in a struggle."

In actual fact, Andrea was floating away on a natural high thinking about how lucky she was having someone to go to bed and wake up with; a true love to go through good times and bad times with, to share the laughs with, while sparing each other the tears. Love was truly a mystery.

"I work so hard," Andrea continued, "that sweat 'pon my shoe and people ask me, how your shoe so wet-up? Yet it's hard making ends meet, because recession deh 'pon my back like trials and crosses. Well, I tried a t'ing to lif up myself an' I find seh it nuh easy. It's tough trying to turn things around to make the salon profitable. I think I might just close it down. I can't make enough money on the hairdressing, so really I would have preferred to expand the business as one of those all in all health centres, y'know? That's the new trend that people are going for, a complete health centre, where they can come in and do keep fit, and where you also offer beauty care and manicures as well as hairdressing. I asked the bank for a loan, but dem tek too long fe come, so me gone."

"How much money do you need exactly?" Beverly asked casually.

"Why, are you offering to give me the money?" Andrea teased.

"You never know," Beverly answered coyly. "Seriously,

how much do you need?"

"Probably about twenty grand, but if I put up ten grand myself, the bank will definitely match that with another ten."

"Ten thousand pounds? I think I can manage that. What do you think Andrea, do you fancy taking on a partner?"

"You're not serious, are you?" Andrea looked hard at her friend to confirm her suspicions, but Beverly was in earnest. "So where did you get ten thousand pounds from?"

"Oh, I've had a little money of my own stashed away for some time now, y'know, for a rainy day. There's lots of things about me you don't know. So what you saying, Andrea? My investment is your chance for business to come back strong. You nuh hear me, man? Partners, always together?"

Andrea thought long and hard before answering. She didn't mean any disrespect, but the salon was her baby. She had set it up on her own, because she didn't really want to depend on any other individual. A partner would mean that things would have to change or be rearranged. Supposing they couldn't agree and fell out with each other? She remembered how they had fallen out over Winston as teenagers. How Beverly claimed that Winston was her man and had blown her top when she discovered that Andrea was sleeping with him. It was all a misunderstanding but Beverly had cursed her for it. "You bitch, Andrea," she had screamed. "You'll get seven years of bad luck for this."

At first, Andrea thought Beverly was simply blowing a lot of hot air, after all she was familiar with idle threats. Andrea's life began to fall apart little by little, however. Winston's attitude towards her had changed completely. He began staying out all night and coming home smelling of perfume. Her dream prince quickly turned sour. Ever superstitious, Andrea suspected then that Beverly's curse was coming to fulfilment. She resigned herself to quietly suffering her seven years of bad luck. Seven years that came to an end when Winston died. But Andrea still watched her step when she was around Beverly, always wary of incurring her friend's wrath a second time.

But then again, what choice did she have? High interest rates were killing her business. Beverly's offer was her only real hope if she didn't want to go out of business. The death of another black business. Jamaicans get the blame for everything that happens. All over the world, people say Jamaicans have the most cocaine, and have the most guns, and kill people recklessly. True, when they can't take the strain of day to day living, certain ghetto youths will turn to crime, but more time Jamaican youths try to make their name with legal shots, and the only way to do it is to get together. Rarely will anyone but your own sistren and bredrin help you to success. Andrea and Beverly were so versatile that they could turn their hands to anything. Together, they could be an explosive team. Andrea decided to accept Beverly's offer and go into business with her friend.

"Maybe it won't be easy," Beverly said, "but we'll work it out."

"I'll call a solicitors up tomorrow, and get them to draw up some papers."

"Good," Beverly shouted as she took her leave. "I won't have my hair done today in that case, I'll come back tomorrow when I'm part of the business. It's free then, I hope."

"Oh, of course."

The two women laughed.

"By the way," Beverly remembered, reaching into her handbag. "You left your comb at my house when you came 'round the day before Carnival remember? I've been meaning to get it back to you, but I keep forgetting. Sorry about that."

Andrea took the comb. She had looked for it all over, but couldn't remember where she left it. The last time she remembered using it was when Max came in to get her hair done on the Friday before Carnival.

Andrea stood in the entrance to the salon, watching her friend climb into her gleaming new, baby blue BMW. Beverly was a strange one, Andrea thought. She could have sworn that her friend didn't have much money, but she had gone out and bought herself a brand new luxury car recently, and here she was offering to put ten thousand pounds into the salon. Well, what a turn up for the books.

What a way Beverly could lie. Sure, she had the ten thousand pounds. Sure, she was going to invest the money in the salon. But it wasn't out of any love for Andrea. Beverly checked in her rear view mirror as she pulled away. She could see Andrea waving her goodbye. If only the bitch realised what she had up her sleeve. Beverly hated Andrea as much as she hated Max. Unable to forget how Andrea had ruthlessly robbed her of Winston, the first boy she ever loved back in their schooldays, Beverly had always held a grudge against her friend.

"Good things come to those who wait," she chuckled to herself. "Time soon ripe for me to show my strength and fling my might. When it drops, Andrea's going to feel it. She won't know what hit her."

Unlike the rest of the crew, as a teenager, Beverly was innocent and lacked confidence with boys. After many false starts, she met Winston. He was a couple of years older and only interested in getting his end away as many times as he could before his next birthday. Beverly had lost her virginity to him. It was sacred to her at the time, and she felt that he belonged to her. But he soon turned his attentions to her friend Andrea, who was only too willing to oblige. It resulted in the two girl's relationship being strained for months, until Merlene, with a little help from Max, managed to get the two women to call a truce, or so they thought. Andrea claimed it was a misunderstanding, an unfortunate mix up; she didn't know that Beverly was interested in the boy. As far as Beverly was concerned, Andrea had used her, tricked her, and then robbed her. Though Beverly agreed to kiss and make up, she knew she would never forgive the Andrea she had once adored. She was vexed. She knew that one day she was going to come out on top. She would pay Andrea back, if it took forever. Like a stalking lion, she had spent the next seven years waiting for an opportunity to pounce on her.

She took her time and wooed Winston back to her. She knew that one day he would keep his promise and run off to the Caribbean with her. So they had embarked on a secret relationship which she had nurtured over the years. By the end of his life Winston loved her more than anything in the world and would have done anything for her.

She had taken a chance with the money, but, as she thought about it now, she decided it was divine retribution if the money from Andrea's boyfriend was the same money used to bring about her downfall.

Not wanting to drive around with thirty-four grand in his car, Winston had deposited the money round at Beverly's late on the afternoon of his crash, after banking the cheques Merlene had given him into several false accounts. Winston hadn't told Beverly he was seeing Merlene, or that the thirty-four grand came from her office. Beverly was the love of his life, that was all he was interested in. They would run off to the Caribbean together and build a home on a plot of land near the beach. They would live happily ever after. 'Yes', Winston had thought to himself, 'we really will.'

Winston thought he was in control of the situation, but in fact Beverly made him fall in love with her by whispering those sweet nothings that tickle a man's ear, and by making love to him like he had never been made love to before. In reality she cared little for Winston but she enjoyed thinking about the hurt her affair would cause to Andrea. She was surprised when Winston showed up with thirty-four grand in cash.

After Winston's death, Beverly sat on the money, not knowing what to do with it. She didn't have a clue where it came from, but she wasn't exactly intending to return it anonymously to a police station. How many people would? It's not everyday that you see thirty-four grand in one lump sum fall in your lap. If she hadn't taken the chance, she would have had nobody but herself to blame when later on in life her kids came up to her and said, 'Bwoy, wha'ppen mek you nevah do it?'

Keep your friends close, keep your enemies closer.

Beverly smiled happily to herself as she eased herself into the driver's seat. As she put her foot on the accelerator she told herself, 'From hereon in, it's my show'.

END

MAN'S BEST FRIEND

"It's just a dick *thang*, you wouldn't understand..."

As if breaking up wasn't hard enough for Troy, he had to be cruel. He summed up the nine months we had devoted to each other with those five little words:

"It's just a dick *thang*."

It didn't just hurt me, it crushed me. Damn near killed something inside me.

It was Thanksgiving and I had invited him to dinner at Luigi's, not far from my lakeshore Chicago apartment. The relationship was finished, worn out and burned out, but there was no reason why we shouldn't stay friends.

That's not Troy's style. He was used to being the one who said 'It's over'. But I beat him to it and, out of spite, he and his bruised ego were going to make me pay.

"It's just a dick *thang*, you wouldn't understand."

"Well baby, here I am, try me."

But he simply repeated himself. All that fancy education and that was the best he could do.

There was nothing more to say so I left him to play with his 'dick *thang*' and walked the three-and-a-half blocks back to my apartment through the winter snow. As far as I was concerned, Troy was history.

So here I am a year later, a new year, strapped into a first class seat, thirty thousand feet up in the air, on my way to starting a new life. Otis is declaring how strong his love is through my headphones and I am just about to lose myself in the latest Terry McMillan. Then 'Mr Ebony Man' leans over from his seat across the aisle and touches my arm lightly.

"It's a good book," he says, and smiles.

I look up briefly, long enough to indulge my ebony fantasy (sparkling, confident smile, shiny bronze skin, thin moustache, rich hazel eyes and smoothed-back relaxed hair), then smile politely and drop my gaze back to the book hoping that he'll work just that little bit harder to break the ice.

He isn't just good looking, but also elegantly dressed in a dark suit, clearly tailor-made to fit his broad physique with ease. He has to be an executive on a business trip. Or maybe an athlete with very good taste in formal wear. Either way, he's the only other African-American in first class and I'm curious to find out more.

"Everything Terry McMillan writes is good," he adds. "I must have read that three times already."

"She's not *that* good."

"No, really, Alice Walker's serious and deep and Maya Angelou's poetic and all that, but Terry just tells it like it is from a sista's point of view. I'm sure that if more brothas were to read her they would appreciate the special woman in their life even more."

Is this the latest pick-up line for a better class of black partner? I wonder. I put my book down and look into his eyes suspiciously, waiting for the punchline, but the man seems earnest. He introduces himself:

"Hello, I am André Brown."

Lieutenant André Brown, he tells me. The youngest homicide officer in the Chicago Police Department. A cop who dresses in Yves St. Laurent? I'm intrigued. He pulls out his Chicago Police Department badge to prove it.

"I always wanted to be a cop, ever since I was a kid."

"They must be paying police officers well nowadays," I say, catching a glimpse of the diamond-studded Cartier beneath his shirt cuff. "I'm impressed."

"Oh, the Mack Daddy pays for everything," he replies

with a wide smile.

"Mack Daddy?" I answer innocently. "Who's he?"

"Lieutenant Mack Dadier, in the Mack Daddy detective novels?"

André can see I need a little help at this point.

"The Mack Daddy thrillers are what some people call trash fiction. I write them in my spare time."

He takes a paperback book from his briefcase and hands it to me. *Mack Daddy In The Bronx*. On the cover is a handsome African-American who could pass for André's brother with his NYPD gold badge in one hand and a smoking pistol in the other. The back cover notes explain: 'When three homeboys are mysteriously clubbed to death in the South Bronx, a new type of cop is needed to solve the crime. Enter Lieutenant Mack Dadier, a ruffneck cop with attitude and his own set of rules...'

"Andrew Berry... that would be you?"

"That would be me," André answers, grinning from ear to ear. "Mack Daddy pays the rent and a bit more besides."

As he strokes his suit jacket to illustrate the point I notice there's no ring on his wedding finger. Maybe he sees the glint in my eye, maybe he doesn't. But by now I am more than a little impressed and more that a little interested. André is more than just a pretty face and a natty dresser. This brotha has class.

"By the way, André..." I stretch out my hand invitingly, "Hello. My name is Dee Robinson."

Maybe I can still find Mr Right in America after all.

Getting a man isn't the problem, all I've got to do is whistle. But a high calibre African-American man is hard to find. Either they've all been snapped up already or they're not into women.

"You gotta be kidding me!" Glenda exclaimed down the line from San Francisco when I told her that I was taking the job in London.

"Maybe you won't find Mr Right in Chicago, but you've got the whole of America to go looking, girl. Try New York, LA, DC. Why not move to Atlanta? Dee, baby, that city is *live*. It's got the highest number of eligible, upwardly mobile black men in America. I read that in *Essence*. Sister, if you can't find what you want in the USA you won't find it overseas, believe me. Remember, Uncle Sam sent me to Germany for three years. I *know*."

It's funny, I was always the one giving my younger sister advice. How to get through high school with as little pain as possible, who to date, what to wear and how to survive and stay alive.

Then Glenda went into the army.

When she went in she was the feisty teenager from Baton Rouge who, together with two of her homegirls, earned the nickname 'triple trouble' in the neighbourhood.

When she came out she was a card-carrying all-American model citizen, married to Harvey, six foot five inches of corn-fed US Marine prime beef and a veteran of Operation Desert Storm. Now he's a decorated sergeant and she's a housewife bringing up her twin three-year-old boys on an army salary.

Now she's giving the advice, trying to help me find a man 'just like Harvey'. It's great having a kid sister who's also your best friend, but when it comes to dating, I can do bad by myself.

"How do you know there are any decent black men in London?" Glenda continued long distance.

"I told you there were. I went over there a month ago to check things out, and you know what, I met some pretty cool guys," I assured her.

"And you know how the English are, right? They always sound so polite and educated. I just love that accent."

"Are you trying to tell me something, sis? Did you met

4

someone 'in particular' over there?"

"No," I echoed, mimicking her, "nobody 'in particular'. I just have a good vibe about London. I had a great time over there and I think the change is going to be good for me. New experiences, new places to see, new people to meet…"

"Well honey, I love my African-American man too much to go fishing in a smaller pond."

When I thought about it, maybe Glenda was right. Maybe I hadn't given the US male a fair chance. But I had lost patience with the brothas.

I had been going around in circles, dating men who couldn't deal with an independent black woman who earns more money than they do. I worked hard to get to where I am, and I believe I should be able to enjoy my money in any way I please. But every man I've dated finds that a problem, especially since I became creative director at Frazier Clarke Advertising. Being a success is great, but I want to share it with someone. That doesn't mean I'm going to hang around for that person to come along. Where I'm at in my life right now, finding a partner is important to me, but it's not everything.

Troy was really happy for me when I got the job. We had been seeing each other on and off for a few weeks at the time. He was a tall, athletic Denzel Washington lookalike, press secretary at City Hall for Chicago's African-American mayor, Richard Wilkins. I was working as a copywriter on the mayor's springtime re-election campaign.

He suggested that we discuss the media campaign over lunch – a casual rendezvous which turned out to be the first of many. But our first official date was Mayor Wilkins' victory ball after the election. Oprah and Steadman were among the many celebrity guests who were there that night, but Troy looked so elegant in his tux that he outshone even the brightest stars for me.

He teased me all evening, telling me that when we we married he'd make sure I wore the same Yves St Laurent evening dress for dinner every night. As we danced to the live Dixie jazz band, he gently pulled me close to him and kissed me lightly on the lips. It wasn't our first kiss, but this was the *one*. This one was *intimate*. I knew what was going down, we both did. And Troy knew that I knew. I wanted it also, I wanted it bad. We held hands discreetly throughout the evening, but by the end of it Troy was holding me tightly enough to be noticed. 'It won't be long now', I figured, maybe an hour, maybe sooner.

As soon as we could slip away from the reception unnoticed, we would be undressing each other slowly, either in my apartment or his. I didn't mind which. I thought about his toned, strong body gripping me tightly, the taste of his sweat and the warmth of his breath on the nape of my neck. Every part of me seemed to tingle in anticipation, I could barely wait.

"No really Dee, writing a novel ain't that difficult," André was insisting.

We had only been talking ten minutes but already we were chatting away like old friends. André had so much to say and had a way of talking that made what he was saying sound like the most interesting thing.

We shared the joke when we discovered that we had each had our first class ticket paid for by our employer. André was on his way to Paris, as he had been invited to lecture to a criminology class at the university there. He was a little defensive about it, which I thought was sweet.

"I do speak French, you know" he said, reading my thoughts. "*Est-ce que vous parlez français aussi?*"

A linguist as well? Could he really be perfect?

"But don't you have to go on a course to learn how to write novels?"

"Sure I could have, but I didn't. Look, you wanna know how I started writing? My niece Jennifer, my sister's daughter, is only ten years old but she loves reading detective novels. I don't know why. She's just one of those bright kids who outgrew all the books for her age group too fast. So every time I went over there to babysit, I would pick out a really good paperback thriller for her. That's when I discovered that there are hardly any black detective novel writers. Did you know that?"

"It hadn't even occurred to me."

"As well as that, I want her to have a balanced education because most of the learning she gets in school is culturally biased.

"She's read all the Chester Himes books and she loved his stuff, you know, because she could relate to it. And she's gone through all Walter Moseley's novels and even figured out the endings before she came to them. This really is one bright kid. Then one day I ran out of books to buy and I sat down in front of my computer and tried to put together my own detective novel with an ending she couldn't figure out."

"Did you succeed?"

I was hooked, and despite my secret fear of flying I barely noticed the turbulence which was tossing the jumbo up and down like it was made of paper.

"Boy did I succeed," André laughed. "She had to keep reading until the last page to solve the crime."

As the captain switched off the 'fasten safety belt' sign André caught me staring a little too deeply into his eyes. He responded with a warm, embracing smile.

Damn it.

All the time I was wondering if life could really be so cruel as to torment me like this. Here I was flying to London, a single woman with the 'man-I've-been-looking-for-all-my-life' sitting right next to me on his way to Paris.

I'd only just laid eyes on him and already I had spotted

that André had good looks to spare, style, manners, intelligence, ambition, good prospects *and* he wrote novels. My old sorority girlfriends from Michigan State would die if I told them about this. A writer was the kind of man we all fantasised about settling down and starting a family with.

"You must have been a pretty bright child too, André. To be able to just pick up and start writing, you've got to be smart, right? Were you always interested in writing as a kid?"

"That's just it, I wasn't," André insisted. He did his best to assure me that he was just a regular guy. He didn't think he was doing anything special when he investigated a homicide, neither did he think he was doing anything exceptional when he wrote a Mack Daddy thriller.

His take on it was that if he could pick up a pen and start writing a novel, then anybody could.

"So, the way it turned out, my niece enjoyed the first Mack Daddy story. Then she gave it to her mother to read. Mom sent it to a literary agent and the next thing I heard about it was when I got a call from a black publishing company called Rex Publishing. They had just set up an office in New York, and offered me a deal.

"You know, when you find your feet in London you should check out those guys, because they're from over that side. They're just a couple of regular guys with a jammin' little company putting out books for the black community. They're always telling me how they want more novels from women, so when you're in London, if you come up with an idea, call them up."

I laughed, as modesty kicked in.

"I write copy for advertisements. I couldn't write a novel."

"No? And why is that? You've got stories to tell, haven't you?"

"Definitely, lots of stories. But writing's just not my

8

thing. I would really prefer to read Terry McMillan than write myself."

"Well, I guess if anyone had asked me about it, which they didn't, I would have told them I didn't think I could do it either. But I would have been wrong if I'd said that…" By now that winning smile was in play again. "… If I'd said that during the conversation I never had, that is, with the person who never asked…"

When we'd both managed to stop grinning like teenagers he remembered what his point was going to be.

"Look at it this way, Dee. We need more black stories for the kids coming up to read. We've got no time to waste."

Troy and I had had a good thing going, and plenty in common. We were both young, successful and ambitious. We were both perfectionists and shared a love for modern jazz, Italian cooking and African art. And we were both great conversationalists, so we rarely shared a dull moment together.

It *seemed* like our relationship wasn't going to be affected by the usual pitfalls of money worries and infidelity. For the first six months especially, I was thanking the Lord for answering my prayers and sending me the most eligible man in Chicago. He had ambition, a life plan. He had a master's degree in law from Howard University but he had his sights on higher things than a career in the legal profession. His job in charge of Mayor Wilkins' PR was a stepping stone.

A committed Democrat, Troy really wanted to become a politician himself eventually. He planned to 'increase the peace' in Chicago's South Side by lobbying big business to pay for improved education and better job opportunities there. Some payback for the community they were earning so much from.

Although he was only a couple of years older than me, he was already being spoken about in Illinois' black political circles as one of the brightest new stars on the horizon. And I wasn't doing too badly either, with my career in corporate advertising. We were the 'perfect couple' at all the social gatherings we attended and many of my girlfriends envied me for having him.

But then I got promoted to creative director after the success of my campaign for Color Creatives: 'Black By Popular Demand'. Suddenly I had all this power at one of the top advertising agencies in the midwest, and a high-roller's salary to go with it. I was beginning to earn much more than Troy.

He kept telling me how proud he was to know that his woman was big in the advertising industry. But things started changing in our relationship; suddenly it was me that was getting invitations to different functions and Troy was accompanying me as *my* partner. He didn't like that and I soon had to get used to attending the various industry parties on my own.

It didn't take long before the media started getting interested in the 'dynamic young creative director' from Frazier Clarke. In an industry with very few black men or women in meaningful positions, I was good copy myself.

Things really began to change between me and Troy after the lifestyle article that *Essence* magazine did on me. It really bugged him that I had described him as my partner in the interview.

We were lying in bed in my apartment doing the *Chicago Sun* crossword together when Troy picked up that issue of *Essence*. Any desire he had to get more intimate disappeared as he read the article.

"How could you say that? How could you say that?"

"Well, it's true isn't it?" I asked incredulously. "That's exactly what you are, so I didn't see any point in denying it. I can't understand why you're so upset."

"I have my career to think about as well, you know, Dee. I am Troy Adams, I am *not* Mr Dee Robinson. And I don't intend to be 'the man behind the successful woman', because I happen to be pursuing my own political ambitions. Didn't you think you owed me the courtesy of asking me about it before you started discussing my private life in a national magazine?"

I thought he was overreacting.

"Get real, Troy. It was only an interview. If you don't want me to mention your name again, I won't. Anything you say; I just don't have time to argue about this."

I got out of bed.

It didn't end there. Troy had a sour taste in his mouth for a long time afterwards. He began to complain that I was spending too much time at work and too little time in the relationship.

"Baby, I'm really happy for the way your career is taking off," was how he explained it to me. "But where does that leave me? Where does that leave us? Do you expect me to hang around and wait for you to reach the top of the career ladder or what. Because it doesn't seem like you've got much time to devote to making things work between us."

So Troy, who was single-minded about becoming the first black president of the United States, and who seemed to see our relationship as something of a diverting hobby, had now really understood that I had my eyes on the prize too, and he was upset about it. He didn't mind opportunity knocking, but he was getting awful sniffy about me opening the door.

"What the hell are you saying, Troy? Are you saying that this relationship isn't working? Is that what you're saying?"

I was angry. Hell, I was fuming, and I left Troy in no doubt that I wasn't going to take this crap. Well, that took him by surprise, and he backed off. No, he wasn't saying that exactly. It was just that he felt that I had changed with my new job and new responsibilities and new salary and he wasn't sure if he liked the way I had changed.

Troy made it sound like he was saying all this for my benefit. What a politician he was going to make! But I had read between his lines, and I knew that the problem between us was fundamental. The notion of power had changed in our relationship. All that had happened was that I had been promoted at work, something that happens to people every day. But the reality of that situation was that I had ended up earning much more money than my partner, and Troy — like so many millions of other men — had not been brought up to be able to deal with that. Nobody had ever taught him that life could be like that. He didn't want to admit that he was on the macho 'black man as a breadwinner' trip, but that's really where he was coming from.

As he searched for a way to redeem himself, everything he said started to stink like horse manure.

"Dee, baby, I want you to be successful and all that, but you gotta see things from my point of view. You're my squeeze; I thought we had something strong together, that maybe someday you would walk down that aisle and find me waiting at the altar in front of the preacher. That's what I want to happen. I want us to settle down and have a home and raise some kids together. But I can't see how that's possible any more. Since you got promoted you've only had your mind on work, I can't see when you'll be able to find the time to settle down now that you're a high-flying advertising executive."

That was straight out of the blue. When did Troy start thinking about marriage and kids? And why was he only telling me about it now? I wasn't buying any of it.

"So you think the job I'm doing means I can't settle down when I want to? Is that what you think?"

Troy searched around for an answer and avoided my gaze when he replied.

"Baby, I want to marry someone who's got time to

spend thinking about me and taking care of me, someone who's got time to raise my kids, not someone whose job comes before her family. A woman earning more than her partner is a recipe for tension and disaster."

Poor Troy. Poor helpless modern man. It wasn't about kids and a family at all, but about economics, pure and simple. Instead of losing my cool, I took pity on him. For a man with so much education he had a lot to learn about sistas like me.

"That's just too bad. Black men better get used to that – you had better get used to it – because some of us are leaving you behind, earning double, three and four times more than you are. That's the facts, baby, and we're not taking any shit with it either."

"Well, let me see, you might have seen my magazine adverts for Karl Kani jeans, the ones with Naomi Campbell. I like working on advertisements like that, but, you know, advertising is culturally biased also," I said.

The stewardess came over and filled up our champagne glasses again. I glanced at my watch. We would be landing in New York in a few minutes, but my fear of flying was altogether gone, and I was wishing the flight would last longer, much longer. It was shocking to me that I was so completely wrapped up in someone I had only known for such a short time, but it was thrilling too.

André was the most charismatic man I had ever met, and I was telling myself that I wasn't going to let him go when we got to New York. We had already exchanged addresses and numbers, and if he didn't have the chance to visit me in London, a dinner date with André would be right at the top of my agenda whenever I returned to Chicago.

"In the old days none of the big corporations wanted black people in their advertisements. It was only when black consumers started voting with their feet and taking their business elsewhere that the burger chains and soda companies saw how important the black dollar was to their business. Even now I think you would be surprised how many companies tell us that they only want us to use black models who don't look 'too African'."

"Are you kidding me?" André asked.

"Sure. You must have heard the three cardinal rules of advertising: 'If you're white, that's all right, if you're brown stick around, but if you're black…' "

" 'Stay back'. " André completed the rhyme.

"Exactly."

"Do you enjoy working in an industry like that?"

"I have a great time, because advertisers with those kind of backward views usually know to stay well away from me. I had always wanted to be in advertising, and now that I've got up the ladder to a position of power I'm going to use it and enjoy it. It's just like what you were saying about writing novels, right now we need more black achievers in advertising because the image that comes across to the kids isn't always positive."

I would rather not have been talking about work; there were other things, much more important things, *pressing* things, that I wanted to tell him. One or two things I wanted to show him, too, when the time was right. But that wasn't going to be right now. I had already decided I wasn't going to lay all my cards on the table for him to see, not yet. I hardly knew him at all, but I surely knew there's a difference between what looks good and tastes good, and what does you good.

Snow was falling as we descended on JFK. It looked beautiful, with thick white flakes blotting out the early evening winter sky. I shifted my seat into the upright position and turned to André who was smiling at me inquisitively.

"Snow always makes New York look so clean," I said as

the plane eased down gently closer and closer to the runway.

"Me too. I love it when it snows," André said. "Except when I'm flying."

The plane touched down with a violent shudder and seemed to skid for the longest time before the pilot slowed it down.

"You see what I mean? I like to think of myself as a real man, but when it comes to flying and snow I'm as nervous as a child."

"At least we've landed safely."

"It ain't over until the fat lady sings," André warned.

It wasn't until we were inside the terminal that I saw what he meant. The snow had closed down JFK and ours had been the last plane to land. Now there would be no more flights landing or taking off until the morning, and the entire airport was filling up with frustrated would-be travellers.

I began considering my options. I *could* call my cousin Ira all the way up in Harlem and stay there the night. But it was a long way to travel and then I'd have to come back out to the airport the next day. It would be better to stay at a hotel overnight and take the first flight out of JFK in the morning. Of course, André was still with me, and he wasn't going anywhere either. Or so I thought, until he revealed one of the advantages of having a police badge. Holding it ahead of him, he used the gold shield to cut a clear path through the crowd and straight to the front of the queue at the ticket desk.

"Hi, I'm Lieutenant André Brown of the Chicago Police Department."

The woman behind the desk examined his ID for a minute, and let André see how impressed she was that the handsome young black man in front of her was a high-ranking police officer.

"How may I help you Lieutenant?"

He nodded in my direction.

"My assistant and I are on our way to Europe to take part in an urgent operation there," he explained quietly. "Now it's very important that we arrived there in tip-top shape, as we'll be going straight to work when we land. Of course, I understand that you can't do anything to get us there tonight, but I would *really* appreciate it if you could find us a couple of decent hotel rooms nearby. We can at least make some progress with the paperwork."

He placed the first class tickets on the desk, and gave her that 'you and I both know how vital this is, right?' look, and then he stopped talking and let her get on with it.

The crowd behind him had appreciated the performance, and watched as the woman picked up the phone on her desk and called her superiors. After a moment she put down the phone and smiled politely at André.

"Lieutenant, the airline would like to offer you and your assistant complimentary rooms at the Larriot Hotel for tonight. If you would just take these vouchers and walk through the exit doors behind you there, you'll find a courtesy limousine waiting to take you to the hotel."

André turned to me and smiled. I smiled back, impressed. André certainly knew how to take care of himself.

By the time we reached the exit door, everyone else in the queue had got the idea too.

Things had never improved with Troy. Looking back on those last few months together, I can't understand why we didn't just end it. I guess that Troy still had most of the wonderful qualities I had admired in him in the beginning. He was still intelligent, he could still become an important black political figure in America, and he could still be charming and witty when he wasn't too busy trying to compete with me.

I still reckon he had no good reason to end the relationship. Of course, I had been at social functions where people were just as interested in me as they were in Troy. But he didn't seem to see how that had made me a political asset. Troy was still consumed by the need to assert himself in our relationship. And he was still talking horseshit.

"Women who have more money than their partners are more likely to be unfaithful," he said. That was one of my favourites.

So for a while I humoured him, hoping he would come to terms with things. But he just got more distant and moody, and the little time we spent together became fraught with tension.

It all reached a head that Thanksgiving a year ago. We were having dinner together for the first time in weeks at Luigi's, one of the top restaurants in downtown Chicago. I still hoped that we could make each other happy again, the way we used to. I worked at it that night. And it was going well. But then suddenly, in the middle of the main course, as the waiter filled our wine glasses, Troy dropped his bombshell.

"Kids."

"What?"

"Haven't you ever felt that way, Dee? Like despite everything you've done in life, in your job and with all your possessions, there's still something missing? I just feel that I want to start a family and start one now... with you."

Uh-huh. So now he wants kids and he wants them now. Well go ahead Troy, I ain't stoppin' you. You get pregnant and you give up your job to look after your child.

"When you've been in a relationship a while, you have to either get married and have kids or end it," Troy implored, "otherwise what else is there?"

Married! Kids! This was not how I had expected a

proposal to be. It wasn't what I expected, and it wasn't what I wanted either. I didn't even have to think about it.

I loved my life, I loved riding the shooting star of my career, I didn't want to change, and I certainly didn't want kids now. Like any thirty year old woman I felt that biological clock ticking away, and I knew that I wanted a baby... eventually. But at that moment there were enough hassles in my life without bringing in new ones.

That wasn't all, though. I also knew that the idea of a child scared the hell out of Troy. It always had. When we first started dating he had made it clear that he wanted things to be uncomplicated. He told me that one of the things that had attracted him to me in the first place was that I seemed to be different from all the other women he had dated who had wanted kids at the end of the relationship.

So why the big change? I asked him straight out, and Troy denied that it was about trying to make sure that I wouldn't earn more money than him and hence couldn't be 'unfaithful'. He became defensive and uncharacteristically coarse when I told him I'd thought about it, but I was more interested in my career than in becoming a housewife.

"Then you'd better think about it a bit longer," he said. "Because, yeah, this is something that I would end the relationship over."

I couldn't believe that he could be so arrogant. I sat silently for a moment before I responded.

"There's no need for you to end the relationship, Troy, it's over. Nobody talks to me like that. You understand, Troy? I'd be crazy if I married you and had kids with you. You want a wife that is inferior to you, someone you can push around. Honey, I ain't tha one."

Troy wasn't expecting what he heard. He took a deep breath and I sensed his anger rise up from the pit of his stomach and rush up into his head.

"Bitch!" he hissed. "You're so high and mighty with your big job and your big salary, but all you are to me now is a bitch anyway."

At first I mistook his venom for volume, and I was taken aback and looked around embarrassed, but the other diners were still wrapped up in their own conversations. For once Troy had almost stopped being a politician. Almost, but not quite. He was speaking the truth all right, but he was still real careful about who heard him say it.

"You think a bitch like you could really get a man like me? Bitch. You weren't even that good in the sack, that's why I had to go balling a different babe every week. You didn't know that, did you? Well now you do. Get real, bitch, it was just a dick *thang*."

I had heard enough, and I grabbed the carafe of red wine from the table and emptied it over his sorry head. Then I stood up and paused for a second to admire my work before turning and marching out. I remained, of course, perfectly composed throughout, and completely forgot to pick up my coat on the way out the door. I tried not to cry as I hurried home, and I tried not to get frozen to the bone too, but there was no avoiding either one. Fresh tears melted a trail back to my apartment that Thanksgiving.

I went back a couple of days later for my coat.

"Thank you, Lord," I said to myself when I realised that I had been given more time with André. Delay in my journey, what delay? Inconvenienced, *moi*? There were going to be lots and lots of flights the next day, so what was the problem? And it was a limousine, then it was going to be a hotel, then it was going to be... well, I probably wouldn't say no to an invitation to spend the night with André, if one came my way. I saw the glint in his eye when the hotel man asked if we were together and would like to share a suite, and I guessed that André was thinking more or less what I was thinking. He looked across and winked at me before informing the desk clerk that we were 'just good friends'.

Good friends. GOOD FRIENDS! That's the last thing I want to hear. But, then, the night is still young and I haven't made myself totally irresistible yet…

We decided to give each other two hours to shower, freshen up, and take a little nap before we would meet again in the hotel bar. Once in my room, I fell on the bed exhausted and for a moment just lay on my back, looking up at the ceiling, asking myself a big question: Is going to London really the right thing for me or, new job aside, is what I'm looking for right here in the States after all?

After I ended things with Troy I had been 'between relationships' for almost a year.

There seemed to be a limitless supply of men available when word got around that I was on the market again. My network of friends and family made sure that every eligible man for a hundred miles got given my number. But I didn't want *a* man, I wanted *the* man, and, for one reason or another, each contender got eliminated after one or two rounds.

Of course, I was making more money than most of the men I dated, which didn't help. Well, it didn't help *them*.

Like Trevor, the thirty-year-old TV producer who thought his penis made up for the difference in our incomes. He didn't need to deal with the problems in our relationship because his manhood wasn't just power to him, but was also worth at least a hundred grand more than I was earning. A man whose penis means that much to him is never going to mean that much to me, and I didn't have time to waste time on someone I really wasn't into while the interesting men were slipping away. Trevor lasted a month.

I was learning, though, not to even talk about money with the men I dated. Even with Lance (thirty-three years old, corporate lawyer, earning a six-figure salary), who liked to play as hard as he worked and seemed in every respect to be my intellectual and social equal. For me, his designer clothes and expensive cars were just status symbols, boy's toys. But in his mind they were quality contributions to our relationship. He didn't feel that he needed to work on feelings and emotions. He didn't like to show his feelings and couldn't deal with anyone else's, even his woman's. Then he started to be less giving of himself. I knew what I was worth on the singles market and felt I deserved more than expensive presents from him. So, one night I asked him what was on his mind, but that was all too much pressure for him and he said he wanted to end the relationship.

Things went kinda quiet for me in Chicago after Lance and I broke up. I didn't think it would leave me feeling empty inside, but I had invested too much emotion in those three months together to simply shrug my shoulders.

Next thing I learned was that I didn't have time for one-night specials, either. I simply had too much to do job-wise for these short bursts of sexual exploration.

Chicago began to feel stale and I began considering moving on. I called around to some of my girlfriends, sorority sistas who I had kept in touch with since college after we had each gone our different ways to pursue our dreams. Larianne, who was teaching in DC, warned me down the long distance line that she hadn't met a man worth talking about in six months.

"The black man is in short supply in this city, baby," she told me. "You better keep your little ass in Chicago, girlfriend."

LaToya had moved down South after college to marry a millionaire record producer twice her age, then divorced him a year later and became extremely rich in the process. She urged me to come down and check Atlanta out.

"Our cup runneth over with black men," she joked down the line, "but the competition is stiff for the successful, upwardly mobile, single black male, honey. They're snapped up as soon as they come on the market."

The more I asked around, the more I felt sure that taking the advertising job in London was the right thing to do. The USA was all filled up with attractive, successful, ambitious and upwardly mobile black women, sitting around with passion in their hearts, waiting in vain for the right guy. And I wasn't about to let myself go to waste because of a man or the lack of a man. Also, I liked what I heard about London. It sounded like a cool city with no guns and little violence, where people were polite to each other and there was much more history and culture than Chicago. On top of which, the job at Splash was way too good a career move to turn down.

"Why is it that men are prepared to risk everything they've got in a relationship — love, their woman, even their children — for one careless night with another woman? Why is that?"

André raised up his hands innocently. He was muscular but elegant even when he wore black slacks and a cashmere sweater. I had changed into a wool jumper long enough to wear as a dress and knee-length black boots which never failed to attract attention.

"Hey, hold on, you have all kinds of men out there. Don't put us all in the same bag."

We found a table in a dimly-lit section of the piano bar, where a happy-faced brotha on the keyboard was strolling through a selection of soulful seventies ballads. *Me & Mrs Jones* wafted across the room.

"But it's true, men can not control their sexual urges."

I sipped the champagne that the hotel had provided on the house once they had discovered that André was a high-ranking detective on an international mission.

"How about the women?" André asked.

"What about them?"

"I mean, I know a lot of women who also can't control their sexual urges."

"But they don't tend to risk everything that is dear to them just for sex. There are too many talented, attractive sistas sitting around getting dissed by men who can't see further than gratifying their sexual desires."

André smiled again. He was still charming, even though some of his views were typical male hogwash. Not to worry, though. So far I'd seen nothing that I couldn't re-programme out of him, given a little time.

"You know what, you can spend your life trying to find a man who would never be unfaithful, but you'll miss a lot of good possibilities. If fidelity is really the most important thing to you then I'd say keep on looking and good luck with it, but if it's not, you might end up cutting off your nose to spite your face."

"It's easier for a man to say that. Because in a man's world he gets his props if he has more than one woman. But women don't get praise for that sort of thing. Would you introduce a woman that had more than one man to your mother?"

"Good point," André admitted. "But the fact remains, underneath all our differences in approach, men and women want the same thing at the end of the day. You want to be loved, I want to be loved. You want to be cared for, so do I, and we both want to be respected and appreciated."

"Ain't that the truth."

Me & Mrs Jones faded away and the piano player followed that with The Chi-Lites' *Have You Seen Her?*

Tonight was special, almost magical. I felt so good

about being with André as champagne mixed with talk and laughs into the early hours of the morning.

The music finished up with a perfect impersonation of Nat King Cole's *When I Fall In Love* and by then we were the only couple left in the bar, with chairs piled on tables all around us. Light-headed from the champagne we made our way arm in arm through the foyer to the elevator. André looked good enough to eat. As the doors closed behind us, I felt sure André must have been feeling what I was feeling.

"It's been such a romantic evening," he began unsteadily as the elevator raced up the floors. "I wish somehow that it could continue."

He paused and stared hard at me.

"You know what I mean?"

Yes, don't I just know exactly what you mean. There's magic in the air and champagne always makes you want the evening to go on for ever.

"I would want nothing more than for this evening to continue, but…"

Oh no, I've heard this before.

"I'm unavailable right now. I'm engaged and in love with my fiancée."

I should have known. Men like André don't just walk around. There's always going to be a woman waiting at home.

"So… what's she like?" I asked, trying not to choke on the words as they came out.

"Oh, Shawna? She's fun, you know, we have a good time together."

André had a look of warmth in his eyes as he spoke.

Damn, damn damn, dammit. Well, maybe you're about to tell me that the two of you fight all the time and she snores!

I decided not to ask any more questions about his fiancée, I had heard enough. His life in Chicago was a thousand miles away and even that wasn't far enough for me.

"I'm a faithful kinda guy, even when I know my woman won't find out."

Suddenly I sobered up. What was I doing? My time spent with André had been so perfect that I wanted to spend my last few hours in the United States with him. Lying in bed beside him, with his powerful arms around me and my head on his chest, listening to his heart beat. I was even prepared to forget that he was another woman's man.

"I'll be sad to see you go," I said to Mr Oh-so-fine-but-taken-by-another-woman, trying to hide my disappointment. "I'm leaving early tomorrow morning." I handed him a company business card from my handbag. "If you're ever in London, look me up."

"Hey, you know what, Dee… I've had such a great time tonight. When you get back to Chicago, call me at the precinct and we'll do dinner. I'll send you the complete set of Mack Daddy books to the address on this card, okay?"

We embraced each other as if we were old friends, warmly and tightly. Then I slipped my key card into the lock.

"Have a safe journey," he said as he made his way along the corridor to his room.

"Hey!" I called after him teasingly.

He spun around, waiting.

"Oh… nothing."

The next day I flew to London with a hangover. It seemed like I'd found the right man six months too late.

SHAME AND PRIDE

Carol sighed nervously and looked at her watch again.

"If you just take a seat, Ms Ballantine, Miss Ridgley will be with you in a moment," the receptionist said with a polite smile.

Carol sat down, placing her shoulder bag down carefully. Two tense-looking white youths, dressed up for a job interview, were eyeing her cautiously, 'sizing up' the competition. Carol hardly noticed them. She had her mind on other things. She had used her maiden name so as not to arouse suspicion.

She had chosen to wear her navy business suit and a simple white blouse with a blue and white polka dot scarf and sensible black shoes. The weight she had put on over Christmas had meant the jacket would no longer close across her waist, but it didn't bother her that the suit no longer fitted her well.

At the age of thirty-four, after nearly eight years of marriage, Carol Edwards was a single woman again. Neville had decided to drop the news that he was leaving her on Christmas Eve, just as she was preparing what *was* to have been a family Christmas. His parents had been invited and also his brother who was coming with his own wife and two kids. Her mother was also going to be there. She had bought all the presents, the food, and all the little things that they would need with seven extra people to entertain. She had planned to cook a special Christmas jollof rice with spicy turkey cutlets. The whole family knew that Carol's cooking skills were unparalleled and, with the children's love of her desserts in mind, she intended to make a strawberry tea cake with ice cream for them. Despite the sad significance of Christmas Day for her and her husband, Carol had been determined to make sure that they would be as happy as possible. As always, Neville had left all the finer details to her. He was too busy with work right up to Christmas Day to have time to help her with the Christmas tree and decorations which she was hanging up even as he broke the news to her.

"I've got another woman and I'm leaving you today," he said. "You can have the house, but that's it. Everything will probably turn out all right for you."

Standing on a stool, straightening up the star at the top of the tree, Carol thought she had misunderstood what he was saying. Lately, Neville hadn't been able to make up his mind one way or another about their life together.

"I love you, but I'm not *in love* with you," he would say. "You're the woman in my life, but I don't love you." Then there was: "You're my sister, my friend and my lover, but not my woman." Not to mention: "We are *too* close to each other, we've become *too* close, *too* intimate."

She turned to face him. He simply stared back at her. The words didn't t really hit her until she saw the look on his face. As the penny dropped, Carol's legs gave way.

"Oh shit!" said Neville, who played fly-half for his company rugby team. He dived across the room and caught his wife before she hit the floor, and laid her down on the sofa.

A moment later, when Carol opened her eyes, she found herself staring up at the irritated expression on Neville's face. Something snapped inside her and, unwilling to stop herself, she lifted her head up and spat in his face. Before he could react she was on top of him, beating and pounding at his ears and face as hard as she could. She took him by surprise and gave him little chance of protecting himself.

"You bastard. Bastard!" Carol screamed at him again and again as she continued to strike out at all of Neville's sensitive areas. He grabbed her arms, but could only hold her for a moment. She twisted to face him again and shot her knee up into his groin. He doubled up, rapidly losing the will to fight, then felt the weight of her on his chest and the impact of her fists in his face again. "You bastard. You bastard! Bastard! Bastard!" she repeated with every punch. Tears were streaming down her face, so she didn't see Neville lift his elbow up and hammer it with all his remaining strength into her face.

The blow lifted Carol clean off of him.

Neville lifted himself up shakily, his teeth red with blood.

"You stupid cow!" he cried out. "What did you make me do that for?"

He didn't wait for an answer.

She heard him go up to the bedroom and pack his clothes, then into the bathroom for his electric toothbrush and shaver. He paused in front of the mirror to examine the damage. Carol had left both his face and his Bruce Oldfield pinstripe two-piece suit bloodied and torn. In fact, he was beginning to look a lot like Christmas… in hell.

His suit pockets hung by their lining. He spat out a mouthful of bloody saliva and counted his teeth in the mirror. They were still red. He kissed his teeth, then went next door to his study where he packed his papers and a few books.

With his belongings all stuffed into a rucksack, he headed back down the stairs, taking them three at a time. He didn't want to spend another minute in the house while his wife was acting like a maniac. He looked down at her lying on the carpet, still sobbing, surrounded by tinsel and the battered remains of the Christmas tree.

"You've got yourself to blame," he said without pity.

"You're to blame for the death of my son. Think about it, if Junior was alive I'd be at home with the kid, being a father. Remember that when you're cursing me tonight. Take a look at yourself, you've become a fat cow. Do you really think any man would want you now? You've got to be kidding."

As he light-footed out into the snowstorm a big glass ashtray sailed through the door behind him.

"You're so full of shit," she shouted through the broken door glass after him, then fell back on the carpet, exhausted. She began to think about all the arrangements. Should she call everybody up and cancel? Or go ahead with the festivities and tell everyone as they arrived that her husband had left her? And what the hell did it matter anyway.

Neville's parting words haunted her.

How could he have been so cruel? However little he thought of her, she didn't deserve to hear that she was to blame for Junior's death, especially on the eve of the first anniversary of that tragic day. Neville was ignorant, but he had spoken knowing the impact his words would have. She was still lying face up on the carpet when she burst out crying. Her arms and legs were heavy and cramped and her face had begun to swell and throb with pain. In between her heart-wrenched sobs, she called out the name of the son she had carried for nine months, the son she had nurtured, cared for and watched over for five years, that most cherished part of her which was now buried deep in a cold grave.

For those who have to live with it, sickle cell is a dread illness. The doctors equate the pain suffered in a sickle cell crisis with that of a woman undergoing natural childbirth. Every sickler learns to live with this pain. Little Junior had bravely faced death before when a crisis had resulted in a heart attack. He finally succumbed to a sudden sickling in the brain, his young life ending on Christmas Day. Carol was devastated. For five years she had watched helplessly each time her son had cried with pain as sickling had attacked his chest and his knees with a vengeance. Hospitals had become a major part of her life but her heart still pounded with fear every time she climbed into an ambulance to accompany him to casualty. The doctors had warned that every crisis was potentially fatal, indirectly if not directly, as it slowly wore down other organs. But that was hardly something you could discuss with a five year old. Carol had frequently found herself agonising when Junior begged her to "make the pain go away".

She didn't know anything about sickle cell to begin with. Then, through leaflets, she learned the disease was found amongst people from countries with the malaria mosquito, Africans especially. When twenty-five million Africans were kidnapped and shipped to far-off corners of the world as slaves, the sickle cell genes went with them, replenishing themselves through the bloodstream, handed down from generation to generation.

Whether you were born in the Caribbean or the States, in Camberwell or Carlisle, sickle cell came to you as a malicious reminder of where you really came from, whether black, brown, red, yellow, mellow or damn near white.

As far as Neville was concerned, nobody in his family had ever had sickle cell anaemia. Even when the trait was found in his bloodstream, he refused to accept that he was anything to do with his young son's illness. He blamed everything on his wife. After all, not only did she have the trait, but she also had a history of sickle cell in her family. This put paid to a marriage which had once looked like the 'perfect relationship'.

Neville became more and more irritable with everything his wife did. He saw faults in all of her actions and would criticise her for being too timid one minute and too aggressive the next, or for being too clever one minute and too stupid the next. On top of that, she was getting fat and her clothes weren't sitting on her properly, which annoyed him.

"Our sex life is shit," he complained one night after

they had made love. "Is it?" she asked. She was hurt, but she agreed. Everything about their relationship seemed to be shit these days.

They had met while at university. Neville had been a handsome economics student studying for an MA when Carol was a first year law student. He had met her at the freshers' ball, just as she was regretting not having applied to a bigger city university. Durham was one of the finest universities in the country, but it was already clear to her that she was not going to see much black culture — the social, political and historical awareness that was as vital to her as the air that she breathed and the food that she ate — in dry old Durham. It was a white town, and the university desperately needed a Black Students' Alliance.

Carol was determined to be the first person in her family to go to university, even though all her friends back home in Tottenham told her that it would change her totally, saying that when she came back she would not want to socialise with them. There was Frankie to think about, too. He was the most worried because he had the most to lose. Frankie and Carol had been together since school and he didn't like what was happening to the girl he had fallen in love with. Raving was no longer at the top of her list of priorities and she was way too busy with 'all this studying business' for his liking.

Neville had asked her to dance to a smoochy soul ballad at the freshers' ball. He was also from London, and Carol was relieved that here was someone that she at least shared something in common with.

"You're not going to believe this," Neville began in a middle class accent, as they danced slowly and closely on the floor, "but my ex-girlfriend from last year is over by the bar with her new man."

Carol saw a tall, leggy blonde girl exchanging loving looks with a broad-shouldered white guy.

"She's trying to make me jealous. The relationship is

over but she's playing games."

Carol simply carried on dancing, not knowing what all of this had to do with her. She was only dancing with the man, and really didn't feel like hearing about his ex.

"Would you mind if I kissed you?" Neville said suddenly.

"What?"

"It's just that I want her to get the message once and for all that it's over."

Carol stared up at him. What a cheek! If he wanted a kiss why didn't he just ask her straight out? Why did he have to involve her in his jealousy game?

"That's got to be the worst chat-up line I've ever heard," she told him, declining the invitation. She had come up to university to get a degree and she wasn't about to begin cavorting with some stranger in her first week.

After that first encounter, Neville kept his distance for most of the rest of their time at university. He spent a lot of his time playing rugby and cricket. When they did bump into each other in the library they would exchange pleasantries. He would ask how her course was going, and she would ask about whichever game he was playing that term.

Then Carol finished her first year and didn't see him again. He got his degree and went back to London, and she heard that he had taken a job in the city.

There were few distractions for a young black woman up in Durham, so she got on with her studying for the next two years and kept herself to herself, spending a lot of time in the college library, searching out 'additional reading' and consuming as much information as she could. She went back down to London when she could afford it, to visit family and friends, and did what she could to keep her flagging relationship with Frankie alive if not exactly kicking.

Despite being separated, her parents put aside their

differences and came up together for her graduation, the reward for her three years hard work at Durham. With tears in his eyes, her dad cheered louder than any other parent when his daughter's name was called out during the ceremony. Nobody could have been more proud. After all his years as a bus driver in England, seeing his beautiful daughter walk confidently up to collect her degree certificate from the university chancellor with a mortar board on her head and her long flowing black gown... well, it was his reward too. Mrs Ballantine, Carol's mother, was quiet and smiling, her heart crying the tears she refused to allow her eyes to shed. Her baby's finest hour was too precious to witness through misty eyes.

She had worked hard to ensure that her children were would want for nothing. By day she typed schedule sheets at one of the government ministries and in the evening her job was as a mother: cooking and cleaning, doting and disciplining. Mrs Ballantine always knew that Carol would do well, but she had come through with flying colours. Very few students called up to the stage had been awarded first class honours.

It was five years after that when Carol ran into Neville at a networking dinner for black professionals in a small basement wine bar off Regent Street. The place was packed from on this Wednesday evening with already-made-it and up-and-coming careerists. It was Neville who introduced himself.

"You were at Durham, weren't you?" he asked.

She didn't recognise him at first. The short-cropped beard he had at college had gone, and a dark pinstripe suit, a pair of wide, striped braces and a colourful tie had replaced the rugby shirts and tracksuit pants.

"Don't tell me, I'll remember in a minute. It's on the tip of my tongue... Carol! You're Carol Ballantine!"

"And you're Neville Edwards, I haven't forgotten you. We danced together at the freshers' ball."

"Is that when we met?"

Neville had no recollection, and only faintly remembered the blonde-haired, blue-eyed, leggy ex-girlfriend. He now worked for an American bank in the city, he explained, buying and selling currency. To him it was a job like any other, a means to an end — the end being to make enough money to retire by the age of forty then spend the rest of his life doing all the things he really wanted to do.

"Weren't you reading law at college?"

Carol looked up, surprised that Neville could have remembered that.

"Yes, that's right. But now I'm working as a researcher for Beverly Marshall."

"The MP? That must be really interesting work, but what's the pay like?"

"I happen to like the job," she retorted. "I'm interested in pursuing a career in politics myself, this is the best way of getting a foot through the door and learning the ropes. It doesn't pay that well, but money isn't everything."

"No, it's not everything. But it's the only way black folk get respect in this country."

Carol had gone to network, but ended up spending three hours talking to Neville. They chatted like old friends about characters from their college days, and each admitted wishing that they had gone to a college closer to home. He insisted on toasting her each time he lifted his wine glass: "To the scholar, Carol Ballantine"; "To old acquaintances"; "To new friendships". It was all done in good taste, and quite amusing, Carol felt. At the end of the evening her memory of their first meeting at college was so distant that she agreed to a dinner date at his club in Soho the next week.

He was the perfect gentleman, holding car doors open for Carol and pulling her dinner chairs out before sitting down himself. Then, after dinner, he helped her on with her coat. When she protested that she wasn't entirely helpless he insisted that he was only acting out of respect and affection for her.

It took several dates before Carol would agree to consider their relationship as anything but platonic, even though she enjoyed his company and his attention. Neville was everything she wished Frankie had been — well-read, charming, eloquent and confident. Frankie had used every excuse not to better himself, and kept on whining about how she had changed, as if his not having changed at all were something to be proud of.

Frankie and her friends had got it all wrong. It wasn't university which changed her, it was education. She had spent three years at university doing what she most enjoyed doing, learning. She had loved the experience, and never stopped appreciating the opportunity. So, when college had finished, she had finished with Frankie too.

That had been the start of a five-year break from men and relationships. She was more interested in travelling, her work, and her girlfriends than she was in dating. She and Frankie had been together for so long that he still featured heavily in her thoughts, and he called several times after they split, hoping that she would reconsider, but he really wanted what she had been, and not what she had become. That was clear to her, so that was that.

Neville's timing was spot-on. After five years, Carol was feeling ready to be the focus of a man's attention again. He proved that he knew how to treat a lady and showed that he was prepared to work hard to become her man. He would call her from work five times a day for no other reason than to say, "I love you," and he was always coming up with interesting evenings for them to enjoy together: an evening at the theatre followed by a leisurely river cruise had been one of her favourites.

She finally consented to start seeing him officially after he sent her twenty-six cards, one for each year of her age, on her birthday. Each card had a different message: 'You spice up my life — happy birthday!'; 'I want you to get to know me better'. Then there was a single tulip with the message 'My two lips long for yours' under the windscreen wiper of her car when she stepped out of the house. Carol smiled to herself when she read the card.

She had never been romanced like this before, and before her next birthday she had became Mrs Carol Edwards and they had moved into a cosy two-bedroom house in a fashionable part of Wimbledon.

Even though they were married they behaved like lovers for the first year, playing romantic games together, eating breakfast by candlelight and having dinner in bed. They were both overjoyed when Carol became pregnant. Neville must have been the proudest father-to-be in London. He was sure the baby was a boy and quickly made plans to put the lad's name down for Eton at birth. In the evening he would bring home a bottle of Dom Perignon to celebrate another day of his wife's pregnancy, and when he had to work in New York for a couple of weeks, he had a fresh red rose delivered to his wife every morning, each one with a different message attached.

When Junior came he seemed to be a healthy child in every respect, except for his jaundiced eyes. The doctors soon discovered that the cause was sickle cell anaemia. Neville said that it was impossible. Didn't there have to be sicklers in both parents' families before the child could inherit the disease? That wasn't the case, they discovered. Both parents only had to have the sickle cell trait.

Carol accepted the fact that it would play a major part in Junior's life. She didn't apportion blame, and she got on with the business of being a mother. Even after their blood tests, Neville was convinced that the doctors had made a mistake in his case, and it began to eat away at him.

Nothing could have prepared them for the shock of seeing their son during a crisis. Junior was in and out of hospital continuously and had to undergo several blood transfusions, a dangerous procedure for such a tiny baby.

Carol had to resign from her job as Beverly Marshall's researcher in order to stay at home to look after Junior full time. Neville got a promotion and was earning more than enough money to support the family comfortably, so she didn't need to work for financial reasons anyway.

Of course, their relationship changed. Neville denied that it had anything to do with her, and told her he was suffering the same pain in his head as his child was suffering in his joints and in his chest. But whatever her husband was going through, Carol knew that it was *nothing like* what Junior was suffering. The doctors explained that sickle cell was like no other pain a human being suffers.

After she had joined a sickle cell organisation, one veteran sufferer had tried to describe the pain for her.

"Your chest feels like it's on fire and the pain in your joints is similar to someone stabbing you in the core of the bones in your body," the woman had explained. "The pain is *so* intense that if someone offered to chop your hand off to get rid of the pain, you would say 'yes' right away. It consumes your entire body. The painkillers don't really help, at best they take the edge off the pain, but it is still there. Sometimes they don't have any impact at all."

What had happened between her and Neville wasn't the worst of it, but it was bad. Their life together had changed so much, and so quickly. They didn't laugh and joke as they had previously done, they hardly ever went out together, and they made love only occasionally and at the weekend. Neville simply didn't seem interested. He had once said that he loved her curves. Now he said she was fat.

Carol was putting every spare ounce of energy she had into studying the illness which so regularly sent her child into hospital. She would try to lose the weight she had put on since childbirth with wonder diets, miracle milk shakes, and powders and pills, but whatever she tried didn't work. All she was losing was Neville, who became more and more of a part-time husband.

Junior's illness would abate every now and then, but it never went away, and as he got older the pain he suffered during a crisis seemed to intensify. One thing Carol and Neville did still have in common: either one of them would have changed places with their son in a second to take the pain for him. But that wasn't an option, and they did all they could. Which amounted to standing by helpless, powerless and useless.

Then Junior was five years old, and he died.

Neville became like a stranger in his own home. Trying for any more kids was completely out of the question. Carol suggested that they adopt a child. Neville wouldn't hear of it. If he couldn't have his own blood to continue after him, he wasn't interested. They weren't even sleeping in the same room together any more. Neville had begun to sleep on the floor in Junior's room.

He didn't seem to know or care how his wife felt. He told her to go back to work, even though he knew how hard that would be for her after five years at home. Even going back to her old boss, Beverly Marshall, was out of the question. The MP had lost her seat.

Carol still held out hope that someday her husband would accept their baby's life, and his death, for what it was. If they could say goodbye to him together, she believed, then perhaps they could go on together too.

She tried everything to stimulate his interest in her again. They hadn't had sex for so long that she took matters in her own hands one evening. When Neville came home from work, Carol greeted him at the door wearing a big red ribbon and nothing else. His face twisted in disgust and he rushed through the door as quickly as he could in case any of the neighbours saw. Then he went straight up to his study without giving her a second glance. He just wasn't interested and nothing was going to change that. As far as he was concerned he was performing his marital duties by bringing home money every month, he told her grimly, and that should suffice.

So, Carol tried the other way to a man's heart, and guess what: that road was blocked too. Neville proved utterly indifferent to her culinary creations, turning his nose up at her creamy mustard chicken and rice, and even at his favourite old-fashioned salmon patties with broccoli sauce. Even the cakes didn't do the trick, 'though he had always had a sweet tooth for them. She baked everything from orange blueberry country muffins to coffee cakes, but all Carol ended up with was a craving for her own food.

A month before Christmas she had discovered that Neville was having an affair. He told her he was going on a trip to the bank's New York office, but he clearly didn't even respect her enough any more to cover his tracks. Two return-trip airline tickets to the Canary Islands fell out of his suit pocket when she was preparing it for the dry cleaners, one in Neville's name and the other for a J. Ridgley, Neville's secretary.

So, there she was on the carpet, with nothing to look forward to and only memories of heartbreak, misery and tragedy for company. They say if you love someone, set them free. Carol had set him free, and he had flown away to the Canaries. Was that what they meant? Was that what was supposed to happen? He had gone, but then he came back and made her wait until Christmas Eve before he told her that he was leaving her.

After all they had been through together, he had gone out of his way to destroy her entire Christmas on the first anniversary of her son's death. She spent most of that night phoning everybody to cancel Christmas, patching the front door glass, and hoovering up the remains of the tree.

Christmas Day was quiet and lonely, thinking about her

marriage, eating mince pies and fruit cake, drinking rum and praying for her son who was no longer alive. Her heart yearned for Junior so much, she burst into tears whenever she thought about the brief time they had had together.

"Ms Ballantine?" the blonde woman asked with a pleasant smile when she came out to reception.

Carol looked up. She knew immediately that she had got the right woman.

"My name is Carol Edwards. You've been sleeping with my husband."

The blonde woman's face dropped and she looked around nervously at the other people in the reception area, hoping that Neville's wife wasn't about to create a scene.

"We best talk about this some other time."

"No. No other time. Do you make a habit of having affairs with married men and breaking up their homes? Because if you do, people should know about it."

She didn't get to answer. Her mouth was open to speak when Carol picked up her shoulder bag and swiftly hurled its contents over her. Looking around at the swathes of black gloss paint on the carpet, the telephones, the windows and all over the secretary's long blonde hair and beige dress suit, Carol felt the first down-deep-from-the-belly laugh she'd had in five years beginning to force its way up and out of her.

And when she stood there laughing, watching a huge round dollop of black paint dripping into the top of the fizzing, sparking computer terminal in front of her, she felt, for the first time, that maybe the worst of it was over.

She had put a stop to it.

Carol didn't hang around for security to get there. But on the way out of the office she was already wishing she had brought another tin of paint for Neville. She skipped across London Bridge to catch her train back to Wimbledon.

When she got home there were already a couple of angry messages on the answering machine. "You need your bloody head examined," Neville screamed down the line. "If you come near me or Jennifer again, I'll call the police."

She wiped the tape and called a locksmith. She didn't know how she was going to do it yet, but she was going to pay Neville back for the way he had treated her.

And paint was just the beginning.

DON'T HOLD YOUR BREATH

One thing I know for sure, I'm not going to be young forever. I've got to use what I've got to get to where I want to be, while I've still got it. Nobody's going to notice you in a small town like Bristol. You've got to go to where the action is — London.

When I finally decided to leave Wayne, it was painless. Yet again, he had come home so late it was early and flopped into bed after another "ruff session" at the Bug Out Club where everybody knows him as Bad Bwoy MC John Wayne.

"It was pure roadblock down there tonight, y'know, Donna," he had explained sleepily, "and I had to work 'nuff-'nuff to set the crowd on fire. But me have some *sweet* loving for you in the morning, baby."

Wayne insisted that he didn't "want no downtown and no sixty-nine", no matter how much he loved his woman, and his idea of hard work was rapping on a sound system every weekend. It made him feel massive and 'broad'. Big deal. He spent the rest of the week chewing on the end of a pencil, writing rhymes — that was overtime. So there he was 'working overtime', loafing, and there I was working as a waitress and bringing in the money. I put it all together that night as he snored softly in the bed beside me — reeking of smoke and Dragon Stout. He was easily satisfied, while I was made for better things and was wasting my time hanging around the neighbourhood going nowhere.

Contrary to popular belief, women are quicker to terminate a bad relationship than men. And when I flicked through the past year of my life with Wayne, seeing images flashing in front of my eyes like snapshots in a Kodak ad, I was sure we were reaching the end of the roll. I am a romantic realist, and I knew then that I was going to London alone.

I had been all ready to move to London when I met Wayne — 'Mr Cool an' Deadly', or, more appropriately, 'Mr Mention' — twenty-five years old and with skin as smooth as fine leather. He was exciting to be with, and he seemed to want the same things as me. I knew an agent who had said that she could get me work dancing in music videos. That wasn't going to make me rich, but at least I'd be in the right places, meeting the right people, rather than in Bristol twiddling my thumbs.

Love is a woman's weakness, and what I felt for Wayne at first was something close to it. He was the only one in the bar when he swaggered in that first time, mobile phone in hand, and ordered a 'Blueberry Hill' in a cone. Maybe it was his seductive smile, maybe it was the twinkle in his eye. It's funny to look back on it now, but yeah, I admit he had me weak at the knees. I dipped into the freezer for his order, he passed a few complimentary remarks, I told him to behave himself, and we exchanged mischievous glances. Before I knew it, I was giving him my home number.

Strictly sexual attraction, you understand.

I wanted to sleep with him. I thought, what the hell. I had a whole summer to kill in Bristol, I may as well enjoy it. That intimate summer together was the best we were gonna get. I got to know and like Wayne more each day he came into the bar for his 'Blueberry Hill', and in the evenings at the movies, in the quayside cafés, and with me simply resting my head on his bare chest in his parked car in the woods overlooking the city.

Sex, of course, was safe. Wayne was one hundred percent lust and lustful, he knew exactly how to give the agony and make it hurt so good.

He was going to move up to London in the New Year, he said, to try his luck in the music business. We got ready to move to the capital together, allowing ourselves six months to save up cash to take in case we didn't get work immediately. I worked two jobs and saved as much as I could. I even moved in with Wayne because it was cheaper. I kept prodding him along, until I saw he was depending on me to do just that. One day I stopped pedalling like hell and looked around, and there he was sitting on the back of the tandem with his feet up, riding *my* ideas and *my* dreams.

Wayne was still deejaying at weekends, but he was spending the money he earned during the week.

"Don't worry 'bout dat, baby," he replied every time I asked him how his saving was going. "Everyt'ing is taken care of."

Of course, he hadn't saved a penny. But when it all came out in the open, he shrugged and said that he wasn't all that bothered about going to London after all. If it happened it happened, but he was in no hurry as certain things were happening for him in Bristol and he wouldn't mind hanging around waiting, if necessary.

"But Wayne, for goodness' sake, why didn't you mention this before? We've spent six months planning to move to London. You know what it means to me, and now you tell me that you're not bothered. Thanks for nothing, Wayne."

He made out that he had only just decided it was better to be a big fish in a small pond than to try to compete with the millions of other people in London.

"I need time to sort myself out," was what he said.

I want an unspecified amount of time to carry on raving to my heart's desire and to 'deal' with any admiring females I come across on my travels.

Was what he meant.

The bottom line? Wayne was scared of leaving the town he grew up in. If he had his way he would rarely leave the familiar surroundings of St. Paul's, let alone Bristol itself.

That was where all his friends were and that was the place he called home, and he was just afraid of disrupting his life too much by moving to the big city. I had to face the facts: while I was with Wayne, I would never get to London.

I'm not a woman that hangs around waiting for something to happen. I'm independent, spontaneous and adventurous; when I see something I want to do, I go for it because no amount of dreaming is gonna get it. I want variety and excitement in my relationships, and I want to make the most of my life.

Which means that Wayne and I weren't exactly made for each other. We were each made for other people would be more like it. Whenever I made demands on our relationship, Wayne would always reply in a whiny voice, "I'm too busy", "I'm too tired", "Maybe next week", "I want to be romantic, but I'm just too forgetful."

And then along came Donald, at a New Year's Eve party in Clifton where I was shocking out in a black wet-look shorts and blouse combination and a peroxide blonde wig.

So I looked at him and he looked at what he probably thought was me and I knew right away that something was going to go down. We danced a couple of slow numbers together, after which he coaxed me into the bathroom on the pretext that he had "something serious" to say. Inside, we stood kissing deeply and intently for several minutes. It was hardly a romantic setting, but I felt romantic enough. In fact, I hardly noticed the other party-goers taking turns to bang on the door. He was an all right-looker, but nothing special and I told him that I was other people's property. He didn't seem to mind that at all, and said that we could be discreet, that nobody but us would know if we had an affair.

"I can take you places you ain't been before, baby," he offered.

I told him that I was only interested in going to London and asked if he had a car.

He said fine, he could deal with that.

"My car is at your disposal."

By the end of the night, I had weakened. Donald lay the seduction on fast and thick, and I knew that it was either go back with him or go home to an empty bed, which is no way to see in a new year. We did it at his house, and he seemed to enjoy it, but for me it wasn't exactly memorable. He did promise to take me places I ain't been before, but I certainly don't remember writing any postcards home.

Wayne stumbled home with the milkman again the following night, and I made up my mind to call Donald early and tell him I was ready to go the following day.

Almost immediately, I regretted agreeing to drive to London with Donald. He pulled up in an ice-cream colour VW Golf with a humungous boom box and some mad mix tapes of all the latest junglist music.

"Nice car."

I didn't recognise it in daylight.

"Yeah, man," he said proudly, stroking the white leather steering wheel. "Nice, y'know."

We loaded my gear into the car. Wayne was upstairs sound asleep, his body drained after a night of passionate love… Well, I had to give him something as a going-away present.

I had left him a note without a forwarding address. I didn't want him coming looking for me. That was the whole point of embarking on a new life without him. I didn't want to be dragged back to the way we were, emotionally or physically, ever.

I knew one thing for damn sure. If I didn't put my feelings for Wayne aside, my dreams could never come true.

We hadn't gone far down the motorway before Donald started acting odd. His hand slipped from the gear shift onto my thigh. He gave my knee a gentle squeeze and flashed a toothy smile.

"I really enjoyed making love after that party," he said. "I'm looking forward to the next time."

He winked at me knowingly, then as if to get me in the mood, pushed a cassette of X-rated ragga music into the Golf's stereo system.

Having sex with him was a mistake. I know what good sex is and that wasn't it. And, as far as I could see, Donald had nothing else to offer me.

When it comes to love and sex I know what I want and how to get it. If you've got a positive attitude, you'll attract partners. But you mustn't try too hard to find someone. If I was interested in Donald he wouldn't have had to ask:

"So how interested are you in me?"

I looked at the motorway sign. It was still a long way to London, so I leaned back on the headrest and let Shabba's bassline tickle the base of my spine before answering. When I did speak, I was diplomatic about it.

"Well, I'm looking forward to us becoming really close friends…"

That didn't exactly satisfy Donald.

"Friends? Friends! Forget dat, lovers is what we are."

He started moaning about black women, how they were dissing the brothas and how they had to stop it and start supporting them to the fullness instead of playing games and teasing and misusing. I began to fear that Donald would expect a payment 'in kind' for driving me to London. I had already given him petrol money, but I thought I'd better offer to take him out to lunch when we got there.

"I don't want you having to go into debt just to treat me

47

well," I said, but he didn't catch my drift.

"Don't worry," he replied, his eyes fixed on the road, "I'm going to *nyam* my lunch when we get to London or before, take your pick!"

He slapped my thigh hard and grinned to himself, then turned up the music some more as Shabba's voice came over the speakers singing 'Mr Loverman'.

Donald thought he was being smart when he turned off the motorway suddenly and pulled into a lay-by. I had to play smarter. As he yanked his handbrake up till it clicked, I was reaching over in the back seat for my handbag.

"Look, Donny, could you be a dear and turn your back for a minute?" I said in the sweetest little lovey-dovey voice I could manage. "It's just that, well, before we… well, you know… before we… do the sex, would you mind very much if I changed my Tampax? It's just that, you see, I've been bleeding really heavily all night long, darling…"

I peeped at him over the top of my economy-size box of tampons, and hit him with my most cutesy-wootsy smile.

I guess he was just no longer down with 'gettin' down'.

An expression of acute distaste came across his face, and next thing he was dropping the clutch just as hard as he dared. He spun the steering wheel all the way round and with his tyres screeching executed a hasty U-turn back to the motorway.

Which was the only rubber he was gonna burn for a while, if I had anything to do with it.

He was rather quiet for the rest of the journey. He kept his mind on the road, and Chaka Demus and Pliers replaced the X-rated stuff on the stereo.

I had to diss him one more time, however, when we arrived in London. He started talking his funny business again and said that he was going to come down the next week to check me for his 't'ing'. I told him that I didn't have an address, and lied that I would call him when I had one. But Donald wasn't quite as dumb as he was horny, and he wasn't going to be fobbed off.

He said that, in that case, he would keep my luggage for me in the car and drive it back with him to Bristol until I called.

Shit!

Double shit!

How was I going to get out of this one? The last thing I wanted was to give this creep my new address in London. As we waited at a red traffic light, my salvation came in the form of a police car.

"I'll just ask these cops the way," I told Donald as I wound down my window.

"Excuse me, officers. We're from Bristol and we're a bit confused… We were told that you can drive in London with no MOT on your car. Is that true?"

"What… the… fuck…?"

Donald was going seven shades of purple. But there was not very much he could do to keep his horny hands on my holdalls now. The two officers in the patrol car indicated that we should pull over to the side.

Donald obeyed meekly, cursing me under his breath, perspiration dripping from his hands and neck. I didn't waste any time. As the cops were giving the VW a thorough inspection I was flagging down a taxi and flinging my suitcases inside.

"Y'know, I told him those tyres were bald, officer," I called out as I hopped into the taxi, confident that I would never see Donald again.

'Yeah... I wouldn't mind a bite of that.' The cab driver glanced in his rear-view mirror at his elegant passenger. She looks nice too, he thought, checking her out. He hadn't even minded when she asked him to re-tune his radio from Jazz FM to a soul station.

That was how good she looked.

Dee sipped from her Evian thoughtfully as the cab drove through the south London suburb. She hadn't been to this part of town before, but from what she could see of the quaint little Victorian cottages and the quiet tree-lined streets, Wimbledon seemed pretty fashionable.

The cab pulled up in the middle of a grey-brick terrace, and Dee checked the house number. Yes, this was it. She told the driver to keep the change and rang the bell.

Carol switched off the vacuum cleaner and waited, listening. The bell rang again as she unplugged the Hoover and shoved it hurriedly into the cupboard under the staircase.

She briefly studied the business-suited woman with the 'ring of confidence' smile on her doorstep.

"Hi. I'm here to see about the room."

"You must be Dee."

"That's right, and of course you're Carol. I am so pleased to meet you."

Dee stretched out her hand. Carol led the way into the house.

"Let me show you around upstairs first," she said and made her way up, the visitor close behind her.

"Mm-m-m-n!"

Dee was immediately impressed as Carol opened the door to the spacious bedroom. The decor was immaculate:

a spotless, fitted, white lambswool carpet went well with the walls, which were also white with a subtle hint of yellow. In the centre was a double bed and to one side a dressing table. The dark green velvet curtains hung down to the carpet.

Carol took her through the rest of the house, to the upstairs study and the bathroom, then back down to the split-level open-plan living room and the kitchen to the side and the little refectory at the back overlooking the large garden.

Carol smiled. The American woman seemed nice, and certainly liked the place, but she wanted to know a lot more about anybody who was going to move into her house with her. They sat together in the conservatory.

"This place is really nice, believe me. I've been looking at a lot of places, but this is the best I've seen, I've got good vibes about this place already, and I would really like to take the room."

Carol poured out two glasses of iced tea from the decanter on the glass-topped wicker table beside her, then offered Dee a slice of home-made double chocolate cake.

"So, Dee, tell me, which part of the States are you from?"

"Oh, I'm really from Baton Rouge, Louisiana, but I've lived in Chicago for about seven years."

"Chicago, hey?" Carol said with a glint of recognition. "Al Capone... The Untouchables."

"Please, honey," Dee retorted, playing up her Southern drawl and pointing a disapproving finger at her hostess, "Ain't nobody in Chicago 'untouchable', and the only Al I know is the guy who owns the local deli on my block."

They laughed together over their glasses of iced tea.

"And how do you find London?" Carol asked.

"It's a beautiful city. Really. The buildings are so old and there are lots of really quaint places to visit. I just love Buckingham Palace. But so far I haven't had much time to socialise, and I haven't really been able to meet too many black folk. You know I'm working for an English company, and most of the people I meet in advertising seem to be of the 'caucasian persuasion'."

Carol wasn't the only one who wanted to know a little bit about who she was going to live with.

"It's my turn to ask you a question," Dee smiled. "Why are you renting out the room?"

"My husband walked out and left me. So I need the money."

"I'm sorry." Dee said quickly. "I really didn't mean to pry."

"Oh, that's all right. It's not a big deal. I read that two out of every three black marriages end in divorce, so I shouldn't have been surprised. And I'm really not bitter about it any more; breaking up is the best thing that has happened to me for a long time. I finally put an end to all those wasted years with him. Have you ever been married?"

Dee shook her head.

"Lucky you. All the things I could have done if I hadn't married… Men get the best deal out of marriage, because becoming a husband is better than becoming somebody's wife. Anyway, I'll never have to look at another dirty pair of men's briefs in the laundry basket. That's why I specifically requested a female flatmate in the advert, I've had enough of men."

Dee was sorry she'd asked. Carol was trying hard to make light of it, but if she's not bitter then I'm Hilary Clinton, she thought to herself. Maybe she could do with a friendly ear.

"He left you for another woman, right?"

"Yes, his secretary — blonde hair and blue eyes, long legs, big tits, you know the score."

"Oh, jungle fever," Dee remarked with a sigh. "Another brotha with a white woman. What's the deal with all this inter-racial dating anyway? It seems like half the brothas I've seen in England are dating white women. You see a lot more of that here than in the States."

"Who knows? I've heard all kinds of explanations, that white women give them an easy time..."

"Please," Dee cried out, raising her hand to say 'enough'. "I ain't falling for that tired old talk, girlfriend. Nobody's as easy on the black man as the sistas. But when we ask for a little respect in return, the next thing we know they're running after some white woman because of all the pressure."

The two women enjoyed the joke together.

"You know what the hardest thing about becoming single again is, Dee? You waste so much time going back over what went wrong in your relationship that you don't get anything done. I know it's wrong, but I feel like my husband's still got his claws in me. And looking back, you don't just see what he did to you, either. That's part of it. But you see yourself in a different light as well. I've started to really question why I ended up ignoring my first impression of him, which was *not* favourable, and then wound up married to him. He was such a big part of my life for so long, and now even though he's gone, and I don't even want to think about him, he's still right there in my mind every time I turn around."

Dee disagreed.

"Ungh-ungh! That way's not for me chile. I've got better things to do with my time than think about my ex. 'Cause he's history and I've gotta keep on movin'. Let me tell you something, since I broke up with my man I've been going places, 'cause I shut him out and focused my *full* attention on my career. I think that's what you've got to do."

It looked to Dee like black women in Britain and their counterparts in the States had plenty in common. She and Carol obviously shared the same problems and the same desires. And suddenly it was like they were life-long buddies. She poured herself more iced tea and went on:

"Whatever the situation, you must admit that black men come up with some lame-ass excuses. My ex in Chicago had some good ones. Things never worked out between us. Sure, he was a good looker and he had potential, but the thing was he wanted me to make all kinds of big concessions. His favourite excuse was, 'You know, it's difficult to have a true intimate relationship as a black man, we're already so *exposed*'."

Carol agreed that was a good one, and they both laughed. She could tell that they would have a lot of fun together, and was about to offer Dee the room when the doorbell rang again.

"Hello there. I'm Donna."

Eyes. Clear, dark, round eyes, looking right at her without a flicker.

For about half a second, which is a lot longer than it sounds, Carol stood looking puzzled into those eyes. Then she saw the rest of the picture: a brown-skinned woman standing on her doorstep in impossibly high heels, flimsy black bell bottoms and a minuscule white blouse. With three suitcases.

"Pardon me. Can I *help* you?"

"It's me, Donna," the girl said, blinking her large, bright eyes excitedly and flashing a million-dollar smile, in between chewing gum rapidly. "I've come about the advert... remember, I called up yesterday? You have got a room, haven't you?"

Of *course*! Carol had completely forgotten about the talk they'd had on the phone. She took another look at the younger woman's 'distinctive' dress style. Donna was the type of woman who was going to get noticed wherever she went. Anyone who judged books by covers would know what to make of *this* slim volume right away. Just standing there she was making Carol feel like someone's grandmother.

"I'm sorry, my dear, but the room has just gone."

My dear? She thought to herself, astonished. *I've never called anyone 'my dear' in the whole of my life!*

Disappointment was all over Donna's face.

"But you told me that you wouldn't be making your decision until everyone had been in to see it."

Carol had forgotten that also. She felt uncomfortable, but what could she do? She had made her mind up about Dee, and that was that.

"I'm afraid the room has gone."

"But I've come all the way from Bristol…"

"Then I'm sorry you've had a wasted journey."

But that didn't sound like a granny, she realised. It came to her. *That's what Neville would have said.* That startled Carol. Neville would have been polite but firm. He would have seen the clothes and the suitcases and sent her packing straight away. Maybe he was still part of her life in ways she hadn't even thought of.

Carol was thinking quickly now, adding up. She had intended to see everyone who came before she chose a flatmate. And she hadn't actually offered the room to Dee yet. But then she *was* going to offer Dee the room. And sharing her beautiful house with a spike-heeled, gum-chewing, cartoon-strip good-time girl had *never* been part of the plan.

But then she looked into those eyes again. First impression. First impression. First impression. Not what you think you see, or what you hope or expect or want to see. But what is. Carol flashed back to that first half a second, time-travelling. She had seen good things in those eyes. Not things that Neville would have seen. And she wasn't about to do what Neville would have done. Not any more.

"Look, Donna... I've just made a jug of iced tea, why don't you come in for a minute, take the weight off your slingbacks?"

She grabbed up the bags, and Donna teetered into the house behind her.

"Oh, this place is just perfect," said Donna, looking around her at the luscious living room and through to the conservatory.

"Hi, I'm Dee," the American said, offering her hand. She had overheard their conversation on the doorstep, and Donna's arrival had placed her in an uncomfortable position.

"Dee, this is Donna. I'm afraid there's been a bit of a mix-up. Donna's come quite a long way, but I was about to offer the room to you."

"A hundred and twenty miles," Donna stressed.

"Is it really as far as that?" Carol asked, trying to keep it light, but managing only to create a lengthy and painful silence in the conservatory.

"That is such a shame." Donna plonked herself down on one of the cushioned wicker armchairs. "I've got a feeling about this place, it's just right."

"That's exactly what I said."

"So you've moved to London?" Carol asked.

"Yeah, today. Been trying to get up 'ere for about a year... finally, you know... just left... Best way. Don't think about it, just go."

Dee giggled quietly.

"Y'know, we were just saying the same thing about men!"

"I'm all for that..." Donna was warming to the subject, "... but you ladies *do* realise that there's a national shortage, don't you? And if you're planning to change horses in mid-stream, you do need more than one horse, or you just end up all wet with nowhere to go!"

Carol chipped in:

"Well, Dee, at least you come from a country that has men like Blair Underwood, Denzel Washington and Larry Fishburne."

"Oh yeah. But those guys aren't exactly standing on every street corner. Believe me, I've looked. And if I'd found one of them over there, I certainly wouldn't be comparison-shopping over here."

They laughed and each woman admitted that they would see nothing wrong with a little bumping and grinding with Wesley.

"Every woman should get at least one chance in her life to actually meet a man like Wesley," Donna added.

Neither Dee nor Carol could see anything wrong with that either.

Carol had begun to feel she had made the right move, inviting Donna in. The younger woman seemed bright and cheerful. Maybe she would be fun to have as a flatmate. She was already acting like one.

"You know what you want to do with this place," Donna volunteered. "You want to get rid of the carpet in the living room. What have you got under there, floorboards? Yeah well, I would sand down the floorboards and polish them with some clear varnish and that would make a wicked living room."

"You think so?" Carol asked. Well, the youngster was bound to be cheeky, but she had no side to her. In fact, Carol had thought about doing the very same thing herself, but had never got around to it.

"So the room has gone, then, has it?" Donna wasn't going to beat about the bush. There was that silence again, till she chirped up: "Got any other rooms, then? I mean, I wouldn't take up very much space. I'm quite small really, I just look tall, that's all. 'Cos I mean, I'll be honest, I am desperate. I was kind of counting on seeing this place and I've got the deposit with me. Plus which, I've got nowhere else to go."

As Carol and Dee had by now both figured out.

"I mean," Donna continued, "I'll take anything you've got. I could even just crash in the living room, or right here. I could get a little mattress, which I'd fold up every morning and fold out late at night after everybody's gone to bed."

That was definitely *not* a good idea, Carol thought.

"Look, I feel really responsible about this whole thing," Dee offered. "I don't know how you feel about this, Carol, it's your house, but I don't mind sharing my room with Donna at all."

Carol shook her head. No, that wasn't necessary.

"Why are you so desperate for somewhere to live?"

"I had to leave Bristol. I was in a relationship which wasn't going anywhere, with a worthless man. It was stifling me, being stuck with a man without ambition, who couldn't see that I needed more. Where's your black man when you want some emotional support, eh?"

"Well, what's a real man?" Carol asked. "Men think they know, but they can't define it."

"A real man," Dee began, "is a responsible person who can stand alone if necessary, a man who can be warm, comforting and kind, a person who doesn't need to prove his masculinity all the time, a man who doesn't give his penis too much attention, because that means he gives his woman too little attention."

"You can't cure a cocksman," Donna added.

"I know exactly what you mean," Dee said, pouring out some more tea. "A lot of black men hate to admit it, but hey, the truth is the truth. Sometimes I think that the only reason I don't act like the men do, is that a woman in my position doesn't get that many chances."

So they talked together like sisters, unaware of the hours ticking away. They all agreed that the implications of falling in love quickly were more complicated for women and that, while the men were big on the 'love at first sight' syndrome, they, as conscious black women, owed it to themselves not to fall for the same old flim-flam. Finally Carol decided that there was just one way for *both* of her new-found friends to move in. She turned to Donna:

"There is another room, but I'm warning you, it's tiny. It's a study at the moment, but we can move the books and computer..."

"Believe me, that would be just fine," Donna insisted. "All I need is a wardrobe-size room and I'm happy."

So Donna went upstairs with Carol to view the room, liked it, and they shook hands on it immediately.

"I really have to thank you for this," she said. "I don't know what I would have done otherwise. You don't mind if I move in right now, do you? It's either that or a park bench!"

"Yeah, I had kind of guessed that," Carol admitted, then they all toasted their future together with a bottle of chilled white wine.

INDECENT PROPOSAL

One of the first things I need to know when I meet a man is what kind of a relationship he has with his penis. Men take their sexual organ much too seriously because it's the only childhood toy they get to keep and play with for their entire life. Forget what they say about dogs, the penis is truly man's best friend. It never deserts him, even when his woman does. Maybe that's why a lot of men are willing to risk everything they have, everything they've built up — their career and their home and family — just to keep their penis happy.

I soon realised that I was the only black face at Splash Advertising. And even as I was being shown around the firm's large, bright, open-plan office on the fifth floor of a Croydon high-rise block I spotted a couple of guys nudging each other and leering at their new creative director in an explicitly sexual manner. That was the first time, and it was going to be the last time too. I was prepared to show them that this was one sista who could take care of herself.

I had no trouble fitting into the company. The job was basically what I was doing for Frazier Clarke in Chicago; the accounts were equally large, and the salary was considerably larger.

I had no complaints, except one. There were no black people in the company. Every now and then a black motorcycle courier dropped in to pick up some artwork, but apart from that I was on my own.

I never felt so isolated as I had in those first two weeks in London. I would go to Splash every morning and come back to an empty hotel room every evening, with no one to offload onto, no one I could relate with. A couple of times

I even went out with some of the people from the office when they asked me to, but it wasn't the same. At the end of happy hour I would take a cab home to my hotel room with an empty heart, to spend another evening alone. My new friend, Helen, one of the receptionists, was always suggesting that I should go out 'raving' with her on the weekends, but I didn't take her up on it. I wasn't really enjoying myself or meeting the kind of people I wanted to meet. Helen wanted to go downtown to the pubs in Covent Garden. That was her idea of a good time, but not mine, so I came up with excuses to make sure that our social contacts ended after work.

"A lot of women wish they were in your shoes. They'd like to have your looks, your chances in life, your job, the way you attract men… and you're complaining."

"But where are all the black folk?"

Julian Phillips was too typically British to understand where I was coming from, but when he asked me if I was enjoying working for the company I told him straight that I was disappointed not to see at least one or two other black faces.

He was young for an account executive but older than his years, and he always liked to give the impression that he wasn't just in charge of the department but also always available to give advice on domestic problems. I wouldn't say I actually *liked* him though, especially after I turned round one morning and caught a glimpse of him admiring my behind. But I decided to let that one go for now.

Julian seemed shallow and self-centred, but what really put me off in the first two weeks of working under him was that he didn't seem to have good professional judgment. His main task was to explain agency thinking to the client and client thinking to the agency and to act as a focal point for the agency's activities. But his mission in life seemed to be acting as an unelected agony uncle.

Julian was always offering to 'lend an ear or give a friendly word of advice' on any personal issues, but only occasionally displayed an interest in creating brilliant ad campaigns and keeping the firm profitable. He made a show of wandering around the office, praising everyone when things were going well. But on the few occasions when we genuinely needed his help he never seemed to be around.

He offered to drive me around to some of the more 'ethnic' areas in London after work one day, and I had nothing waiting for me back at the hotel, so I accepted. We cruised around Brixton, Peckham, Battersea and Streatham in his elegant dark green Jaguar. Even from a distance, curled up in the comfort of the leather passenger seat, I could tell that I would feel right at home in these neighbourhoods.

We decided to stop at a brasserie in Brixton for a drink. Julian said that I would like the place, and he was right. For the first time since I landed I found an abundance of elegantly dressed black men and women who looked like they were going places. While I was making plans to come back — without Julian — I noticed his lips moving.

"Pardon me?" I yelled over the music from the loudspeakers. He tried again.

"I've been out with a few black women, you know,"

Big deal. Am I supposed to be grateful that he has graced Black Womankind with his attention, I wonder?

I was still sipping my first glass of white wine. Julian was on his second or third beer. He flashed me a self-assured smile as we moved to an empty table further away from the sound system.

"Oh yes, I consider myself an 'equal opportunity dater', you know…"

If he goes on like this, I'm going to have to seriously consider throwing up.

"And I've noticed one thing. My black dates seem to dress better and are less frequently overweight than my white dates. Now why do you think that's the case?"

I told him that it didn't surprise me.

"And I've known black women who weren't earning that much but who were spending half their salary every week on getting their hair done."

What does he know?

"Is that so?"

I mean, he wasn't telling me something I didn't already know

"So how do you really like your job with Splash? Come on now, you can be frank, it's off the record. Don't think of me as your boss."

I looked around me in the brasserie, at the young black couples in their his and hers Karl Kani 'college' outfits, sitting whispering sweet nothings to each other over bottles of wine. I sipped my drink. Yes, I could tell Julian exactly what I thought about the job. I didn't think for a second that he would understand, but I could tell him.

"I like it. I am really enjoying myself. I'm having a great time being in London and the people at Splash are cool, I've met some really nice people."

I stopped before I got caught in my own exaggeration. Julian smiled.

"I'm sure you're going to be very happy at Splash, and I am sure that we are going to be very happy with you."

He touched my hand gently as he was talking. I didn't know whether he was just trying to reassure me, or trying something else altogether. Either way, I didn't care for it. He caught the waiter's eye and indicated that he wanted another beer,

"You'll find us very reasonable… and you'll find me very fair. I don't expect much."

He laughed, thinking about it.

Julian was surprised to see that as a black woman I was

more attracted to black men than I was to him. I didn't try to hide that, and I did explain that it wasn't a political thing, it was just a preference.

I told him that white men and black men have to compete for my time on equal terms; the days when marrying white would have been a stepping stone to social advancement for me are long gone. I would date a white man who appealed to me enough, I explained. That just wasn't something that had happened yet.

The drink and the music were loosening Julian up nicely. If he had been sober he would never have given me such a clear picture of his scheming and dealing. I knew what to do; I just sat back and smiled, and let him talk, picking up all the information I could along the way. He told me all about how good he was at his job, and all about how he would deliberately lose at golf just to get an account.

"That's how it is out there in the real world," he said proudly. "Forget all that politically correct crap about the proper way to do these things. It's dog eat dog out there and I don't intend to be any dog's dinner. That's why I'm trying to set up a breakaway. My own agency. And if I do... *when* I do, I might just take you along."

The time must have whizzed by, because suddenly it was 11.30pm. I looked at my watch when I noticed Julian's head jolt back after he nodded off briefly.

"Are you all right?"

He hiccoughed and said he was fine, but he clearly wasn't. I had stopped counting after three or four beers plus the liquor shots, but the waiter who was clearing the table raised his eyebrows and held up eight fingers for me to see as he saw me looking at Julian's car keys. Terrific; how was I going to get back to my hotel now? He was in no condition to drive his Jaguar.

To be honest, I was pissed at having to accompany him in the cab. Julian was practically asleep by the time I got him a taxi, and the driver said he wouldn't take him anywhere unless I was going too. What could I do? I pushed Julian in, climbed in after him and shook him awake for long enough to find out his address.

He slept all the way home.

It was midnight when the cab pulled up outside Julian's penthouse apartment overlooking the Thames at Surrey Docks. I told the driver to wait for me while I pulled, pushed, dragged and coaxed Julian up three flights of stairs. He was tall, and heavier than he looked, and I was suddenly very glad to have put in all those hours working the free weights at the gym.

His apartment was immaculate, with pale blue carpets throughout that looked like they'd never been walked over, pale blue walls that looked like they had been recently decorated, and a Swedish television set and stereo. His furniture all looked like it had only just been unpacked.

The moment Julian flopped lifelessly on his brand-new bed I took off his tie so he wouldn't choke, rolled him into the recovery position, dumped his house keys on the coffee table and got my butt out of there — only to find the taxi driver had done likewise.

Damn. I had only been gone a few minutes. I looked all around, the streets were deserted. There wasn't a single car in sight. Aside from the river waves lapping softly behind me, there was silence. I walked around looking for a payphone or a cab, but Julian seemed to live in the middle of nowhere. I found my way back to his apartment building and leaned on his doorbell for seven or eight minutes before he answered, sounding jacked.

"Julian, it's Dee. Buzz me up."

"Dee? Oh... Dee, come up."

The door clicked open.

"What happened?" he asked, dazed, as I reached the top of the stairs. He was still dressed the way I had left him, in his crumpled grey suit and white shirt. He still stank of alcohol.

"I couldn't get a cab," I said stiffly, trying to contain my anger at being compromised into this situation.

"You'll have to stay here," he suggested, with a concerned look on his face. That didn't seem like a good idea at all. So he gave me some numbers and I tried calling for a cab, but every taxi firm I tried said they were rushed or had nothing in the area.

"Look, trust me, you can stay here. You can sleep in the bedroom and I'll sleep here on the sofa."

I had heard lines like that before. Every time a man says 'trust me', alarm bells ring in my head. But I didn't have much choice. I was tired, it was late and I didn't know the area well enough to take my chances on the cold, dark, quiet streets.

Julian gave me a nightshirt, toothbrush and towel and I washed my face in the bathroom. I was too tired to think of anything but sleep and soon flopped down on his ample bed with its satin sheets.

The next thing I knew, there was Julian standing butt-naked over me in the near-darkness, about to climb into bed. I looked up at his scrawny white body ambling towards me with his manhood standing to attention in front of him, and did the second thing that came into my head. Because laughing out loud just wouldn't have had the effect I desired. I rolled out from under the duvet and lashed out, feeling the heel of my left foot jolt as it made contact.

The noise he made straight away told me what it had made contact with. Julian decided it would probably be best to crawl back into the living room, which took a little longer than he had anticipated on account of him having to keep one hand between his legs to prevent uncomfortable testicular pendulations.

I rolled back into bed, pulled the cover over my head to

keep out the terrible groaning sounds he was making in the other room, and went back to sleep.

I woke up early as the sun streamed through the bedroom window, dressed, and tiptoed through the living room where Julian was wheezing lightly through a deep slumber, then slipped out of the door without waking him.

I took a taxi back to my hotel in town and freshened up, before taking a train out to Croydon. When I got to work, my office had someone else's name on the door.

"Helen, what's going on?" I asked.

"Morning, Dee. I was going to ask you. We got a call from Julian saying you were going to swap offices. Something about a mix-up."

I asked where my things were, and she pointed to a tiny cubicle across the hall, in the darkest part of the office. I was fuming.

"Right. Where is he?"

I was ready for war.

"Oh, he's not in yet."

"Well, honey, as soon as he steps through that door, I would like you to let me know. Could you do that for me, do you think? I'll be... in there."

I didn't mind waiting. I hadn't come all the way from the States to be messed about by Julian or anybody else.

Julian kept a low profile for the rest of the day. I didn't really feel like working too much either. Not until this 'mix-up' had been resolved. So I went and sat in my cubicle with a blank sheet of paper and a croissant, brainstorming copylines for my new campaign.

I waited for him all day, and the next day also, but he didn't show. By the time he dragged his sorry ass in on the third day, I was ready for him.

I caught him on the way into the building. He snapped off his mobile phone in a hurry as he saw me bearing down on him in the lobby, and I cornered him in front of the elevators.

"What the heck are you playing at, Julian? I would like to know, right here, right now, why you've been going behind my back and playing games with my office."

In a typically stiff upper-lip British manner, he asked if I would mind very much discussing the matter in his office. I followed him in.

"I must say that I'm disappointed, Dee. As your line manager, I really must insist that you address me in a more respectful manner while we're at work."

"Cut the bullshit, Julian. Why have I been moved to that shoebox?"

I was steaming, the anger had been boiling up in me for two days and at that precise moment I didn't care if I got fired. I was ready for the worst.

"As I explained to Helen, there's been a mix-up," he said. "I had simply overlooked the fact that the office we allocated to you initially had already been earmarked for somebody else. I *do* apologise."

I looked at him hard, his eyes were laughing at me. I knew he was lying, and he knew I knew.

"Be brave, Julian, and tell me the truth. You'll feel so much better about it if you admit that it's because you couldn't make it with me the other night."

"As I told you, Dee. It was all an unfortunate mix-up. But surely you must know that it pays to keep your superiors happy."

His eyes laughed at me again.

"Julian, there's nobody else here but me and you. How about you just letting me know where I stand? If I had let you have sex with me the other night, would I still be in my original office?"

Julian was pleased that I was catching on.

"Exactly."

"And if I keep you 'happy', my time here will be happy?"

He smiled again.

"You're getting the picture." He moved behind me and caressed my shoulders slowly with his hands. "And if I'm not happy, you won't be happy, because you'll be without a job and without your job you'll lose your work permit."

I turned around and pushed him away. He laughed it off, no doubt believing that I'd come crawling back when I'd accepted that he held all the cards.

Well, when I came back, it wasn't gonna be crawling.

I went all the way to the top man, the managing director, showed him my tiny tape recorder and sat in his office while I watched him play the tiny tape. The old man almost choked on his cigar. He didn't need to hear more, he knew what the implication was. He buzzed his secretary and asked her to call their lawyers immediately. The lawyers arrived after an hour, by which time Julian had been summoned. He didn't know for sure what was going on, but when he saw me there he decided attack was the best form of defence.

"I was going to let you know as soon as possible, Maurice," he addressed the managing director, "that with regret I was forced to sack Ms Robinson earlier today for gross misconduct."

"Don't worry about that now, Julian. You've been working too hard, much too hard." The old man patted Julian on the shoulders like you would an old and faithful hound. "You're going to be going away on holiday for a while, old chap."

I almost felt sorry for Julian. Almost.

SCREWFACE

Carol looked on enviously as a typical 'renaissance black family' passed her by in the fruit section of her local supermarket. Dad looked proud pushing a trolley laden with food, with a new-born baby in a sling around his neck and a little girl hanging onto his hand while she sucked her thumb. Mum checked her list as she selected the week's provisions. That was how it should be, Carol thought. It was a living picture of everything she had ever wanted. Surely she had as much right as anyone else to a loving relationship?

Going to the supermarket every Friday evening had become one of the highlights of Carol's week. Donna and Dee's rent money meant she could once again buy little luxuries like crab meat, fresh pasta and smoked salmon. Her sister, Janice, told her that supermarkets had become a popular meeting place for singles — they provided an opportunity for people to make eye contact several times without commitment, and without having to speak to each other. Since then, Carol had half-seriously kept one eye out, scanning the aisles for furtive couples swapping phone numbers and bodily fluids, but so far she hadn't seen any 'action' between the fresh pasta and the baked beans.

"If you shop at the same stores, at the same time, then you'll meet the same people."

At this time of night there were quite a few men popping in to the supermarket for groceries on their way home from work. The contents of their shopping baskets would often show which ones were planning to eat alone. Janice had also recommended laundrettes and bookshops for meeting single black men.

As she stood in the queue at the check-out, Carol felt someone staring across at her from the next checkout. She tried to ignore it, but the back of her neck was burning, so she turned to see who it was. A tall, dark-skinned, average-looking, thirty-something man in a grey pinstripe suit smiled at her warmly. She thought she recognised his face from somewhere.

"Carol? Hello... You don't remember me, do you? Kelvin, Michelle's brother... Michelle Johnson, Hornsey Girls, remember?"

Of course, a blast from her school days past. It must have been twenty years at least. She remembered Kelvin, Michelle's older brother. When you are fourteen, you readily give your heart to sixteen-year-old boys.

Nobody, but nobody, knew about her secret teenage crush on him — a crush which had come back to haunt her at regular intervals ever since. Years later she would think about him and wish she could have turned back the clock and gone with him instead of Frankie.

Kelvin helped her to load the carrier bags into the back of her Escort, then they stood chatting about the old days.

"So how are you doing?"

"Fine," Carol said with a smile, "really fine."

"Hold on a minute. Yeah, I remember now," Kelvin recalled, "didn't you once have a bit of a crush on me?"

"Did I?"

"Yeah, you did. My sister said it was a big secret and told me I wasn't allowed to let on."

"Are you sure that was me?" *Oh... bloo... dy... he... ll!* "I don't think so. I'm *sure* I would have remembered something like that."

Kelvin was rubbing his chin with a big smile on his face. Enjoying watching her trying to wriggle out of it.

"Yeah, I am pretty sure it was you. And I'm pretty sure she said it was a crush."

She suffered through it until he showed mercy by

71

changing the subject and talking about work. He explained that he was now a pensions salesman and said that he was doing it for the money, which was really good.

"Do I remember somebody saying that you got married? How is your husband?"

Carol lied and said fine.

"What a pity. I was hoping you might be free and single so that I could ask you out. But I don't suppose your husband would appreciate another man inviting his wife out to dinner?"

"No, I don't suppose he would."

She didn't give Kelvin any room for manoeuvre and they said goodbye to each other without exchanging numbers.

Men had proved to be a disappointing experience for Carol, even though she had tried hard to make her relationships with them work. She hadn't found Neville that attractive while they were at college together, and had even kept her distance when he sought to begin a relationship with her. Looking back, she had seen how many fundamental differences of opinion there had been between them, about money, religion, and politics — he wanted to raise Junior as 'black British' while she wanted to raise their son as 'African-Caribbean', for example. But at least they enjoyed each other's company and had fun together at times when they weren't worrying about their son. They gave each other plenty of space, and the relationship offered them both time to relax and chill out.

But then, after Junior died, everything changed. Neville's personality became like a huge iceberg, with so much lying beneath his skin. They seldom went out together and when they did he openly flirted with other women.

Junior's death had brought Carol close to the face of death. It had made her realise that the one important thing in life was love. No matter how Neville behaved, Carol had been emotionally tied to him because of the son they had shared. If anything, she now loved him more deeply to fill the emptiness of their joint loss. She tried to be everything he wanted her to be and made sure she said "I love you" to him first thing in the morning and last thing at night. He was hurting too, he also needed healing. By the time she had accepted that, she had become irrelevant to a large part of his life. She felt too old to become a single woman again, so she kept up the 'happily ever after' pretence to friends, family and herself.

Nobody said marriage was going to be easy, but she and Neville had known so many couples who had managed to make it work, who had learned the ability of making it through thick and thin, together for richer and for poorer, and stayed happy.

It was hard to go suddenly from spending every night for eight years with someone to being on your own. During the day when she was alone in the house, Carol would lie on the living room sofa playing her Billie Holiday until it made her cry. Who feels it knows it, and Billie *knew* it, her mournful voice the echo of a thousand shattered dreams, a million broken hearts. Like Billie, Carol knew that she had to forget her no good man and pretend that he had never existed, but she couldn't help flicking through their wedding album, trying to relive the memories of the good times. At least she had got the house.

After the episode at his office, Neville didn't want to have anything more to do with his wife and he got his lawyers to begin severing all links. He was only too eager to accept her lawyers' demand for the house to be transferred to her name and for papers to be quickly drawn up for an out of court settlement. The bank had been having a very good year, and he was flush with money after receiving an extremely generous bonus, so Neville had been able to pay off the mortgage.

So she came out of it with a roof over her head. But

Neville had abandoned her when she had needed him most, and said things which she could never forgive him for. His lying and cheating and insensitivity, and his willingness to use their son's death as an excuse for his own infidelity, had destroyed her faith in black men.

She had been almost consumed with thoughts of revenge, constantly planning ways to make his life a misery. But the more she plotted to make him pay, the more she felt that Neville was still in control of her life. What she needed to do was to live her own life instead of wasting her time trying to destroy his.

It was time to explore her options. Like Kelvin, for example.

Why had she not encouraged him? Even as she rejected his advances out of hand, Carol was wishing that she hadn't. Dinner with an old flame would have been just what the psychoanalyst ordered. But, as much as she needed the healing, her memory told her that her life depended on not deepening the wound.

When they said 'dinner', too many men meant 'oral sex'. And Carol strongly felt that she had nothing to win by taking a chance. Her hurt had been so deep that she would have to re-learn how to love, one small step at a time.

Carol woke up in a passionate sweat. It had been so long since she had slept with a man. But that wasn't what she wanted in her life either. She was still young and there were countless things she wanted to do. She would deal with being single by engaging in other activities. She could adopt a child on her own, or go back to school part-time. She would continue her work with the sickle cell support group which had helped her so much during Junior's suffering. A friend had asked her to review films for the local newspaper and Carol had become something of an 'expert' recently. She would earn some money and go on trips to Africa and Asia, or out to dinner, or to the theatre. She would have any hairstyle she wanted, after all she no longer had a partner to stand and criticise it if he didn't like it. She would improve her physical appearance by shedding the extra pounds she'd been accumulating for the last few years. She would learn a foreign language and even learn to play the guitar, just for fun. She would go up to Birmingham to visit that old school friend she hadn't seen for years, and visit family and friends more regularly. And she would pamper herself with small luxuries. But never again, she vowed, would she give up any part of herself to someone who did not truly love her.

She had suspected that something was going on for months before Neville admitted it. He stopped asking her how her day had been and they no longer made love, for, while she sat in bed needing a hug, Neville snored in Junior's room. While he slept, she went through his diary, sniffed at his shirts and searched his hard disk for clues that would confirm her suspicions of his infidelity. She found nothing, not even after going through the counterfoils in his cheque book.

She came within an inch of throwing everything away and having an affair herself. It was the summer, after they'd been fighting a lot. Neville was away on business, and Carol thought, 'What the hell, I'm going to a bar to see if I can get lucky.'

As she was preparing to head out for the evening she removed her wedding ring. It took her nearly five minutes to do it. As she fought with the gold band, it occurred to her that she had never had that ring off her finger in all the time that she had been married. She stood in the doorway holding the ring, before going back inside believing that her marriage was worth more than a casual affair.

BOOPSIE

Men don't see nothing wrong with a little bump 'n' grind unless their woman's doing the bumping and another man's doing the grinding. But hey, I just wanna have fun. I'm in London and I'm having a fantastic time. I've landed on my feet, with a great place to live, earning just enough as a waitress and it's that time of year — Spring — when women come out to play. I'm not gonna turn down so many offers from men who want to do "anything" for me.

I didn't really want to live with two women in case they felt a way about me having several partners at the same time, or even one after the other. A lot of women can't handle someone who can jump in and out of relationships at the toss of a coin. But Dee and Carol are cool. They pretty much get on with their own lives and don't mind me getting on with mine.

What's a girl to do?

Everywhere I go some guy toots his car horn and offers to give me a lift or carry my bag. Every time I go raving, bouncers chat me up in the queue then just wave me through without paying. All of this happens because I like to dress in a way that attracts men, not for their money but more for what they can do for me.

Alex is as close to a 'boyfriend' as I've got. The others are just casual flings, but Alex is a real buddy.

We met at a house party up in Hampstead. After work one Saturday night at Corrina's, the Clapham Common restaurant I wait tables in, a bunch of us piled into two cars and ended up in an expansive house on Haverstock Hill. Four different sounds played, one on each floor — junglist in the basement, soul on the ground floor, ragga on the first floor and rap on the top. The place was live and so were the people. Alex had gone there with some of his arty friends. He was doing a fine arts post-graduate course at the Royal College of Arts in Kensington and he was dressed suitably artistically in a purple denim Chairman Mao jacket with a back to front baseball cap on his head. His dancing was as sensitive as his nature. While everybody else bopped to the ragga in rowdy fashion, Alex sort of flowed with the bass line to a rhythm that was not from the speakers but in his head.

We shared a rum and coke out in the chilly darkness of the garden and our joking somehow developed into a challenge to see who could come up with the best insult jokes: "Your boyfriend's so ugly his doctor is a vet," Alex threw in.

"Your sister's so stupid I told her it was chilly outside, so she ran out with a knife and fork."

"Your boyfriend's so stupid he tripped over a cordless phone."

"Your brother's so ugly when he sits in the sand the cat tries to bury him."

"You're so stupid, on the job application where it said 'sign here' you wrote 'Aquarius'."

We fell about laughing and tickled each other playfully. When it came to be time to go, it was clear to me that I was going to spend the night at Alex's place in Brixton. It wasn't clear to him though and he stuttered for a moment, before getting the courage to suggest it.

His flat was at the top of a four-storey Victorian house on Landor Road. It was small enough, but seemed extra tiny because he shared it with Leo, another black artist from the RCA. Everywhere you looked there were huge paintings of stunning African women with proud expressions on their faces. Those were Leo's stuff, Alex explained, handing me a mug of Ovaltine. I had only half-finished my mug before we were in a passionate embrace on his mattress.

I know what good sex is, remember?

I don't always have the time to drop everything and enjoy sex like I'd want to, because I live such a hectic life. Part of enjoying sex is being happy just cuddling up to a lover and falling asleep in each other's arms. But most of the sex I was getting was just a case of 'in out, in out, and shake it all about'.

I know that the way we made love, Alex had never experienced the like before and because it was so satisfying to him I knew that I had the power of influence over him.

It wasn't just because it took him until the morning to recover, but because he confirmed it afterwards, between gasps of air as he lay on his back, my head cradled in his arm. He hadn't had too many sexual experiences, he confessed, and he certainly hadn't had to work that hard before. He promised that he would run up Brixton Hill every morning to build up the stamina he was going to need.

Me, I 'just wanna have fun', and the next morning I told him so to make it clear.

"I'm enjoying myself too much to think about anything more serious. I've just come out of a relationship that wasn't going anywhere, and I don't want to spend my time locked in another one right now."

Alex nodded, said he understood and that he could accept things as they were.

"Are you sure about that?" I asked. "Are you sure you can deal with seeing me with other men all the time?"

"Look, Donna," he said, "I've had a great time with you and it's going to get better. As long as you know that I'm the guy who really checks for you, I don't mind being 'friends'."

I wasn't convinced but I left it at that. Men are always saying they want to be friends, but it always ends up with them wanting more than that, becoming possessive, and turning up at all times of the night and day and calling 'round unannounced.

But Alex was right, it had been a great night and it could have gone on that way, if the early morning sun hadn't risen.

"Don't get me wrong," I said, "but I don't really believe in all this fidelity stuff. I believe in love and marriage and everything and I want those things one day, but dating Mr Right has lost its significance for me. I don't believe that love means that you have to stay with that same person for ever."

Alex insisted that he agreed.

"I don't expect my woman to stay faithful to me for ever because I know that, just like she needs to take a holiday from work every year, she may need to take a break from me also. As long as she knows that I need to take that break from her as well, everything's cool. I don't think it does any harm, and it probably does some good, because there are people out there whose marriages have been improved by taking a break from each other."

We spent most of the next day together. We started off by having breakfast in bed, staying there to read *The Observer*. He had the broadsheet whilst I read the profiles in the fashion supplement. As it was Sunday we decided to take the underground up to Camden to look around and do some shopping. Alex said that he could see I loved earrings, and that he would like to surprise me some time with some that he had chosen himself except he didn't have the confidence to buy them for me, because my taste in them seemed so personal and wacky. I told him to pay closer attention as we browsed through the market stalls, and he would see the method in my madness.

I first met Lloyd when he came to the restaurant for lunch with a colleague, both carrying an array of mobile phones and beepers. He was only twenty-six, but already owned a

79

string of pirate radio stations up and down the country. I noticed him straight away and kinda floated across the room to wait on his table. As I took his order, I noticed him undressing me with his eyes. It made me tremble slightly. But he eased my discomfort by making a joke about the lack of spicy food on the menu. He had light eyes and fine, crinkly hair. He continued staring across at me throughout his meal and then blew a kiss across to me as he left. After his generous tip, I felt obliged to return the kiss, giving him the green light to pursue what was on his mind. So that's the way it started.

I agreed to meet up with him on a whim, but had to wait a few weeks while he fulfilled his other commitments — ducking and diving out of the courts and paying fines for broadcasting illegally.

On our first date he took me for a long drive in his Mercedes 190. We had dinner at an expensive restaurant in Brighton, and then went on to a private gambling club where he was a member.

It was the first time I'd been in a casino and I just stood there watching the gamblers throwing chips at the croupier and losing them. But somehow Lloyd came out on top and we celebrated with a glass of champagne from the bar before the drive back to London.

On the journey home, with 'dirty soul' filtering softly through the stereo speakers, Lloyd admitted that he had a girlfriend whom he was about to dump "because she's a loser, and ignorant." He also let me know that he regarded me as "sex on legs".

"That's supposed to be a compliment," he added quickly when he saw the look I gave him. "I like your legs, is that a crime? I'm at a time in my life when I need balance and I think you could give me that balance. When I met you I was like, 'Damn, there's something different about this woman and the way she handles herself'."

Lloyd was a much better lover than Alex. He was

confident and knew how to handle himself well. He protested that he didn't believe they made condoms large enough to fit over his manhood.

"Never mind," I said. "See if you can wriggle into this anyway," and tossed one at him.

Compared to Alex, this was mature, adult sex, as dirty as it gets. I'd had sex like this before, but I'd never met anyone who would interrupt a lovemaking session to answer his phone.

Dating older men wasn't always a good idea. Vernon was forty, and a bank manager. He wasn't exactly handsome, but that didn't bother either of us over-much. And as far as he was concerned, his main asset was his income. He was old enough to be my father and he handled me gently and tenderly, but he couldn't understand that we weren't suited. He desperately wanted children, but the thought of settling down tied a knot in my stomach. I told him straight.

"Vern, honey, I ain't the one."

On our third date, he produced an engagement ring and said that he loved me. I told him that I loved him too, but I didn't want the ring. Well, it wasn't the first time I had lied to a man, and it wasn't going to be the last. I believe in telling them what they want to hear. Talk is cheap, and it makes them happy.

I got the shock of my life when he appeared at the restaurant the next day with a big high pile of wedding magazines for us to look through. I spluttered something about everything being rushed through so quickly and that, anyway, I was too young to settle down.

He looked dejected but assured me that he wasn't going to give up that easily. He was determined to "make an honest woman" out of me, unless he found someone who better satisfied his needs and was equally attractive in the meantime.

In the end I just laughed in his face. I couldn't believe he was serious, but Vernon didn't see the funny side. He disappeared, embarrassed, and I never heard from him again.

FITNESS

Dee was picking up provisions at the late night store. As she stepped out of her black Audi she heard a man who was standing next to a spanking new BMW shout after her: "Baby dat booty bad!"

She turned around angrily, staring the ebony-skinned man dead in the eyes. He wore a string vest over his T-shirt and dark glasses, and he sported a row of gold teeth; gold 'cargo' hung from his neck, wrists and ears, and a phone sat on his belt.

Dee hadn't learned everything about British customs and she was still not used to that particular flavour of behaviour that was distinctly Black London.

"Do I know you?" she asked angrily.

The man smiled nervously when he heard her accent.

"You a Yankee, then?" he asked, but Dee didn't stop to answer him.

"Look, asshole, you wanna talk about somebody's booty, you talk about your mama's, 'cause this is one behind you just can't touch."

He smiled.

"Baby gimme your number man, I like your style."

Dee blanked him and walked into the store.

It was late when she got home from work. Carol was sitting in front of the television watching *Imitation Of Life* and crying her eyes out, cuddling a half-empty glass of red wine.

"Hi, honey," she said, laying her briefcase down on the coffee table. "How's your day been?"

"Oh, nothing new," Carol answered, looking up from her tissue. "How was yours?"

Dee kicked off her shoes, flopped down on the sofa next

to her flat mate and complained that her job was still demanding more of her time than she had expected.

"I don't know why you watch that film, girl. It always makes you cry."

Carol wiped a tear from her eye and said that was exactly why she always watched it.

"Your sister, Glenda called, by the way. Nothing important, she just wanted to see how you were doing."

"I'm surprised she didn't ask you if I was dating anybody in particular."

"Well, actually…"

"You're kidding me."

"'S'true. But she said by the time you find someone you're happy with she will have to accompany you down the aisle in a wheelchair."

"That's what I get for coming from a large family of sisters. You know I've organised weddings for four of my sisters and been at the births of thirteen nephews and nieces. That's one of the reasons I had to get out of Chicago – because all I got was pressure from family and friends to get married. I've been through so many relationships which may have ended in marriage but for whatever reason didn't."

Carol smiled. She understood. Dee was one of a growing number of young and upwardly mobile thirty-something black women in the dating game and still single who had personally suffered due to the shortage of eligible black men in the professional classes.

"Hey, don't rush it, Dee. You should take all the time you need before deciding to marry. Take a tip from me, that's one thing you don't want to rush into."

"I hate it when old friends say something like 'Oh I thought you would be married by now'. Why would they say that if they know you're single? What purpose does it serve? Everybody wants to know what's wrong with you and how they can help you find a man."

"Oh yeah... but the one thing they don't tell you," said Carol, almost bitterly, "is that if you don't choose carefully, you're gonna be a *lot* better off single."

"Carol, as busy as I am right now, I would gladly make way for a family if the time were right. But, to be honest, I think that me marrying and having children becomes less likely as time goes by. It makes me sad, but I really believe sometimes that I will never get married... unless it's to Wesley of course."

Carol laughed. She, Donna and Dee had found out early that they shared a crush on Wesley Snipes, and would often talk about what they would like to do if they got hold of him. They would strap him to a bed all night, or get him in a bubble bath or a sauna, or ski down a mountain slope with him butt naked.

"Finding the right person just when the time seems right ain't easy," Dee continued.

"I've been searching for so long."

She always selected men who she thought were on the same level as she was intellectually or financially, she explained. Then she started talking freely about the crazy schemes she had come up with over the years to land a suitable partner.

"First you have to capture a man's attention. Then you've got to arouse his interest. And then you've got to make him desire you." That was Carol's contribution to the debate.

"But honey, you know my job is to sell anything. I sell myself as easily as I sell advertising, by using the most effective methods. But I want the man to sell himself too."

The conversation went like this for a while, before Dee decided to get her bag and go to the gym. She encouraged Carol to go along too.

At the gym, they only had time for a quick game of squash before closing time, but that was all Dee needed to work off the tension that had built up in her after a hard day at the office. When they got home, she soaked in a deep herbal bath with the bathroom light off, thinking of nothing and everything for an hour. She had an early start the next morning.

Carol also felt better for the exercise after the pounds she had gained recently – a by-product of all those irresistible chocolate chip cookies between meals. She had nothing planned except another trip to the gym with Donna the next day, so she sat down to watch another video before calling it a day.

Upstairs, Dee had just finished looking hard at the lines on her forehead in the bathroom mirror. Yet another sign of that biological clock ticking away. She returned to her bedroom and picked out an outfit for work the next day; the knitted navy skirt and jacket, stockings and low-heeled shoes made an appropriate outfit for a woman in her position. Preparations done, she turned to the package that she had brought home from work.

It was from Rex Publishing. She opened it to find a collection of Mack Daddy books.

"You know, you're putting on weight," Donna said in her usual frank way.

Carol grimaced.

She didn't need to be reminded that, instead of watching what she ate, she had been eating everything she could see.

They were showering in the changing rooms after a strenuous aerobics session at the gym. As usual, a number of male onlookers had been watching as the fifty or so women went through their routine.

"I'm telling you as a friend, Carol. You gotta keep in shape if you want to get a man and regain your confidence, because men only care about how 'fit' a woman is. It's all about the size of your breasts and the shape of your hips for them. And if you don't look good, your black man will never be yours entirely, he's gonna look around.

"You've got to smile and make them see your dimples. Didn't you know that smiling makes you look more attractive?"

Carol smiled. Donna's concern for her welfare was touching, but she was already getting back on her feet. She had started writing film reviews for the local paper, which gave her the opportunity to get out and about more, and could feel herself becoming more assertive every day.

"But your dimples are in such great shape. How am I supposed to win if I'm competing with a curvy young thing like you, hey?"

That was one reason why Donna always had a host of horny would-be boyfriends scratching and sniffing around her. But Carol was ten years older, and felt that it might be another ten years before she felt good about dating again.

"Look, Carol, it's no good being attractive and getting a lot of sex but no love."

"Better than being overweight and getting no love and no sex, though."

"Yeah, well... er... yeah. I've never really looked at it like that before," Donna admitted.

"When you've gone through some painful experiences, as I have, you'll know that men figure quite low in the order of things."

"Hey, Carol, I've been through some painful experiences also, y'know. The difference is I don't want to carry it all around with me. I wanna have some *fun* in my life, without thinking of all the worthless men out there who I've allowed to diss my life in some way."

Having changed, the two women walked out together through a throng of body-building men, one of whom whistled in their direction.

"You see that?" Donna asked. "He whistled at you."

Carol smiled. Did he hell.

"You know what I think?" Carol continued. "God should have made men menstruate. If they had a period to deal with every month they would have to cut out all the macho male bullshit and become a lot more sensitive."

Donna was laughing.

"Oh, you have got to be joking. Most of them would top themselves. They couldn't deal with that."

"Even better, men should be the ones who give birth. They should be the ones who worry about getting pregnant and suffer morning sickness and carry a child for nine months. If men suffered the pain of childbirth, they wouldn't carry on their lives having casual relationships here and there and everywhere. They'd have to think carefully before having their end away."

Donna laughed even louder.

"That wouldn't stop them. They love sex too much. No amount of pain is going to stop them getting it."

Carol thought for a moment.

"Yeah, you're right. All they want out of a relationship is good looks and sex, but they make out like they want the same things as women do like charm, maturity, honesty, warmth. You have a wide experience of men. Have you ever met a man who really wanted any of those things?"

"Errrr… no, not yet, no."

"You see what I mean?" Carol continued. "Right up to the day he died, my grandfather used to bring my grandmother breakfast in bed every day and he would always lay a fresh rose on the tray. When I asked him why he did this, he said he wanted to make sure that whatever happened during the day, she would know that he had woken up that morning in love with her."

"Mmm, isn't that a wicked story," Donna said dreamily, "your grandfather sounds like the kind of man I've been looking for all my life."

Carol hadn't met any other man who held a candle to Grandad either. For most men, romance seemed to be about having a huge dick and fucking like crazy.

Donna listened as Carol drifted off in her own thoughts. A sadness in her housemate's voice revealed the sorrow in Carol's heart.

"Your husband, Neville... he's still crawling about somewhere under your skin, isn't he?"

"Neville? No, I'm over him..."

Donna gave Carol her 'oh yeah, right' look.

"I wouldn't give him the mud off my shoe," Carol insisted. "It's just that my whole marriage would have been pointless if I haven't learned anything from it. Maybe I do want to find another man, but right now I don't want to be out there looking for a man and ending up with someone just like Neville."

"Maybe you should lower your expectations and just do like I do. I date for fun. Me, I can let a man think that I am really crazy over him, but I'm actually just in there to get what I want from it and then 'see you later'. Every now and then I make a man scream all night with pleasure, just because I'm having such a good time myself."

Donna and Carol had a good laugh about that one on the rest of the short walk home.

LET'S TALK ABOUT SEX

The postcard from André was waiting for me at the office when I arrived for work the morning after I moved in with Carol and Donna. It was the first contact between us since our evening together at the hotel in New York. I read it with a smile as I was once again reminded of him – the man my heart and mind told me was the one I had been looking for:

Hello Homegirl,

You're on my mind at the strangest of times. Wish we could have had more evenings together.

If you're in Chicago, give me a call.

Lots of Love

André.

The picture on the front was a scene from the movie *When Harry Met Sally.* I read André's words again unsure of their meaning. He hadn't mentioned his fiancée, which left me hanging confused.

I resolved to drop him a card with my new address.

The deal at work was this: Julian got paid off and laid off and I was promoted to account executive, with a higher salary and a company car. That way the firm would never hear anything about a lawsuit for sexual harassment. That sounded fine to me. I managed to keep Helen as my secretary also and got them to throw in a salary raise for her at the same time. After all, she had suggested the tape recorder trap when I told her about Julian's real motives.

In many ways, my new job was less demanding than being creative director. The only problem was that, as account executive, I had to lead the team and inspire them. I was used to working with a bunch of white guys, either on the same level as them or as their superior, so that part was nothing new.

But here I found myself responsible for motivating a bunch of advertising guys who really didn't want to sell anything. Just why are the British so embarrassed about selling themselves? Splash's creative minds spent their time dreaming up witty and clever TV and radio commercials but found the hard sell 'distasteful'. The agency had managed to hang on to its existing clients only because it was more convenient for them than going elsewhere. But that wouldn't last for ever.

Clients weren't going to care about how many awards the agency won if nobody was buying their product. I thought it was time the agency made a choice. Either sell the product or make a clever ad. In the States, the three rules of advertising are sell, sell and sell: *'You gotta a headache? Try this, it will make you feel better. You haven't got a headache? Try this, it will make you feel better'.*

Basically, the public weren't going out and buying the products that Splash worked on. The PR company of one of our clients had indicated unofficially that the client was about to review all of its existing advertising commitments. Which meant that they were almost certainly going to fire us. That was serious. I had to get tough. I called a meeting for the whole department, to announce the start of a new campaign.

They were all in the boardroom on time, the creatives, the media planners, media buyers, photographers, artists and illustrators.

"The first thing I want to say is that you all know me by now and you all know my name is Dee… I've heard all the jokes about dee-*cease*, dee-*feet*, dee-*lay*, dee-*kay*, dee-*light*, dee-*liver*, dee-*note* and dee-*va*. Unless anyone objects, I'd like you to finish enjoying the joke today, so that we can start working from tomorrow."

I looked around the room at each person one by one. I had made up my mind to kick butt. Now the only question in my mind was how hard.

"Next, the business we are in is advertising." I spelt it out in big and bold capital letters on the board behind me. "Translated, that means selling something that people don't want to people who can't afford it."

I looked slowly around the room at puzzled faces.

I hadn't expected them to appreciate it, but it was at times like this that I was grateful for what I remembered of my Master's degree in Communication.

"Consumers don't always know why they buy a product. That's why we all get paid nice fat salaries to tell them what they want."

The clients needed to know that they were getting what they wanted, which was increasing sales, and I had to explain how it would be done.

It was time to deal with the individual jobs. I started with the planners and worked my way up.

"So how come this production is going to cost much more than the client said he could afford?"

The planners are the people who research the product to start off with — what kind of people will buy it, *why* they will want to buy it and what socio-economic group they belong to. Planners are usually new college graduates desperate to get into advertising who feel that they can do everybody else's job better than them. They also decide which magazines are suitable to place our advertising for each product.

I stopped speaking and held their attention until one of the planners couldn't stand the pressure any longer.

"We ran into unexpected costs, the product had to be fully researched to make sure there was a market for it; and then we decided that if the client spent more money on the campaign we could do a thorough job. I'm sure people in Manchester would go for it but the budget was initially for London alone. With all due respect, Dee, every client says they can't afford a penny more but, when push comes to shove, they usually can."

"That's not the point," I fired back.

"The client pays your salary, he calls the shots. From now on any 'surprise' increases in budgets are going to come directly out of your salaries."

I heard somebody curse quietly, but I let it go. I had more fish to fry.

"Another thing. Stop producing reams and reams of paperwork; it's impossible to go through all those figures and statistics anyway. What I need to know from the planning department is whether people like the product or not, and which people liked the product and which people didn't."

Every copywriter is a failed poet and, as such, is very sensitive. But that didn't trouble me, I was on the warpath — determined to introduce professional US business methods to the English. It was the copywriter's job to write the words used on an ad or spoken on a radio or TV commercial. Everybody thinks they can do the job, but to do it well ain't that easy. I decided that it was about time someone knocked the egos of these 'writers-in-residence'.

"Maybe you should consider getting a job on a poetry magazine," I chastised the one copywriter who spent his days dreaming up fancy captions that couldn't sell anything. He blushed a deep red and avoided my gaze, probably thinking, 'who the hell does this Yank think she is?' They hadn't come to terms with having a woman superior, let alone a black woman superior, yet.

Well it was time they came to terms with it. I intended to make sure they knew who was boss and what I expected from them, right here, right now.

I pulled out a couple of books on copywriting from my briefcase and threw them across the polished table at the copywriters.

"Read them. If you can't come up with a good original idea, steal one from these books. If it was a good ad once, it's still good now, because people don't change that much. So spice it up and spin it 'round."

I looked around the room once more at each anxious face as it dawned on them that this was a totally new regime, and wondered what some of them had been doing all day. I made a mental note to let some of them go, because we didn't need more people; we needed better people. Besides, I would need empty rooms for the new people I was going to bring in.

Out with the dead wood, in with the new blood.

My art director was staring moodily into space, as he had throughout the meeting. He had an expensive habit of calling in freelancers when he was stuck for an idea. As the art director, he should never be stuck for an idea. That's what he was getting paid for. Well, he was already gone, so I left him to dream on, then closed the meeting by asking for suggestions for the new project, to be on my desk by the close of business the following day.

Every night for the next two weeks, I lay in bed thinking about André. I wondered what he was doing, and whether he was doing it with his woman; if he was...

Lucky her.

I wondered if he thought about me as much as I thought about him and whether, if I tried hard enough, I could will him to give me a call.

Could a man I had only spent one day with, a man I hardly knew at all, really mean this much to me?

Was that what love was?

Well, maybe it was something to do with the fact that I was away from home in a foreign country. Maybe I was lonely, or homesick, and just didn't know it. Or just the tick-tock of the biological clock inside me getting louder, reminding me that I was thirty years old and still single. Now it was my turn to start brooding and questioning what I was doing with my life. I started longing to be back home in the States, if only to get the opportunity to convince André that I was the perfect woman for him.

No way was I going to blow another opportunity with that man.

I couldn't believe what I was doing. Here I was, driving back to Wimbledon in my Audi with a handsome young man at my side and kissing and cuddling every time I pulled up at a stop light. I hadn't even intended to go to the brasserie in Brixton after work, but it was Friday evening and nothing special was happening and suddenly I was there, relaxing with a drink in front of me and watching the lively 'thank God it's Friday' early evening crowd coming in.

Maybe I *was* hoping to meet someone, but it was still a surprise when a handsome young hunk of a man with a charming smile and a polite nature about him came over to me and asked if he could buy me a drink. I looked up at him and smiled.

"No thanks," I said, pointing to an almost full glass of beer, but wishing I had said 'yes'.

"Well, would you allow me to bring my drink over here and join you?"

Now, I'm not normally in the habit of picking men up in bars. But I told him to go ahead, he went to fetch his drink and sat down opposite me. He introduced himself as Harvey and explained that he had just popped into the brasserie for a drink on his way to a party. He was a part-time model and a full-time student at East Herts University reading mathematics. He wasn't stupid enough to rely on his looks for success, like so many other male models.

"Quite a few models are really clever businesswomen, but male models have kind of a bad reputation for not having anything between their ears," Harvey admitted.

"And when you meet most guys in the business, you understand why. Generally speaking, the handsomer they look, the stupider they are."

I laughed when I found out he was only twenty-three and said that I was old enough to be his lecturer. He looked me straight in the eye, holding his gaze for a moment.

"I think I would like that very much," he said firmly.

I thought about it for a second, but decided it was best to let it drop. We continued talking. He seemed very interested in what I was doing and knew a lot about advertising.

"You know, if you're ever looking for a black model for one of your campaigns, maybe you could give me a call. Working helps me pay for my studies, you know."

He said that it made a change meeting a black American woman in London, and that he had always wanted to visit the States. He had a sister in Philadelphia who was always inviting him over, but he had never made it across to see her.

"That's what I love most about modelling," he said. "Despite all the long hours and hard work, it gives you a chance to travel. The places I've been to, I'm telling you, one moment in Paris, the next in Milan, and I've even been to Tokyo one time for a magazine fashion shoot. I could never have afforded to go to so many places without the job."

I couldn't exactly say when I decided that I was going to go home with Harvey that night. Neither of us said anything, but 'sex' was in the air. Harvey said he shared a tiny room in Clapham with a friend, which left me no choice but to invite him home to Wimbledon.

I started thinking that maybe I'd been a little hasty thinking of going back Stateside.

When we arrived back in Wimbledon the lights were all out. It looked like Carol had gone to bed and Donna was out as usual on a Friday evening.

The reality of what I was doing hit me as I stood in the familiar surroundings of the living room. I was bringing home a man for the first time to my new London home, a complete stranger.

It was crazy.

Whenever girlfriends in Chicago had confided that they had picked up men in bars and gone home with them, wasn't it always *me* who told them *they* were crazy? Here I was doing exactly the same thing. But I felt totally safe. It was hard for me to imagine a man with a British accent as anything but a gentleman.

"Maybe this isn't a good idea…"

"Anything you say," Harvey replied. "I'll stay for just one cup of coffee, then I'll phone for a cab."

I thought about how many times I had heard a man say that and how many times it hadn't turned out that way. I should have shown him the door immediately if I was serious about it being a bad idea, but I couldn't suddenly just send him packing after driving him so far out of his way. And Harvey had managed to chase away my blues and cheer me up when I was low. I thought for a moment about the postcard, and the Chicago police lieutenant whom I really wanted in my life. But André had Shawna, his fiancee, and I had nobody. I was longing for some intimacy in my life.

Harvey made himself comfortable in the living room flicking through the issues of *Pride, Newsweek, Essence* and *Marie Claire* on the coffee table. I took in our drinks.

"So Harvey, you read *Pride* magazine regularly?"

"I just like looking at the photos in women's magazines."

"Pride is the best black woman's magazine I've seen," I said. "The States has got *Essence* magazine, and that's good, but I couldn't believe there was a magazine for me in the UK which was even better."

Harvey waited patiently for me to finish my coffee before he put his arm around my shoulder and began gently massaging my back for me. For a man of twenty-three, he knew what he was doing and he gently probed all my tense spots, relaxing me. It wasn't long before we were kissing passionately on the sofa. Next thing I knew my hesitancy was gone.

Harvey wouldn't be riding a cab home that night.

Before I knew it I was sitting astride his lap with my skirt hitched up to my waist and his zip pulled down. I was glad he was sensible and had taken a condom from his pocket. My whole body seemed to explode as he entered me, slowly and stiffly. It seemed to go on for ever before he was fully in, deep inside me. I felt excited and confused as I moved slowly up and down on him, only just managing to catch myself from exhaling a loud and long-awaited sigh of pleasure.

It was nerve-racking.

What if Carol heard a noise and came down? I put my fingers up to my lips as Harvey's breathing became heavier and louder until he was almost gasping for breath.

It was going to be very hard to stay as quiet as we had to be. Hell, it was just going to be very hard.

I continued cautiously but firmly, raising my hips higher and letting them down harder and faster each time. I ran my fingers through my hair, enjoying every minute of it. I wanted to thank Harvey, because it felt so good. But there were more ways to love a black woman, and I wanted to roll around with him on my mattress, unrestrained and without anxiety. I coaxed Harvey upstairs. He was so powerful that he lifted me up, still inside me, with my legs knotted tightly around his waist, and carried me up the stairs effortlessly, his muscles bulging under his shirt.

I ran my fingers across them and felt the tensed-up power. I was in heaven and I didn't want it to end. We went as softly as possible along the upstairs corridor. But the loose floorboard outside Carol's room betrayed us.

"Who's that?"

"Oh, Carol, it's... mmm... oh-oh-only me," I called back, catching my breath for a moment. Talking was somewhat of a challenge, as he seemed to be filling me up as far as my throat.

"D-don't... bother getting up, I'm going to bed. See you in the morning. Good night."

Harvey carried me the rest of the short way to my room and, still locked together, we continued to make beautiful love on the bed.

The sun streaming through the window woke me up at midday. It was Saturday so it didn't matter that I had overslept. Then I remembered the night before. Harvey, it seemed, had already got up and gone. He was nowhere to be found. Neither were his clothes, my pocket book and my car keys.

And neither was my Audi.

WAKE UP AND LIVE

The stereo in the living room was turned up to full volume. It was the middle of the day and Carol was alone in the house dancing and singing to *I Will Survive* along with Gloria Gaynor.

Everything was turning out fine. She had just accepted a place at law school in the autumn to pursue the career she should have followed after her degree, she had two great girl friends as flatmates, and she had succeeded in banishing Neville from her thoughts. Their split was his loss. She knew what she was worth and she would never again settle for less. If she was interested, there were lots of men out there who were a lot more giving than Neville. And a lot of bastards who were better looking than he had been too, if she got really desperate.

It was like being given a new lease of life. And she was taking much better care of herself, too. There was a strict 'no crisps' rule in her house, and she'd been sticking firmly to her regular fitness programme down at the gym. She had even got rid of the wide-screen colour television in her bedroom, which had comforted her with romantic late night movies during her difficult time. The next door neighbours' kids were delighted when the lady next door presented them with the TV.

Carol hadn't felt this good in years, fresh and 'born again'. She intended to have fun in the few months before she became a student again, and she was determined not to allow any man to mess up her vibes.

She had made herself feel good for herself, likewise she aimed to make herself look good for herself.

She splashed out on miracle anti-ageing creams and beautiful clothes, she went and got her hair done once a week and started using make-up again. And as she got fitter, she threw out everything in her wardrobe and bought a whole new set of what she considered to be classy clothing but which Donna described as 'dry'. She even got her teeth straightened as she had wanted to for so long. It made a big dent in her meagre savings, but she would have borrowed the money to pay for it if she'd had to. It was worth every penny.

Her self-confidence had also been boosted by borrowing Dee's American self-improvement tapes — *Learn To Love Yourself* and *Success In A Month? Ask Me How.*

If she could feel good and better by herself, she could get on with her life without having to consider any man.

She read voraciously during this time, books of African fiction and travel as well as her favourite romance fiction.

"Yeah," she said aloud as Gloria's vocals faded out.

"I'm a survivor."

Her sister Janice had started coming around more regularly when Carol's marriage had broken up and she encouraged her to think positive.

"You're just a spring chicken," she said. "You're only thirty-four, with the whole of your life ahead of you."

Janice was twenty-eight and had been happily married for eleven years to Ollie. They had two kids, Shannon, ten, and Martin, seven, and had managed to stay together despite their differences. Ollie was the old-fashioned type who believed in the husband being the breadwinner and he was always complaining that Janice didn't need to work because he earned enough money for the both of them. But Janice had always been staunchly independent and Ollie had known this back in their schooldays when they first met. She loved nursing too much to quit, and still harboured dreams of one day becoming a doctor.

Recently, Janice had begun to invite herself around to

her sister's in the company of Ollie's unattached friends.

"Oh, me and Greg were just passing by, so I suggested we drop in for a cuppa," Janice said with a wink to her sister.

Carol didn't mind her sister dropping by any time she wanted to, but as she had already explained several times, she had better things to do with her time than "run after men all day long." Janice seemed determined not to take the hint.

Greg was thirty-five and, like Ollie, a powerfully-built fireman. The first thing Carol asked him when Janice brought him over was why he wasn't home looking after his kids, then she made the tea.

He assured her confidently that he didn't have any kids.

"You mean you don't have any kids anywhere?" she asked as they sat around the coffee table in the conservatory.

"Nope."

Carol could see Janice staring at her intensely, indicating that she should change the subject, but she ignored her.

"There's no little Greg junior somewhere who you've forgotten about?"

"Definitely not. That would hardly be something I'm going to forget about."

"So what's wrong with you then?" Carol said sharply. "Medical problem, is it?"

"Nothing like that. I guess I just haven't found the right woman."

"Well, you'd better not let me keep you from looking then. I mean, you being thirty-five and all, you're not getting any younger, are you?"

Janice looked at Greg sympathetically. Greg looked at Janice helplessly. Janice shrugged her shoulders and fired an icy stare in her sister's direction. Carol wondered if she had gone too far, but it was too late to begin regarding Greg as a potential date.

"Look, Janice asked me to come up here. I was doing her a favour," the fireman said coldly, getting up to leave. "She said you were desperate. I guess it's not hard to see why."

Greg didn't even bother to thank his hostess for the tea.

Janice turned briefly to look at her sister and shook her head, before following the fireman out.

"I didn't say 'desperate'," she called out with a warning finger, "I said 'available'."

Even after that, Janice didn't give up; when it came to finding unattached men, she seemed to have unlimited talent. She believed that there was a good man out there for her sister, and that all she had to do was find him.

Victor called because Janice had given him Carol's number. He was a thirty-eight year old stand-up comic with a sense of humour that could come in useful. He had obviously been briefed on how difficult Carol was going to be. He responded to her lack of enthusiasm over the phone, by sending twelve yellow roses around the next day and then passing by later that evening to check that they had arrived.

With the fragrance of fresh flowers and a reassuring smile he stood on her doorstep.

"Hi, you must be Carol," Victor said to Dee, taking off his hat.

Dee looked him up and down. He was dressed and groomed impeccably and had a wide smile to go with his happy face.

"Hold on," the American woman replied and went in to let her flat mate know that "a cute brotha" was standing on the doorstep with another bunch of yellow roses.

Carol sighed when Victor introduced himself at the door.

"I thought I told you not to bother coming around."

She was wearing her stony 'black man done me wrong' look.

"I'm not here to distress you," Victor joked, raising his hand, "I just forgot to send these along with the delivery this morning."

He presented Carol with another dozen roses.

She took them reluctantly, thinking that he had overdone the flowers slightly. She didn't mind being surprised with a rose once in a while, but gifts didn't impress her; anything she needed she could get herself.

"You're not going to ask me in?"

Carol studied him for a moment. It wasn't that she had anything against inviting him in, it was just that Donna and Dee were at home arguing about Donna's overuse of the telephone and Dee not returning Donna's hairdryer, and she didn't want this man embarrassing her with any corny lines in front of her friends.

"Well, I'm just on my way out," she lied.

"Well, why don't you let me accompany you?"

"Suit yourself," Carol said, and she went inside briefly for a jacket, before stepping out into the early evening.

She kept up a steady pace, walking down the road, with Victor keeping up as best he could at her side.

He said he would prefer to walk hand-in-hand. That sounded really stupid to Carol, so she ignored him and continued walking. She didn't know where she was going, just going for a walk anywhere until Victor had had enough and left her alone.

"You see, I'm a bit of a romantic..." he said, panting slightly to keep up. "As I'm sure you know, being a romantic is very unusual for a real black man."

Carol was unimpressed.

"Who says so? Did you read it somewhere? Did your father tell you that? Did you see it in a film?"

"No, nothing like that." Victor protested, "I just thought that that was common knowledge."

They hadn't gone far when he suddenly announced that he was unattached.

"Why are you telling me that?"

"I was just letting you know for future reference," Victor said sheepishly. "Bwoy," he said slapping himself on the forehead, "yuh is hard work, yah know dat. I can't understand it, I always seem to chase women away."

Carol took pity on him briefly.

"Look, it's not you, there's nothing wrong with you, you're fine, it's me. I'm just *not* interested."

She turned and walked back to the house, leaving the comedian standing by himself on the pavement.

But Victor didn't give up that easy. The next day she got home to find the whole of her answering machine tape filled with Victor's unique live rendition of *It Wasn't Me.*

Donna and Dee were already clapping in time to the message when she arrived. Fortunately, Carol saw the funny side of things. Her friends both thought that it was a romantic gesture which Carol should respond to positively. But she wasn't ready. She hadn't been asked out in a long time and all of a sudden she was inundated with offers, but preferred to wait for the right time and the right man with the right attitude.

Victor sent her a different parcel every day for a week before he gave up. First it was a box of matches, the next day it was a wall thermometer, then a bottle of tabasco sauce, then a kilo of chilli peppers. Finally he sent a postcard of a lazy beach in the Caribbean.

On the back he had written: "I've got the hots for you."

However much Victor huffed and puffed, he wasn't able to blow this woman's mind.

Janice believed that Carol would have relented and put him out of his misery if this was any other time, but her marriage break-up had hardened her heart.

"Are you sure you've managed to come to terms with life after Neville?" she asked Carol.

"Have you really put him far enough behind you? Because you don't want to keep that bad attitude with you. You gotta change that attitude because you're scaring all the men away."

Carol assured her sister that Neville was history, and tried to explain that now she was older and wiser she just didn't have any more time in her life to waste on the wrong man.

"I don't need a man. Not unless he's nineteen years old, wears corduroy trousers, has at least one broken marriage behind him and speaks with a French accent. Look, I just enjoy being single, I don't want a lifelong partner and I don't need a part-time man."

"Sis, I know what your problem is, you don't want to sell yourself short, you want to make a good catch first time. Well, I have come here today to tell you to get your fishnets mended, because I have found just exactly what you're looking for, and his name is Dalton Browne!"

Carol sighed. "I was joking when I said it before, but you really *don't* know when to give up, do you?"

Janice said she would give up if her sister at least took a look at Dalton. Then she gave a detailed list of his selling points: imaginative, insightful, communicative, affectionate, harmonious and supportive, with VGP (Very Good Potential).

Carol thought about it for a moment.

"Okay, but this is definitely going to be the *last* man you fix up for me."

"Sure, sure. Don't worry about that."

"And he's only getting one chance to make an impression. No second date."

"He won't need one. You'll see," she said, smiling. "I *know* you'll like him – and as long as you're not expecting Einstein, he won't expect you to be Naomi Campbell. And this time, I'll set everything up."

Janice called the next day; she had spoken to Dalton

who was amenable and free any evening. Carol agreed on a day and time. A few days later she received a formal invitation from Janice 'requesting the pleasure of her company' with the day, time and address. *Dress strictly formal.*

Had Carol met Dalton anywhere else, she may have treated him to the same disdain as her earlier suitors. But she had never been on a river boat restaurant before and she was looking forward to the experience.

Dalton was already there to greet her as she stepped out of a black cab on the Embankment, dressed in an elegant black woollen two-piece. He looked impressive with Dax-oiled hair slicked back and shiny, an immaculate dinner suit with dress shirt, and well-shined black shoes.

However well he hid it, Carol could always tell when a man fancied her. It was in their eyes. And it was certainly in *his* eyes. She caught Dalton stealing surreptitious glances at her bosom and behind even before they climbed onto the deck of the *Caribbean Queen.*

As the boat moved off on its cruise eastwards down the Thames they sat down on the restaurant deck amongst the other diners, watching the lights of the city drift by. A jazz pianist provided some mellow atmosphere.

"You know what my fantasy is?" Dalton began. "It's to leave the rat race and get a little sailing boat and to sail over to the Caribbean and just go island-hopping for a few years. Y'know, my only worry would be where to go next — Port of Spain, Georgetown or Negril."

"So you're a dreamer?" Carol asked, unable to resist a little irony.

Dalton Browne was thirty-seven and a partner in a firm of chartered accountants in the City. The tall, well-built Jamaican looked like a black James Bond and carried himself like someone of means. He was a single woman's dream and he owned a luxurious flat and an expensive car. But all his net worth meant nothing, as far as Carol was concerned. She was having a pleasant evening out and that was all that mattered.

A uniformed waiter took their orders.

Carol went for the fish, with a side salad. Dalton ordered the chicken, no salad. The conversation was cordial throughout and touched on the situation in Haiti, with America declaring itself 'the world's police', and the latest theatre openings in the West End. Carol was on her best behaviour, giving her companion an opportunity to show whether her first impression of him — bright, easy-going, open and sensitive, and not exactly hard to look at either — was a true one.

"Don't you dream?" he asked when the food arrived.

"Not really. Not any more."

"Pity," Dalton said."I found that dreams kept me alive when my wife left me."

"It took me a long time to trust women again, after the way my ex-woman handled me," he continued, slowly and deliberately. "I don't understand how she could have been cheating for so long. Y'know, all that time she told me she was attending evening classes…"

What cut him up, he explained, was not just that his woman had been unfaithful, but that when she told him about it, she already had all her bags packed and was ready to move in with her lover. He hadn't suspected anything because she was his woman; why should he suspect anything? If she wasn't happy, why didn't she talk to him about it?

"You've got to trust your partner, haven't you, as much as your partner's got to trust you."

"Were you ever unfaithful during the relationship?"

"Never," Dalton insisted.

The conversation had touched so close to her own situation that it made Carol uncomfortable. Neville was the last thing she wanted to think about tonight, while she drifted down the Thames feasting on salmon and champagne.

"Usually, it's the men who think nothing of lying and being dishonest," Carol said finally, unsympathetically. "Isn't that all part of the game that you've been playing in relationships since the beginning of time?"

" 'You' who? I haven't. You know, Carol, there are *some* black men out there who respect their women too much to behave that way."

She saw she'd hurt his feelings and changed the subject. "So how comes you haven't found anybody since?"

"I'm more careful now. I can't afford to make a mistake the next time around. I still want to build a family and share my life with someone special. I want someone I can really devote myself to, but I'm too old to be disappointed again."

Carol smiled. It was sweet that Dalton, despite his marital experiences, still believed he would fall in love and live happily ever after, and still valued the traditional elements of love such as fidelity. He really was a dreamer.

"If only it were that simple," she said half to herself. "I always thought accountants were supposed to be practical. Is there really such a thing as a romantic accountant?"

"Why, shouldn't there be?"

Carol didn't reply.

"Something's troubling you?" Dalton said as they walked and talked on deck after dinner, a gentle spring breeze following them on their way back up the Thames to town.

"Oh, you know, I've been going through some things recently," Carol said, her head light with champagne and becoming momentarily sentimental.

"Why don't you tell me about your problems. Maybe I can help you solve them."

She could have told him so much. She could have said that she was a casualty of love, worn and battered and no longer willing to suffer the low moments of a relationship just in order to experience the occasional 'highs'. She wanted to weed out the 'no hopers' from her life and find someone who could fulfil her emotional needs and not just scratch those physical itches. Carol could have told Dalton all these things, but she chose not to.

"Look, never mind all that right now. Let's us just enjoy this beautiful night," she said, leaning her head back over the safety rail.

"Tonight is not about problems for us..."

Carol was right, it was a magical night and they were both still staring up at the night sky when the boat pulled into its mooring at the Embankment.

Back on the street, Dalton flagged down a black taxi and they climbed in the back. Carol said that he didn't have to follow all the way to Wimbledon, but he insisted.

"I wouldn't dream of abandoning you," he said.

"I won't even be able to invite you in for a cup of coffee, because my flat mates will be in bed."

"I'm not doing this so that I can be invited in for coffee."

The taxi came to a halt at a red light by the Houses of Parliament.

Dalton was talking about how many children he someday hoped to have when Carol felt eyes upon her. She looked out of the window on Dalton's side and saw Neville's blue Mazda sports car also waiting at the light. He was staring right into the back of the cab, straight at her.

Carol snaked her arm around Dalton's waist and pulled him towards her, locking her mouth on him in a long, passionate kiss. He was clearly taken aback, but it didn't take him long to catch her up, and he made sure that his embrace was warm and considerate.

Carol found herself enjoying it.

It had been a very, very long time since she had been so close to a man.

RAGGA TO RICHES

The make-up man said he had never seen a face like mine, so perfectly shaped and skin so unblemished. It would be his pleasure to work on my face, he said. He mixed the colours expertly on the back of his hand with a soft brush and set about making me look sexy.

It was my first video shoot, and I was on my way to achieving what I came to London to do. The make-up man worked on. I stared into the mirror and waited. My stomach was full of butterflies as my face slowly took on a new beauty I had never seen before.

I felt like a star.

Dancehall fashion doesn't pretend to be 'fashion'. It's more like 'bare as you dare' — anything you feel comfortable with. Clothes which other people call tacky or slack are *haute couture* in the dancehall. Sequins, see-through clothing, fishnet stockings and extra tight leather shorts are definitely in, baggy clothes are definitely out. Church people are always describing dancehall queens as coarse, crude and rough, but check how the thing's turned. Nowadays, everyone wants to book dancehall 'models' for shows, thanks to dancehall videos.

If you're gonna get noticed, you need to dare to bare more than anyone else. That's why I dress more extravagantly than anyone else, and why I dance more outrageously. That's why men are always describing me as 'sexy', despite my having thighs some people would call 'chubby' and a big bum. But I'm proud of my body and men like it that way.

I was wearing my favourite peroxide blonde wig and green contact lenses, with a tight dress and panty hose, dancing in the middle of the dancehall at the Bass

Academy — one of the successful new clubs that had sprung up in south London — when I was spotted by Colin, who was tall and skinny with round wire glasses.

"Are you a model by any chance?" he shouted in my ear above the boom of the music.

I looked at him suspiciously before answering. I had heard so many different chat-up lines, and that was one of my *least* favourite. I nodded my head and he handed me his card, which stated that he was a photographer.

"I'm doing a video for Reggie Fury," he yelled. "I want you to be in it. Give me a call."

I nodded and said I would. Reggie was one of my favourite artists, a sexy soul singer with a reputation for being able to hit a woman in her 'G Spot' and make her moan, 'oooh' and 'aaah'. I had seen his videos and knew that they fully deserved their reputation for being steamy and unsuitable for those of a delicate disposition.

I rolled up at the west London warehouse where they were shooting. Colin had asked me to come in my most outrageous outfit, so I dressed in a bright orange leather batty rider over fishnet stockings and a low-cut matching top, short enough to leave my midriff bare. I wore a diamond stud through my nose, oversize earrings and a ruby in my bellybutton. Topping off the ensemble was another peroxide blonde wig, this one cut short to a bob, and I took along a selection of spare outfits wrapped in plastic. It was a very long day. Me and the six other models danced seductively for hours as Reggie lay on a bed covered with satin sheets wearing nothing but a G-string and miming to his latest tune, *XTC*. When everything was through and we were preparing to leave, Colin came over and asked me to stay behind so that he could try out some alternative shots with just me and Reggie.

As I turned to join Reggie on the bed again, I heard the cameraman whispering, "She's got the best tits in the video, her figure is unbeatable."

112

The cameraman circled around as I snogged away with Reggie on the bed, trying to get perfect angles for every shot, and made us do it over and over again until he was satisfied. It wasn't hard to tell that the other models were pissed off at all the attention I was being given.

After the shoot was finally over, Reggie drove me home in his Range Rover. He looked great with his clothes on, too, wearing designer everything, including boxer shorts with his name across the waistband, clearly visible above his baggy black denims.

"Tell me, er, Donna..." Reggie said, peering over his Ray-Bans at me as he handled the steering like an expert through the near-deserted streets, heading south, "...do a lot of men lust after you?"

I asked him what kind of question that was to ask a lady and he replied that he didn't mean any offence and that it was just that I had turned him on all the way through the video shoot.

Reggie looked at me hard. He turned down the volume on the stereo, until the music from the swingbeat tape merely rocked gently.

"You see, I have a lot of women lusting after me. Pure lust. And everything they want to do with me has something to do with sex."

I giggled.

"I'm not surprised, though. Are you? After all, you are the 'G-spot' man, aren't you?"

He smiled.

"Good point. I am. And I hate to admit it, but being able to get any woman I want to is ruining the loving and caring side of my nature."

"I personally don't mind if a man lusts after me," I assured him, "but some of my girlfriends might feel offended if a man came on to them that strongly. Man shall not live by lust alone."

I tend to be more interested in sex than most of the me

113

I meet. Long after they think the job's done, I'm still craving for more, teasing and taunting them until they give me what I want.

Sex for me has always been hot and heavy.

"Is it a problem for you having sex very early on in a relationship?"

I turned to Reggie and studied him for a moment, trying to decide whether I really fancied him or merely lusted after him. All these questions could only be leading to one thing, but he was keeping his cards close to his chest. A lot of people have to wait and hunt around for years before they find that one relationship which is exciting and special, someone who is unlike everybody else they've ever met.

But here he was, Reggie himself, successful pop star and sex symbol, and it seemed like he had just fallen out of the sky into my lap. What woman would turn him down? Every time I thought about the fact that I was actually being driven home by him in his jeep, it blew my mind. I couldn't just let him slip away.

When I see a man I fancy, I just walk up to him and chat him up. That's the kind of woman I am. But now Reggie was in the driving seat. He had to make his move, so that I could find out exactly what he was after.

"No, Reg," I replied. "Sex early in a relationship doesn't bother me."

He didn't add anything to that, but kept his eyes on the road and kept driving, scratching his goatee beard every now and then, as if he was considering different propositions. I think he forgot to slow down for the next sleeping policeman, though.

When we got home to Wimbledon, Reggie parked up pavement right in front of the gate. He quickly and went around to my side to let me out. He e his move.

ure you won't be too lonely by yourself

114

upstairs?" he asked as we said goodnight.

"Oh, no, I'm quite used to it. Why, are you offering to keep me company?"

"Yeah. I am."

"Well, then, come on in," I said.

SKINTEETH

Carol shook her head again. She was ten years too old for the outfit. It was too revealing, the colours too bright.

"It's not exactly… me, now is it, Donna?"

"That's just the point, my dear. We came here to *find* something which wasn't you, remember?"

Carol frowned.

Donna was right.

She wasn't herself any more, anyway. Now she had to start thinking like a single career woman if she was to *be* a single career woman. A new Carol was emerging, and if she was going to start partying, she would need some new party clothes. But even so, she was wishing she had gone shopping for clothes with Dee instead. They were closer in age and had similar tastes.

"It's a bit too flash. You try it, Donna."

Donna sighed. They had been traipsing around Finsbury Park all morning. Like so many other fashion-conscious black women, she frequented the Greek and Turkish wholesalers on Fonthill Road, looking to purchase the latest styles at wholesale prices. But they had been to a dozen different stores already and Carol had still not seen anything she liked enough to buy.

"I am telling you, Carol, this dress is *you*, gyal. You can go to any dance or party with this and have men's heads *spinning*."

"Maybe what I need is a dress which will only get a couple of guys to turn their heads. Maybe something a bit… mmm… looser."

"But then what did you go and lose all that weight for? All that aerobics and weight training? Honey, now you've got it, you've got to show it."

Donna could see that she wasn't making much impact on her friend. They belonged to two different traditions of black beauty. Carol belonged to the old school, but she was going to have to put on the new style to make any kind of impact on the dating scene.

"If you wanna look cool, you've got to wear something that's wild."

Donna was way ahead of the fashion industry. She didn't just wear the latest clothes, she put them together in combinations that nobody had even thought about, and before the designers picked up on it she had moved along to something else.

Carol knew that her flatmate believed in always being impeccably dressed and in shopping as hard for men as she did for her clothes. Donna was hung up on clothes and spent much of her time looking at and thinking about clothes and men, but Carol couldn't see how the men were treating her as anything but a sex object.

"Looking your best is important, you don't want to spend the rest of your life tied to a stove," Donna insisted. "When I was younger, I was the ugly duckling. I went to an all-white school outside Bristol, and the other girls bullied me because I was bigger, blacker, taller, fatter and goofier than them. No boy would look at me, because I wore all the wrong clothes, so everybody laughed at me and I was as miserable as sin.

"Until I turned fifteen. Then all of a sudden things started to look up for me. For some reason boys suddenly started finding me attractive, and suddenly I became really popular."

The two women had now been chatting as they darted in and out of the tightly-packed row of fashion shops on both sides of the road for nearly two hours. Donna was waddling along carrying a number of large shopping bags filled with the latest creations at knock-down prices, but Carol had still to make her choice. Finally she chose a dress that made her look sensible but hardly sexy. But Donna had planned for that. She had managed to hide a really raunchy Carol-sized dress in amongst her other purchases.

One way or another, Carol was going home with at least one dress which would make her irresistible to men.

Carol had been up all night working on her film reviews. She had clean forgotten that it was her birthday until she came downstairs in the morning to find cards from Donna and Dee. She appreciated the thought, but a birthday when you're thirty-five is hardly cause for celebration.

"Another year. Great. Another reminder of how time is running by me."

"Oh, don't be such a grouch," Donna snapped. "You're only thirty-five. That's no age at all. You're almost still a teenager."

"That's all right for you to say," Carol retorted. "You *are* almost a teenager. Wait until you hit thirty and start to count how long you've got left."

Carol put a brave face on her new age. A birthday is easier to bear when you've got your best friends there to turn it into a celebration.

"So, what do you want to do this evening?" Dee asked, "I'm coming home a bit earlier from work, and I'd like it if we could all maybe go out together."

Carol said that it would have been a good idea, but she already had a date. Donna and Dee were delighted for her. It was the first time Carol had been out in a long while.

"You go ahead and have that date," Dee urged. "Don't worry about us, girl child. It's about time you went out meeting some men, show 'em what you got, honey."

"It's not exactly like that..." Carol said quietly.

"Well, anyway. If you're not going to be here this evening, perhaps you better get your presents now."

Dee pulled out a little packet from her briefcase.

Inside a jewellery box was an oversize necklace made out of beads and looking very African.

"Oh, I love this necklace," Carol said enthusiastically.

"It's not a necklace," Dee advised her, "it's a 'gri-gri'. You wear it around your waist, next to your skin, and you never take it off. It will protect you and keep you fertile and help you to realise your dreams. It's an old African thing."

Carol lifted up her shirt and slipped the gri-gri around her waist.

"I can feel something happening already," she laughed.

"Don't mess with the spirits of our ancestors," Dee warned, "those things are for real."

Donna brought down a large package from her bedroom. Carol's face broke into a huge smile as she recognised *the* most outrageous dress that she and Donna had seen on Fonthill Road. Donna insisted that it would suit her perfectly, but Carol declined, saying that she was too old for that type of thing and that, in her day, you would have been done for streaking in an outfit like it, but that it was very sweet of her nevertheless to get it.

Carol embraced Donna and kissed her on the cheek, but was absolutely adamant that she would never ever be seen dead wearing it outside the house. Dee urged her to put it on. Eventually Carol conceded. Both Donna and Dee thought she looked wicked with the gri-gri around her waist visible through the see-through top.

"All you need now is a brand new wide-brimmed hat, a pair of high heeled shoes and maybe some Ray-Bans and you'll soon have those heads not only turning, but revolving."

"I can't see any man resisting you looking like that," Dee agreed, impressed; it really was the best she had seen her friend. Carol seemed a million miles from all her personal worries. For the first time, she really *looked* like a new woman.

Though the dress was nothing like what she would have chosen herself, Carol couldn't help feeling that she looked fabulous wearing it.

Then Donna came up with the idea.

"I know... let's have a party."

"Party for what?" Carol asked sceptically.

"Just a party, to celebrate. It is your birthday, isn't it? The day of your birth? The day you were born! That's enough of a reason. Let's just have a good, jamming party that people will be talking about for years to come. Let's invite all the decent men we know and all the single women we know, that's the recipe for success. Let's just have a party," Donna insisted.

Dee backed her up and said that she had not really been to a 'black' party in all the time she had been in London, and it would be nice to compare how the British did things over here with the way they threw parties in the States.

Carol wasn't sure she wanted a whole heap of strangers traipsing all over her nice clean house. She said as much, too.

"Just give me some time to think about it, all right?"

Dee snapped her briefcase shut and made her way out to work. Before departing, she turned around to Donna, no longer able to resist speaking her mind.

"Child, that wig looks *damn* foolish," she said frankly.

Donna shrugged her shoulders and flicked her long peroxide blonde wig.

"It ain't what you wear, babe. It's how you wear it."

The police finally found my Audi in Scotland after a week. Harvey had stolen the radio and all my CDs. I thought it best not to be too specific about the exact circumstances of the theft, but I was surprised how unconcerned the firm's fleet manager seemed about the loss of a $40,000 vehicle. They were used to cars being stolen in London, their fleet manager explained.

"We've got the worst record in the world. Cars are stolen as often in this country as hamburgers are eaten in the States," he joked.

I was looking forward to working on a new account that promised to be the most interesting yet. Rex Publishing had moved their advertising to Splash and made it clear that they had only done so because they had heard that Splash had a black woman account executive.

The first thing I said when I met the two young black men who owned the company was that I knew one of their authors.

"Oh, you know André?" said Devon, the taller, darker partner. "Yeah, wicked writer. He's going places. Give him some time and he'll end up being one of the most successful authors in America. Wait and see."

It was mostly the other, more laid back, partner, Simon, whom I dealt with on the account. He was the business half of the partnership and seemed to know a lot about advertising and what he wanted the agency to do for Rex. He had sent me a full set of Rex books so I could come up with some ideas for them to consider.

"We're 'the publisher with attitude'," he explained, "so we've got to have memorable adverts even if it upsets some people."

Of course, I had already read all of André's novels as soon as I received them, but I spent a great two weeks going through the other books that Rex published. I hadn't read black fiction like this before, not even in the States. Their stuff was snappy, exciting, entertaining and a great read. I couldn't wait to get started properly on the project, this was going to be fun.

"Which book did you like best?" Simon asked when I told him how much I had enjoyed reading them.

"It's got to be *Pickney*," I replied. "I really liked the Vincent Kelly gangster books, but I'm not so familiar with the type.of life he writes about. But *Pickney* was a really universal topic."

"But you got an idea of the type of books we publish? That's good. You understand, what we want to do with this advertising campaign is to assure our readers that when they see our logo they are buying the genuine article and not a fake by one of our competitors. The important thing is to develop brand loyalty amongst our readers."

I had suggested that they continue to advertise their product exclusively in the black media — on cable television, pirate radio stations and the one or two black legal stations, and print media — as well as beefing up their street flyposting.

"Yeah, and I strongly feel that a re-design is one thing we really must prioritise," I told him. "If we are going to make your brand stand out, we need to freshen up the visual impact we're making. Trust me, hiring a really hot designer will pay dividends as soon as we get our new image seen out on the streets."

Simon agreed and said that he had designed their advertising himself though he wasn't really a designer.

"I'll tell you what, Dee, I'll leave everything in your hands. Give me a call when you're ready to show me something on paper and I'll take you out to lunch to discuss things. How does that sound?"

I said it sounded fine.

I had already encouraged our art director to take a holiday so he could maybe get the 'staring dreamily into thin air' out of his system on his own time. Now getting the Rex Publishing account gave me an opportunity to test out a young black designer who had brought his portfolio in for me to see the previous week. He was only too keen to come in and work on the project on a freelance basis and he had already read all Rex Publishing's books, which made things a whole lot easier. Marc was only twenty-one, heavy set with a goatee and dressed like a cross between an art student and a be-bop jazz musician. But I liked his book: to me he seemed like a really talented designer with great ideas.

His speed and skill on a Macintosh were formidable, and if I could house train him out of spending half the time chatting to his girlfriend on the telephone he might just carve himself out a full-time job.

I returned home late from work one Tuesday evening to find Carol's copy of *The Voice* spread out on the coffee table. As usual she had left some of her home made low-fat oatmeal raisin cookies on a plate for me. She wasn't around and neither was Donna. I was tired but didn't feel like going up to bed. There was nothing interesting on TV, so I settled down to reading the week's news in 'Britain's Best Black Newspaper'. I flicked through the pages — the letters page, the Tony Sewell column, Sister Marcia's gospel page, and through the entertainment section and culture page. I finally came to the 'Heart To Heart' dating page and scanned through the ads looking for cheeky ones:

SEE ME YAH 6'1", handsome male, athletic, witty, passionate, 26, G.S.O.H., seeks romantic, affectionate, humorous female to become one in mind, body and soul.

FULL-FIGURED, plump, black woman, size 18 or over, needed by attractive, professional, mixed race male, 45, for fun-loving, long-term relationship. London area.

WANT KIDS SOON? Crazy, tall black male seeks adventurous, young girlfriend. Laughter and cuddles essential. All nationalities welcome. Pregnant girl considered. London-ish. Write before it's too late.

EVER DREAMED of a caring, professional, witty, mouth-watering, black British male, 32, who'd appreciate your every embodiment of femininity? Why dream? Harmony awaits you. A.L.A.W.P.

SEXY RAGGA man, 25, with own flat and lonely seeks 'fit' ragga lady. Must be over 25, 5' 9". Call me, let's flex! Jamaican/English only.

ATTRACTIVE black hunk, 30, lonely but not desperate, seeks confident, level-headed, employed, childless, caring black woman to share life's ups and downs.

SPORTY black male, 50+, seeks lively ethnic or mixed race companion for two weeks jaunt to Spain in Oct/Nov. Interested?

CAN you make up for lost years? Single Nigerian male, 26, enslaved for years by loneliness and inactivity seeks liberation. N/S female, 20-30.

I'M A PLAYFUL, slim, 28, coppertop, widower and don't like being on my own. I gotta lot to give to the right woman.

AGORAPHOBIC black male, 30, seeks female company,

any nationality, for intimate dates in tiny bedroom. All replies answered.

IRRESISTIBLE large, damned fine black man, 29, looking for love, affection and a good woman who enjoys life. Midlands/London.

PROFESSIONAL white male, 32, 5' 11", fit, seeking sexy, feminine, dark Jamaican lady, with weave-on, painted nails, batty riders and tall boots, who wants lasting love.

EARTHBOUND astronaut, own rocket, young crew, heading to stars and galaxies beyond, awaiting space-woman, 25-35, 5' 7"+, for long-term cosmic travel. Countdown commencing.

GOOD LOOKING professional, black male, 28, tired of giving, willing to share, seeks employed, conscious, classy, intelligent, cultured, black beauty. Christian values.

STILL looking? Educated, employed, 'street-wise', well-endowed, 5' 7"+, 25+, childless, African/mixed race beauty? Enjoy mental, physical, aesthetic escapades? Music? Black issues? Black engineer, 5' 8", 30+ needs you.

TALL black man, 35, seeks slim, attractive woman to share time and space. Confidence and positive attitude more important than age.

SITTING on the dock of the bay watching the tide... Black male, 43. Want to waste time with me? You: gorgeous, sexy black woman. Birmingham area.

ALL this love going to waste, it's a crime. Someone should arrest this pale prince, 31, bring him to justice. Reward includes diverse qualities.

BLACK male, 25, 'uncut diamond', seeks SBF 20-25, to polish off his rough edges. Ladies, are you up for it?

I hadn't taken much interest in dating again after I got taken for a ride by Harvey. But as I read all those ads I started to look at things in a different way. I was thirty years old, I was living in a foreign country, and had everything going for me, yet I was single. However much I enjoyed being in London, I knew deep down that I wouldn't be completely happy until that empty place in my life was filled permanently. One of the adverts caught my eye.

MALE, black, professional, slim, tall, 29, handsome and a gentleman, seeks 'likewise' female. Strong, gentle, solvent, quietly confident, for friendship and going out on social occasions.

I dialled the toll number underneath. I guess I was mainly curious, but I also thought it would be good to have one black male friend who didn't want anything from me, someone whose company I enjoyed on a platonic basis. I listened to the polished English accent on the taped message.

"Hi, my name is Trevor. Thank you for responding to my advert. I shall be brief, because my advert says it all. If you're an open-minded and adventurous black woman with a career who enjoys the high life but are tired of going to concerts, the movies or the theatre by yourself, then leave your number and I'll get back to you. If you're the right woman, we'll soon be enjoying a pleasant 'no strings attached' date in town. I'm a professional man, and I think you'll find me interesting, widely-read, intelligent and good company. So don't waste time, leave your number."

126

I left my number, then regretted it as soon as I put down the phone.

But then it was too late.

Trevor called about an hour later. I was surprised but interested. He seemed eager to meet up. He said that there was a new Wesley Snipes film showing at the Prince Charles cinema in Leicester Square. I agreed that sounded good, and we decided to meet outside the cinema. I would be carrying a copy of *Newsweek* magazine and he said he would be carrying a copy of *New Nation*.

The next evening, I had only stood outside the cinema for a moment when a short Spike Lee-lookalike with thick-rimmed glasses and a New York Knicks baseball cap poked his head out of a beaten-up old Japanese car parked by the sidewalk, waving a copy of *The Voice* and the *New Nation*.

"Hiya… you must be Dee," he said with a broad grin, pointing to my copy of *Newsweek*.

"I'm Trevor."

He climbed out of the car and stretched out his hand to greet me. I looked him up and down, unable to believe that this was the same guy who had described himself so appealingly in the advert. It looked like a case of what we call in the advertising business 'bait and switch'. You advertise one thing to get people in through the door, then sell them something else.

Trevor saw the expression of displeasure on my face, and hurried to explain.

"Yeah, I know…" he began. "The paper made a mistake and mixed my description up with somebody else's. There was nothing I could do about it."

I wondered why he hadn't corrected the mistake on the answering machine or told me on the telephone that he wasn't 'as advertised'. He assured me that he had only just seen the mistake on his way to meet me when he picked up a copy of *The Voice* at the newsagent.

He seemed earnest, but I wasn't totally convinced. I could turn around and go home, but didn't want to diss him if he was telling the truth. Besides, I had psyched myself up to fantasise about Wesley on the big screen for ninety minutes, and what harm could there be in a social date with a man I didn't feel the least bit attracted to?

I made a point of going Dutch with him. The last thing I wanted was for Trevor to feel in any way that he had 'invested' anything in me by paying for the tickets. As we sat through the trailers waiting for the feature to begin, he explained that he was a British Telecom engineer, but had only recently relocated to London from a small town on the south coast.

"Coming to London to work is like a big adventure," he enthused. "But I haven't found many people who I really want to go out and have a good time with. You know what I mean?"

I said I did. I was in the same situation after all. The one thing I didn't say was that I *still* hadn't found anybody who I really wanted to go out and have a good time with in London.

Trevor did most of the talking. He had an irritating habit of reading my lips when I spoke, following my words and finishing off my sentences at the same time as I did. But I didn't mention it.

"I love films," he said, "I've seen thousands of them, but I don't like watching them on video, you know what I mean? It's not the same thing. So what's your favourite film? Mine is *Casablanca* with Humphrey Bogart. I mean, it's got everything, hasn't it? It's got the thriller and romance elements — and you're not going to see a much more thrilling or romantic film — and of course it's got the music with old 'play it again Sam' — the token black man — playing it again, and then Bogart and Bergman, what a team, eh?"

As much as I wanted to take Trevor seriously, I was past being excited about meeting up with him and couldn't help feeling more than a tinge of disappointment. He really was nothing like what I had expected. There was worse to come. When a couple of cinemagoers brushed past us to get to their seats, they knocked Trevor's baseball cap off, revealing a shiny, bald head with hair only on the sides and back. I tried *real* hard to focus on Wesley up there on screen for the rest of the evening.

I already knew when I said my goodbyes that evening that I wouldn't be seeing Trevor again. I had run my minimum requirements through my mind so many times that I knew exactly the type of man I wanted to socialise with, and Trevor wasn't he.

I was looking for someone cute, ambitious, charismatic and sincere. A real professional, even just to socialise with, someone on my level, someone who most of all wasn't a telephone engineer.

Silly me. I had given Trevor had my home number, and for the next two weeks he laid siege to our telephone, leaving messages on the machine and asking Donna and Carol to have me call him. I never returned his calls and he eventually stopped ringing.

The day finally came when I had to make my presentation to Rex Publishing. Simon sent his chauffeur down to pick me up and I was driven in the silver Mercedes to a nice Caribbean restaurant in Chalk Farm where Simon was already waiting to have lunch. I hadn't been to Cottons before and, as I looked about me, I was thrilled and delighted that the other diners were almost exclusively black professionals. We shared a 'Belly Nah Bawl' meal for two, after which I showed him the portfolio. He went against every one of the suggestions. He wanted the company logo written larger and he wanted a different colour scheme. He didn't see things the way I did at all,

129

and felt the series of photos of black celebrities with their favourite Rex novel captioned underneath was the wrong approach.

"Just because Jane Public has bought a product in a certain way in the past doesn't mean she's going to continue doing it that way, does it?" he said. "Our readers trust our product because they know we publish entertaining black fiction, so we should have photos of ordinary readers with *their* favourite Rex books."

I fought for my ideas as hard as I could and protested that celebrities were the best way to sell a product, but he wasn't convinced. In the end I conceded that he was right.

"To be honest, I have a deep disrespect for advertising agencies," he said. "I sometimes wonder if I couldn't do the whole thing myself. It's only the time factor that stops me finding out. But I suppose you hear that from all your clients?"

"Oh yeah... especially when we present them with the bill."

Simon smiled.

"Dee, I hope you're not one of those ad people who lives, eats and breathes advertising. I hope you're able to go out and enjoy yourself sometimes as well."

"Sure," I said. "All the time."

It wasn't the truth, but advertising is all about telling people what they want to hear. I continued using my fork to pick at the curried vegetables and rice on the combination platter.

"So which clubs have you been to since you've been in London then? Moonlighting? The Roof Garden? Gantons?"

I admitted that I hadn't yet been out to let my hair down properly, but had mostly been to the movies or to the theatre when I had time.

"But that's because I haven't really had a chance to discover the club scene."

"Well, you must come along to this little party one of our authors is having at his place on Saturday. I think you'll like it if you're interested in meeting black professionals. Why don't I come by to pick you up about seven?"

Simon didn't have to ask me twice. As much as I was looking forward to meeting a crowd of 'my kinda people', I was also daydreaming of getting to know Simon 'off-duty'.

MOUTH TO MOUTH

Janice and Ollie finally arrived to collect the kids. Martin and Shannon knew that they could get away with anything when they were at their aunt's house. She always spoiled them. Despite the fact that their mother had expressly told them and her sister that they weren't to have any sweets, they sulked wholeheartedly until Carol conceded that one ice cream wouldn't do them any lasting harm. They took a walk down to the local newsagent where Martin was quick to choose the largest and most expensive ice cream in the freezer, and his sister selected her favourite, which was somewhat cheaper.

If Carol thought she was buying peace and quiet, she was mistaken. Once they knew they could get away with almost anything with their aunt, the kids set about turning the house upside-down. Six-year-old Martin was clever far beyond his years.

Carol believed he didn't fully understand what it meant that his cousin Junior had died the previous year. But it hadn't escaped his notice that his aunt now doted on him as if he were her own son. He looked forward to going around to Auntie Carol's, it was like Christmas there all the time.

Shannon was ten, and she understood. She missed Junior and tried her best to be a good girl whenever her aunt babysat. But she was a tomboy and couldn't resist joining in with her brother when he began kicking his football around in the conservatory. She would tease and torment the little fellow until he started a fight, which she would inevitably win. It wasn't that she enjoyed seeing him cry and bawl out. She truly loved her little bro. She just wanted to show him who was boss.

"Unnnnnnnnnghhh!" Martin wailed, tears streaming down his face.

Carol looked up and shook her head.

"What is it *this* time?"

"Auntie... C-C-Carol..." Martin began slowly and purposefully, stressing every syllable and gasping for air in between.

"Sha...nnon took...ungggghhh... my football from me... unnnggghhh... an' now, now she says she won't give... unnnggghhh... it back to me unt...il I'm big e...nuff to take it... Unnnnnnnnnggggggggghhh!"

"Shannon!" Carol called out. "Give Martin back his ball and give it back to him now."

"Pardon, Auntie?" Shannon cried out from the top of the stairs, pretending that she couldn't hear a word.

"I said give him back his ball... Do you hear me?"

"Sorry Auntie," Shannon called back, "I think I've gone deaf... I can't hear anything you're saying."

"Shannon!!" This time there was threat in her aunt's voice and the little child threw her brother's ball back to him.

"He's such a baby," the young girl called out.

Carol lay her head back on the sofa. She was tired. She thought about Junior and wished he was here to play with his cousins. Having Shannon and Martin around for the evening had made her yearn for her own child all over again. Well, Junior was with God now, there was nothing she could do about that, but would she ever get the chance to mother another child?

At that moment the doorbell rang and Martin rushed to the door to open up for his mother and father.

"Daddy, Daddy! Look what Auntie Carol gave me," Martin cried out as his parents stepped in, proudly displaying the watch that his aunt had bought him.

"You're going to end up spoiling that child you know." Ollie was a tall and powerfully-built British-born

Grenadan of twenty-nine, who lived for his wife and family first and foremost.

"I have told her that," Janice quipped. "You better take care of that watch, Martin," she turned to her son, "because you're not going to get another one."

"And you better learn the time quick," Martin's father added, "because from now on, I'm not going to use my watch again, I'm just going to be asking you the time."

"I know how to tell the time," Martin said with a cheeky smile.

"No he doesn't," Shannon teased, "silly boy doesn't even know his times table... hahaha!"

Martin turned to his sister and kicked her squarely on the shin.

"Yes I do."

Shannon screamed as loudly as she could.

"What did you just do?" Ollie asked his son incredulously. Martin simply rested his hands on his hips and stood his ground defiantly.

"You are not looking at me like that, are you?" his father asked.

Martin knew who he shouldn't mess with. He dropped his hands by his side. Shannon continued screaming as if she were about to die.

"All right, all right," Janice comforted her, "don't overdo it, Shannon, or we'll have to take you to the hospital..."

"I *wa-a-a-ant* to go to the hospital," Shannon cried through her wailing.

"Well you're not going," her mother countered, "so you'd better get well quickly. We've got to go home..."

Ollie was still dealing with Martin.

"We've been standing here for two minutes and you still haven't apologised to your sister."

"But she started it."

"I don't care who started what," Ollie said, "where do

you get off kicking your sister? Who taught you that? You've got five seconds to apologise to her and I'm talking a real apology, because you've just done something to your sister which you should be ashamed of."

Martin took the full five seconds to think about it, but when he apologised he made a proper job of it.

"I'm sorry, Shannon."

He thought about it for another second, then he hugged his sister. "I love you."

Shannon hugged her brother back.

"And I'm sorry, too, Martin."

"I'm sorry about all this, Carol," Janice said. "Have they been troublesome?"

"They've been all right. I wish I had your problems."

"Not with these two you don't," Janice assured. "You don't know the half of it. You don't have to live with them full-time."

"So how was the show?" Carol asked.

"It was really good," Ollie said, nodding. "You should go and see it."

Janice and Ollie had been out to see a production of *Carmen Jones* at a theatre in East London. The production starred a UK-based soap opera star, who had won rave reviews for her interpretation of the classic musical. Carol said she would think about it.

"But you're going to have to go on your own," her sister said, "because you done scared away every eligible man from Wimbledon to Watford."

"Not *every* man..." Carol protested.

"Oh? Don't tell me that things have turned out sweet between you and Dalton? I don't believe it."

"Nothing like that."

Carol smiled.

"No, I can tell it from your eyes," Janice countered. "You *do* like him, don't you? You actually like him." She laughed. "Well, good for you."

Ollie coughed. The kids were getting fidgety and they had their beds to go home to.

"I'll call you tomorrow," Janice insisted. "I want to know all the juicy bits."

From the doorstep Carol waved goodbye to her sister and the family in their Volvo estate.

Everything seemed quiet in the house once the children had gone. Suddenly, Carol was full of energy again and she decided to make the phone call she had been looking forward to all day.

"Hi, Dalton, it's me," she said.

"Hi there. What are you doing?"

"Nothing, I just thought I'd call to see how you were."

"You can call me any time," Dalton said.

Dalton had thought he'd got lucky when she suddenly turned around and started kissing him in the taxi cab. But he had another thing coming. Once the cab pulled away from the lights, Carol completely withdrew her advances. When he pressed her, she couldn't deny that she had enjoyed the embrace. Neither did she deny that she wanted to do it again, but when he made an attempt to resume, she stopped him and said she just wanted friendship and that he was pushing their intimacy too fast. He asked her whether it was because she found him unattractive.

"No".

"Average then?"

"No, I think you're very attractive."

It had been so long since she had been so intimate with anyone. Feeling Dalton's warm breath in her mouth as his tongue toyed sensitively with hers had reminded her of how much she had missed having someone who could make her feel secure, but also excite her at the same time. Like any other woman she needed a big hug every now and then to make her feel she was the most important person in the world. And being in a position where she was meeting available young black men was preferable to staying at home moping.

She was pleased that Dalton had continued to take an interest in her, but Carol just couldn't bring herself to trust a man a hundred percent after Neville. Anyway, it was never too late to get 'dirty' with Dalton. After all, men never 'just say no' and when a woman does offer sex, even if they would prefer to wait, they will always say yes.

"I've got a few questions to ask you," Carol continued down the phone line.

"Sounds intriguing," Dalton replied. "Don't you trust me yet?"

He was getting used to it. He had now dated Carol twice and both times he had felt like he was under interrogation. As well as that, they were always spending time discussing things over the phone, but they never ended up doing anything. Carol explained that she felt entitled to question him, and reminded him that she had already made her mistakes in life and couldn't afford to befriend a man she didn't know.

"Fire away, then."

"Who did you make love to last night, a girlfriend or a casual acquaintance?"

The line went silent for a moment, before Dalton let out a loud laugh.

"How can you *ask* me that?" he spluttered. "What do you expect me to tell you?"

"The truth," Carol said, unamused. "You've got nothing to hide from me, it's not like we're having an affair. Or can't you even be honest with your friends?"

"I slept in my bed alone last night," Dalton answered with a sigh.

"And the night before?"

"Same thing."

"When was the last time you made love?"

Dalton dodged the question as much as he could, said

that Carol was going too far, and anyway it had been such a long time ago, he couldn't remember."

"Try."

"Well... I suppose after my wife left me, I went a bit crazy... spite sex, you understand... I don't know, maybe six months ago."

"So what have you been doing since then?"

"What?"

"You know, you're a man... How have you been satisfying yourself since then? Do you masturbate?"

"I can't believe this. I'm thirty-eight years old, I'm an accountant. You think I've got time to spend pulling at my plunger every night?"

"There's nothing wrong with it. Everyone knows that everyone does..."

"Well, what about you, then. Do you masturbate?"

That shocked her.

"When I have to."

The line went silent again.

"Well then why don't we just get it on?" Dalton asked finally. "You don't need to do those things, Carol. Why don't you just pick up the phone when you're feeling lonely and call me?"

Carol had wondered the same thing herself. It seemed so easy, and yet it felt out of the question. She was waiting until the right time for sex in their relationship. She just didn't feel like having sex without a partner she loved, and she just didn't know about Dalton.

He seemed nice enough. He was the type of man who would always pull out her chair for her and hold the car door for her. He was a professional, and had both education and social status.

But did she like him enough to make love to him? Or did she just want friendship? She wouldn't jump into bed with Dalton until she was sure.

Neville had made her less interested in sex. When he

first started becoming distant after Junior's birth, she attempted to be better at sex, because she had read in a woman's magazine that having a good sexual relationship was the best defence against your partner playing away from home. When they made love, she made sure she always asked him what he enjoyed, and how she could make the sex for him even better.

For her, sex was a poor substitute for her real need, which was intimacy. Nevertheless, Neville, had enjoyed the opportunity to try out new and varied sexual experiences with his wife.

Back on the phone, Dalton said that postponing sex wouldn't affect his feelings for her. Anyway, why didn't she come around to his place for dinner at the weekend? She accepted, as long as sex was not on the menu. He said that it was a good job he was old enough to understand her old-fashioned attitude, and pointed out that the "make them wait" approach would not go down too well with a lot of other men. She said goodbye, but warned him that if he couldn't just be friends he was obviously not the type of man she needed.

Two days later, Carol received a formal invitation to dinner from Dalton. He had taken a leaf out of Janice's book:

You are invited to my house for a night of romance. The evening will begin with dinner and drinks and conclude with a classic romantic movie... There will be absolutely no sex on the menu. No cancellations allowed. Dress formal.

Dalton lived in a beautiful three-bedroomed maisonette above a shop on Camden High Street. The apartment was huge, particularly the attic living room which opened out to a beautiful rooftop patio filled with tall plants in huge pots. Carol was suitably impressed.

"I got it really cheap a few years ago when the prices

were low," he explained, ready with a glass of champagne for Carol after taking her raincoat.

They sat down to a pleasant candlelit meal of fresh pasta and spinach with caviar.

"Look, Carol, I know something about what you're feeling," Dalton said suddenly as they ate. "Remember, my partner left me too. And when you're together with someone as long as we were, you never really forget them. But one thing I've learned is that you can't keep torturing yourself. You've got to start a new life. If you find someone special, take my advice and hold him tight. Don't be stingy with your affections."

He paused briefly, studying Carol for her reaction and then he told his story:

"I used to come home from work, give my wife a brief kiss and sit down to dinner without realising that she was unhappy. I just assumed that, because we were together and she wasn't nagging, everything was all right. I thought that the more I could afford to buy her, the more she would love me. Boy, was I wrong."

"It's a fabulous place," Carol said again as she helped him to clear the table after dinner. Dalton told her that it felt huge since his wife had walked out. He was always trying to find uses for the two extra bedrooms now that his plans didn't include children.

Before they sat down for the video, he cooked some popcorn in a pan. Carol rummaged through his larder looking for ingredients. She said that she could knock something up quickly which would go well with popcorn. Dalton looked on in awe as she prepared her renowned caramel topping. He dipped his finger in the sauce for a taste.

"My God, that is ab-so-lutely delicious," he said. Then he hit the lights and they snuggled up cosily in front of the fireplace to watch an old Sidney Poitier movie.

It was the most romantic evening Carol had experienced for years. She didn't need a man with diamonds and gold rings, because that would never last; what she needed was a big, strong hand to lift her to a higher level and make her feel like a queen. A romantic evening like this brings you close to another, whether you welcome it or not. If she and Neville had had evenings like this they might have been able to sit down and work out the problems in their lives.

"Just answer me one thing," Dalton began after the movie. "Do you consider me as just a friend, or am I a bit more than that?"

Carol looked at him long and hard; her resistance was almost broken.

"Just a bit more than that."

"I hope so, because I'm fed up with talking to my cat all the time."

Dalton had rolled out the spare futon and spread a blanket on top for them to lie on. Carol looked at her watch and said she had better be going, but it was only a half-hearted suggestion. She made no attempt to stop Dalton filling up her champagne glass once more. For the next hour they lay on the futon, having intimate discussions, but nothing more, enjoying Joyce Sims singing *Come Into My Life* softly in the background. Slowly, they began touching each other and then caressing and gently petting, but mostly they talked. They gave themselves enough time to lounge and laugh and, in a way, learn to love in bed.

He said that he had strong feelings for her and that he was going to do everything in his power to make their time together the most beautiful, the most warm and the most intimate of any relationship. They should not try to manipulate or control each other, he insisted.

"I vow to support and nurture this relationship through its growth and changes. I promise to be there for you always."

"As far as I am concerned you can never say 'I love you' too often," she said, finally allowing him to come into her life. She had *so* much love to show him. She wanted to inspire him with her love. She wanted love to create an 'us' and not to destroy the 'me' that was there.

Before they went any further, Dalton hit the tape button and the sound of Mozart filled the room.

"This stuff is great for making love to," he said, joining her again on the futon.

"Did you see that TV documentary on Aids?"

The question stopped Dalton in his tracks, coming as it did out of the blue.

"How has the fear of Aids changed your sexual behaviour? What are you doing to protect yourself from catching Aids, Dalton?" she asked.

She had been meaning to bring up the topic earlier, without making him think she was trying to find out if he was in a high-risk category. But she had found herself in this compromising position, drunk, relaxed and horny, before she had had a chance to raise the topic. So she'd blurted it out like that: well, there went the evening.

He calmly reminded her that he had been as good as celibate in the last six months, and that she had nothing to worry about. Nevertheless, she insisted, "No glove, no love."

Besides Aids, she had still to consider sickle cell trait. Her beloved son had died of sickle cell anaemia, and to make a mistake and get pregnant by Dalton without a blood check could have further tragic consequences.

It didn't take too long for Dalton to conjure up some condoms from the bathroom downstairs.

When they made love he caressed her body as though it were a rare and priceless musical instrument, following the classical music's highs and lows. He started off fast and passionately and wound down to a conclusion, soft and gentle, breathless and light. *The Jupiter Symphony* has four movements. The first was strong, passionate and energetic and it soon got them going. They slowed the pace right down as the second movement came up.

They were both moaning ecstatically as the symphony came to a resounding finale.

They lay still, side by side, staring up at the ceiling.

Exhausted.

Drained.

Happy.

DICKIE INSPECTION

With each new partner the possibility that this could be Mr Right is always at the back of your mind, especially if he's a good lover, good-looking, good-natured and good value. That's why a lot of single black women like me keep shopping around and wondering: should I get involved, can I trust him, is he worth it? Alex puts it down to 'cock fixation', that I can't get enough. But then a man would say that, wouldn't he, rather than accept that he ain't adequate.

Reggie over-rated his penis. He felt that introducing me to new positions such as the 'roast duck' and 'the stag' was sufficient. He didn't need to work any harder at it, he thought, because his penis did the rest.

You could loosely describe me as his 'woman', as I had dated him a few times. But he kept stressing that he was too much of a sex symbol for his female fans to find out that he was with one particular woman, so our relationship was never 'official'. I was an 'accessory' to him, useful whenever he needed to be noticed at an event. If you want to be noticed, you get yourself a stunning date as well as a flash car and clothes. Reggie could afford to have a stunning girl as just another asset or status symbol.

I was accompanying him to an 'exclusive' party later that evening, so in my bedroom beforehand it was a case of 'wham, bam, thank you, ma'am' as Reggie graced me with his presence. But that was just not good enough for me. If a man couldn't turn me on, I wasn't interested.

When we made love he moved so fast that I didn't have a chance to come. But I didn't want to say so for fear of bruising his ego. As soon as he entered me he turned from a national sex symbol into a Grand National jockey. All he thought about was crossing that finish line before anybody else. Then he rolled over on his side, sweating, exhausted. After a while he opened his watery eyes slowly and panted:

"How was it for you?"

I simply smiled, looking into his eyes deeply.

"You came, didn't you?" he asked.

I had to stifle a laugh.

Sure I came, I nodded ironically. Sure I came.

"I knew it, I could feel it… it was *great*."

Like most men my age, twenty-four, he thought that being good in bed was the most important part, maybe the only important part, of a relationship. Reggie took his cock far too seriously. He always had to convince himself that he was a real stud (drinking more than anybody else, smoking the most ganja, too). And when he was in that mood I couldn't really get close to him because he was too busy thinking about his dick. It was as if he lived to perpetuate the image of the Jamaican man as ever-hard and ever-ready, even though he was 'Mr Once All Night'.

I would have to put him right. Teach him a thing or two about tenderness, warmth, emotion and closeness. I would have to teach him about love, a foreign concept to Reggie.

I rarely volunteered to have oral sex with any man, but Reggie had asked so many times and I felt it might arouse his interest. So I decided to allow him this one moment of pleasure. He lay his muscled body back on the bed, our eyes locked momentarily. Very slowly I began licking his penis. The warmth of my mouth stimulated him immediately and his manhood stood erect. I slipped the penis head into my mouth gently and teased with the tip of my tongue darting around under the edge of the rim. Eventually I took the whole penis into my mouth carefully, sucking it and moving my lips up and down the sturdy shaft as Reggie sighed repeatedly with pleasure, murmuring, "Yes, oh yes… oh yes, oh yes, oh yes…" I couldn't have got the whole penis into my mouth without gagging, so I held the base of it with a hand, stroking it rapidly up and down and with my other hand fondled his balls lightly. Reggie began to breathe heavily, his pelvis jerking to a rhythm of its own and his balls dancing around uncontrollably. I knew that I had only thirty seconds at the most. I moved my mouth rapidly up and down and then quickly pulled out just before a spray of semen and a long, mournful sigh attested to the pleasure Reggie had enjoyed.

Whatever he said otherwise, I knew he didn't love me. He was just enjoying being a hot pop star with women falling over him all over the place.

But I was getting what I needed out of the relationship. Through dating Reggie, I was meeting all sorts of people who could be useful in my career. I figured I could handle being his status symbol, and, if I couldn't, I'd get out quickly.

Sleeping with Alex was preferable, though he was less experienced. Yes, I was still sleeping with Alex, the way you do with a good friend who you know isn't the right man for you, but you're so intimate with anyway that sex doesn't feel bad. I wouldn't even know if he was sexually aroused when I dropped by his tiny apartment, until I noticed his penis getting hard as we sat down to drink coffee. He wouldn't know it either, from the look on his face, until he felt his jeans becoming tight. He didn't want to admit that I was able to control him with sex, but it was true. I had the power in the relationship and I made him bend over backwards for me. Though Reggie didn't know I was sleeping with Alex, Alex knew about Reggie.

Though he wasn't overjoyed, he accepted that he was my 'bit on the side' and that I would date other people, as long as I never stopped coming around to see him. I felt bad about the situation, but I was only getting half of what I needed from each of them, so why should I have to dump either one?

I always felt close to Alex; he was the sweetest man I

had known. I was relaxed and myself with him, and I enjoyed talking to him for hours before and after sex.

"What do you enjoy most about kissing my body?" I asked him as we lay naked on his mattress. He paused for a moment just as he was applying his lips gently to the base of my spine. He replied that my body was like a cure for his lovesickness.

Reggie had promised that he would have me on his next video, and I had been eager for him to get back from tour so shooting could start.

He came around to our house as soon as he got back from tour. He said he knew where his duty lay and was ready to give his woman the "good bed-work", so we got straight to it. I tended to his penis by mounting him, facing his feet as we rocked the bed during intercourse, massaging his inner thigh and tickling his balls while his cock was safe and warm inside of me. Though Reggie was stiff and hard to start off with, he quickly went soft — to his embarrassment.

"Just because I don't have a hard-on doesn't mean that I'm not horny," he said dismissively, when I wondered why he wasn't interested. "That's the problem with women, they think if a man hasn't got a hard-on, there's something wrong. If a limp dick is the worst thing in your relationship, you're livin' large. Cho. It's not easy having a cock that's out of control, y'know. I don't know what's wrong, it gets hard when I'm on stage or driving in my jeep... but you're not around then, and by the time I get round here, it's gone."

Which got me thinking.

This man doesn't find me attractive any more — that's why he's got a limp dick. Okay, his dick wasn't working, but there were lots of other ways he could interest me sexually. Why couldn't he give me a back rub? Why couldn't he go downtown on me?

It was the same thing the next two times we met up.

After that second time, Reggie broke down crying and told me how he wished women would stop wanting him just for sex. The 'G-Spot' gimmick had been taken too literally because now women were only interested in the novelty of sleeping with him. He almost felt he had to get married just to change his image.

From that evening on, I watched my whirlwind romance with Reggie get all out of breath.

I always ended up choosing the same type of men over and over, some of whom did and some of whom didn't satisfy my needs. When Reggie found out that he wasn't able to get his dick up he was so embarrassed he just disappeared. He also changed his mobile number, so I couldn't get hold of him for weeks. When I finally tracked him down, he just said:

"Look, I can't talk now. I'm busy."

I figured that I had been dropped. When I asked him if all this was because he couldn't get it up, he got very angry and shouted down the line that it was because he couldn't date a woman who was a sell-out to her race and thought she was white and walked around with a blonde wig.

"You're beautiful, baby, just beautiful," Colin coaxed as he peered down the lens of his camera at me. I was dressed in a Calvin Klein see-through slip dress that was falling off one shoulder and a white micro-bikini underneath, barely able to contain my figure, and my hair was pulled back.

I had decided to concentrate on modelling. There was no point in waiting to get more work on Reggie's videos, so I turned to Colin, who didn't seem to mind that I was no longer Reggie's woman. He was still prepared to help me and thought I had a good chance of making it as a model. He said he enjoyed working with me because I had a beauty and shape which was unique, and because, unlike other models, I always knew which make-up to use for which occasion and which dresses to wear.

"I'm going to take these photos to a friend of mine," Colin said. "His agency is looking for some sexy black women for a catalogue. I'm sure they'll love these shots."

Long gone were the days when using a black face to sell a product in Britain was unthinkable. Agencies were now actively looking for black models. Because now it was common knowledge that black kids, black women and black men set the trends which everybody else followed. Multi-national clothes companies now sought approval for their products from the black community. Car companies wanted a sexy black woman to sell their cars, and phone companies were using upwardly mobile black females to sell their services. They had finally figured out what a difference the support of black consumers, and the pulling power of black style, could make to their business.

"Just do what you think is best," I told Colin. I trusted him and, ever since we first met that night in the club, I had regarded him as a photographing friend who I could talk to.

He continued clicking away as fast as he could. My every twitch was captured for posterity. Several rolls of film later he was still not finished.

"Okay, keep that smile..." he said. "That's brilliant... really brilliant... yeah, hold it for a couple more... that's incredible."

At the end of the session Colin promised to send me a contact sheet, and said he would let me have personal copies of any shots I liked.

"Just one thing," he said, grabbing my wrist just as I was about to disappear behind the screen in the studio to get changed.

"Reggie said that you give really good head and he doesn't mind if you give me the same, 'on the house'."

JUST WANNA HAVE FUN

The idea for the party came from Donna's favourite rap video, in which everyone dressed up as characters from seventies blaxploitation films. She sent her housemates out to buy a huge Afro wig each, and the invitations urged their guests to do the same. Dee was up for it and added that they ought to go the whole way with fluorescent mini skirts, satin hot pants and thigh-high go-go boots. It would be a costume party where everybody had to dress Seventies-style, the men in flares and the women in hot pants or minis.

Carol frowned and explained that she had in fact actually dated guys who wore bell bottoms and huge Afros. She didn't think she could take the whole thing seriously, but she would go along with it.

It was settled then. They would throw an unforgettable party. Dee got to work designing and printing the invites. Donna did her bit by sorting out the music. She had enough contacts in the business to sort out a free sound for the night.

Carol also contributed by calling up all her girlfriends, some of whom she hadn't seen for years. Many of them were attached, but agreed to come as 'single'. It was difficult choosing which men to invite. They told all their girlfriends to invite men who they themselves weren't interested in. The only requirement was that they would invite men who, to their knowledge, had never dissed a woman, but as hostesses they wouldn't invite any of the men they were dating either.

There was no shortage of single men, however, and in the event there were slightly more men at the party than women, which was just fine.

The party was in full swing. The guests drifted in throughout the evening; familiar faces had transformed into Shaft, Superfly, Cleopatra Jones and any number of other blaxploitation characters from the seventies.

The sound system operator stuck, as requested, to the theme of the party: Sly & The Family Stone, Motown, Stax, the *Car Wash* soundtrack, James Brown, Hot Chocolate's *You Sexy Thing*. Those who remembered how, danced 'the bump' and 'the hustle' from yesteryear.

There was a cross-section of guests: journalists, civil servants, lawyers, advertising people, accountants, shop managers, nurses, one or two doctors, and a few people who seemed to have drifted in uninvited.

Some of the guests had come simply to party and were more interested in 'getting down' amongst the other 'wicky wacky' people. But others had definitely come to find a partner and spent their time out in the conservatory talking, or in the garden, or standing with their backs against the wall in the living room trying to attract the attention of some of the dancers. Other guests were there because they had heard that there would be plenty of good food and free drinks all night long. But that was all right for Donna and Dee: everybody was welcome.

By midnight, the ravers were all wet with sweat. Some who couldn't take it were in a corner sitting down, having had as much as they could possibly take. Others refused to leave the dancefloor and started shouting "Here we go, here we go, here we go!" as the sound operator teased them with tune after tune that took them back down memory lane to their soul boy/girl days. In between records, someone shouted out that there was no way they were going to let 'Mr Deejay' go home tonight. The deejay laughed and said, that tonight he was going to "disturb the neighbours" with music they couldn't resist.

Donna was standing in the conservatory with a broad-shouldered, red-skinned man with a shine on his deep-tanned face, who carried himself as if he was somebody important. Tony St Paul looked immaculate and confident enough about himself behind his dark glasses, and Donna could hardly take her eyes off of him. They had danced close together for a full hour in the living room before retreating to the conservatory, and Tony had shown himself to be adept at the slow, seductive 'wine'. Whatever record was playing and no matter how fast the rhythm was, Tony stuck to that one, slow, intimate dance which he did so well. He was in his forties, in London on business, and the owner of a group of Jamaican holiday hotels specialising in couples-only resorts.

"Only the Jamaican government employs more people than I do," he boasted above the noise. "All this from having started with a run-down little hotel in Negril... Most things that I put my mind to I end up doing... I've been having a ball all my life."

He confessed that another reason why he was in London was to see if he could find a decent woman for himself, "to powder me every time I come ah England. A woman who knows that there are more than sixty-nine ways to love a black man... a woman who can give me unconditional love and elegant eroticism."

He raised his eyebrow. Donna continued smiling, wondering whether she should grant him his wish or not. She would be the first to admit that he wasn't exceptionally attractive, but he had so much else to offer...

"So," Tony said, "what's a guy got to do to take a woman like you out to dinner some time?"

"You don't have to be perfect," she told him, "you've just got to keep trying."

Dee would rather have been enjoying herself raving, but instead was engaged in a heated argument out in the garden with Roger, a twenty-eight year old barrister, over the Clarence Thomas issue. He said that whatever had happened between the black Supreme Court judge and Anita Hill, she should have done something about it at the time, not wait until he was about to be elected as the first black judge on the supreme court and then start to destroy his career.

"There are too few black people in those top positions for us to diss them when they reach there. What does that look like to the kids who want role models? It doesn't look too good, does it?"

Dee said that that wasn't the issue; it was an issue about a woman who wanted to live her life without being sexually harassed by a guy in a stronger position.

"You know, *so* many women have to go through that every day in the workplace."

Then Roger turned to Robin Givens on his 'bash the women' crusade and the whole Mike Tyson thing. He said he didn't like the way Robin had "shafted" the people's champ.

Dee countered that he didn't know anything about what went on between Robin Givens and Mike Tyson in their private lives... It wasn't like Tyson denied it when she told the whole world on prime-time TV that he was physically abusive to her, even though he was sitting right there beside him.

"And, as we can see from the whole Desiree Washington rape episode, Tyson proved to be the kind of man who would do something like that anyway. Women have to be protected from Tyson and all men like him."

Roger insisted that he had watched her testimony in court and just didn't believe her. She must have known what she was doing when she went up to Tyson's room, and she must have known that he had a reputation for being insatiable. Why else would he invite her up to his room in the middle of the night — for coffee and cookies?"

Dee was furious. She couldn't believe how backward

Roger was.

"Whatever she may or may not have known about Mike Tyson's history, she had every right to go up to his hotel room and not be raped..."

"Okay, okay... maybe we should continue this discussion over dinner one evening," Roger said out of the blue.

Dee couldn't believe what she had just heard. If this was Roger's way of chatting up women, he was going to be single for a long time to come.

By the time Carol finally dared to come downstairs in her seventies drag — hot pants and platform shoes with hooped overknee long socks — it was early morning and there were only about three good-looking men left amongst a number of less desirable ones. There were, however, still a number of attractive women, and the competition suddenly got stiff for men whom no one would have bothered with earlier. Carol didn't mind, though. She had gone through a half bottle of Bacardi upstairs in her room as she built the confidence to come down, and, when she had drunk too much, all men, even the less attractive ones, began to seem highly desirable. Everybody said that they'd had a great time at the party, but none enjoyed themselves as much as Carol, who danced the rest of the night away as if she was still seventeen.

MAMA USED TO SAY

Tension had got so tight over Rex Publishing's advert that the art director and the copywriter had a fight — an honest-to-goodness physical fight — right there in the office. I couldn't believe it and went out to mediate. The copywriter had insisted on having his words splashed all over the ad and a tiny photo, but of course the art director had done the opposite and squashed the copy into one corner. I eventually had to overrule. I wanted less copy used and the photo improved if we were going to use it at all.

The launch date for the Rex commercials finally arrived, with twenty huge street billboards in key black areas in London, Birmingham, Manchester, Leeds and Nottingham, all featuring the slogan: "Rex Appeal", and with a different black celebrity reading their favourite of the publishing company's books.

I had been juggling my business life with my personal. Seeing Simon regularly had meant that the one was merging into the other.

Simon seemed genuine. We enjoyed each other's company so much that we would be happy going for long Sunday walks together along the river or on Blackheath, just holding hands and talking. We joked and teased each other about our lifestyles, our families, our dreams and ambitions, and got close to each other over the next few weeks. He said that sometime in his life he wanted to buy a boat and sail around the world.

"Take a few years off from everything and just sail at my leisure. It probably won't happen until I'm about sixty and I've been married and had kids who are grown up. But you know, you've got to have your dreams, haven't you?"

I told him that my dream was to have my own magazine one day.

"It would be something like a 'Lifestyles of the Rich and Famous' for black folk. The magazine would show the private lives of successful black role models with photographs of them at home with their families and that kind of thing. I know a lot of my friends who would buy a magazine like that."

"And I bet it would go down well with advertisers as well," Simon added.

"That's exactly my point."

"Well, what's stopping you from going for it?"

"Money, of course. A magazine's going to take time to develop and a lot of cash to get off the ground."

"You should check out Rex Publishing," Simon smiled, "we're always interested in new projects."

"I might just do that," I said.

My mother had always said that you should judge your men by the way they treat their own mothers. She would have *loved* this guy. After my first date with him, Simon drove by his mother's house to check up on her. She was living alone in a small flat in Camberwell. She was a youthful looking sixty year old whose sad eyes brightened up the moment her son let himself in through the front door. She welcomed me in warmly and proceeded to bring out an old family album with photos of her son as a baby.

"He was such a cute child," she explained, "and wherever I took him women would fall in love with him."

"Oh, Mum, I don't think Dee wants to see those old photos," Simon said, embarrassed.

"My mother is the most important thing in my life," he explained as we drove south to Wimbledon afterwards. "If it wasn't for her I wouldn't be here today. When I think of some of the things that woman has been through to raise her kids, I know that we're never going to be able to pay her back in this lifetime. So me and my brothers and sisters take it in turns to check up on her every evening. Tonight was my turn."

I know exactly what type of man I am looking for, and I've got used to being disappointed. But I always had a great time dating Simon. Life was like a big party with him, especially in bed, where it always got pretty hot because my satisfaction was one thing he always took seriously.

For a moment I thought I had found Mr Right, the man of my dreams, who appreciated that I was an attractive and highly sought-after woman. After a long romantic drought, Simon was just what Doctor Ruth ordered. He had all the right qualities and mixed with all the right people. So, I told him straight that I was looking for a 'fine black man'.

"I think you found him," he said with a cheeky smile on his face.

"No, I'm not kidding... I'm looking for nothing less than the very best — no compromises."

He said that, from what he had heard, African-American men weren't much competition and I had to admit that American men were more concerned about walking around like studs while, from what I had seen, English guys seemed to give their women a lot more attention.

With me, it's nearly always 'feast or famine' when it comes to relationships. There are times when more people are interested in me than I can handle, and other times when it feels like no one is interested. This was definitely feast time. Simon called me at work and said André was in town for a crime writer's symposium and that he wanted to get in touch with me.

"That's right, Dee. And he wants to know where's the most romantic restaurant in London so he can take you there."

"That might be a bit embarrassing," I said hesitantly.

I had to explain the situation. That there was nothing going on between André and myself and there never had been, but there *almost* had been, and maybe André was thinking that there still could be.

"Does that make sense?"

"No," said Simon, laughing. "I bet you just don't want to admit that you've had a fling with him. Come on, admit it," he teased.

Joking aside, we still had a problem. If André and Simon didn't already share the publisher-writer relationship it might not be so difficult, but now...

"Why don't we go on a double date?" said Simon. "I'll tell you what you do, invite one of your flatmates along to be my date and I'll come up with some excuse to André that it was arranged from time, then everybody's happy. He still gets his romantic evening out with you and you get to have dinner with him, without it becoming compromising in any way."

It sounded like a good idea. I said that I would speak to Donna and Carol and see which one of them wanted to date 'my man' for the evening. Simon laughed and told me not to be jealous, and reminded me that he'd be keeping an eye on me and André the whole evening.

André hadn't changed one bit, and as soon as I saw him at the French-African restaurant in Kensington, I started catching those feelings I had previously held for him again. I wasn't just glad to see someone from back home; I still had a thing for him. Even though the whole set-up seemed awkward, I tried to keep my cool.

He said he liked my new hairstyle. I thanked him without revealing that I had kept the style short since I accidentally burned off half of my hair with my curling tongs. I had even grown some feminine sideburns to go with the style, because they were in vogue.

We sat to eat dinner, all four of us — myself, André, Simon and Carol. André wanted to order the most expensive meals on the menu and the best wine, "or why not some bubbly?"

If André had known me better, he wouldn't have taken the liberty of ordering my meal for me, just because he spoke French. I let him sound off for about three minutes, giving the waitress instructions on what I was to have and how it should be cooked.

"Believe me, Dee, when you taste this, it will make you fall in love with Moroccan food."

Not if Moroccan food means that you don't respect my independence and judgement, homeboy.

I waited until the food arrived. There were trays and trays of it, meats of every type all neatly arranged in separate plates.

"I'm a vegetarian," I said calmly, looking at the food.

"What?!"

"I don't eat meat."

André was embarrassed.

"You didn't give me a chance to tell you..."

He was flustered. His customary self-assured nature had taken a knock, if only temporarily. Fortunately, there were enough vegetables to go with the cous-cous for me to enjoy the meal. I didn't mind, and Simon, who had been engaged in a serious conversation with Carol, offered to eat my share of the meat.

"Do you remember that night at the hotel in New York?" André whispered. He said he had often thought about it and wondered if the sacrifice of not sleeping with each other had been worth it.

"So how is Shawna?" I asked, reminding him of his commitments. "I know your woman must be longing to see you."

"That's just the point I'm making," he insisted. "I gave up an opportunity to get close to you, and I got back to the

States to discover that Shawna no longer wanted to get married and had left me. Of all the times to break up... The wedding details were already being arranged and it seemed like my life was more tied to Shawna's than ever before... But it taught me never to depend totally on another person for my happiness."

I told him that I was sorry to hear that things didn't work out with his fiancée, but that I didn't know what all of it had to do with me. He began telling me intimate things about himself that I didn't care to know.

"It's just that you get to a point when you get tired of the bachelor lifestyle — going out, meeting beautiful women and dating. It's time for me to settle down and start a family and have children... I had such a great time with you in New York, at the hotel. I'm too embarrassed to tell you how many times I've thought about that night since... before I go to bed at night... Do you ever think of having kids?"

I was surprised that André brought up the subject. Usually men get scared at the very mention of children, seeing kids as an attack on their freedom. However touching his desires seemed, I had to make it clear that, as far as I was concerned, it was too little too late.

"Well, I do want kids and a family sometime," I admitted, "but you know what, I'm seeing someone here."

"What, a British guy?" André exclaimed.

"Yes. Something wrong with that?"

"Now, let me get this straight. Twenty million black American men aren't good enough for you, homegirl?"

I said that there were lots of African-American men who were good enough and even too good for me, but they were all hitched up, as André had been previously. What was a poor girl to do? But now I had met a guy and I didn't know where it was all going to go, but I wanted to check it out.

"But we had a thing going, Dee. I know what you felt

for me and I know what I feel for you. Now, I don't know who this other guy is, but you've got to make sure that he's offering you more than I am, that he feels for you as much as I do and that he's gonna love you as much as I will if you give me the chance. Is he willing to have kids with you? Just answer me that. If a man's not willing to have kids with you, he's not worth it, believe me."

At this point, Simon, who had been deeply engaged in a discussion with Carol, suggested that because dinner was finished maybe we ought to go on to his private club in Soho. André finished his drink and 'remembered' an early appointment he had the next morning. He got up to leave, and looked straight in my eyes.

"Well, Dee, I probably won't see you before I go back, but you've got my number in Chicago. I'll be waiting to hear from you."

He said his goodbyes and left the rest of us feeling a bit uncomfortable. The double date had obviously not been a success.

THE REAL McCOY

When you come out with a winner, you want to go home and tell your friends, "Look at me, girl." Aware that there was always the possibility that things weren't going to work out with Dalton, Carol decided there was no point in raising the temperature at home.

"My wife? Oh you must mean my sister," Dalton said when Carol enquired down the phone line.

She had followed Dalton discreetly after work the previous day, just keeping tabs on him. He had jumped into a cab and she had hailed another to follow him. At Euston station, Dalton's cab waited as he alighted. He returned a few minutes later with an elegantly dressed black woman on his arm. They had climbed back into the cab and headed west. Carol's driver lost them in the madness of the early evening traffic on Marylebone Road, but she had seen enough and drew her own conclusions. From his description of her, Carol suspected that the woman was Dalton's estranged wife, but he denied it.

"You saw us at Euston? You should have come up and said hello. I've told her all about you. She was down in London for the day from Birmingham and, you know, every time she comes down I take her out to dinner at an elegant restaurant. I try to give her a good day out because it's the only break she gets from her kids."

Dee and Donna weren't convinced. If it was his sister, why hadn't he mentioned her before? Carol knew that her friends were right but she convinced herself otherwise. She had given up too much of herself, too much trust, hopes and feelings, to assume the worst. Even if it was his wife, it didn't have to mean much, did it? But then again, why couldn't he come clean?

"I was being sneaky checking up on him like that," Carol said, "so I've only got myself to blame if he's sneaky back."

The next day Carol went to the hairdressers to have her hair cut in a new short and sexy cut which everybody said took ten years off her age. On the way home she stopped by the beauty store and picked up a fresh selection of miracle creams. At home, she waxed her legs for the first time in ages, perfumed her entire body with a fragrance called Irresistible and, dressed in nothing but satin underclothes, she lay on her bed for hours, thinking of all the things she had been through, then threw an old overcoat on and headed up to Camden.

Dalton was clearly not expecting her, but buzzed her up anyway. The walk up the three flights of stairs seemed to go on for ever, every step a reminder to Carol that she could still turn back before making a fool of herself. But no, she had decided to swallow her pride and let Dalton know in no uncertain terms how much he already meant to her. She would be any woman he wanted her to be, as long as they stayed together.

There would be no embarrassment, however; Carol was going to get to keep her coat on. The door to Dalton's apartment was already open when she got there. That was not surprising, it was usually like that once he had buzzed somebody in. She made her way up the next flight within his maisonette, taking her up to the living room, where Dalton was sharing a bottle of wine with a handsome, bronze-skinned man with a handlebar moustache and wearing a sleeveless T-shirt through which his well-oiled muscles bulged.

"You must be Carol," the muscle-man lisped, looking her up and down. "I'm Darnell, Dalton's 'other half'."

He gave Dalton a playful squeeze on his thigh. "Thanks for taking care of him while I was away. We both appreciate it, don't we Dalton?"

Dalton had been trying to avoid Carol's gaze. He nodded. At first Carol thought she had misunderstood. She searched Dalton's eyes for an explanation, but he wouldn't look at her.

"Me and Darnell are going through a romantic journey," Dalton said. "The kind of journey you couldn't take me on."

"But..."

"Look, honey, I'm a swinger," Dalton explained. "When my wife left, Darnell was there for me when nobody else was."

Carol stood stunned for a moment. There was nothing to say. She felt cheap, used and abused, and wanted to cuss Dalton for not telling her before. How could he have allowed her to keep thinking...? How could she have let herself...? But she didn't say anything. After a long while, she turned and went back out the door.

Outside the flat she found a lager can lying crushed in the gutter. Just what she needed to scratch the word 'bastard' all the way along the flank of Dalton's beloved Ferrari parked on the street outside.

A week later she registered at Goldsmith's College in New Cross as a mature student. She had forgotten what it was like to be a student, but this second time around she was determined to enjoy the social life as much as the study. She had decided to do an MA in Law as a refresher course in the subject, before she decided whether to go on to law school afterwards.

She hadn't been at the college long before one of the young black male students called out to her after a meeting of the Afro-Caribbean Society — "Slim body gyal, you ah look good..." It made her feel good that young men who were ten or fifteen years her junior found her attractive. Okay, maybe they weren't serious, maybe they were just flirting... but even so.

If Carol had thought that beginning at college would at least get her off the subject of men and sex and dating, she was mistaken. If anything, she was reminded of her single status even more. At Goldsmith's, sex was a hot subject — everyone else at college seemed to be doing it or talking about it.

She had only been at the college for a couple of weeks when one night, to her surprise, the unmistakable figure of her old boyfriend, Frankie, walked into the bar. She knew him immediately, despite the fact that she hadn't seen him for more than ten years. She surprised herself and him by walking up to him and giving him a tight hug.

"Fran-kie... wow, wow, wow, I just can't believe it. What are you *doing* here? How are you, how have you been?"

Even though he looked very much himself, Frankie had changed. He wasn't dressed the same way, but in a casual jeans and sweater. He had also mellowed. He was thirty-eight, though he could pass for thirty, and he seemed mature. She invited him over to her table and they sat and talked over a couple of pints of beer. She thought she had forgotten him, but she hadn't. Sitting opposite him in the smoky student bar, it came home to her that she had lied to herself all this time.

Frankie explained that he was in the final year of an economics degree at the college. It had hurt him losing his woman because of his reluctance to educate himself all those years ago. And then he'd had a daughter with a woman, and now his daughter was old enough to come home from school and start asking for help with her school work. Frankie felt embarrassed that one day his daughter would come home from school and he wouldn't be able to help her any more. That spurred him on and he took A-levels in maths and physics, because he had always enjoyed those subjects from school days.

"Carol, you know, I really want to thank you. You were the only person who encouraged me at the time, the *only* one who believed in me, but because I could only think of college as selling out, I never appreciated what you were trying to do for me."

He explained also that, as a single father, it was down to him to bring up his kid. He felt he had to set her an example by going through college first, otherwise how could he expect her to appreciate education herself? Carol was well impressed; was this really Frankie, her ex-boyfriend who had refused to read anything — not a single book or even a newspaper — in the last two years of their relationship? Frankie, who was more interested in smoking ganja than in working for a living? She thought of something nice to say about his moustache, which was one of the main ways he had changed. He was still very muscular, so he must have kept up with his kung fu, she assumed.

First impressions are important. The last thing that Carol was expecting to see was Frankie, of all people, with a striped college scarf hanging from his neck and sitting in a student bar somewhere talking about his finals. It made an impression on her, and he seemed even more good looking than she remembered him.

He reminded Carol how, after university, she had decided that she deserved somebody with the same potential as she had, both intellectually and financially. She callously broke off their relationship because he was of lower market value.

Carol was embarrassed by that, but Frankie assured her that she had no reason to be.

"I would have done exactly the same thing if I were you," he insisted. "I didn't realise what it felt like — how when you get a bit of education suddenly the things that meant so much to you before mean so little. You're on a higher level, and you find that you don't have anything to say to those around you who have not reached that level. They just become less and less important to you. The things you used to do, you won't do any more, and the food you used to eat..."

He asked her how her love life was going; he had heard that she was married.

"Great," she answered without hesitation.

They chatted all evening until the bar closed, and found that they liked being together and talking to each other as much as they had ever done. Carol hopped on a train to take her back to Wimbledon, and Frankie headed off in the other direction to Elephant and Castle, where he lived with his daughter in a high-rise block.

Carol promised to meet him the next day and take him out to a nice little Caribbean restaurant across the road from college where they served a pretty decent fried chicken, rice and peas, and even ackee and saltfish.

EYES ON THE PRIZE

From an early age I saw a lot of deceit in relationships, so I decided never to tie the knot with anyone and just have a string of lovers instead. Men don't like that kind of attitude in a woman, but I know a lot of other women who have come to the same conclusion.

By the time I was fifteen, I had already stopped believing in love. That was when I fell for Floyd. He was two years older than me and had left school to start working as a car mechanic. To a fifteen-year-old girl he was seriously cool. I had already had lots of boyfriends but falling in love was a different thing entirely, and when Floyd assured me that he felt the same thing, it was easy to give up my virginity to him in one intimate moment.

Wendy was my best friend at the time. We had known each other since the juniors. We spent most of our time together, playing netball and sewing raving clothes for each other in my bedroom, and we trusted each other with all our secrets. Wendy more or less lived round our place, eating there and even sleeping there. She could come by anytime and my mum would treat her like a daughter. Then, one Sunday, her boyfriend Danny came banging on our door after Wendy had gone home, asking where she was. She wasn't at home and she wasn't at my house. Then my mum arrived and said she had seen Wendy going into Floyd's house. Danny asked what she could have been doing at Floyd's house.

My thoughts exactly.

By the time we had walked the few blocks to Floyd's, Danny had worked himself up so much that he didn't even wait for us to knock, but broke the front door down when we reached it. We rushed into the house to find them sprawled out on the living room floor, Wendy astride him, groaning and gasping and bouncing up and down as if her life depended on it and Floyd down below in a passive role, his hands clasped on her buttocks.

I couldn't believe it. Up to this day it hurts bad. The only thing that saved Wendy that day was Danny, who had to pull me off to stop me gouging her eyes out, and the only thing that saved Floyd that day was me, because Danny had to let him go to restrain me.

Reggie, the small-minded bastard that he was, had passed it around that I gave good head, and the rumour spread like wildfire. Everywhere I went, I kept coming across people who had heard about me. Of course, things soon became difficult. Nobody took me seriously when I went for dancing and modelling work. Complete strangers would come up and proposition me at auditions — even women. Shit! I was ashamed. How low can a man go? I had no choice but to keep a low profile and didn't even want to go back to work at Corinna's. Instead I started staying at home a lot more with Carol. She loaned me her old sewing machine which had been up in the attic gathering dust and I set about making alterations to some of my clothes for want of anything better to do.

For the first time in years, I had no interest in men and had enough time to concentrate on what I wanted to do. That was when Carol saw what I was doing and said it was good enough to sell and why didn't I give that a try? Well, never again would I think that the only way I could achieve anything was through a man.

Not every man appreciates a woman who dresses like I do. But then again, not everybody likes dancehall music. I love dancehall, because that's how I relax. And when I go to dancehalls, I like getting dressed up, and the more outrageous the clothes the better, because I like to do the opposite of what everyone else is doing and wear the opposite of everyone else.

That has always been my passion. But now it's also my business. I can make money from my creativity. Dancehall doesn't have to be X-rated clothing, just imaginative combinations. I dress to feel good and look sexy. When a man tells me I look sexy, I take it as a compliment, it's not necessarily a come-on. Least of all in the dancehall nowadays, where you're gonna see more flesh than fashion. At least amongst the women anyway, who think nothing of wearing a bra, a G-string and mesh stockings just to see who can show the most flesh and get away with it — bare as you dare. Some would say it's unnecessarily explicit, but when all the artists are singing about how your body looks so good, you want to be even more daring.

I dress according to how I feel. But I also dress according to the body I have. I wish I had a body shaped like a Coca-Cola bottle, but I don't, and I'm not putting my body through a lot of emotional stress by dieting; plenty of fruit and vegetables keeps my body healthy. So I've got to get the clothes right.

I always knew I didn't have to be a knockout beauty to attract men, all I needed to do was to wear certain clothes, like a tiny mini skirt. Yeah, men always go for that, and some lace leggings...

Some women would definitely not look good in the clothes that I wear and design. But then I wouldn't look good in the ones they wear. There's something for everyone if you look hard enough, isn't there?

A lot of people might consider what I wear vulgar and men think that you're a sex machine, but that's their business. If you wear hot pants or batty riders and revealing tops or see-through dresses and silk stockings with long gold lamé thigh boots, people are going to start saying something.

Even internationally renowned designers are getting into dancehall fashion now. That was Carol's reasoning, and if they were making money with our fashions, I could too.

I got paid fifty pounds for my first creation, a red leatherette batty rider with chains on the side, which a friend of Alex's ordered. It wasn't a fortune, but it was a start. The same woman ordered a glittering 'pussy printer' outfit to go with a pair of knee-length suede boots she had just bought. I had to wait a while for word to get around that I could design funky clothes at reasonable prices, but before long I began getting three or four orders a week.

Rap fashions have become everyday, and, who knows, with my help, dancehall fashions from the reggae arena could too.

BROTHAMAN

Simon wasn't too happy when I started mentioning kids to him. He said he felt that I had only brought it up because André had talked about it at dinner and had wanted to have kids with me.

I said that maybe he was right. Maybe it was André's words that had got me brooding, but there it was. I *was* thinking about kids and couldn't help it. I was a thirty year old woman who was wondering whether it was time to continue the relationship we were having together, whether it would lead somewhere, or whether it was going nowhere at all and I might as well just give it up.

I told Simon that I wasn't interested in just having an affair that had no purpose. I was too old for that and, much as I enjoyed going out with him, maybe the best thing for both of us would be to continue seeing each other as 'just good friends'.

Simon was intelligent enough to know that I was fishing for some kind of declaration of intent. We had been dating each other for several months now. My first anniversary in England was coming up, too, and although I had a glittering career to show for it, I had a deeper sense of fear that I was 'missing the boat' now than I had ever had in Chicago.

I told Simon I wanted a partner who wanted children. Simon told me that he didn't want to be pressured like that.

I had heard it all before, but still it hurt me a little that, after all we had been through, Simon had the nerve to tell me that he still wanted his freedom, that he didn't want to be hassled, that things were going on fine as they were. Why did we have to change it, he wanted to know?

172

"Because I haven't got time to waste on a relationship that's not going anywhere," I almost screamed at him.

My mood didn't change anything. Simon stopped calling me and I stopped calling him. The relationship, I guessed, was fizzling to nothing.

What was I left with, then? I thought about André, my next choice. If he was as serious as he said he had been over dinner, perhaps it wouldn't do any harm to call him. I was going to go back home for Christmas, anyway, and while I was in the States it wouldn't be too hard to make my way over to Chicago, even though I didn't have an apartment there any more.

I rang his number.

You know how these things go, I didn't want any more surprises. I wanted him to know in advance that I was coming over, and that I was available. I didn't want to ram it down his throat, you understand, but I felt I had to be clear about it.

"Hi, how yah doing? I'm sorry you can't get through… just leave your name and your number, and I'll get right back to you," André's voice came from the answering machine.

Well, he still lived by himself.

That was a good sign.

I left the most alluring message I could come up with.

"André, sweetie, it's your UK homegirl… I'm just checking up on how you're doing and seeing where you're at and all of that. I wanted to let you know that I will be arriving back in the States on Christmas Eve and I will be over for at least a month while I figure out whether I want to go back to work in London or not. You keep promising me dinner at some elegant restaurant in Chicago, so how about it? Call me when you get this message and we can arrange something."

The sound of the phone ringing brought me out of my deep slumber. I had fallen asleep on the living room rug in front of the fireplace, with the radio on low.

I answered the phone.

It was André.

"Hi…"

He sounded upbeat.

"Dee, baby, it was so good to hear your voice again… So how are you doing? Have you married your British guy yet?"

I was embarrassed. Of course that would be one of the things that André would want to know, but, nevertheless, I hadn't really expected it.

"No, I haven't. In fact, that is all over. We're still good friends, you know, but things didn't quite work out… How about you?"

André said that he had some good news. He had just come from Shawna's house; they had ironed out their differences and had just agreed to fly out to Reno the next morning to get married in one of those quickie weddings.

I puffed out a deep sigh, in spite of myself.

"What's the matter ?" he asked.

"Oh… nothing, I was just wishing you well… I hope you two are very happy. I know how much you care about her."

There wasn't much to say on the phone.

I had missed my final opportunity to get that ideal man.

WHEEL OF FORTUNE

After making it to college despite all the obstacles in her way, the last thing the typical sista wants is to find herself pregnant by a partner who is unwilling to take his responsibilities seriously. The sista didn't spend three years studying for a degree in order to spend the rest of her days changing nappies and cooking. She's clearly overqualified for life as a baby mother, yet so many young sistas end up doing exactly what they swore they'd never do, and sidestep out of successful careers the moment they hit twenty-six, as soon as they start dreading old age, to have babies with sub-standard men.

Frankie told Carol that he had a child when they met at college. He said he was now a single father, that his life revolved around his wonderful daughter, six year old Femi. Things hadn't worked out with her mother; they were still friends, but Jenny now lived in the States with a new man and had left Femi behind in Britain to get the benefit of a good education.

"Traditionally, the single mother gets more stick when it comes to relationships. The minute a man finds out you've got a child, he runs a mile. Men immediately think that you're looking for a father for your child and that you're out to trap them. But fathers, too, are feeling what it's like to be overlooked because they are single parents," Frankie explained.

"So tell me, Carol, do you think about getting married again?"

By now Carol had come clean with him, and confessed that her marriage had been a disaster that she had lived through for seven years, but now she was glad that she was well out of it and able to carry on her own life.

"I do think about marriage, but more important for me in my life is to be at peace with myself," she told him.

They were taking a stroll through the park, just talking. Since they had first met up again, they had been seeing each other, just on a platonic level, getting to know each other all over again.

Carol was still embarrassed every time Frankie teased her about her dumping him just because he couldn't get a decent education. But whenever he mentioned it he would go on to say, "God works in mysterious ways". Now, looking back, he saw clearly that her getting rough with him had been the cue for him to start studying. The way she left him had such an impact on him that it drove him on to get his O-Levels and A-Levels. Even after Femi was born, he would sneak off to his evening classes, just to make sure that he got the degree that everybody, except him, seemed to have. And the funny thing was, he added, that since getting the piece of paper, he had begun to behave just like she had done. He could no longer check the type of women he used to check who only seemed to be interested in clothes and raving. Studying had dragged him up to another level. It had been a hard, long slog for a mature student to get through, but he had persevered and it had truly been worth all the work and all the sacrifice in the end.

"Don't think that educated and successful women don't get dumped by men as well," she warned him. "I've been dumped like everybody else, remember. The single life that I'm living wasn't out of choice."

Carol couldn't deny that she still had feelings for this man. Frankie was exactly the way she wished he had been ten years ago. If only he had shown an interest in studying back then, they would have had no reason whatsoever to break up.

Was it better to string Frankie along before accepting his advances, or should she seize the magic moment?

When he showed some romantic interest in her she felt like, 'No, it can't be true.' After all this time, he still held a torch for her as she did for him.

She decided to still play hard to get, and set about running her quality control checks on him, just to find out if his heart was in the right place.

Frankie said that he wanted a second chance. He was sure that they could make it work this time.

Carol didn't disagree, but listened, neither encouraging nor discouraging, wondering whether she was about to choose her mate for the future.

But then... nothing.

They were stuck in a romantic stalemate, each person waiting for the other to make the next move.

Feeling the time running out, Carol broke the deadlock. She sent him an expensive wristwatch accompanied by a perfumed card, which read: *I will always have time for you.*

That was it, there was no holding back now, and Frankie quickly responded with his own present, a Zippo lighter inscribed with the legend: *Come on baby, light my fire.*

"We'll start dating," Carol said. "But if you miss one birthday or one anniversary, you pay for it for the rest of our time together..."

Frankie smiled and said that he thought that he could deal with that. That he would give her one hundred percent, always.

"Why not a hundred and fifty percent?" Carol asked.

Frankie really boosted Carol's ego, telling her continually, repeatedly, how much he fancied her and how he couldn't understand how anyone could have left her, or cheated on her.

Yes, there was no doubt about it, he was the someone she needed who believed in her even when she didn't believe in herself.

Frankie had always been handsome, but he seemed to have become more good-looking with time. Some days she would do nothing but gaze at him dreamily when she ran into him between classes at college. That's how good looking he was.

"You're acting like what we did didn't mean anything..." Frankie said.

They had met up in the pub across the road from college, in between classes. It was the day after they had made love for the first time in years. Now Carol was regretting it and wanting to just stay friends.

"I did *not* go over to your house to make love to you... What was I supposed to do? You wanted to make love as well."

Carol still didn't think it was a good idea. She had sat in her classes all day, wondering what she had let herself in for. After so long apart, they should have taken a lot more time to think about it before they decided to make love.

Frankie tried unsuccessfully to reassure her that everything between them was just like it had been before they made love. They were friends, first and foremost, and everything else would develop by itself.

"We've known each other long enough, Carol. I don't have to consider it, I know that you're the woman of my dreams. You're the woman I've been thinking about all these years," Frankie said.

Carol listened quietly but thoughtfully. She had to admit that she felt the same way as he did. She really didn't have to consider what she thought about him, because it was the same feeling she'd had when they first met all those years ago and became childhood sweethearts. Like it had then, her heart now told her that being with him was something she couldn't do without.

"At least let me take you out tonight," he asked her. "I've got a couple of tickets for that pantomime they do every Christmas — *Pinchy Kobi and The Seven Duppies?* I went last year with Femi and I bought a ticket to surprise her this year, but she said that she would rather go to a friend's birthday party instead."

Carol agreed to meet up with him after college and they planned to go straight to the theatre, then try to talk things through after the show.

The theatre was packed, and they had two of the best seats in the house, right up front by the stage. The side-splitting humour was fast and frenetic. Suddenly, in the middle of the pantomime, the rest of the cast stood motionless while Pinchy Kobi walked directly up to Carol in the audience.

He announced loudly:

"I have been asked by the man on your left to stop this production and ask whether you will marry him."

Carol thought it was part of the pantomime and waited for the punchline. Instead, the spotlight shone on her, and the entire audience fell silent as each and every person realised that this was not part of the show at all.

Carol turned to Frankie.

He had a cheeky smile on his face.

In front of her and the entire theatre, he went down on his knees. There was an affectionate roar of approval from the women gathered there, followed by many of them nudging their partners to ask, "How come *you're* not that romantic?"

"Answer, woman!" Pinchy Kobi shouted. "Answer, yes or no, we don't have time for any maybe. Will you marry this man?"

So many thoughts and emotions were racing through Carol's mind. Sure, she wanted to marry him, just as soon as her divorce was through. She had wasted the last ten years; it should have been Frankie all along.

She didn't need to think about it any longer.

The entire theatre roared with approval as she turned to Frankie and nodded enthusiastically. He pulled her close to him and hugged her tight and long.

They were getting on well and Carol found that she didn't need to insist to Frankie that his daughter, Femi, was always to come first in their relationship.

Frankie was a model father and always made sure that Femi was well taken care of. The way he treated his daughter was the way that he might treat a child of theirs if they had one. When she had told Frankie about the death of her son, Junior, he had assured her that he'd had a blood test for sickle cell anaemia anyway, and that he didn't have the trait. Carol was happy and, even though it was sometimes inconvenient having to stay around his tiny flat in Elephant and Castle to help babysit his daughter, she didn't complain.

Femi was a wonderful kid, and she and Carol took to each other immediately. If she had been a complete brat things might have been different, but, as it was, the child seemed to know to stay out of the way of her father and his new woman as much as she could, and never argued when Frankie told her it was time to go to bed.

Frankie was proof that the caring black father was still alive and well.

"Everybody wants to make out that black fathers are useless and that they are never around when their kids are growing up. I'm living proof that they're wrong," he said reassuringly.

"I will love you and stay devoted to you and I will be a role model for my children and bring them up together with you in the best way we know how. Not every black man is irresponsible. After all, there are a bunch of black men like me with kids by the same woman and with love for their kids."

Carol was impressed. Like many men, Neville seemed to think that he'd done his bit as soon as Junior was conceived. After that all he had to do was discipline the child every now and then — but otherwise the duty was on the mother's head to make sure the kid ate right and had clean clothes to go to school in. But Frankie was different. He understood that there were other problems in being a black father, and that there were things that he would have to teach his children about dealing with life as a black child.

During the next few weeks, Frankie and Carol gave each other as much love and attention as they could. They weren't putting on a show, they really did look like the happiest couple in the world, already together for richer or for poorer, even though they were not as yet legally married.

"Let's get married African-style," Frankie suggested when Carol came by one evening. "We can wait to get the official marriage papers signed when your divorce comes through, but why don't we get married in the ways our ancestors did? And let's do it soon."

Carol was taken aback. She asked what had brought all this about so suddenly. Frankie showed her a holiday brochure.

"I went out today and bought us a honeymoon," he said with a cheeky smile.

Carol read the page hesitantly:

The 'Gold Vacation' it said in the brochure. "You will fly to the Sandy Lane Hotel in Barbados, where you will be picked up at the airport by a Rolls-Royce... with champagne accompanying nearly everything... and including an airplane tour of the island and a ride in a submarine..." The cost was only three thousand pounds per couple.

Carol couldn't believe it. But Frankie's eyes confirmed it, he had done it. He said he had sold a few bits and pieces and that Femi was coming as well. The only thing was that the flights departed on Christmas Eve.

The wedding arrangements were rushed. Frankie already had an idea of what he wanted, but he discussed it thoroughly with his bride-to-be and she was agreeable. It would be unusual and interesting, and she agreed that the African-style ceremony would declare to all who knew them exactly where they were coming from. Carol got Dee to help with the details of the ceremony while Donna contributed by getting the material to sew a series of African costumes in the same pattern for all the guests present.

Carol and Frankie were married a few weeks later in the woods on Hampstead Heath in front of about seventy guests who braved the chill to witness the spiritual, homemade ceremony inspired by African wedding traditions.

Their colourful silk outfits, based on royal African wedding clothes, were designed by Donna from original drawings. Frankie was escorted to the ceremony by his daughter, followed by the bride who was accompanied by a banjo player.

As she arrived, several of Carol's female friends formed an aisle for her to walk down. Standing in two parallel lines, they were dressed in identically patterned African women's clothing. As Carol walked between the women, each knelt and placed a small piece of African cloth on the ground for her to step on.

"You're starting a long journey," each one of the women chanted in turn, "may the first steps of your journey be blessed."

As the wind blew through the trees, the couple were married in a ceremony which they wrote, orchestrated and officiated themselves.

They burned sage incense and passed around a conch shell, into which they asked each of the guests to speak so that their words would be trapped, like the roar of the ocean, forever. Afterwards, the guests walked with them to a reception at a hotel. Many sang, carried sunflowers and played drums or tambourines.

Everybody said how much they had enjoyed the ceremony and people went home with their friends and partners grateful for having witnessed a little slice of tradition.

Dee had still not decided whether or not she would return to London after the Christmas break. Her whole family was bound to be waiting to find out if she'd had any romantic success in the UK. It had been something of a disaster in that department. How could she explain to them that, whenever true love seemed to be coming over the horizon, it never quite reached her? She leant her head back on the club class headrest and closed her eyes.

"This is your captain speaking. I have a question for the lady in seat 8D. May I please have your attention?

"The gentleman in seat 10D would like to know whether you will marry him."

Dee listened up like everyone else in the plane at the unusual announcement, not realising at first that she was in seat 8D.

She looked around and saw that all eyes were on her.

She glanced at her seat number and then spun around with surprise, only to find Simon smiling at her from seat 10D, two rows behind her.

END